Critical Acclaim for

MIND THE GAP
A NOVEL OF THE HIDDEN CITIES

"A pitch-perfect blend of fantasy and realism. Golden and Lebbon craft a riveting tale of adventure that is both gritty and magical."
—Kelley Armstrong, *New York Times* bestselling author of *Personal Demon*

"Super-fast pacing and creepy touches [give this] adventure plenty of character."—*Publishers Weekly*

AND FOR AWARD-WINNING AUTHORS
CHRISTOPHER GOLDEN *and* TIM LEBBON

CHRISTOPHER GOLDEN

"Christopher Golden is one of the most hardworking, smartest, and talented writers of his generation, and his books are so good and so involving that they really ought to sell in huge numbers. Everything he writes glows with imagination."—Peter Straub, author of *In the Night Room*

"A new book by Golden means only one thing: the reader is in for a treat. His books are rich with texture and character, always inventive, and totally addictive."—Charles de Lint, author of *Promises to Keep*

"A master of his craft."—SciFi.com

"Harkens back to classic Stephen King."—*Dark Realms*

"Tim Lebbon is an immense talent and he's become a new favourite. He has a style and approach unique to the genre."—Joe R. Lansdale, author of *Lost Echoes*

"A firm and confident style, with elements of early Clive Barker."—Phil Rickman, author of *The Fabric of Sin*

"Tim Lebbon is an apocalyptic visionary—a prophet of blood and fear."—Mark Chadbourn, author of *The Hounds of Avalon*

"One of the most powerful new voices to come along in the genre . . . Lebbon's work is infused with the contemporary realism of Stephen King and the lyricism of Ray Bradbury."
—*Fangoria*

"Beautifully written and mysterious . . . a real winner!"
—Richard Laymon, author of *The Beast House*

"Lebbon will reward the careful reader with insights as well as gooseflesh."—*Publishers Weekly*

"Lebbon is among the most inventive and original contemporary writers of the dark fantastic."—Ramsey Campbell, author of *Secret Story*

"Lebbon is quite simply the most exciting new name in horror for years."—*SFX*

"Tim Lebbon is one of the most exciting and original talents on the horror scene."—Graham Joyce, author of *T.W.O.C.*

"Lebbon has a way of throwing staggering images at you which you almost have to pause and think about before you can fully grasp."—Paul Kearney, author of *This Forsaken Earth*

"It's rare indeed to witness the conventions of fantasy so thoroughly grabbed by the throat and shaken awake the way Tim Lebbon has done."—Steven Erikson, author of *Reaper's Gale*

"Lebbon has etched a powerful new version/telling of the traditional magical quest, whose tortured twists and turns will (alternately) disturb and electrify its readers."—Sarah Ash, author of *Tracing the Shadow*

"Tim Lebbon writes with a pen dipped in the dark stuff of nightmare."—K. J. Bishop, author of *The Etched City*

"Lebbon is an author so skilled he definitely belongs on auto-buy. . . . His prose is alternately poetic and flesh-slicingly real. His characters always strike a nerve and have the sort of heft that makes you feel as if you might have met them or the real people they were based upon—even if they were not in fact based on real people. And finally, for me the killer, Lebbon's novels offer places you can go back and visit."—*Agony Column*

"One of the most talented authors working today."—*Horror Channel*

"I've come to admire Lebbon's masterful blend of beauty with the horrific."—*Talebones*

A NOVEL OF THE HIDDEN CITIES

Christopher Golden
and
Tim Lebbon

BANTAM BOOKS

THE MAP OF MOMENTS
A Bantam Book / February 2009

Published by Bantam Dell
A Division of Random House, Inc.
New York, New York

Book design by Catherine Leonardo

Library of Congress Cataloging-in-Publication Data

Golden, Christopher.
The map of moments / Christopher Golden and Tim Lebbon.
p. cm.
ISBN 978-0-553-38470-3 (pbk.)
1. New Orleans (La.)—Fiction. 2. Hurricane Katrina, 2005—Fiction. I. Lebbon,
Tim. II. Title.

PS3557.O35927M37 2009
813'.54—dc22
2008034913

Printed in the United States of America
Published simultaneously in Canada

www.bantamdell.com

BVG 10 9 8 7 6 5 4 3 2 1

"Amid the devastation, you have to look for hope."

Chris Rose, *1 Dead in Attic—After Katrina*

We'd like to thank Marcy Italiano for her help, and our editor, Anne Groell, for seeing clearly into the Hidden Cities. Also thanks and respect to Chris Rose, Douglas Brinkley, and everyone else who continues to tell their story.

The Map of Moments

chapter

1

In Max's dream, Gabrielle still loves him. And she is still alive.

They're in the attic of the wood-frame house on Landry Street, making love on top of a decades-out-of-fashion gown that her mother had worn to some ball in her debutante days. Gabrielle had dragged it to the floor and positioned it carefully to avoid getting splinters from the old boards. Golden light streams in and makes her cinnamon Creole skin glisten, and Max's heart catches in his throat as he moves inside her. She's the kind of beautiful that clouds the minds of men, and makes even the most envious woman marvel. Yet she has a wild, desperate need in her eyes, as though a fire burns inside her and she believes he might be able to give her peace.

"Don't ever stop," she says, gazing up at him with copper eyes.

Stop what? Making love to her? Loving her? He's known her only a handful of weeks, and already he realizes that he will never be able to stop. The spell she has cast over him is irrevocable. He suspects that he has opened himself up to anguish, but he drives on with abandon. Better to have her and suffer forever if she should cast him aside, than to never have her at all.

Confusion touches him, makes him blink. This isn't how it was. The ball gown is right, all sequins and charm, and Gabrielle shudders with pleasure, her breath hitching, and that is very right, indeed. She wears a tight tank top with lace straps, her socks, and nothing else. So sweet, and only nineteen . . . but the wisdom and confidence, the sensuality in those eyes belong to a woman who truly understands the world. Gabrielle is the first woman, Eve; the temptation for which Max is willing to risk his reputation and career.

But the light shouldn't be like this. It should be night, with the sounds of car engines and pounding music from the street below. Instead, there is no sound at all, save for her heavy breathing. It's like listening to a dead phone line——not just an absence of sound but a vacuum.

A heavy knocking comes from the door into the attic. Eyes glazed with love and lust, Gabrielle doesn't hear it, but Max falters.

"No, no, baby, come on," she urges, closing her eyes tightly.

The light has changed. Her skin has a bluish tint, but he blinks and it's gone.

Her fingers twine in his hair and she pulls him down. He loses himself in the hunger of her kiss, but when they break apart the wrongness still troubles him.

The attic is too clean.

Gabrielle flips him over and settles down onto him, and he can *feel the heat emanating from the place where they are joined, and the dark ringlets of her hair brush his face as she bends to kiss him again. Max rises to meet her, eyes drifting closed . . .*

But the attic is too clean, and the knowledge stabs him. This is a moment of magic for Max, like nothing that's ever happened to him before, but Gabrielle keeps the attic of this old place clean, which makes him wonder how many men have been here before him, and how many felt the same way he does.

Floorboards creak, and the attic has changed. It's impossibly huge. Posters hang on the walls—things he'd had in his office at Tulane University—and in the shadows of the eaves, figures loom. Then, somehow, he can see through the shadows, and he knows these silent observers. He recognizes some of his colleagues and students; Gabrielle's cousin, Corinne, two men from Roland's Garage, the bar on Proyas Street where she'd taken him once and he'd been the only white face in the place. They watch, but he feels no menace from them, only sadness, as if they've come for a wake.

One figure remains in shadow. Max cannot see its face, which is fine, because he doesn't want to. He's too afraid.

He focuses on Gabrielle, shutting them all out. He wants to give her all of him, to bring her joy, and he touches her face, thrusting up to meet her.

Only then does he feel the wetness beneath him.

Frantic, he glances around and sees water flowing up through the spaces between the floorboards. The arms of the ball gown float like butterfly wings. An old leather shoe drifts by his head.

He tries to ask where it's all coming from, turning to look up at her. But when he opens his mouth, water spills in. The attic is flooding. Max is drowning. Panic surges through him for a moment, but up through the water he sees that Gabrielle is still rocking on top *of him, smiling as she presses her hands down on his chest, holding him down, keeping him under. He cannot breathe. For a moment he fights her, but then his panic shatters, leaving only the debris of sadness.*

The world inverts.

Gabrielle is still above him—he can see the beams of the attic roof, and he can still feel the floorboards beneath his back—but as though the house has turned upside down, she is now the one under the water. It fills the top of the attic and she begins to sink upward, arms still reaching for him as though beckoning him to follow.

She is wearing her mother's old debutante gown now, and it billows around her. Then the roof tumbles away, down into a pit of nothing, and she slips into black waters and is gone.

And he wakes . . .

. . . with a deep breath, as though coming back to life. Max had a moment of dislocation, and then his seat jostled and the hum of the passenger jet's engines filled his ears, and he remembered it all.

"Jesus," he whispered, opening his eyes and surrendering to consciousness.

The obese woman in the seat beside him shifted, absorbing even more of the space he'd paid to occupy. It seemed she'd actually gotten larger since the plane departed Boston, but of course that had to be impossible.

Don't be a prick, he chided himself. Such thoughts were out of character for him on most days, but most days he wasn't pinned into his seat by a woman of such immensity. Most days he wasn't returning to a place he'd sworn to leave forever, traveling to the funeral of the person responsible for both the greatest joy and the greatest pain he'd ever known.

So if he behaved like a prick, he had a feeling he'd be able to live with it.

The landing announcement came through the PA system. Max managed to get his seat upright. He rested his head against the window frame and stared down at civilization below. It should have been New Orleans, but ten weeks after the hurricane, getting a flight into that city still presented complications and doubts. In the seven months he'd lived in Louisiana, Max had never been to Baton Rouge, and as the plane descended over the state's capital, he found himself wishing he could have avoided it forever.

Did I ever really know you? he thought. And though the question was meant for Gabrielle, it could easily have applied to the city of New Orleans. He'd barely scratched the surface during the nearly two semesters he'd taught at Tulane, figuring he'd have years to explore and understand the mystery of what had once been called the Big Easy. It had been a city of music and exoticism, a place of both excess and torpor. He thought he'd gotten more intimate with New Orleans than the average tourist, but he'd been fooling himself, like a john falling in love with his favorite hooker.

Such thoughts led to dark corners of his mind, and he forced himself to move away from them. Gabrielle had hurt him so badly that he'd fled home to Boston, taking a new position teaching at Tufts University. But comparing her to some back alley whore made him cringe. She wasn't entirely to blame. Yes, she'd told him that she loved him, and pulled him into her life and her bed with a fervent passion he had never before encountered. But Max was thirty-one years old when he met Gabrielle, while she was only nineteen. He'd been her professor. He'd known the rules, and had broken them with abandon.

Yet despite the way everyone who discovered the relationship had seemed willing to give him a pass, Max blamed himself. He'd looked into those bright copper eyes and *seen* the love she felt for him, believed it wholeheartedly. When Gabrielle had told him that she'd dreamed of finding a man who would leave *her* breathless, and that she'd found him in Max, he'd believed her. When they'd made love in the attic on Landry Street, and she'd wept and clung to him afterward, and wished them away to someplace where no one else could ever reach them, he had felt like the man all men wanted to be—the hero, the knight, the lover and champion.

What an asshole.

One thing he'd learned in his time in Louisiana was that New Orleans was a city of masks. Everyone wore one, and not just for Mardi Gras. Only the desperately poor were what they seemed to be. Otherwise, how to explain the way the populace had so long ignored warnings of their beloved city's vulnerability, or the libertine air of sexual and epicurean excess and music that fueled the tourist trade, while sixty percent of the city remained illiterate, and thousands lived in shotgun houses slapped together like papier-mâché? New Orleans had two faces: one of them a stew of cultures and languages, poverty and success, corruption and hope; the other, the mask it showed the world.

How could he have been fool enough not to see that Gabrielle also wore a mask?

Max had asked himself that question far too many times while back in Boston. He ought to have been settling in, enjoying the preparations for his new job, and trying to move on. At his sister's Fourth of July barbecue, he should have listened when she'd told him her single neighbor, Jill, had taken an interest in him. But he'd been too lost in that question to pay attention, beating himself up, wondering how he had fallen in love so fast and hard. Wondering how long it would be before it stopped hurting.

And then August had come, and with it, hurricane season. Watching the television reports as Katrina moved into the Gulf of Mexico, he'd wondered why no one seemed as terrified as they should have been. Weren't they watching the same reports down in Louisiana? Couldn't they see the monster about to make landfall? But even as those questions rose in his mind, he understood. Some of the people in New Orleans would put their faith in God, others in luck, and others would simply chalk it up to fate. If the storm was meant to take them, it would. And some would just be stubborn; until someone called for a mandatory evacuation, they weren't going anywhere. And maybe not even then. Someone would have to round them up to get them out of there.

For too many, no one ever came.

Max had sat in his little faculty apartment on the Tufts campus and watched the anguished aftermath of the storm.

He had little faith in the spiritual, but Max had felt a soul-deep certainty, in those initial few days, that Gabrielle had not survived Hurricane Katrina. Days turned to weeks, shock turned to numbness, and numbness to mourning.

Hurricane Rita arrived at the end of September, flooding parts of the city all over again. Chaos had still not released its hold on the Gulf Coast, and it seemed order might never be restored.

On the 18th of October, just over seven weeks after Katrina, Max's phone rang. Without even realizing it, he had gotten into the habit of holding his breath when he glanced at the caller ID window. That night, the readout had said *unknown caller*, but what struck him was the area code: 504. Louisiana.

Max had picked up the phone. He'd hated himself for the hope in his voice when he said, "Hello?"

"It's Corinne Doucette."

And he'd known. "She's dead, isn't she?"

For a moment, the line went silent. Then, just as he'd begun to think they'd been disconnected, Corinne spoke again.

"I told her to get out of there, but she wouldn't go. Said she couldn't leave, that it was the only place she'd be safe. They were saying all the neighborhoods in the bowl could be flooded, but she just went up into that damn attic and wouldn't come down. I told her she was crazy, Max, but you know Gaby. No talking to that girl."

Corinne's voice had broken then.

"The water got that high?" he'd asked.

"High enough."

Max had listened to Corinne as she told him about evacuating to Houston, and how she'd called and tried to get the police or someone, *anyone*, to go by and check the house on Landry Street. Most of her family had left New Orleans, and of those who planned to return, none of them wanted anything to do with Gabrielle, dead or alive. Except for Corinne, her family had written her off years before.

In late September, Corinne had reluctantly returned to New Orleans. And so she'd had to identify the body.

At last, when Max had heard enough, he'd finally spoken up.

"Why did you call me?"

It had brought her up short. "What?"

"After what happened. Why would you call me?"

Her nerves had to be frayed. She'd laughed, and the sound was full of hurt and anger. "Jesus, Max. I called you because I thought you'd want to know. Maybe she fucked with your head, but I figured you were the only one . . ."

Her words trailed off.

"The only one what?" Max had to ask.

"The only person in the world besides me who would cry for her."

Max had wanted to tell Corinne that he'd done his share of crying for Gabrielle when she was alive. That it hadn't helped then, and it wouldn't help now that she was dead. But he couldn't get the words out.

Nearly three more weeks had passed, and now he found himself on this airplane, about to touch down in Baton Rouge. During the layover in Memphis, he'd almost turned around and caught the next plane back north. At least, he'd pretended to himself that he could do that. What a joke. He could no more turn around than he could snap his fingers and make the grief go away. Leaving the way he had, this chapter of his life had *never* felt closed.

Gabrielle's funeral might finally put an end to it.

He'd grieve, but he would not cry. Perhaps it was a good sign that he couldn't shed any more tears for her. Or maybe it meant he was dead inside.

"I hate landings the most," said the woman beside him.

Max blinked and looked at her. She'd said nothing the entire flight, and now she wanted to strike up a conversation? The cynicism that had been building in him all year began to form a reply, but then he looked at her, and he *saw* her. The woman had kind, intelligent eyes, and wore an expression of nervous self-deprecation. He wondered what brought her to Baton Rouge. There must, he knew, be other people on board who were coming to Louisiana for funerals or to rebuild. And some who were returning to search for still-missing loved ones, lying undiscovered in mud or in some other attic.

"Don't worry," Max told her, smiling. "This close to the ground, even if we fall the rest of the way, the worst we're gonna get is bruises."

She gripped the armrests and stared at him, wide-eyed. "Don't even say that!"

Then, with a squeak of tires, the plane found the runway. The woman let out a breath and chuckled. "Was that your attempt to set me at ease?"

"I'm afraid so."

"You're not very good at it."

"Never have been," he confessed. "But still I try."

They shared a smile as the plane taxied toward the terminal.

"What brings you to Louisiana?" she asked.

Max glanced out the window. "A woman."

Corinne drove south on Interstate 10 with the windows down, making a wind tunnel out of her beat-up old Chevy Corsica. Max didn't complain. The car had no airconditioning, and the afternoon was warm and humid. Back home in Boston, November meant chilly days and chillier nights. But that Louisiana day, winter felt a whole world away.

"Thanks for coming to get me," he said, fifteen minutes south of the airport.

"Not a problem. Guy like you, if you'd gotten a rental, you'd probably have been carjacked before you got anywhere near your hotel."

Max stared at her, waiting for the smile.

It didn't come.

"You're serious."

Corinne kept both hands on the wheel and her eyes straight ahead. There'd been precious little small talk at the airport, and even less since.

"We're a little short on jokes down here, lately," she said. "So yeah, I'm serious. It's rough. The city's still reeling." She trailed off, but Max sensed that she had more to say, so he gave her the silence in which to speak. After a pause, she did. "They've got hundreds of dead folk in a warehouse over by the Superdome. Doing DNA tests, supposedly, trying to figure out who they all are. If I hadn't laid claim to Gaby, she'd probably still be over there. Maybe forever. French Quarter's back up and running, other parts of the city, too. High ground. You'll be fine in your hotel. But some areas, it's still a war zone. Might as well be in Baghdad. A lot of the folks that left, maybe most of 'em, aren't ever coming back. Some places, it's like the apocalypse came. There's talk of rebuilding, but it's never gonna happen. That's the first sign of a crumbling empire, Max. Cities fall and nobody builds 'em up again."

He kept staring at her, but Corinne still didn't turn to him. Max became keenly aware of his hands, as though he should be able to do something with them, maybe try to offer her comfort, or send up a prayer to God. But he barely knew Corinne, and he and God were strangers.

After a couple of minutes, the time when he should have said something in reply passed, so he stopped seeking the words.

Corinne and Gabrielle were cousins, Creole girls who'd never be mistaken for white but whose skin forever marked them out among the black population of New Orleans. Max had never understood the politics of hue, and always feared expressing an opinion on the subject. He was white and from Boston, and he couldn't claim to know a damn thing about New Orleans. So he kept his mouth shut. All he knew was that even before he'd met Gabrielle he had thought a mixed race heritage produced the most beautiful children, and that there must be some lesson the world should learn from that. Meeting Gabrielle had cemented this belief.

Riding in the car beside her, Max saw some of that same beauty in Corinne. They'd met half a dozen times when he'd been involved with Gabrielle, but he'd never really noticed her looks. She simply didn't have her cousin's presence. Gabrielle had burned brightly; Corinne had been in her shadow. But apparently it hadn't stopped her from loving Gabrielle.

Abruptly, she turned and shot him a hard look. "Why do you keep staring at me like that?"

"You look a little like her," Max said.

"I'm *nothing* like her!" Corinne snapped, turning her gaze back to the road ahead. The hurt in her voice didn't surprise him, but the anger did.

"Are we really going to be the only people at the funeral?"

Corinne softened. "Our family shut her out; you know that. The ones who are still in the city, they live Uptown. When she was alive, they'd cross the street if they saw her coming. Now that she's dead, they won't be going out of their way to say good-bye. Could be some of her friends'll have heard and come along and surprise me, but I doubt it. Lots of people have been shipped out. Those who *are* still here are looking after themselves and their own. It's all right, though."

Max looked out the window, watching the side of the highway where wind-downed trees and abandoned cars remained, part of the debris left behind by the storm.

"Two people," he said quietly. "How can that be all right?"

"Ah, she wouldn't mind so much," Corinne said. "She didn't have but the two of us who really loved her. *We'll* be there. That's as it should be."

Max swallowed hard. His throat had gone dry. "I'm not sure—"

"Don't even start. She put the knife in you deep, man. I know that. But don't try to tell me you stopped loving her because of it. I know better."

Irritated, he narrowed his eyes and studied her. "You think so?"

"You're here, aren't you?"

Max opened his mouth, but closed it again. The Doucette women had a habit of leaving him speechless.

The French Quarter of New Orleans had established a reputation around the world. Some of it had been born of fame, thanks to the Quarter's unique architectural mélange and the delights of its restaurants, and some had sprung from the infamy of Bourbon Street, where the drunkenness and breast-flashing of Mardi Gras had spilled into the other 364 days of the year. Max had never been interested in Bourbon Street. One walk along that road, with its faux-voodoo shops and tourist puke-fest bars, might have put him off of the city forever, if not for the rest of what the Quarter had to offer. The terraced balconies and narrow streets could transport him back in time, and the tiny restaurants with their succulent gumbos delighted him.

The Quarter had sustained hurricane damage. There were restaurants and bars that were still closed, some of them boarded up, and more than one shop stood empty and dark, the owners having given up on New Orleans forever. The wind and the rain had taken their toll, but the Quarter hadn't flooded. When the city was ready to receive tourists again, Bourbon Street would be there.

For now, though, Max found it eerie as hell. Even in the rain, there had always been street performers here; saxophone players and steel bands, dancers, mimes and jugglers. The afternoon he arrived, the sun was shining, but as he walked into his hotel the street outside was silent. New Orleans had lost its music. It might as well have lost its soul.

Next morning, Corinne picked him up and they drove out of the Quarter, following Esplanade up through Faubourg Marigny. Their route took them mainly through areas that had remained above the floodwaters, and thus far he'd not encountered the level of devastation he'd seen in photographs and on television. He wondered if Corinne had been purposely sparing him that, or if she'd just rather avoid it herself.

When they reached Holt Cemetery, however, there was no way to avoid the reality of what had transpired in the city. Max had driven past it before, had seen the rows of tilted crosses and slate-thin headstones, but he'd never been inside the gates. In most of the Catholic world, All Saints' Day just meant another trip to church. But in New Orleans, every first of November brought massive gatherings to the city's cemeteries. People went there to decorate the graves of their loved ones, to leave flowers and notes and photographs, or just to remember.

As Corinne drove the car slowly along the narrow cemetery road, Max shuddered to think what November

1st had been like this year. Markers were down, and many were probably far away from the graves they were intended for, lying on brown, lifeless grass.

"The whole cemetery was flooded," Corinne said.

Max didn't need telling. In his mind's eye, he could see the crosses slowly being submerged as the water level rose. In some places the water had worn the topsoil away, and the upper edge of a coffin could be seen. If any bones had been brought to the surface by the flood, they'd been removed or reburied. With so much of the city's population driven from New Orleans, Holt Cemetery had probably been quiet on All Saints' Day, but someone had been tending to the worst of it. Someone had hope.

"There are no aboveground crypts here," he said, glancing around in surprise.

Corinne laughed. "Not everyone can afford to be buried in style, Max. Holt's full of poor black folks. Some of the markers have lists of names on them, bones from half a dozen generations in a single grave."

"Your family's not poor."

She put the car in park.

"Our grandparents and my father are buried in the family crypt in Mount Olivet Cemetery. I tried to get Gaby's parents to let us put her there, but they refused, and they wouldn't give a dime for her burial. Even my mother wouldn't give me a dollar for Gabrielle's coffin, and the girl had been her favorite once. Made her laugh more than I ever could. Gaby used to sleep over and we'd do my momma's hair. Now that she's dead, everyone turned their backs on her."

Her voice cracked, tears threatening.

"I don't understand," Max said. "When I was seeing her, I was aware of some rift, but she never talked about it. Now you tell me her family hated her so much they won't even come to see her laid to rest. But *why?*"

For a second he thought she might tell him, and the idea brought a darkness to her eyes that made him think maybe he didn't want to know. Then the moment passed, and Corinne shook her head.

"It's family business, Max. I start talking about family business, and when my time comes I'll be buried out here with her. They're already turning cold to me because I won't pretend Gaby never existed. I'm just hoping once she's in the ground, we can all put it behind us."

"So you can forget her?"

Corinne glared at him. "I won't ever forget her. But I want *them* to forget. It's the only way they'll forgive me. Now, come on. They're waiting."

She exited the car and started off across the ravaged cemetery, stepping over a warped, bloated wooden sign that had once marked a grave. Max watched her go, trying to ally the picture she was painting of Gabrielle with the girl he'd known. At nineteen, she hadn't only been stunning, she'd been spectacular, one of those people who seemed loved everywhere she went.

Maybe she never went anywhere she wouldn't be so well received.

There might be some truth to that. In the months he and Gabrielle had been together, the only member of her family she had introduced Max to had been Corinne. But he had never realized the full extent of the rift in the Doucette clan. Now that he did, he couldn't help wondering not only what had caused it, but what it had cost Corinne to ignore it.

Max fixed his tie and adjusted the cuffs of his jacket. Even in November, he felt too warm in the charcoal suit he only ever wore at weddings and funerals. Perhaps the New Orleans weather was to blame, humid and warm today. Or maybe he just felt out of place here, the jilted ex, much too old for the dead girl to begin with.

The eight people standing by Gabrielle's open grave watched him without expression as he approached.

Corinne spent a few moments in quiet conversation with the priest, by which time Max had arrived at the graveside. From there he could see the other road through the cemetery and the two cars parked there, one of them a hearse. There had been no wake and no funeral mass.

No longer able to deny its presence, he at last focused on the coffin that sat on the ground beside the open grave. It was a simple metal box, but he suspected it was better than a lot of those interred at Holt would have had. He stared at it, tried to imagine that Gabrielle lay inside, and could not.

His throat closed up, emotion flooding him. Grief and anger mixed into some other, unnamed thing. Memories began to rise of their time together, making love in the attic room of that empty house, strolling the backstreets of the Quarter, drinking in bars in Marigny or listening to music in Bywater clubs. She'd hated all the tourist spots except for Cafe du Monde; their beignets were better than crack,

Gabrielle had joked. At least, he'd always thought she was joking. She'd make breakfast in the nude, but get shy if he walked into the bathroom while she was showering. She loved flowers that grew wild, but thought gardens pretentious.

How could anyone not have loved her?

How could he ever stop?

"Are you all right?" Corinne asked.

Max flinched, looked at her, and then slowly nodded. "I will be."

"You don't look it."

He smiled, keeping his voice to a whisper. His words weren't meant for other ears. "I thought I was being a fool, coming down here. What kind of guy travels this far for a girl who slept with someone else, you know? But I'm glad I came."

Corinne touched his arm gently. "She was hard to understand."

Max only nodded. That was the understatement of the year. He glanced at the other mourners. "I thought you said it'd be just us."

"Father Legohn's congregation is mostly gone. The one with the nice shoes is the undertaker. The others are what's left of the church, just here to help carry her, say a prayer, and put her in the ground."

The truth of this hit Max hard. Despite the warning Corinne had given him, the idea that there was nobody left in New Orleans who cared enough to say good-bye to Gabrielle was bitter and ugly. It boded ill for the city, and spoke darkly of the dead girl. At least Gabrielle's body had been identified, not left amongst the hundreds of corpses remaining unclaimed, identities unknown.

The priest took his place at the head of the grave, Bible clutched in his right hand. As he began to speak, Max leaned toward Corinne.

"At least she had you," he whispered. "If you hadn't paid for it, who knows where she would've ended up."

"I didn't pay for it," Corinne said. "The storm left me with nothing."

Max blinked, confused, listening to the priest with one ear as he tried to make sense of Corinne's words.

"Then who did?"

She gave the slightest nod toward the hearse. A third car had pulled up on that cemetery road, a little white two-door coupe that looked forty years old. The man who stood by the car must have been thirty years older, with hair as white as his car, and skin darker than his funeral suit.

"Who's he?" Max asked.

One of the congregation members hushed him. Corinne was focused on the priest and didn't answer. Max looked back across the cemetery to the old guy and his little white coupe and wondered why, if he'd paid for the coffin and the grave, he didn't come and listen, and say good-bye.

But then Father Legohn began to talk about Gabrielle— what little he knew of her from Corinne—and he segued into talking about the days of loss they'd all put behind them and the many more days that lay ahead. And Max let himself be seduced by the man's eloquence and heart, and again slipped into the past, into his own memories of Gabrielle.

When the funeral ended, the undertaker and the handful of members of Father Legohn's congregation accompanied the priest back to his car. Several men piled into the Lincoln with him and drove off, but others remained behind with the undertaker. They stood by the hearse and smoked, waiting for Max and Corinne to depart so they could put Gabrielle into the ground. One of them offered a cigarette to the old man by the white coupe, but he declined.

"I could use a drink," Corinne said. "And nothing pleasant. No fucking margaritas for me. I want whiskey."

Max looked at her. "I'm with you. I'd like to take a minute, though. Is that all right?"

"Take as long as you like." Before leaving the graveside, she touched her fingers to her lips and then brushed them against the lid of Gabrielle's coffin, a last kiss for a cousin who'd been more like a sister. Then without glancing back at Max, she turned and walked back across the storm-and-flood-ravaged cemetery to her car.

Hands stuffed in his pockets, Max stared at the coffin. No headstone had been erected. From the look of Holt Cemetery, it seemed more likely Gabrielle would have some kind of marker set into the ground, and maybe that would be the best thing. If someone put up a cross or a stone, the next storm surge might just knock it down. And any fool could see there would be a next time.

"I hate you a little," he whispered. "For what you did, and now for dying." He chuckled softly, ashamed but unable to pretend he didn't feel these things. With Gabrielle dead, he'd never know why she'd hurt him, or how she really felt. He'd never be able to confront her about it.

"Sometimes I wish I'd never known you." But he knew, even as the words came out, that they were a lie. What he wished was that he had never learned the truth.

A cough startled him. The polite, sorry-to-interrupt-you sort of cough.

He turned to see that without him hearing, the white-haired old man had come over to the graveside. Max stood at the head of the grave, where the priest had prayed a short time before, and now the old man stood at the foot, with that gaping hole between them and Gabrielle's coffin off to one side.

"You're Max Corbett," the man said. His skin was so dark his hair looked like snow on top of tar. Of all the things Max might have expected to come out of his mouth, this wasn't it.

"That's me. Who are you?"

The old man nodded toward the coffin. "Girl was a friend of mine. Sweet thing, and gone too soon."

Max nodded. Gabrielle was full of surprises.

"You have questions for her," the old guy said. "Things you wanted to ask her."

Uncomfortable, Max glanced at him. "Why? Did she talk about me? Give you a message or something?"

"Some, but nothing like what you mean." The old man touched the thin metal of the coffin, stared at it for a moment, then looked back up at Max. "I'm just saying if you have questions you want to ask her, it might not be too late."

chapter

2

Max had no intention of going anywhere with this strange man. He'd just buried the girl he'd once loved, and Corinne's suggestion that they get a drink—probably more than one—sat well with him just then. Besides, this guy was . . . spooky. And obviously a little deranged.

"Look, no offense, but—"

"Your lady's gone," the old man whispered.

Max glanced at the coffin, thinking he meant Gabrielle. But then he heard the sound of a car starting and looked across the cemetery to see Corinne driving slowly away. She didn't turn to look at him, but neither did she seem in a rush to leave. Almost as if she'd forgotten he was even here.

"Time to talk, Max," the old man said. Max was not sure whether it was posed as a question or a statement.

"How d'you know my name?"

The old man shrugged, in a smug way that Max knew would become bothersome very quickly.

"And what do you mean when you say—"

"I know a nice little bar," the old man said. He stretched, and Max was sure he actually heard bones creaking. "Not far from here. Least, used to be nice. Since the Rage, the whole city has gone sour."

"Rage?"

The man rolled his eyes at the clear blue sky. "The storm. Katrina. Such a sweet name."

"Why would I go anywhere with you?"

"'Cos you're intrigued," the man said, shrugging again. Then he smiled. "And 'cos your lady's gone."

As he climbed into the passenger seat of the white coupe, Max realized that he had made no plans beyond the funeral. He'd arranged the trip, booked the flight and hotel, spoken with Corinne about her picking him up from Baton Rouge airport, but his focus had always been on the moment that had just passed. He had watched Gabrielle's coffin as words that meant little to him were spoken across it, and now that it was over, he was lost. He'd figured today would be taken up with the funeral, and whatever gathering might take place after it. But there wasn't going to be any gathering, and Corinne had just taken off and left him in the cemetery. And what the fuck was that about?

Two days remaining in New Orleans, and nothing left to do.

At some point, back in Boston, he'd presumed he would at least go by and visit the colleagues he'd worked with at Tulane, see about their welfare after the storm. But he'd barely been in contact with them since he left, and wondered if he'd be welcome.

Beyond that, he hadn't thought about what he would do after saying good-bye.

Max closed his eyes for a moment and saw her face, and the idea that he would never see her again cut him in two. Since leaving, he had lived with the certainty that she was out of his life forever, but at least she had still existed in the same world, still shared the same atmosphere with him. He was still *aware* of her. And now she was gone, completely and finally, and when he sucked in a breath it contained nothing of her.

The old man drove slowly from the cemetery, steering around grave markers that had been washed onto the road. He turned left, eventually edging them past the muddy ruin of City Park and driving so slowly that Max thought they could probably walk faster. He glanced across, and the expression on the guy's face was one of quiet contemplation.

"You said it might not be too late," Max said at last.

"Hmm?"

"To ask questions of Gabrielle. What did you mean by that? And who are you, anyway? An uncle or something?"

"Something like that," the man said, smiling. He exuded

calmness and peace, and Max wondered how he'd made it through the past couple of months. Because he had no doubt that the old man had been here before the storm, and had not left since. There was something about him that attested to that, some New Orleans quality that Max had just started to recognize in people before he fled back to Boston.

"If you're not going to answer——"

"Bar's called Cooper's. I've been drinkin' there some thirty years, and it was there long before that. Cooper's long dead an' gone, but his boys still run the place. It wasn't the nicest place you'll find in the city, even before, but . . . it's one of the best. You can smell the honesty when you walk in. Know what I mean?"

Max didn't, but he saw where the old man's non-answer was leading. "All right. We can talk when we get there. But do I get to learn your name?"

"You can call me Ray."

"Ray," Max repeated. The framing of the answer wasn't lost on him. He'd asked for the old man's name, but he hadn't given it. Just something Max could call him.

Ray gave that haughty, one-shouldered shrug again, and kept his eyes on the road, the little coupe crawling along the streets of New Orleans.

Cooper's looked dead. The sign had been blown away, leaving a bent metal hanger above the entrance door, and most of the windows were boarded up. Three others were exposed, glass grubby and surrounded by what Max first took to be bullet holes. Then he realized that they were nail holes, punched into the frames and walls when the windows were covered before the storm. Behind one window was an old neon beer sign, swathed with brightly-colored paint to give it some semblance of life.

Someone had spray-painted WE SHOOT LOOTERS across the façade, the double "oo" of "shoot" missing now that the entrance door was unboarded again. Just below that stark warning, two feet above sidewalk level, was the grubby tide mark that Max had already noticed around the city. It showed how high the waters had come. The limits of life and death.

The edge of the sidewalk nearest the road was piled with broken things: air-conditioning units, smashed-up floorboarding, picture frames, chairs, ceiling fans, and the remains of a wooden bar, all of them tainted with filth or swollen from immersion in water. It looked like someone's insides laid bare.

"Place got off lightly," Ray said. He slammed the car door and stood beside Max. He was a good eight inches shorter, but a palpable energy radiated from him. For someone so old who drove so slow, he certainly seemed very much alive.

"Doesn't look that way."

Ray pointed along the street. "Ground level falls the farther you drive. Half a mile down there, water was ten feet deep."

"I don't want a tour," Max said, immediately regretting the comment. How could he not expect Ray to want to talk about the storm? The Rage, as he'd called it.

"Good," Ray said, and Max knew that he meant it. " 'Cos life and death move on." He opened the door to Cooper's and beckoned Max inside.

You can smell the honesty when you walk in, Ray had said, and Max had not really understood. Upon entering, however, he knew exactly what the weird old man had meant. This was a place where the sweat and blood of life were laid bare, and the lie of casual acceptance had no place. It no longer looked like a normal bar, if it ever had. Floorboards had been replaced with thick plywood flooring, joints rough, nail holes already filled with dirt and cigarette ash. The furniture was a mishmash of plastic garden chairs and tables, wooden benches, a couple of church pews, metal chairs with timber seats tied on with wire, and round tables made from piled car tires and circles of the same plywood used for flooring. Flickering candles sat on each table and on rough shelves across the walls, providing a pale illumination.

Along the back wall was the bar itself: beer crates stacked five high, and an open shelving unit screwed to the wall and containing dozens of liquor bottles. A tall, thin black man sat on a stool beside the pile of booze, a cigarette hanging from his mouth and his eyes half-closed. Another tall man walked the room, collecting empties, chatting with the dozen people there, and fetching more drinks. These, Max assumed, were the Coopers. They had refused to let their place go to rot, and had instead reopened it as best they could. No illusions here, no pretense; this was a place to drink and talk. It stank of sweat and spilled beer, because there was no power for air-conditioning. It stank of defiance.

Everyone here lifted their bottle or glass before they took a first drink, toasting their barkeepers.

A few people glanced around at the new arrivals, then returned to their conversations.

"Bother you, bein' the only white face?"

"I thought you'd been drinking here for thirty years?" Max asked. *So where was the welcome? Where were the raised hands from the Cooper brothers, or the other patrons?*

That shrug again. "Keep to myself."

"Okay," Max said, unconvinced. "And no, it doesn't bother me."

"Good," Ray said. " 'Cos if you looked bothered, it'd bother them. Drink?"

"Yeah," Max said. He wondered whether Corinne was drinking now, and what she was thinking about, and why she'd left him with Ray.

"Water?" Ray said, a twinkle in his eye.

"Whiskey."

"Partial to Scottish single malt myself. But hereabouts it's mostly bourbon. Folks are suspicious of anythin' that goes down too smooth."

"Whatever." Max looked around and spotted a plastic table in the corner of the room, two old school chairs upside down on its yellowed surface. He nodded that way, then left Ray to buy their drinks.

Max walked between tables, nodding a greeting as a couple of men looked up. They tilted their beer bottles in apparent welcome, but watched him a moment longer. He remembered walking into Roland's Garage for the first time with Gabrielle on his arm, how all the eyes had settled on her and he'd felt as though he hardly existed. But she'd looked at him and made him glow, because that night she only had eyes for him.

He took the chairs down from the table and sat, and Ray came across with a bottle of Jack Daniel's and two glasses. Max wasn't a big drinker. But right now, it was just what he wanted.

Max had a hundred questions about Cooper's, but a thousand about Gabrielle. And Ray saw that. The old man sighed and sat down, pouring them both a double shot, and lifted his glass.

"What?" Max asked. "A toast? To Gabrielle?"

"If you like," Ray said.

"For now I'll just drink. And listen."

Ray nodded, his face suddenly serious for the first time since they'd met. Max wondered whether this was his natural look.

"Gabrielle's truly one of New Orleans' lost souls," Ray said. He drank his whiskey.

"You mean a hurricane victim?"

Ray shook his head. "I'm not talkin' about that, not now. This goes deeper, and further back. Right to the heart of this place." He smiled, and gave a more casual version of that annoying shrug. "But you ain't from New Orleans."

"No buts, Ray," Max said, trying to keep his voice level and low. "And no more of this mystery man crap."

"Oh, I'm not sayin' I'm not going to tell you. Already

decided that, in this old head of mine. All I'm sayin' is, you won't understand."

Max wanted to stand, leave Cooper's Bar, and walk as far and as fast as he could, following the terrible tide marks to higher ground and finding his way out of this city once and for all. When he'd lived here, he'd enjoyed being an outsider, trying to learn the city. Now Corinne's talk, the way Gabrielle's family had abandoned her, and Ray's condescension just made him want to get the hell away.

"She could have been so special," Ray said.

"She *was* special."

"You can save her, boy. If you choose to do as I say, if you're willin' to follow the path and go here an' there, now an' then, you can save her from herself."

"She's dead," Max said. "By now, she's in the ground."

"Dead now, yeah. But she *was* alive, *so* alive. More'n any woman I ever met." Ray stared into his glass for a moment, seeing unknown pasts in the swish of the amber liquid. Then he drank the remnants of his whiskey and poured some more. He filled Max's glass as well, which Max was surprised to find empty.

"I don't know what I'm listening to here," Max said, drinking the whiskey in one swallow. It tasted good, felt better. It burned his insides, and he imagined parts of his body glowing when the lights went out.

"There's a man who can help you, name of Matrisse. He's a conjure-man."

Max paused with his empty glass halfway down to the table. He looked away from Ray, glancing around the bar at the other drinkers. Most were in pairs, a couple drinking alone, and they all found something amazing in their glasses, whether empty or full. When they were tired of looking at each other, they could look into their drinks and see themselves.

"Magic," Max said. "Right."

"Not magic like you know it. Not that tourist shit. Matrisse, he don't have a shop front on Bourbon Street selling charms and magic dust. He's known in the city, but only to some." Ray leaned forward across the table and lowered his voice. "True magic, boy. None of this meddlesome fakery peddled to wannabes. His heart is tied with the heart of this city."

"And he's still here after the storm?"

"Yeah, boy, still here. His heart aches, but he can never leave this place. It's a New Orleans thing." Ray sat up again and smiled, pouring more whiskey into his glass. They'd got through a third of a bottle already, and Max was feeling the effects stroking the extremes of his senses. The candlelight looked brighter, the outlines of the other patrons sharper, but the door looked much farther away than before.

"True magic's an oxymoron, Ray. No such thing. Even if there was, what do you think this guy can do for Gabrielle? Make her a zombie?"

"Hollywood!" Ray spat, his smile no longer holding any trace of humor. "Forget all the stories you think you know. Matrisse, he has ways an' means to do more than you can imagine, boy. An' one of those things . . . well, he can open a door to the past. Maybe get a message through."

His chin tilted down, so his eyes were lost in shadow.

"Maybe get a *man* through. It ain't easy, and he don't do it too much . . . but he'll do it for you."

"For Gabrielle, you mean?"

"Yeah, for Gabrielle. He don't even *know* you."

"Why?"

"I told you why. 'Cos she could have been special." Ray drank more whiskey and filled his glass again, no longer topping up Max's.

It was a hell of a fantasy. Send a message back to Gabrielle, warn her what was coming. But fantasy couldn't raise the dead.

Max stared at Ray. "Even if I believed any of this, how would I find this Matrisse?"

"He'll find you. First, though, there's a map you have to follow. You got no magic about you. No aura. You're from outta town, but in cases like this that can be good. An advantage. You're a clean slate."

So sincere, and already talking like Max had agreed to go along with this bullshit. Max almost scoffed, but stopped himself. He was asking the questions, wasn't he? Maybe it was the whiskey talking, but he couldn't prevent his mind from following where Ray's words led, and wondering.

"Clean slate for what?" Perhaps it was their surroundings, lending that honest power to everything the old man said. Or maybe it was just the deadly combination of grief and Jack Daniel's.

"For gatherin' magic to you. I can give you the map, if you commit to following it. Follow it, magic yourself up, like runnin' your feet along a carpet to build up static, and at the end of the map you'll find Matrisse. Then maybe he'll help you through."

"And I can get a message to Gabrielle, back before any of this happened?"

"Or maybe you bring it yourself." Ray raised his glass and looked into the liquor again, hypnotized by the candle-light refracting gold and amber. "Right place, right time . . ."

Max wanted to laugh. He wanted to mock this old fool, tip the table over, and storm from the bar. But he could not. And he knew it wasn't just the whiskey keeping him in his plastic chair. It was something about the old man and his words, and the fact that he obviously believed every one of them.

"Why are you telling me all this?" Max said. "You knew Gabrielle. You obviously cared about her. Why don't you do it?"

" 'Cos it's dangerous, and I'm old, and I doubt this body could take it," Ray said. "You want to see the map?"

"Yeah. But . . . won't it all be changed?"

Ray grinned. "This ain't a map of places, boy. It's a map of moments." He took an envelope from inside his jacket, extracted a folded sheet of paper, and spread it across the table. He glanced around just once, and for an instant Max saw something like danger in his eyes. Ray had smiled, and grinned, and looked serious . . . but now Max sensed that he could be deadly as well, if the time and need called for it.

Max took another long swig of whiskey. *This is crazy,* he thought. But hadn't his love for Gabrielle been a kind of craziness as well? Back in New Orleans now, why not let that insanity continue, just for a while . . . ?

He leaned over the table and looked down at the map. "That's just a tourist map of the city."

"Look closer."

Max did so. Wavering candlelight seemed to make the Mississippi flex like a sleeping snake, and Lake Pontchartrain loomed across the top of the map, dark blue and menacing. He started by trying to locate exactly where they were now, with Holt Cemetery, and Greenwood and Metairie Cemeteries, close by. Then he moved farther out, tracing roads with his finger, until he came to a marking he did not recognize across City Park:

The First Moment:
Even Before the City,
the City Shows Its Heart
July 15, 1699

"What's this?"

"One of New Orleans' most magical moments," Ray said. "You can see it, sense it, feel it. You can watch it, and gather some of the dregs of its magic to you. Moments like this echo through history, 'cos time don't bow down much to magic."

"How can I see something that happened——?" Max began, but Ray cut in, an element of impatience in his voice.

"It's your choice now, boy. I've told you enough, and I can't hold you down an' make you do this. I ask one thing, though." He smiled at the empty bottle of whiskey. "You owe me half a bottle, so do this one thing for me. Go to the first place, an' the first moment. You'll know where an' when that is when you study the map. Drink this before-hand, an' it'll help you."

Now Max did scoff, too loudly, fueled by whiskey. "Magic potions? You're shitting me." Every head turned to look at them.

Ray paused, hand holding a small clay bottle halfway to the table. He spoke quietly. "Don't believe in them?"

The other patrons turned away again, and Max sensed a tension in the room now. Maybe they *did* all recognize Ray. Maybe he *had* been drinking here for thirty years.

"Just humor an old man," Ray said. "Ain't nothin' in this bottle to hurt you. And you know I ain't lying, just like you know the rest of it's true."

Max frowned. Somehow he *did* believe it when Ray told him nothing in that bottle would harm him, but he couldn't avoid the suspicion that the old man's words only sounded like the truth because Ray himself believed them.

"You're crazy."

"Thank you." And Ray chuckled, an infectious laugh that came from somewhere deep and shook his whole body.

Max stood, and the whiskey hit him hard. His legs shook and his head seemed to sway atop his neck, and he wasn't sure whether everyone was looking at him, or everyone was looking away. He grabbed the map from the table and folded it, then snatched up the small clay bottle. It seemed the right thing to do.

"This . . ." he said, waving the bottle before Ray's face. But the old man was still chuckling, and he watched as Max edged his way across the bar.

Standing by the front door, conscious of the poor light

inside and the harsh sun without, Max glanced back at the old man. There was a fresh bottle of whiskey on his table, his glass was full, and he was talking at the chair Max had just vacated. He gestured with his hands, nodded, and gave that annoying, dismissive shrug once again. *Talking to himself,* Max thought. *Now I know he's nuts.*

Then Ray did a curious thing. He reached inside his jacket pocket and pulled out a small glass vial. Carefully, he poured a few drops into the glass Max had just left behind, and followed it with a dash of whiskey. He slid the glass across the table, toward the empty seat, and smiled.

Nutjob.

Max tugged at the door and stumbled outside. The stark autumn sun blinded him for a moment, and he slid down the wall and sat on a sidewalk strewn with litter and grit. He shaded his eyes to try to see, and a shadow passed before him. It seemed too large to belong to just one man.

Ray chuckled again and started the coupe, the engine seeming to match its owner's laughter.

As the car moved away, Max's sight returned, and he was just another midday drunk, washed up on the shores of New Orleans.

He sat there for a while, dazed, trying to go over what Ray had said but finding no sense there. It felt like a dream. Several times he turned to stare at the front façade of Cooper's Bar, listening for voices from inside, almost convincing himself that the place was empty and he'd imagined it all. But then the door would burst open and someone would stumble out, or a lonely shadow would walk along the street and enter, and he knew that the place was real. No one spoke to him, and no one paused to see if he was all right.

He dozed, the drink befuddling his senses and confusing him every time he woke. Was the sun *really* farther back than it had been when he'd nodded off? Was the tide mark across the street *really* three feet higher?

At last the need to urinate brought him around. He got slowly to his feet, holding his head in case his brains leaked out. He had not drunk so much in a long time, and certainly not so quickly.

He heard Gabrielle giggle at his hangover, and he spun around in case she was there. His head throbbed even more. He was alone.

Walking along the street, looking for somewhere to piss, Max at last noticed the small bottle grasped in his hand. He'd been holding it all along, like some kind of talisman. It was gray and bare of markings, and it had a corked top. He paused on the sidewalk, staring at the bottle, and the silence crowded in to stare with him.

A pack of dogs trotted up the street from where the ground was lower. A couple wore collars, others bore open wounds on their muzzles and necks, and they all looked mean. They passed him by without a glance. Their presence only brought home just how deserted this street, and this neighborhood, really was.

He went to throw the bottle away, but his arm refused to obey the command. He thought about pulling the cork and sniffing the insides—not drinking, just taking a slight whiff to get the measure of what it contained—but something about that did not feel right, either. He had no idea what was in there. He was alone, and vulnerable, and the only person in the city who had offered to help had left him alone with a crazy old man.

"Fuck it," Max said. "Fuck it all." He popped the cork and sniffed the bottle, and it smelled of nothing. He'd been hoping for more whiskey, at least. "Magic potion." He tried to laugh, but could not, and then he tipped his head back and upended the bottle.

He readied himself to gulp and swallow, but what came out barely touched his tongue, light and insubstantial as a lover's gasp. He closed his mouth and staggered a little, head spinning again. The bottle still smelled of nothing, but now it felt much lighter. He tipped it up again, felt nothing, and then threw it as hard as he could across the road. It bounced once on the concrete, hit the opposite curb, and shattered, a dozen parts losing themselves amidst the muck and shit already there.

"Crazy old bastard," Max muttered, and was answered by the sound of a motorcycle roaring somewhere far away.

He slipped between two buildings, stumbling over a pile of refuse from a gutted dwelling. Someone's refrigerator leaned against one wall, its edges taped shut and several fridge magnets still exhorting the wonders of Six Flags and Joyce's Gumbo. He passed the fridge and pissed with his head resting against the wall.

Turning back to the road, he noticed the bicycle. It was rusty, single speed, and it had the remains of a kid's seat on the back, foam and straps long since rotted away. He looked around, natural guilt pricking at him as he pulled the bike upright. This had to belong to someone, but there was no one here. The buildings were empty, and felt as if they'd been deserted for some time. Cooper's Bar was full, but he had no idea where any of its patrons lived. Maybe they now only truly existed in Cooper's.

It could have been noon or three in the afternoon; he'd lost all track of time. His head throbbed, his mouth was dry and demanded water, and his insides roiled with the effects of too much whiskey; he knew he had to find his way back to the hotel. He had left Gabrielle's funeral and lost himself for a moment, and he needed to center his thoughts again, handle the grief, and look forward to the time when he could move on.

He could not believe how quiet it was. Even inside the bar—he now struggled to remember the sound of voices other than his and Ray's. Had *anyone* been speaking in there? Or had they all been listening?

He started cycling on the soft tires, heading back to Orleans Avenue. But when he reached there he turned left, not right toward the French Quarter, steering without really thinking, and the presence of other people again was good enough for him. A few cars came by, then an army Humvee, and some trucks towing trailers stacked high with filthy kitchen appliances. Other people were using bikes to negotiate their way around town. A couple of cop cars zipped past him, lights off but obviously going somewhere in a hurry. *Someone's day ruined,* he thought, and he was glad he was moving in the opposite direction.

The exercise was painful at first, but then Max started

to enjoy it. He felt the alcohol's effects leveling off to simple drunkenness—an improvement over his previous state of totally shitfaced—and he could handle that just fine. His muscles started to ache, but that was okay, that was right, because he'd let himself go. Since fleeing New Orleans six months earlier, he'd been wallowing in despair. He'd never wanted to admit to himself that he was depressed, but retrospect was a clearer, more honest glass through which to view what had happened.

He pedaled harder, because it was starting to feel good. These past few months in Boston he'd stopped exercising, preferring instead to sit in front of the TV and lose his way in mindlessness. His diet had also suffered, and slowly he'd been piling on the pounds; not a fat man yet, but heavier than he'd ever been. His strength had faded, and tiredness was always close by.

Now he had the wind whipping at his face and sweat beading on his brow, and though the smell of this place was like nothing he had ever imagined, there were sights around each corner that he had only ever seen with . . .

"Gabrielle." He whispered her name and it was lost to the breeze, along with her memory. He had just buried his Gabrielle. She'd felt too young to love, but her eyes had sometimes looked so old.

Somewhere in the distance he heard a gunshot. He braked, and the bike's old wheels squealed in protest. He came to a stop behind an abandoned car, mud and filth dried in a thick coating and obscuring its color and make. Listening, head tilted to one side, he began to doubt what he'd heard, when two more shots came. It was from somewhere to his left, a rapid *crack-crack* that echoed quickly away between buildings.

He remembered Corinne speaking to him on the phone, during those brief but frequent calls when he'd been organizing his trip. *This isn't a good place right now,* she'd said. *You won't recognize it anymore.*

Max had never owned a gun, and never would. Now, though . . .

"Where the fuck am I going?" he mumbled. He'd left the area where there had been a few people and vehicles, and his surroundings looked as though someone had fought a war here and lost.

His impending hangover was already seeding itself, thrumming in his head and sending pain stabbing into his eyes.

There were no more gunshots.

He waited there for a while, sweating, craving a drink of water, when a pickup screeched out of a driveway several hundred yards along the road, coughed dirt across the street, then came his way.

Max edged closer to the curb behind the abandoned car.

The vehicle streaking toward him was old, rusted, and ruined, and it trailed clouds of thick gray smoke behind it. The sun reflected from the windshield, and he could not see who was driving, nor how many others were inside.

He'd heard about the looting and lawlessness, the attacks and burglaries, and the more extreme crimes that rumor dragged out of the water and laid bare for the tabloid press to relish.

The pickup truck sped by, and the passenger glanced at him, then down at the bike. Guilt hit Max, sobering him with images of the vehicle screeching to a stop, the passenger climbing out and pulling a gun, asking, *Where the fuck did you get that bike?*

But the truck went on and so did Max, and he knew exactly where he was going. Lakeview. The house, the attic where Corinne had found Gabrielle's body. The last place Max had seen her alive.

It had been hot and airless that day, the heat lying slumped in the bowl of New Orleans like a sleeping thing. Gabrielle had not called him for four days, and when he tried her cell, she never answered. He'd felt cast adrift, and the only person he'd felt able to speak to was Corinne.

Not my business, Corinne had told him on the phone. *But, baby, if she's sending you a message, listen to it and stay away.*

But he couldn't stay away. So he'd driven down here, down the very street he was cycling along now, to the place where he thought he might find her. Back then there had been trees lining the sidewalks; now there were only stumps. Back then the cars had looked at least serviceable, as opposed to the heaps of mud and rust that were here now. And they had been parked, not slewed across the street, and front lawns had been neat, flower beds planted, porches painted and manned with people content to watch the world go by. Now everything was a uniform gray, the color of dried silt, and there were few people other than Max. Some walkers, a couple of bike riders, and the occasional car full of the dispossessed and lost, curb-crawling for trouble.

Once upon a time, Lakeview had been a quiet, upper-middle-class neighborhood. Now it was a crumbling ghost town, like so much of what had once been New Orleans. The silence of a place so used to noise and bustle, the immobility of somewhere always on the move, was shocking. A pall of emotional dread coated the whole area, as thick and noticeable as the dirt.

If I were sober, I'd get the fuck out, he thought. But there was a comfort zone in alcohol, a numbing of the sense of danger . . . or perhaps an acceptance of it. Either way, he was too far gone to turn around now.

As if to confirm this, he came upon a street sign, one of the few still intact, and saw he'd arrived at Landry Street. As he cycled toward Gabrielle's aunt's house, he seemed to be seeing two views of the same scene. One had Gabrielle waiting for him up in that sweaty attic, wearing nothing but her socks and a welcoming smile. The other gave him nothing but death.

There was a house blocking half of the street. It had been lifted from its foundation and dumped here, gushing its insides across the concrete. Nobody had come to clear it away, and cars and trucks had driven across spilled furniture and memories. As Max moved around the remains of the house, he tried not to look inside; that would be intruding.

He had to go slowly so that he did not miss the address. Everything was different. The place next door to Gabrielle's always had a rainbow explosion of flowerpots hanging and standing on the front porch and garden, and it was only as he passed that he realized there was nothing left. No flowers. No porch. No house at all.

Max slipped from the bike and let it fall in the street. Its impact was a lonely sound.

His heart thumped far too fast, almost hurting his chest.

This was the first time he had ever been here without Gabrielle present, out here with him, or inside with—

Max squeezed his eyes shut, but that only gave the memory a greater hold. He'd been torn that day, part of him hurt by the way Gabrielle had been avoiding him, and the other part worried for her. He'd thought he knew her, and this behavior was unfamiliar. Someone needed to check on her. So he'd gone over to the house and let himself in, quietly. He'd called softly, but no one answered. And yet the house lacked the sense of vacancy that existed in empty places. Someone was home.

He'd started up the stairs, and it was as he reached the landing that he heard the sounds he had come to recognize so well. Gabrielle sighed as she was making love, and groaned, and when she came her groan rose in pitch and volume.

Standing there, he heard Gabrielle giving those noises to someone else.

Max had not bothered keeping quiet then. He'd run up the narrow attic staircase and thrown the door open, and still they had not heard him. Gabrielle had been sitting astride a young black student from Max's class, a pleasant kid called Joseph, and her naked back and butt were slick with sweat, her hair damp and stringy. He'd watched for a while, feeling removed from the world. It was only when he'd turned to leave that they heard him.

The memory gave him pause. He took a breath, then stepped forward.

The house looked so ruined now, so empty, that even ghosts would never call it home. And the only indication that Gabrielle had ever been here was a sign spray-painted across the dormer: 1 IN ATTIC. One. One girl. One woman. One dead.

Even then they'd left her here to rot.

Max sank to his knees on the dirty road. Someone shouted in the distance, a car engine revved, but he was immune to the thought of danger. His head throbbed and his heart thumped, and he thought one must surely explode. The stink on the air was awful. He tried to believe it was muck from the flood or filth from the streets, and nothing else. He did his best not to smell death.

Why had she stayed here? Why not flee? She had told Corinne that it was the only place she'd felt safe, but safe from what?

Rising, he climbed onto the stolen bike, turned around, and started cycling away. On that day of his final visit, there had been nothing here for him; now there was less.

Even the ghosts were gone.

On Canal Boulevard, a group of half a dozen young men stood waving guns at the air, shouting, loaded with threat. They all seemed angry at something, but the target of their anger was not obvious. Maybe they were angry with one another, and just waiting for the first shot to be fired.

Max stopped and pushed his bike onto the sidewalk. He didn't think he'd been seen, but he wasn't sure. Though the men moved and gesticulated, poking the air with their guns, they all seemed frozen in time, waiting for someone to make the next move. There was a pile of trash in the gutter from a ruined shop, and he crouched down behind it, peering out across rusted metal shelving and bloated cereal boxes.

There were a few black guys there, and a couple of Creoles, and a skinny white youth with one arm heavily bandaged. Though they all carried guns, there were no alliances apparent. The rage and fury hung heavy in the air, like dynamite sweating in the sun.

"What the fuck am I doing here?" Max whispered to himself. As if startled by his voice, several huge rats scurried from the pile of rubbish beside him and ran across the street.

Three shots rang out, and spouts of dust kicked up from the road amongst the running vermin. None of them was hit, but laughter erupted from behind Max, replacing the anger but sounding no less threatening.

If they find me hiding here . . . He considered just jumping on his bike and riding by, but he honestly did not think he could ride straight. He might as well be wearing a sign that said *Does not belong.* He would feel a hot barrel against the back of his neck, and there would be another dead rat in New Orleans.

"Fuck fuck fuck!" He did not know this area at all. He'd

always come down here with Gabrielle, straight to the house and then back out again. She hadn't liked the area, saying it stank of money and insensitivity, but now he suspected it was because some of her family lived here. She had never spoken about them.

There was a side road thirty yards back the way he'd come. He could take that and then ride like hell. But if it ended with a dead end? If it curved around back onto this main road? They'd know, and he didn't, and the risk was . . .

The map! Crazy Ray had insisted he take it, along with whatever that weird bottle had contained. *Nothing, there was nothing in there.* But he remembered drinking it, and the memory seemed to touch his tongue.

Max glanced around the pile of refuse. The men—little more than kids, really, teenagers—had gathered together now, and they were smoking and joking, anger apparently subdued for a time. He hunkered down and took out the map. *That's just a tourist map of the city,* he'd said, and Ray had replied, *Look closer.*

He looked closer.

Canal Boulevard was easy to find, but locating himself exactly was more difficult. He was sure he hadn't yet gone by Harrison Avenue, but if he took the side street he'd just passed, he could negotiate the blocks to find it. Then, once on the avenue, it was straight through to whatever was left of City Park and the golf course, then . . .

There it was, that blocked area on the map over the golf course. One of Ray's "moments." Max sighed and shook his head, but as he brought the map closer he had a sudden, brief taste of pure, clear air, like the first breath of his life untouched by pollution or rot. He gasped, swallowed, and then the stink of New Orleans was on him again.

It had been like a feather touch on his tongue, a breath from that smashed clay bottle.

The First Moment:
Even Before the City,
the City Shows Its Heart
July 15, 1699

He had to pass within a block of the spot, to get where he was headed.

"Why not?" he whispered.

Ray's story had been fantastic, and probably ridiculous. But there had been truth about him, and a sense of brutal honesty that could hurt as much as heal.

Max took a deep breath, stretched his limbs, and jumped onto the bike. As he pedaled hard along the debris-strewn sidewalk, hoping that the buildings would offer him cover, he waited for a shout, or the cool kiss of a bullet.

But none came. He reached the side street and swung straight out into the road, not bothering to look or listen for anything coming the other way.

Max rode hard. The street was narrow, and abandoned cars and piles of debris from gutted buildings formed obstacles for him to steer around. He had to concentrate, and that did something to allay the fear that the display of pure aggression had planted in him. He was away, and the feeling of having avoided a confrontation felt good.

There were no signs of life, but plenty of death, spray-painted on buildings above that terrible tide mark.

He followed the street for a while, then took the third turning right, the second left, right again, and he was on Harrison Avenue. He was so close to City Park that he could see its wall and railings at the end of the avenue.

Something called him. He wanted to taste that pure, fresh air again, wash away the stink of death and disaster. *The First Moment,* Ray's strange map said. And, Max supposed, the least he could do was give it a chance.

chapter

3

Max had strolled through City Park perhaps four or five times in the half year he spent living in New Orleans. Only once had he gone there with Gabrielle. They'd had a picnic, which he'd been the one to suggest, only to have her take over all planning and preparation. She wouldn't even tell him what was in the basket until they arrived at the park and he spread the blanket on the grass. It had been warm that day, but not so hot that they sought a shady place. Gabrielle liked the sun, and he supported anything that would make her smile.

The picnic had been an odd assortment of po'boys, corn bread, black bean salad, and locally brewed root beer. For dessert she'd made a good attempt at Max's favorite, key lime pie, though she'd never even tasted it before.

They'd ridden the carousel and strolled the Botanical Garden, and then, walking along a path, she'd taken him by the hand and led him off the trail. Behind a thick oak tree, Gabrielle had shushed him with a kiss, undone his belt, and crouched down to perform the most extraordinary fellatio of his life.

She had become all things to him in so short a time that she seemed almost like a dream, a construct of his imagination. Sweet, kind, and funny, she could be self-conscious and shy one minute, and the next a creature of lust and mischief. Falling in love with her had been the easiest thing he'd ever done.

He tried to keep those memories close to his heart and in the forefront of his mind as he rode the bicycle into City Park. From the slant of the daylight and the dimming of the eastern sky, he knew it must be late afternoon, the time of long shadows. Night was not far off.

Yet as he rode into the park from Marconi Drive, Max faltered. The place had come through better than he expected. There must have been mud everywhere at one point, and downed trees and branches, but whatever organization saw to the care of the place had marshaled their forces far better than the city, state, or federal government. Many of the live oaks had obviously been stripped of leaves, but already some were showing new growth.

Max rode on, soon discovering that not all of the park had recovered so quickly. The salt water that had flooded the area had killed all of the grass. Some roads and paths seemed to have been cleared, but dried mud still dappled the trees and benches. The carousel was closed, and Story-Land looked in need of repair. He paused several times to consult the map that Ray had given him, trying to figure out precisely where, in the park, this First Moment was supposed to be located.

There were people in the park, though they kept to the areas that had been restored. He saw several couples walking hand in hand, and a few mothers pushing baby carriages. These were stragglers, brave and determined people who refused to surrender the lives they had before Katrina.

Max stopped the bike and watched them for a while, hoping that in time they would find that they had been prescient, but fearing that one day they would think themselves fools for holding on to such hope. The park might be in the process of its resurrection, but the city would take much longer.

Gormley Stadium looked a thousand years old. He rode through the Botanical Garden and then north, right up through the heart of the park. Then he worried that he'd gone too far and stopped to consult the map once more. It took him a moment to realize where he was headed: Scout Island, an area of the park surrounded by water. He'd been a history professor at Tulane, and had talked plenty about the city of New Orleans. He knew a little about City Park, but not enough to know if Scout Island was natural or man-made. Probably the latter.

He rode on. The park was three miles long, and Scout Island just west of center, so it took him a while to find it and make sure he was in the right place. He found a bridge and hid the bike in its shadow, glancing around to make sure nobody was paying him any attention. He needn't have worried. There were very few people in the park, and nobody in shouting distance now. With a frown, he hesitated. There might be trouble here after dark, and dusk was coming on fast.

Then he realized how foolish that was. The streets were full of trouble. He'd likely be safer here than anywhere else in New Orleans. Still, he hesitated another moment before starting over the bridge, trying to figure just why he'd come here. But curiosity and whiskey had the better of him. Walking away now would only make him feel more foolish than he already did, so he crossed the little stone bridge.

The moment he set foot on Scout Island he shuddered. A wave of disorientation passed over him and his stomach gave a twist, as though vomit might not be far behind. Yet the taste in his mouth was not whiskey or sickness, but a strangely sweet kind of nothing, more like the scent of subtle flowers than any real flavor. Max blinked, trying to clear his head.

He took two more steps . . .

. . . into the pouring rain.

"What the hell?" he muttered, looking up and wiping water from his eyes. The rain came down so hard it hurt, pelting at his arms and the back of his neck. He shook his head and droplets flew from his hair. *Impossible. The sky was clear. Dusk coming on, and the sky was clear.*

Impossible or not, the storm raged. The wind blew, though not too fiercely, and the rain battered the trees around him. Worst of all, though, in the seconds during which he had been blinking, trying to clear his mind, it had gone from late afternoon to full-on night.

He bore the pummeling rain for a few seconds more to stare at the low, heavy clouds, seemingly lit from within by the dull glow of promised lightning. Thunder cracked like a whip, then rolled, like mountains rising up to war.

Max shook the rain from his hair again, but he was really trying to shake off the impossible. He turned to flee back over the bridge, hoping to find temporary shelter while the worst of it went by, but he'd become confused. The bridge was no longer behind him. He spun around, but all he could see were oaks and cypress trees.

Then he stopped, breath coming hard and fast, because something was very wrong. *Different.* He could see the edge of a marshland, and the grass and trees were a massive tangle of vegetation. The branches around and above him were heavy with leaves. The air had grown hot, despite the darkness and the rain.

A question bubbled up to his lips and was born before he could stop it.

"Where am I?"

He hated the question. Thoughts of that little gray stone bottle and its cork stopper rose in his mind. The whiskey couldn't have helped, but it wouldn't do this. It had to be a hallucination. Even if he'd blacked out and woken up after dark, even if the rain had come in while he'd been out of it, drugged by whatever Ray (*that crazy fuck!*) had given him, what about the marsh? He'd never seen a marsh in the park, and there was no way these trees had been through Katrina. No way.

And just when he thought he might scream, he heard a rustling, something more than the noise of the driving rain, and he turned. Something moved, there in the storm and the dark.

A man.

Like Alice following the rabbit, he pursued that silhouette. Lost and confused in the storm, heart rising into the back of his throat, panic clenching his fists, he gave chase. Thoughts of attack filled him. He'd tackle the guy and demand answers. But he raced amongst trees, shoes sinking into muddy earth that sucked at his feet, and he began to slow.

The man was not running.

By the time Max emerged at the edge of the marsh, the shadow had stopped. The water was high, thanks to the storm, and surrounded the bases of the trees nearest the marsh. The marsh had begun to spread.

The man crouched in several inches of water, hiding himself behind the high grass. Even in the dark and the storm, his clothes seemed anachronistic. Other than a half glance backward, revealing a long, thin mustache, he kept his back to Max, seemingly unaware that he was being followed. The man's attention had been caught by movement out across the marsh, and Max peered through the rain, trying to make out what unfolded there.

He moved north along the edge of the marsh, skirting a tree, trying to get a better view without giving himself away. A pale figure stood fifty yards away, and Max had to step into the water and part the high grass before he began to make sense of what he saw. Three canoes were drawn up onto the far bank, and seven or eight people stood beneath the trees, some hiding beneath hanging cypress branches, all of them hard to see in the dark and the storm. Their clothes were rough, their hair long and slicked by the rain.

Only when the pale figure—shirtless, hair in braids— lifted something toward the thunder clouds did Max realize that they were Indians. For a moment he felt a queer dislocation, and then he told himself this must be some strange tribal thing conducted by a local group.

But moments ago, it had been a cooling fall afternoon, and now it was night and the storm had risen from nowhere. His mind tried to rationalize, but there were simply too many things to explain.

Lightning flashed across the sky and he saw the granite features of the Indian who stood in the marsh, and got a clearer look at the bundle he held up toward the storm.

It squirmed in his hands.

Thunder boomed across the sky. When its roar had diminished, another sound could be heard over the constant patter of rain. A baby had begun to cry—a frightened, angry bleating that grew into a wail.

Max held his breath. Off to his right, the guy with the mustache rose slightly, leaning forward. But Max only glanced at him for an instant before returning his focus to the shirtless Indian standing in the marsh. From the squirming bundle he held aloft, the baby's arms emerged, fists beating the air. A terrible suspicion grabbed Max; perhaps this wasn't any kind of baptism or blessing at all. The woman on the opposite edge of the marsh watched, but wasn't as impassive as he'd first thought. Her shoulders shook with quiet sobs. The rain swallowed her tears.

The Indian holding the baby began to chant in his own language, and immediately the others joined in. Their voices came together not in harmony, but in a unified, prayerlike rhythm.

Something flitted through the dark above the marsh. Trees rustled and branches shook, and then birds took off from the crooks where they'd been hiding from the storm and began to circle like vultures above the Indian and the wailing infant. The chanting grew louder. The mother shouted and stepped into the flooding marsh, but one of her tribesmen grabbed hold of her arm and would not let go.

The chanting ceased.

"No," Max said, for he could feel something awful coming.

The man in the marsh lowered the baby ever so gently, resting the swaddled infant atop the water's surface. And then he let go. Blanket already soaked through with rain, the baby sank in an instant, the water closing over it. The crying ceased abruptly, leaving only the shush of the rain.

Max stared, trapped in a moment of disbelief.

In the distance, deep in the belly of the storm, thunder rumbled.

The hidden man leapt up and forward, wading into the marsh. Max moved at almost precisely the same moment. In unison they cried out, Max in English and the other man in French, as they slogged through the water.

The Indians on the opposite edge of the marsh looked up, all of them staring at the Frenchman. None of them seemed even to notice Max. The baby's mother and the man who had drowned her child did not look up at all, staring at the dark surface of the water where the baby had gone under moments before.

"Save him! You can still save him!" Max shouted, waist deep in the water now.

The night birds screamed. He looked up just as the first of them dove into the water, wings folded back against its sides. Three others darted into the marsh. Max faltered, staring in wonder, as others skirted the top of the water, whipping through tall grass and then rising again, wings beating the air.

Something broke the surface, wings shedding droplets of water. Then more, until four birds emerged, heads dipped low, talons thrust out below them as they lifted the baby from the water by its sodden blanket.

The shirtless man smiled, tilted his head back, and let the rain fall on his face. He raised his arms in silent thanks.

The birds carried the baby aloft. Max could hear it coughing, spitting up water, as they began to descend with their burden again, lowering the child into its mother's out-stretched arms. The moment she took hold of the baby, the birds flapped away, vanishing over the treetops. The child began to cry again in great hitching sobs.

Max wiped rain from his eyes and stared. He took a step back. What he'd just seen simply wasn't possible. Out of the corner of his eye he saw movement, and he glanced over at the Frenchman, whose mouth hung open in astonishment that mirrored Max's own.

The Frenchman lifted his hands, palms up. It took Max a moment to realize why: the rain had begun to taper off. As the shirtless Indian called out to the thunderclouds, a dim growl came from the sky, and that was all that remained of the storm. The clouds had thinned. Even as Max gazed upward, he saw clear spots open above. Starlight glittered through those rents in the storm.

The rain drizzled to a stop.

One by one, the Indians returned to their canoes. As they did so, each touched the squalling infant on the crown of its head. The man who had nearly drowned the child helped its mother into the last canoe. They began to paddle away. Several of them glanced at the Frenchman, aware of his presence but unwilling to acknowledge him. The Frenchman raised a hand and made a noise, as though he wanted to call out to them, to ask what it was he had just witnessed, but he stopped himself.

Perhaps he wasn't sure if he wanted the answer.

None of them looked at Max.

He waded after them. On his third step, the depth of the marsh changed so abruptly that he stumbled forward, catching himself just before he would have submerged completely. Water enveloped him to just below his shoulders.

Cursing, he searched with his feet and found a shallower spot, pulling himself out so that he was only waist deep again. Even as he did, a wave of nausea came over him. He swayed on his feet, blinking, and his throat felt suddenly parched.

He squinted against the light.

To the west, through the trees, he could see the light of the setting sun. For a second, he smelled lilacs.

"What the hell is this?"

He stood in the middle of the narrow river that surrounded Scout Island. A dozen feet away, the water flowed under the little bridge he'd crossed. The bike he'd taken from beside Cooper's Bar stood propped against the stonework.

Max raised his hands to his hair and found it dry.

There had been no rain. No marsh. No Indians, no baby, no Frenchman, no birds. Shaking, afraid his mind had slipped a gear, he forced his eyes closed, open, closed, and open again. The world around him now was solid, but it had felt solid enough before, too. A hundred thoughts filled his head, stories of alien abduction and of fairy mounds, but he discarded them all. Those were just stories.

Blinking, he studied the branches of the old cypress and oak trees around him. The hurricane had damaged them enough that even if some of them were the same trees, he wouldn't have been able to tell.

The same trees? What did that even mean? He'd hallucinated, that was all. Drugs were the only answer. Crazy Ray had given him something in that little stone bottle, and he'd been drunk or stupid enough to swallow it.

Furious with himself, still hazy with alcohol but at least lucid, he slogged to the riverbank and climbed out. *Bullshit,* he thought. *Hallucinations. Can't be anything else.* But Max had always been a child of logic, and as strange as it had been, he'd never heard of hallucinations like the ones he'd just had; a single, richly detailed scene peopled with characters. A single moment.

The Map of Moments, Ray had called it.

He patted his pockets. His pants were soaked through and the shoes he'd worn to the funeral were ruined. Somewhere he'd lost his jacket. He touched the bulge of his wallet, but money would dry out. Then he felt the outline of his cell phone and his gut turned to stone. Taking the phone out, he tried to turn it on. A strange, unpleasant clicking noise came from inside the plastic, and then nothing. He tried it several more times.

"Fuck!"

A bird fluttered from a nearby tree and took off across the darkening sky, roused by Max's curse.

He cocked his arm to throw the phone into the water, then paused. Maybe if he swapped out the battery, he could get the phone dried out and working again. He slid it back into his pocket, thinking about what he would do when he found Ray. The man had a lot to make up for, and a lot of explaining to do.

Max located the map in his front right pocket. He stood at the foot of the bridge and unfolded it carefully, not wanting to tear the wet paper, mostly just trying to figure out the quickest way back to the French Quarter. He figured the ink would have run badly and become illegible, but it was worse than that: the First Moment had vanished altogether.

But a Second Moment had appeared. He was certain this new blocked area had not been on the map before, but now, as though drawn in invisible ink and made to appear by New Orleans' still-dirty waters, here it was.

The Second Moment:
The Pere's Kyrie
November 2, 1769

For several seconds Max stared at this new marking, but the last of the day's light was fading, and he could not understand the words. Or perhaps he didn't want to. With the setting of the sun, the November night had become cool, and he was soaked from the waist down.

Max shivered as he folded the map, glancing nervously at the bridge and across the narrow river at Scout Island beyond, picturing in his mind the almost primordial landscape he'd hallucinated. The wildness of the land in a bygone age. Watching the trees for birds, he slid the map into his back pocket, telling himself he didn't care if the dampness ruined it, even though he didn't believe that would happen. Not until it had served its purpose.

He retrieved the bike and walked it to the path before climbing on. His stomach ached and for a moment he feared another hallucination, or whatever that had been. Another drug-induced vision. Then his stomach grumbled, and he remembered that he'd eaten almost nothing all day.

Uncomfortable, pants stiff and heavy with water, leather shoes tightening on his feet, he pedaled out of City Park, all concerns for his own safety forgotten. Except that, in the back of his mind, he kept a rough image of the location of that Second Moment, and he made sure to go nowhere near.

Max abandoned the bike three blocks from the hotel. His thighs were painfully chafed and he tried his best not to walk like John Wayne. The exercise had burned off enough alcohol that he was practically sober by now, and starving. Questions crowded his mind but he forced them away. It had been a day for impossibilities, but he couldn't think about them until he had a hot shower, a hot meal, and dry clothes.

Walking through the lobby, he tried to pretend there was nothing at all strange about his appearance. He'd kicked a lot of dried mud from his shoes, but they were still filthy, as were the cuffs of his pants. His shirt was untucked, but that couldn't hide the fact that his pants were still wet. He probably stank of muck and whiskey. But he kept his gaze straight ahead, unwilling to acknowledge the stares he knew he must be receiving from the handful of staff and guests in the hotel.

To his relief, Max made it to his room without encountering anyone, and was surprised to find that his key card still worked, despite the soaking it had endured.

Once inside the room he leaned against the door and let out a long breath, grateful for the sanctuary, and wishing that he would never have to go back out again. He emptied his pockets of wallet, keys, change, phone, and map, and then stripped. He dumped his shoes and pants into a plastic bag he found in the closet. It was intended for guests who wanted to send clothes out to be laundered, but Max would simply throw them away. He was tempted to toss his shirt, socks, and underwear into the bag as well, but for some reason, that seemed excessive.

He laughed, and even to his own ears it was an uncomfortable sound.

The room service menu was limited to basics and a few more elegant specials, but the last thing Max wanted was haute cuisine. He ordered a bowl of gumbo and a hamburger with French fries, then opened the complimentary bottle of water on the bureau. A drink had seemed like such a good idea this morning, during Gabrielle's graveside service. Now the thought of alcohol made him queasy. He tipped the bottle back and drank, and that spring water was the best thing he had ever tasted.

Max took a hot shower, scrubbing himself clean of the day's strangeness. He only wished he could wash away his grief and confusion. Afterward, he put on clean underwear, cotton sweatpants, and a T-shirt, and waited for his food to arrive. They had said twenty minutes, but room service estimates were invariably wrong.

His eyes were drawn to the bureau, where the map lay folded beside his wallet and useless cell phone. It had to still be wet. He glanced toward the door, trying to will his food to come, but when no knock followed he went to the bureau and stared down at the map.

After a moment he picked it up and unfolded it. It would dry better if he left it open; that was what he told himself. But what he really wanted was to confirm that those words of the First Moment were gone. He opened the map and stared at City Park, and sure enough, the First Moment was no longer there.

The next one was even clearer than before.

The Second Moment:
The Pere's Kyrie
November 2, 1769

"The Pere's Kyrie," he read aloud. Though he'd never been religious, he knew a Kyrie was a kind of prayer meant to be sung. And in French, *"Pere"* meant father. But whose father?

The questions ran deeper than that. Ray had talked about following the map, gathering magic—*yeah, he said magic*—like static, opening a window into the past so Max could get a message to Gabrielle, maybe even talk to her. No matter how much Jack Daniel's he'd drunk, and no matter what the old guy had given him in that little stone bottle, that part of the conversation remained clear in his memory. Follow the map, and then find some "conjureman" named Matrisse.

He'd never heard such bullshit in his life.

That was what he ought to be thinking, and he knew it. But the map had dried now, and though it looked like a common tourist map of New Orleans, it *felt* like old parchment, dry and rough in texture. It was as if the map he held and the one he was looking at were two entirely different things.

Add in his hallucination in City Park, and logic brought him to answers he had difficulty allowing into his mind. Two plus two equaled four, always and forever. *Dumb-ass. After Lakeview, you should've come straight back here.* But he'd run across assholes with guns . . . and then he'd used the map.

Should've known better.

But how could he have known better? He hadn't believed a word crazy Ray had said.

"That's a lie," he whispered to himself. He threw the map on the bureau. Because he had been drunk enough and full of enough sadness that he *had* believed, just a little. Hell, he'd wanted to believe.

"Yeah, two plus two equals four," he said aloud. Which translated in his mind to another equation. If what he'd seen in the park connected to real events, and if the area had been marsh back then, what he'd seen could have been real, and not just some drug-fueled vision.

He'd spent half a year as a history professor at Tulane, but had only basic knowledge of local history. Still, Max knew who could give him answers. What he had to decide was whether or not he wanted them.

A heavy knock came at the door. "Room service."

"Finally." He'd been about ready to break into the mini-bar and pay eight dollars for a tiny package of Oreos.

Only after he had gotten his food, tipped the guy, then looked for the remote control to turn on the television did he finally notice the blinking red light on his phone. Some-one had called while he had been showering, and left a mes-sage. He hesitated, thinking that it might be his sister calling to check on him, either to see if he was all right or to give him crap for having come down here in the first place. Nei-ther was a conversation he felt like having, but it couldn't hurt to listen to the message.

As it turned out, the message wasn't from his sister.

"Max, it's Corinne. You went off with Ray and never turned up back at your hotel. I came by and had a drink in the bar, called up to the room a couple of times. Anyway, I'm home now if you want to call. I figure you've got an-other day or so down here, and I thought we could get breakfast at Poppy's tomorrow. If you're up for it, I mean. If it wouldn't be weird or morbid or something. Anyway, call me if you want to. If not . . . I'm glad you came down. Thanks for not making me do that alone."

Breakfast at Poppy's. Why was it all the good memories hurt so much?

He ate with the TV on, but Max barely registered the zoetrope shadows dancing across the screen. He spent the time thinking about tomorrow's breakfast, wondering what he should say. By New Orleans standards, his gumbo tasted bland, but the burger was just what he wanted. When he'd finished, he set aside the tray and picked up the phone.

Corinne answered on the second ring.

"Poppy's survived Katrina?"

"Max," she said. "Yeah, it's still there. A little worse for the wear, but Poppy's stubborn, and she loves this city so much she wouldn't know how to live anywhere else."

"Nine o'clock all right?"

"I'll see you then."

Poppy's sat on the corner of Dauphine Street and Iberville, still in the Quarter but off the typical tourist track. Its exterior had always reminded Max of a private club in some European city, tall windows gleaming in the morning sunlight, but with the blinds drawn. Casual passersby would presume the place closed. Its name was stenciled on the windows and painted on tiles above the door, but no operating hours were posted. There wasn't even a menu on display to those who might be walking past.

The message couldn't have been clearer: *if we don't know you, we don't want you here.*

Yet in Max's experience, that wasn't the case at all. In truth, the diminutive woman from whom the restaurant gained its name simply felt that word of mouth had made her little place popular enough already, and that soliciting casual diners would only make Poppy's less hospitable for those who truly appreciated what she had to offer.

"She's not in it for the glory," Gabrielle had once told Max. "She's in it for the food."

When Max walked in that morning, he could not help but smile. The restaurant brought back painful memories, but they were wonderful memories as well. He had never expected to set foot on Poppy's tile floors again, and despite all that had happened in the past twenty-four hours, it felt like a gift. The walls were painted ivory, with olive-green trim, and the floors were inlaid Italian marble. The front of the restaurant was a narrow corridor with a bar on the left and a single row of small tables to the right. He walked through to the hostess at the end of the bar.

The woman looked up, and Max recognized Poppy herself. Her auburn hair had been brighter red the last time he'd seen her, and shorter, and there were lines around her eyes that he didn't remember. But charm still radiated off her.

"Mornin', darlin'," she said. "One for breakfast?"

"Actually, I'm meeting someone." He smiled at her. The woman stood about five-foot-nothing, but had a formidable air about her.

She gave him a bemused look. "I know you, don't I?"

"You have a good memory. I used to come in here sometimes with Gabrielle?"

Poppy's eyes brightened. "Oh, Gaby! Yeah. Haven't seen her for . . ." She trailed off when she recognized the expression on Max's face. He guessed she'd seen that same look many times recently. "She's gone, huh? The Bitch get her?"

Max almost corrected her, but then realized that to

Poppy—and other New Orleaneans—"the Bitch" was Katrina.

"Yeah. We buried her yesterday."

"I'm sorry. She shone bright, that one. You remember her, now! *Nobody* we lost ought to be forgotten."

"She won't be," Max said, looking down at his feet, and the brief silence quickly grew uncomfortable.

"You want to sit, or wait up front?" Poppy asked.

He glanced at the door, but saw no sign of Corinne. "I'll sit, thanks."

Poppy led him into the main dining room, which was as narrow as the front but had room for a row of tables against either side, just eight in all. There were three free, and she led him to one about halfway down and slid two menus onto the table.

"Get you some coffee to start?"

"Café au lait, please."

"Coming right up, honey. And I'm sorry, again, about Gaby."

Max nodded and watched her go. She came back with his coffee within minutes, trailed by a doughy waiter with a goatee, who introduced himself as James. He asked if Max wanted anything else while he waited, then retreated to the kitchen.

Corinne arrived a few minutes later. He'd sat himself so that he'd be positioned to see the front of the place, and the moment she came through the door he knew he wasn't going to tell her anything about the previous day. What would he say? The map felt crisp and stiff in his back pocket, but even if he showed it to her, what would she see? A tourist map that someone had scribbled on?

"Hey. Sorry I'm late," she said.

"I've only been here a few minutes myself."

She slid into a chair and looked at the menu. James drifted from the kitchen as though he had some sixth sense, and she ordered black coffee.

"Do you know what you want?" she asked.

He laughed.

Corinne looked up at him over the top of the menu. "What's funny?"

"Nothing and everything. I don't have the first clue what I want. I thought I did, once, but . . . Anyway, that's not what you meant. I'm getting banana pancakes. Poppy does them wonderfully, with cinnamon on top."

When James returned, Corinne ordered the spicy shrimp omelette—essentially shrimp, cayenne, Tabasco, and ham folded into the eggs. It had been Gabrielle's favorite. Max wondered whether that was why Corinne had ordered it, or if they simply had the same tastes.

"So tell me," she said, when the waiter had vanished again. "Where'd you take off to, yesterday?"

A wave of anger went through him. "Well, you didn't leave me much choice."

Her eyes dropped to her coffee cup, but she didn't pick it up. Hadn't even touched it. "I'm sorry about that. Ray asked for some time with you. He paid to get Gaby buried, so it was the least I could do. Anyway, I didn't think you'd mind." She looked up. "Why, what did he do?"

The tone of the question could have been interpreted many different ways, but Max sensed a real curiosity in it, as though Corinne had a lot of questions about Ray herself.

"How well do you know the guy?"

If it bothered her that he hadn't answered her question, she didn't show it. "Hardly at all. But Gabrielle knew him really well. Up until a couple of years ago, they were inseparable. I know how weird that sounds. I mean, he's gotta be in his mid-sixties at least, and she was just a kid, maybe fourteen, when they started spending time together. But I never suspected anything funny, or dubious. They were like father and daughter. He taught her how to cook.

"We were at JazzFest and he'd set up a cart in the parking lot, selling étouffée he was fixing right there on a frying pan. It was damn fine étouffée, crab and shrimp in there, and Gabrielle demanded to know his recipe. Ray looked at her a while, like he was sizing her up, and then he said, 'I ain't gonna tell you, little girl, but I'll teach you how to make it proper.' That was the beginning. Her family didn't seem to mind—seemed to like the fact she was learning cooking from someone who knew his stuff. But once she got to be seventeen, she didn't see much of him, as far as I know. But obviously he still cared for her.

"Now, are you gonna tell me what you two talked about yesterday?"

Max had not known the young Gabrielle, but he knew how she could get when she wanted something. There was no stopping her. So it was easy for him to picture her going up to the old guy and demanding his recipe, and to understand how Ray could've been charmed by that. The story had a sweetness and ordinariness to it that he wanted to embrace, but the map crinkled in his back pocket every time he shifted, and he couldn't shake off his own experience with Ray.

"Just what you might expect," he said, trying to make his face as unreadable as possible. "How much we loved her, how much we miss her. He told me about teaching her to cook, but not that story."

Max had never been a good liar, so it amazed him how easily the falsehoods came.

"Actually, he got me ridiculously drunk. I had hardly any breakfast yesterday, so by the time lunch came around I was wrecked. I . . . well, I went over to the house in Lakeview. Kind of a farewell tour, I guess."

"Seriously? Damn, Max, you've got to be careful, you know? You should have called me. I would've driven you over."

He chuckled. "I would've been too embarrassed to call you, even if I could've. But I dropped my cell; shattered the thing. It's useless. I put it in the trash this morning."

Corinne gave a sympathetic shake of her head. "Not your week. Look, I know you're in town another couple of days. I have to work tonight, but I'm off again tomorrow. If you need a chauffeur, I'd be happy to help."

Max cocked his head. "Why?"

"I'm sorry?" She seemed irked.

"Why would you want to help?"

"You came down here. I didn't have to say good-bye to her alone. You shouldn't have to, either."

He thought about that, tempted to backtrack, to dig out

from all the bullshit he'd just dumped on the table between them. But so many things were confusing him right then that he needed to hold on to the one thing he really did know for sure, which was that crazy Ray had given the map to him. Whatever he did with it, use it or burn it or just stick it in a hotel drawer, he wanted that to be his choice. Telling Corinne would bring her in on that decision, and he wasn't ready for that.

"Thanks, but I'm just going to visit some old colleagues from Tulane, have a couple of decent meals, and go home. Too many ghosts for me now."

Corinne picked up her coffee mug at last, raised it as if in a toast, and stared at him over the rim. "Too many ghosts for all of us. This whole city's haunted by what it used to be. But New Orleans is used to living with its ghosts, paying respects, and going on living. I guess we'll manage it this time, too. Eventually."

She drank, and if the black coffee was bitter, her face didn't show it.

Their breakfast came and they tucked into their meals. For a while, Max just let himself enjoy the banana pancakes, which were even better than he remembered them being. Poppy came by the table to see how they were faring, and he heaped her with praise.

"Poppy didn't know she was dead," he said when she left, breaking the silence of their meal.

Corinne looked up at him, eyes glistening. "Max," she said slowly, as if savoring his name. Then she smiled. "Never seen her like when she was with you. In fact, I couldn't believe it when you two started up together. She usually kept everyone at arm's length. Aside from me and Ray, there'd only ever been a couple of other people she let into her life." Corinne's eyes were kind. "You were good for her, Max. I was sorry to see you go."

His fork dangled from his fingers. Suddenly, his appetite had departed. He thought about the night he'd walked in on her screwing one of his students, and about the things he'd learned in the past day. Her family had cast her aside, and though she knew a lot of people, she must have been a lonely woman.

"What's wrong?" Corinne asked.

He shrugged. "It's just strange. The longer I stay here, the more I think the girl I came to say good-bye to never even existed."

"That's just foolishness," she chided him. "Gaby *loved* you."

"For a while, maybe."

She waved the words away, as though angry. "Think what you like. You and Coco were the only . . ." She looked away, lips pressed tightly together as if to hold back any more mistakes.

Max sighed. Nothing should surprise him by now. It seemed he hadn't known a damn thing about the girl he professed to love.

"Who's Coco?"

chapter

4

He felt like a fucking idiot. Corinne seemed to be playing him, feeding him information about Gabrielle piece by piece. Whenever he asked about Gaby's estrangement from her family, Corinne said, *It's family business.* And now there was Coco, the guy who'd been in Gabrielle's life before she met Max, and whom Corinne had refused to talk about. *Forget I mentioned his name,* she'd said, nervous and unsettled. *I never should have.*

That pissed off Max. He already felt dislocated and alone, existing in a city that had lost itself and was still struggling to find its way again. And now the more he discovered about

Gabrielle, the more complex and distant her memory seemed to grow. The Gabrielle he remembered was quickly becoming a stranger.

"This isn't the way to Tulane," he said. The cabdriver turned in his seat, offering a grin that displayed no humor.

"You just come back?" he asked, reading Max like a book. *Been here before, but away when the storm came.*

"Yeah," Max said.

"A lot's changed. The New Orleans that's risin' from the waters is a whole new woman. Still got the humps and bumps in all the right places, but the lay of the land has moved around, here an' there." He drove on, settling in his seat and tapping the steering wheel in time with some inaudible music.

"I don't want a tour."

"I ain't giving you a fuckin' tour." The driver turned on the car stereo and gave his fingers something to tap to.

Max sighed and sat back, trying to make sense of things. Morning had shed no light on what he'd seen yesterday. He could still smell the swamp, taste the rain, and feel the cold waters against his legs, and he could hear the cries of the child as it was plucked from the water and given back to its mother. It had the quality of a memory from the past that might have been a dream, or might have been real.

Whatever Ray had given him to drink . . .

"Crazy bastard," Max muttered. What he'd seen had appeared so detailed that he was not sure it could have just come from his imagination. He knew little about the history of this area, but one of his colleagues from his time at

Tulane taught the history of Louisiana. *The marsh, the Native Americans, the Frenchman* . . . Max closed his eyes and rested his head back against the seat.

Yesterday had been a bad day. It almost felt good having something else to pursue, for a while.

And then Coco, he thought. But he was not sure he'd ever go that far.

"You walk from here," the driver said, pulling up at the curb.

Max looked outside and recognized some of the dorm buildings. Windows were boarded up and trees were down, and façades were coated with the same sad dust.

"We're half a mile from the campus," Max said.

"Yeah, and you walk from here."

"Why?"

The driver turned around again, and this time his smile was genuine. "Walk, an' see. The roads? Bad news. They're not washed away, but clearin' the university hasn't been a priority, know what I mean?"

Max nodded and looked along the street ahead of them. There were very few vehicles, other than those parked haphazard along the curb. "Thanks," he said.

"Yeah, well, take it easy," the driver said. "And sorry if I was harsh, y'know?"

"No need to apologize." Max gave the cabdriver a five-dollar tip and got out, watching the battered car turn around in the street and head back the way they'd come.

Half a mile wasn't so far to walk, but he remembered the gun-swinging gang he'd seen yesterday, and he could still perceive the scent of decay on the air. It smelled as if the city was dying.

For some reason, he'd assumed that the university had escaped the worst of the flooding. He hadn't seen it on the TV coverage of Katrina, and though he'd been unable to contact any of his friends or ex-colleagues there during the storm, he'd put it down to the phone systems being down all across Louisiana. And after the storm, when the true extent of the devastation and horror was becoming clear, he'd felt reticent about calling. He'd rationalized it as a fear of being the outsider; he'd only taught there for six months, and he'd left almost four months before the hurricane.

As time went by, and it became too late to call with any pretense at concern, he'd realized he had been afraid. He didn't want to hear that any of those people he'd run away from had died.

But the university had not escaped.

The cabdriver had been right about the roads. As Max walked on, he found himself crossing a strange landscape of dried mud, piled debris, and abandoned cars. The destruction felt different from what he had witnessed in Lakeview, perhaps because he had not expected to see it here, or maybe because he knew this place so well. He could hear engines somewhere out of sight. A couple of rats dodged across the road ahead of him, fleeing one pile of debris to find shelter in another. He winced, expecting gunshots, but there was no roving gang here. Not yet.

He walked past a coffee shop where he'd gotten his caffeine fix many times before. The front window was smashed and the insides were a mess, and on the huge menu black-board the word "Looter" was scrawled in dried mud, with an arrow pointing down behind the counter. Max had no wish to see what the arrow was aiming at.

He walked on, and the sound of engines grew in the distance. He passed a man wearing a gun holster around his waist, three women carrying trash bags slung over their shoulders, and a teenaged boy on a bike who seemed to be making a challenge of leaping fallen trees and cars resting on flat tires. A police car cruised by, and even though Max offered a smile, the cop in the passenger seat stared at him until the car had drifted from view.

Turning a corner into one of the grassy squares, he saw where the engine sound came from. A heavy wagon sat in the center, and a front-end loader was shoveling up mud, broken glass, and snapped branches, slowly clearing the square from north to south. Half the job was done, and Max wondered how long it had taken. It seemed like an endless task.

He walked through the chaos of places he knew, surprised and disturbed at the relative silence of somewhere so used to bustle, noise, and life. When he reached the history building where he'd once taught, the front door was open, and he walked up the steps and entered. It was silent inside. He flicked the light switch but nothing happened, and he could hardly believe that the power was still off. The floor was smeared with dried mud all along the corridor, and ten yards along a door had been smashed, glass speckling the floor. Surely someone should have cleaned that up? Where was the lecturer whose office had been vandalized? Where were the staff?

"Hello?" Max called, because the silence was starting to spook him.

But he'd come this far, and the lecturer he'd come to meet was not one to accept defeat. If anyone would be here, Charlie Baker was the man.

He headed upstairs by habit. As he walked along the second-floor corridor, he began to hear a steady *chink, chink, chink* of something deeper inside the building—metal against glass, too rhythmic to be accidental. *What the hell was I thinking, coming here?*

Chink . . . chink . . . chink . . .

The whole place was shut down. The front door stood open, but no one seemed to be inside, and if that wasn't asking for trouble, what was?

Chink . . . chink . . .

He didn't shout again. Instead he walked on, trying not to give away his presence. His old office was at the end of the corridor, and it felt as though he'd been away for six years, not six months. Everything had changed so much.

Chink . . .

The sound stopped. Something creaked.

"Who's there!" a voice boomed, and a figure leapt into the corridor a few steps in front of Max.

"Shit!" Max stumbled back and almost fell, grabbing on to the windowsill to hold himself upright. "Charlie!"

Charlie Baker, the man he'd come hoping to see, stood before him, leaning back against the doorjamb and tapping the crystal glass in his left hand with his wedding ring.

Max stood up straight and tried to smile. It didn't feel right. "Charlie, it's Max."

"I know," Charlie said. His expression did not change, his tapping continued. Max smelled whiskey. It was barely midday.

"Good to see you," Max said, reaching for something deeper.

"What the hell you doing here?"

"I . . . er . . ." Charlie's manner and tone had thrown him, and now Max was beginning to think he'd done the wrong thing, assumed too much and understood far too little. The storm had changed the landscape of the city, and it could just as easily change the geography of people's minds. "I came here to find you."

"Me?" Charlie had been a garrulous man with a big personality, but now he seemed a shade of his former self.

Max looked around and sighed. "I didn't know the campus had been hit so bad. So you're . . . what, here alone?"

Charlie smiled sadly and shook his head. "Few others in the building. We come in, go through the motions, go home. Same most days. But all the students are gone. There's nothing to do here." He shrugged, and stopped tapping his glass long enough to take a drink.

"I'm sorry," Max said, and he meant it. "How are Lucy and the kids?"

"Living with my folks in Houston." Charlie said no more, as if that were answer enough. The silence went on for so long that Max wondered whether he should say *I'm sorry* again.

"I came back for a funeral."

Charlie nodded. "Has it happened yet?"

"Yeah. Yesterday."

He nodded again. Then he held up his glass. "Drink?"

"No, I—"

"Said you came looking for me. You want to talk to me, we drink. That's my new rule now. Charlie's rule, I call it. You wanna talk, you drink."

"Right," Max said. "Well, okay, just a little one."

"Just a little one," Charlie mimicked, turning back into his office.

Max followed him in. He expected a mess—the exact opposite of what Charlie had been—but the room was pristine. No book was out of place, no files strewn across the desk, and for a beat Max was glad. Then he realized it was because Charlie was not working anymore. In one corner stood a couple of cardboard boxes filled with empty bottles.

"Charlie . . ." he said.

"Don't patronize me," Charlie said, soft but firm. "Really. You have no idea. I saw looting all across the campus, and men with guns, and a body that stayed on the sidewalk for two weeks, people walking right by every day. Hell, *I* walked by, tried not to look at her face. Jim Delahunt, a professor here, Max—a *professor*—didn't even go around one time; he stepped right over her." Charlie poured Max a drink and handed it to him, challenging him to respond.

I should go, Max thought. But though they hadn't exactly been close friends, he felt as though he should do something to help.

"City Park," he said.

Charlie frowned and sat behind his desk. "What about it?"

Max walked around the office, running his finger along the book spines. They were in perfect alphabetical order. *Before or after the storm?* he wondered. "What do you know about the place?"

"Stupid question. What do you want to know?"

"The past. A long time ago, before the city was here. Maybe the French were there?"

"Well, yeah, they founded the city. Early eighteenth century. But . . ."

Max could not help smiling. Had he seen a change in Charlie's eyes already? "A friend of mine is interested, that's all," he said. "And I was looking for an excuse to come out here before I fly home, so I said I'd see if you were still around."

Charlie put down his drink and leaned forward, steepling his hands in front of his face. "Exactly what do you want to know?"

"What did it look like? Who and what was there? Anything you know, really."

"It was marshland, mainly. Swamp. Forest. Lots of oak. Much of it was reclaimed to form the park. Back then, before New Orleans was founded by Jean Baptiste-LeMoyne, you had different Indian tribes there."

Max tried to keep his face neutral, but inside he was translating everything Charlie said into the vision he'd had the previous day. Marshy ground . . . oak trees . . . Indians . . . It all fit, and with every word that Charlie uttered, Max became more scared.

This was stuff he did not know, yet he'd seen it all.

"These Indians . . . did they practice ritual sacrifice?"

Charlie frowned and leaned back, then broke into a smile. This was the man Max remembered. "Never thought of you as a gore hound, Max."

Max smiled back. "I'm not. But my friend is writing a historical novel, and he was just wondering . . ."

"Historical novel?"

"Yeah." Max tried not to look away, feeling foolish for lying.

"Well, there're no real records, to be honest. There are myths and stories of sacrifice, but there's no saying they reflect actual events. I seriously doubt it, if you want my two cents. Rituals, yeah. Offerings. But blood sacrifices and that kind of crap, I'm gonna say no." Charlie picked up his glass and tapped his wedding ring against it again. He looked down into the despair he had obviously been inhabiting, then up again. "You haven't had a drink."

Max lifted his glass and sipped, and he had an intense flashback to the previous day: Ray, the bar, and what had happened afterward. "They didn't mind the rain," he muttered. "And the men wore masks."

"I think the Biloxi wore masks in some of their tribal ceremonies," Charlie said. "There was an offshoot of that tribe here. Though I'm no real expert, of course."

"The Frenchman," Max muttered. He had been so close, he could have reached out and touched him, but the man had still not noticed him. *That's because I was never really there. I was witnessing the moment, not actually there at all.*

"The one I mentioned? Jean——"

"No, no," Max said, waving his hand. He took another drink, and the flashback this time was simply his need to remember.

"So, your friend's novel?"

"Work in progress." Max shrugged, then drained his glass. *I didn't know any of this,* he thought. And yet he remembered the Indians—Biloxi, perhaps?—the Frenchman, and their surroundings. He shivered.

"It's good stuff," Charlie said, lifting the half-empty bottle. "Amazing what you find in fellow professors' rooms."

"Maybe you should go with your family, Charlie."

"Houston? Fucking hate the place. I live here. I was born here, forty-two years ago. Lived in six houses in New Orleans. My house now . . . not too bad. I can live there, at least, though I wouldn't want the kids to see it." He poured some more whiskey without offering Max any more. "Besides, there're 'plans'! The university will rise again from the waters, like a soggy fucking phoenix, ready to . . ." He shook his head and sipped some more.

"It'll be all right," Max said. "Eventually."

"Yeah." Charlie put his glass down again. "You know, I might be able to find you a book on the Biloxi. Dan Pettigrew used to have a thing for them, and he went back to Chicago when everyone evacuated." He stood, swayed a little, and then headed past Max and out into the corridor. "Come on."

Max did not really want a book about the Biloxi. He did not want to walk past the office he'd once occupied, where he'd spoken to Gabrielle on the phone, made plans with her, and daydreamed about their time together, and fantastic sex in that hot attic. But Charlie's eyes had changed as soon as Max had asked his first question. Here was an intelligent man, unable to come to terms with what was happening to the city he loved and desperate for somewhere else to aim his intellect.

And Max had left. After only six months, he'd fled the city this man had loved his whole life.

So he followed Charlie, watched as he appropriated the book about Biloxi Indians from Pettigrew's office, and was glad when Charlie shook his hand and wished him well. "Maybe you can come back here to teach, one day," Charlie said. Max was not sure how much he knew about the circumstances in which he'd left—they'd never been that close—but he nodded, and said maybe, and then it was time for him to go.

As he descended the stairs and went back out into the ruin, he heard the steady *chink . . . chink . . . chink* of Charlie losing himself again.

Max started walking along St. Charles Avenue. He hadn't thought about arranging for the cab to return, and he hoped that he'd be able to flag one down. The odds were stacked against him, though. How many cabs were running in New Orleans two and a half months after Katrina? Not many, and those that were probably stuck mostly to the French Quarter hotels. It hadn't been very long since they'd started letting people back into the city.

The small slug of whiskey haunted the edges of his perception, but as he walked and broke a sweat, it was not the only ghost troubling him. The map was in his back pocket, and it never quite sat comfortably. He was always aware of it, could always feel it, as though it was announcing itself to him. He found himself dwelling once again on the Second Moment, a boxed section of neat, meticulous writing that said *The Pere's Kyrie*. He knew of the Kyrie, but he had no idea who the *pere* might be.

The writing had appeared in Jackson Square, not far from his hotel in the French Quarter. He knew eventually he would go to that spot, try to figure out what the Second Moment was all about, and see if anything strange would happen. He was torn between curiosity and fear. If he went and nothing happened, that would mean last night never happened. But if he went and something *did* happen . . . he would no longer be able to pretend it was anything but real.

He needed to find out about the Pere's Kyrie. But now he walked a little faster, and the day grew a little warmer, and another ghost began to bother him more. This one had a name but no face, a link to his past but nothing by which he could connect. Its name was Coco.

He knew he ought to go back to the hotel. New Orleans wasn't really ready for visitors. It needed tourists, and it needed the people who were the heart of the place to return, but given the pace of the recovery so far, it would be years before things were put back in order. By then, many of the older generation would have died, and many of the younger generation would have moved on to somewhere that didn't have the character, the history, or the finely woven fabric of life in New Orleans.

This city might be dead, Max thought. And the idea hit

him like a blow to the gut. The people who loved it too much to stay away, or so much they never left in the first place, might be inhabiting some kind of necropolis, and not wake up to that truth for years.

God, he prayed that wasn't so, that it wouldn't ever be true. If not for Gabrielle, he never would have left this city. New Orleans could be resurrected, he felt sure of that. America *needed* New Orleans.

Max held the book Charlie had given him against his chest like a schoolboy, thinking about ghosts. His memory of Gabrielle haunted him, but other things haunted him, too, and that was why he couldn't just go back to his hotel and wait out the day until his flight home. He'd never been the kind of man who'd run from his ghosts. The only thing he'd ever run from was Gabrielle, and he'd cursed himself for a coward ever since.

No more running.

But before he went looking for the Second Moment, he had to at least look into the other ghost that was haunting him. It weighed on him, filled him with a nervous energy, like he knew there was something he was supposed to do but couldn't quite figure out what.

Gabrielle had loved him. But the woman he thought he'd known wouldn't have cheated on him with one of his own students. The woman he thought he'd known was loved everywhere she went. Yet Gabrielle *had* cheated. Her family hated her so much they wouldn't even pay for her burial, and she had no real friends.

Had *his* Gabrielle ever really existed? Could the bright, shining intellect he'd seen in those young eyes, the humor and life he'd seen within her, have been nothing but his imagination?

If he went home without trying to understand how he could have been so wrong about her, that would haunt him more than any spirit could.

When Max had pressed Corinne about Coco, she had glanced away, as if she didn't want to meet his gaze. *I only met him once,* she'd said. *In Digg's. He was bad news. Forget I ever said his name.*

Max had heard of Digg's—a bar in the Quarter—and it was as good a place as any to start looking. As if to urge him along this new plan of action, a cab drifted by and slowed down. It was the same cab that had taken him to Tulane.

"Find what you went there for?" the driver asked.

"Partly," Max said.

"Cool. I drove around a little, but not a lot of people needin' taxis today. Maybe I came back to work too soon, y'know, but what else am I supposed to do?"

Max didn't have an answer. "Thanks for coming back."

"Hey, you got places to be and money in your wallet. I'm not out here for the scenery."

The cabbie turned up his music and wheel-tapped all the way to the Quarter.

chapter

5

Digg's was on a narrow backstreet, away from the bright lights of the French Quarter, a block away from a fish market and a Cajun seafood take-out place. This wasn't a spot for tourists. The combination of Katrina and the flood hadn't done much damage here, but the neighborhood felt like it had started holding its breath when the storm swept in, and had yet to exhale.

Max walked past Digg's twice before noticing the doorway. A faded wooden sign was screwed into the brickwork, announcing the name. The door was ajar, and immediately inside a stairway led down, its walls papered with decades of overlapping music and gig posters. Hundreds of names publicized dates long since passed, and perhaps some of those names were long gone, too. The stairway was poorly lit, but standing by the open door Max caught a mouth-watering waft of gumbo and fried chicken, and the familiar scents of bars everywhere: spilled drinks, old wood, good times.

Digg's certainly wasn't doing much to draw attention to itself, but in his seven months here, guided by Gabrielle, Max had come to love local bars and shun the more commercialized tourist areas of the city.

But she had never brought him here.

He wondered whether Coco came here sometimes, sat alone at the bar and thought about Gabrielle. And then he wondered why the man had not been present at her funeral.

Max went down. As he passed the half landing, the sound of subdued conversation, the clink of glasses, and soft laughter rose to meet him. He hoped none of that would stop when he entered.

It was a small bar with brick walls, a vaulted ceiling, and a flagstone floor. The bar itself was brick-fronted, and the furniture scattered around the place was all dark, old wood, well used and comfortable. A candle on each table gave an intimate lighting level. There were maybe thirty people sitting around in small groups or couples, men and women, black and white and every hue in between. A skinny guy working the bar might have been Native American, or some perfect mélange of heritage that gave him skin with the color and gleam of bronze.

Max walked directly to the bar as though he belonged,

smiling and nodding at the barman and receiving a smile in return.

"What'll it be?"

"You do crustas?"

The barman's grin widened, and he uttered a deep, slow laugh. "Do we do crustas?" He went about mixing the cocktail, his movements smooth and fluid without verging on cocky, the product of experience rather than practice.

Max put the book on the bar, leaned sideways, and looked around. He caught a couple of patrons' eyes, and swapped polite nods and smiles. Most of the people here seemed upbeat, but there were enough sad faces to remind the still air of the place that a storm had passed them by. The laughter was low but honest, and to Max it felt like an easy place.

He wondered whether Coco was down here right now, but he thought not. He wasn't quite sure *why* he thought that—he had no idea what the guy looked like—but he'd have a *feeling* if Gabrielle's other love were in the same room with him. A hint. Maybe he'd see a similar loss in that other man's eyes.

"Here you go," the bartender said, sliding a glass across to Max.

Max nodded his thanks and handed over a ten, then took one of the bar stools and sat down.

"Nice place," he said. "You the owner?"

"Been in my family fifty years," the barman said. He swilled the cocktail shaker and dried it, repositioned clean glasses, wiped the bar, always on the move, always working.

His smile looked painted on, but the paint was contentment, not fakery.

"I've only just come back," Max said, then decided not to elaborate. If he admitted to being an outsider, maybe the barman would feel less inclined to help him.

"Yeah, well . . ." He poured a glass of soda, dropped in a slice of lime, and took a drink. "Lotsa people still away. Lotsa people not gonna make it back."

"Plenty." Max drank and sighed, feeling the alcohol hit instantly. Maybe whatever shit had been in that clay bottle had lowered his tolerance. "Actually, I'm looking for a guy called Coco. You seen him around?"

Something changed. The bartender's smile remained, but the muscles used to keep it there altered, strained rather than flexed. He took another drink of his soda, perhaps so that he could look away from Max and up at the ceiling.

Max glanced around the bar again, as if looking for the man himself. He was pretty sure no one else had heard the question, and he wished he'd asked louder.

"What you want him for?" the bartender asked.

Max turned back, and the man was mopping the bar top again. It was clean and dry, but obviously it needed to be cleaner, and drier.

"Just to chat," Max said.

"Don't know any Coco," the bartender said, shrugging.

Max frowned. What was this? The guy was obviously lying. He'd just asked what Max wanted with him.

"What about Gabrielle Doucette?"

"Who?" This time the man's shrug seemed genuine.

"Guess not," Max said.

"Refill?" the bartender said, taking the empty glass. Even his smile had slipped now, and it was clear that he really didn't want to serve Max another.

"I'm good," Max said. "Just hoping to meet an old friend."

"Well, good luck," the bartender said, even before Max had slid from the stool.

Max nodded, then walked slowly back toward the stairs. He glanced around as he went, trying to see what had changed, why this place no longer felt at ease. Maybe it was simply the bartender's abruptly altered manner.

So who the fuck is Coco? he thought. On the bottom step he paused and turned back, considering asking out loud if anyone knew him.

Several pairs of eyes flickered from him, and a swell of loud talk and laughter rose up. Digg's suddenly looked and felt like a very different place.

Max hurried up the stairs and back onto the street, turned left, and headed away from Bourbon Street. He remembered he'd left the book about the Biloxi on the bar, but he had no desire to go back. He was confused and frustrated, because every time he looked into part of Gabrielle's life, it revealed more mystery. The bartender down there had known Coco, he was certain of that, and he'd clammed up as soon as his name was mentioned. *He knew I was an outsider.* But there was more to it than that.

If only Corinne had known more, or trusted him enough to tell him whatever else she *did* know. But he was starting to wonder now if, cousin or not, Corinne had really known Gabrielle any better than he had. There were family secrets and secret histories, but perhaps Corinne had been too far away from both sides to be immersed in either. Maybe the sadness in the woman's eyes was for herself more than for Gabrielle; for her city, and a family she had betrayed for a girl she'd never understood.

He had to find this Coco guy.

Max reached the end of the street and paused. He could hear the sound of a funeral procession, the slow dirge and hymns echoing between buildings, and he stepped up onto the raised sidewalk to show respect. As the procession approached, he wondered whether this was another victim of the floods only just recovered from the ruins.

Funeral marches in New Orleans were usually accompanied—once away from church—by vibrant, upbeat music celebrating the life of the deceased. He was surprised there would be any processions at all in these dark days. But in New Orleans, tradition was everything. The music was an expression of sadness and loss, but he knew that this somber sound would soon turn into a celebration of the life of a lost loved one, not a mourning of their death.

Gabrielle should have had this, he thought. Max glanced at his watch, amazed that it was still only mid-afternoon. He sighed, looked up at the sky, listened to the funeral procession passing by, and then sensed someone standing behind him.

"Don't turn round," the voice growled.

Something pressed against the base of Max's spine. It could have been the person scaring him with their fingertip, or it could have been a knife or gun.

"Lookin' for Coco?" A waft of garlic breath washed over Max, indicating just how close the man was.

Someone in the procession looked at him with sad, heavy eyes, then glanced at the face behind his shoulder and looked quickly away.

"Yeah." He scanned the street, desperate to set eyes on a cop.

"You buyin'?"

Max had no idea what he was talking about, but he nodded.

"Keep walking and you'll find him."

"Which way?"

The man pushed at Max, sending him stumbling into the street. "Just keep walking."

Max was tempted to turn around and ask more, but just because he no longer felt the touch on his back did not mean the threat was gone. So he walked, and as he crossed the road and mounted the opposite sidewalk, he heard laughter.

He turned around, but several pedestrians had gathered on the corner he had just left. They looked toward the disappearing tail of the funeral, and any one of the men could have been his assailant.

Max gasped, breathing deeply and slowly to try and settle his sprinting heart. Then he started walking again, passing shops and bars and restaurants, waiting for inspiration to strike.

You buyin'? the guy had asked. Drugs? Is that what Gabrielle had been mixed up in? It was frightening, and it might explain the way her family had turned their backs on her, but in a way there was also something anti-climactic about it. Gabrielle's mystery was growing in his mind, and something as prosaic as drugs just did not feel right.

Keep walking, you'll find him. But where? And how, if he didn't even know what Coco looked like?

He crossed an intersection and kept moving, staying on the same street, wondering what he'd do when he reached its end. Five minutes later he did, and he waited there for a while before turning around and walking back along the street. He browsed shop windows, then bought a coffee and sat on a wooden bench outside a café, watching the world go by. He stayed there for half an hour, thoughts slowly turning to that Second Moment once more. He could be at Jackson Square in fifteen minutes if he started walking now, and maybe—

Someone sat down on the bench beside him, and he discovered what the unseen man had meant.

Coco had found *him.*

The man lit a cigarette and inhaled deeply, relaxing back on the bench and not once looking at Max. His manner spoke of complete control.

"What's your name?" Coco asked at last.

"Max."

"And you want to buy something?"

"Well . . ." Max trailed off, hit by a moment of indecision. If he pursued this false line, he could get into trouble. Maybe it was better just to ask outright.

"Don't be shy," Coco said, laughing softly. He had a smooth, coaxing voice, nothing like the gruffness of the man who'd pressed something into Max's back.

"Should we be doing this out here?" Max asked. People walked up and down the street, cars passed by.

Coco looked at him for the first time, and there was something about his eyes that shocked Max. They were intelligent, yet distant, as though he'd seen something somewhere else that was much more interesting than the here and now.

"You afraid," Coco said at last, and it was not a question.

"I've had a bad couple of days," Max said.

Coco put his head back and laughed, and Max was conscious of a few faces turning their way. The man rocked on the bench, dropping his cigarette and seeming not to notice, and he had to wipe tears from his eyes. "Haven't we all?" he said, then laughed again.

As Max waited for the laughter to subside, he had a chance to appraise him. Coco was smartly dressed, with hair cut close to the scalp, and a goatee. His skin was smooth and unmarred. He looked strong and fit. There was something chilling about him, but it was more in his manner than appearance.

Max realized there and then that he did not want to fuck with Coco.

"So, decided what you want yet, boy?" the man asked. Max found it strange being called "boy" by someone probably younger than him, but with Coco it seemed to fit. "Got stuff that'll make you see the whole world. Got stuff, it'll take the pain away, if pain's your worry. Got girls who'll suck the pain right outta you."

A drug dealer? A pimp? Surely not Gabrielle . . . surely not.

"Gabrielle Doucette," Max said.

"Ah." The last of Coco's smile filtered away. He withdrew another cigarette, lit it, and leaned back against the café wall, looking along the street past Max.

"You didn't go to her funeral."

"She's dead?" Coco asked, his expression unchanging.

Max was sure he knew the truth. Either that, or Coco was completely unconcerned. Yet there was opportunity here, he could sense that. A chance to find out more of Gabrielle's background, delve into those dark parts that even she had wanted to keep from him, and perhaps to know the woman as he had never known her before. Right then, that seemed so important. It was all part of the mystery that Max sensed nestled around him. And the thicker it grew, the more he wanted to solve it.

"One of your hookers?" Max said, hating the idea, dreading the answer.

"Gaby?" Coco smiled, and perhaps there was even a hint of sadness there. "You really think that, boy?"

"No," Max said.

Coco nodded and smoked some more. Mention of Gabrielle had changed his whole manner, and Max thought it might be caution. Coco looked him up and down, a very frank appraisal that Max found uncomfortable.

"Friend of hers?" the man said at last.

Max nodded. A few more people were sitting outside the café now. It felt busy, but it did not feel safe. He wondered how much of that feeling grew from inside rather than without.

"The people she hung around with . . ." Max said, trailing off, intending it as an opener rather than a question.

But Coco's answer was instant. He flicked his cigarette into the street, stood, and pressed a flick-knife hard against Max's throat.

Max leaned back, head pressed against the café's wall, but Coco came closer, and for a beat Max was sure the man was going to slit his throat there and then. He grunted, trying to call for help but unable to talk. He looked around, certain that someone must be seeing this, but everyone was looking away. People sat drinking coffee, smoking, walking past, driving slowly along the road, and not one of them seemed to be looking at him and Coco. Conversation was louder than ever . . . perhaps to drown out the sound of his imminent death.

He looked up into Coco's face, just a few inches from his own. The man's eyes seemed to be searching deep. He looked all around Max's face, coming to rest on his eyes, his expression totally blank.

"Tordu don't take kindly to people asking after them," he said at last.

"Tordu?"

Coco pursed his lips and tensed his arms, and Max brought his hands up, terrified that this was his last moment on Earth.

Coco batted his hands aside and pressed his nose against Max's. Max could smell his smoky breath, and beneath it something more spicy and exotic.

The knife edge was cold against his throat. It was only them, and the rest of the world. No one interrupted, nothing was said, and Max had never felt so far from the heart of this city.

"Your only warning," Coco said. Then he stood slowly, folded the knife, lit another cigarette, stared at Max for a few more seconds, and walked away. Never once did he look around at the patrons of the café, or those people walking along the street, and he did not look back.

Gasping, pressing his hands to his neck and dreading what he would feel, a sudden faintness blurred Max's vision and dried his throat. He leaned forward and checked his hands, but they were not bloodied. Breathing deeply, head between his knees, he looked down at one of Coco's crushed cigarettes.

Tordu?

When he sat up again, a few people were looking at him. "Did you see that?" he asked. But none of them had. Maybe in the wake of the storm they had become blind to violence and death, like Charlie, who'd walked around a dead woman on the sidewalk at Tulane for weeks. Or maybe, like Max, they were terrified.

Coco was gone, just as quickly as he had arrived. And in his wake he left even more mystery.

I almost died just now, Max thought.

He left the café, and that street, and the people who had seen but done nothing. The thought crossed his mind that he should tell the police, but he had no proof or witnesses, and it would be a waste of time.

But who or what were the Tordu? Some kind of gang? That was a question for Corinne. She would not volunteer the information, but he had a feeling that if he found things out for himself, she'd be more than willing to talk about it. Maybe she *needed* to talk about it.

And then, of course, there was Coco's warning . . .

He walked until he found an old pay phone on the side wall of a convenience store. Digging in his pocket for some change, he racked his brain for Corinne's number. He'd called it often enough over the past couple of weeks, arranging his trip down here, and he cleared his mind and tried tapping it in.

On the third try, he got it right.

"Hey," he said when she answered, "it's me."

"Max. Didn't think I'd hear from you again—today, at least. Meet your friends at Tulane?"

"Yeah, yeah," he said, waving his hand dismissively. "Corinne, what's Tordu?"

Silence. Max shifted and the line crackled. "Corinne?"

The silence continued. He was sure she was still there, but he heard nothing; no breathing, no heartbeat.

"Corinne, I need to know—"

"Go back to Boston, Max," she said. "Really. If you ever listen to anything I say, listen to this: go back to Boston." Then she hung up.

Max dialed her number three more times, but she did not pick up.

"Shit!" He banged down the receiver, looking around to see if anyone was watching him. He seemed to be alone in the busy street.

Dropping the change back in his pocket, he felt Ray's map. He looked up at the clear sky and thought of rain coming from nowhere, and then he remembered the name of the Second Moment on the map: *The Pere's Kyrie.*

He'd only come down here to say good-bye, to close the

door on a part of his life that had left him scarred. Instead, with every passing moment he seemed to be opening more doors, and each one led into mystery.

Max was sick of mysteries. He needed to stop asking politely for answers. He could still feel the point of Coco's knife on his throat, still hear the threat in that silky voice. It should have made him do just what Corinne recommended. Run back to Boston.

Well, fuck that. Corinne obviously had some of the answers he was looking for, and she wasn't likely to cut his throat for asking. And if whatever he'd seen or witnessed yesterday was more than a drunken, drugged hallucination, there was one other mystery he could solve right now.

Jackson Square was ten minutes away. He started walking.

The Square was beautiful. He'd been here a few times with Gabrielle, sitting in the park and eating lunch, throwing down bread for the birds, staring at St. Louis Cathedral and wondering at the history of the place. It wasn't busy now— none of New Orleans was—but there were still a few people wandering through the circular park, eating from paper bags, smoking, staring at their feet.

Even here Max saw the scars of Katrina in the boarded windows, broken trees, and the air of dejection that seemed to flow from the shops and restaurants around the Square. It felt like a place where the last parade had already marched by, and all that remained was the cleanup. Then God would put up the chairs, lock the doors, and turn out the lights forever.

Max really hoped that didn't happen. A lot of people obviously still had faith in New Orleans. And maybe faith could be enough.

He sat on a bench in the park and opened the map. The Moment was still there, and the box it was written in ended in a sharp point in front of the cathedral.

Max looked up. There was nothing out of place here, no mysterious other-world where he would witness events from the past and taste the air of yesteryear. People walked back and forth before the cathedral steps, and nothing disturbed them.

They haven't drunk that stuff from Ray's clay bottle, Max thought. But he shook his head, confused. In the cool light of day, and so soon after having his life threatened, yesterday was starting to seem even more like a dream.

He folded the map, stood, and walked toward the cathedral.

And he heard singing. He paused, head tilted to one side. Was there a service today? Nobody else seemed to be listening, and he walked on, realizing he must present an odd sight standing there in the afternoon sun.

A dozen yards from the cathedral steps he stopped again. Two young women parted to walk around him, and one of them muttered something that made the other one laugh. Max turned to watch them go, and when the taller woman looked back, the smile dropped from her face.

What does she see? Max thought. *What is it about me that dries her laughter?*

He took another step—

—and the rain struck him, driving him to his knees.

Heavy and unrelenting, it battered him down to the rough stones that had been smooth a moment before. The rain, and the darkness . . .

It was daytime in the Square, but nighttime for Max. His guts knotted and he felt sick, but he swallowed it down, tensing his muscles against the spate of cramps that twisted them up.

Twisted . . . "Tordu" is French for "twisted"!

The singing grew louder, a deep, beautiful tenor singing the Kyrie. Lightning flashed and thunder rumbled. Another Moment. Another storm. Once again he had slipped into long ago. The Square here was old, less arranged, functional rather than beautified for tourists. And it was strange. Some of the buildings he recognized, yet even in the downpour they seemed newer, their stone not so weathered and the façades smoother.

A priest stood before the cathedral, hands clasped before his chest as he sang that wonderful chant. *The Father's Kyrie!* Max thought. Before the priest, a group of people were gathered around six rough pine coffins that were lined up in front of the steps. On the steps themselves were the stinking, rotten remains of six human beings.

The priest said something in thickly accented French that Max could not translate, and the people started trying to lift the remains. The bodies fell apart. They must have been here for a long time, lying rotting on these steps with no one removing them—like the bodies left all over New Orleans after Katrina; like Gabrielle in her attic—and Max could not understand why.

Criminals? Heretics? Blasphemers?

But the priest sang on, and the weeping people ignored the stench of the dead to nail their loved ones at last into their coffins.

Shadows moved through the rain and flitted at the limits of Max's perception. They wore armor and carried weapons, but the downpour seemed to keep them at bay. And the rain, he realized, carried the priest's song. His words did not emerge from one place, but all around, coming at Max from left and right, up and down. Each splash of a raindrop was part of the priest's voice, and every touch of water on Max's head felt like a baptism into this man's complete and wonderful faith.

"Who are you?" Max shouted, but nobody heard.

He stood and started backing away. The rain and the voice followed.

The priest and his funeral entourage walked away from the Square, passing out of view along an alley beside the cathedral. As darkness swallowed them, those armed shapes moved again, casting shadows on the rain that were washed away with another burst of that voice. They wanted to get at those coffins and the people who dared join the procession, but the Pere's Kyrie kept them out.

The singing continued, as though every drop of rain was making a small part of the sound, lifting it and echoing it from the sodden ground.

Max backed away some more, his clothes soaked through, and he wondered what song the rain would sing next.

He was lying on the ground, and an old black woman knelt over him.

"You okay, baby?" she asked.

Max blinked up at the clear blue sky. The song was gone, but it echoed in his mind.

"You shouted at me, asked who I am. Then you fell down. Sorry if I startled you. I'm no one, really."

Max sat up and looked around. The Square was real, this woman was real, and his clothes were dry once more.

"Where's the rain gone?" he asked. "There was a storm."

"Sure was," the old woman said. "Sure was. But we'll get by." Then she stood slowly, groaning as her old joints creaked, and walked away.

Max found his feet and staggered back to the park, dropping onto a bench. *That was no dream,* he thought. *That was no hallucination.* He wondered whether, if he approached those steps, he'd see it again. But then he remembered the map. And when he took it out and unfolded it, he was just in time to see the last traces of the Second Moment's ink fading away, and the first of the Third Moment appear.

chapter
6

Whatever Ray had given him should have been out of his system by now . . . unless whatever it had done to him was permanent. That thought scared Max, but not as much as the idea that magic had touched him. Magic was for fairy tales and kids. To Max, it meant card tricks and making coins appear out of thin air.

But it was too late for denials, especially after what he'd seen, what he'd experienced. And he felt it now, too, like static in the air around him. Maybe that was why that woman had looked at him so strangely on the steps of the cathedral. Ray had said something about gathering the magic, and somehow that's what he was doing. Perhaps static was the right way to think about it, but eventually, static would build into a shock.

Steadying his breath, he read the words of the Third Moment:

The Third Moment:
The Sacrifice of the Novices
Mireault Marks the City
February 13, 1823

Nodding, he folded the map. He needed to see Corinne, talk to her, but after what he'd just experienced he could not just break away from Ray's map. If it was real, if these moments really *were* the magical history of New Orleans and he could witness and feel them, maybe the other things the old man had said were also true. Maybe crazy Ray hadn't been so crazy after all.

Impossible hope rose in him and Max chuckled, an edge of hysteria building up inside him. Screw Coco, and Corinne, too. Maybe there was another way to get the answers he sought about Gabrielle. Maybe he could ask her himself.

The Third Moment was only three blocks from here, on the corner of Chartres and Ursulines. In fact, if he wasn't mistaken, he knew precisely which building that address and those words referred to.

He slipped the map into his back pocket and headed out of the park, past the black wrought-iron fence, and up to the corner of Chartres and St. Ann. He hesitated in the shadow of the cathedral, wondering if he would hear the

Pere's Kyrie again. But that moment had passed. He felt its loss, and he wished there was music in the air to take its place. Once, he wouldn't have been able to leave Jackson Square without having heard a brass band playing, or at least a sax player on the corner blatting out something for the tourists. But in what was perhaps the most telling sign of the catastrophe that had befallen New Orleans, the musicians had fallen silent.

Max hurried up Chartres, long past the time when he could have appreciated the balconies on either side of the street. The little barbershop where a barrel-chested old Cajun had once cut his hair—reluctant to be pulled away from the chair on the stoop of his storefront—was boarded up, the brown water mark on the wood only a foot above ground level. GONE TO TEXAS had been spray-painted on the boarding, and Max wondered what that old man would do in Texas, so far away from his culture and his city.

It took him only a few minutes to walk to the intersection marked on the map. He passed other people on the street, but not many. Some drove cars through the Quarter, looking as if they were on some kind of safari, afraid to get out but wanting to see the place, just the same. Max wanted to shout at them, direct them to Lakeview or the Lower Ninth, today's *real* New Orleans.

As he walked, it occurred to him how few police cars he'd seen since he'd arrived. He started wondering where the cops were now. GONE TO TEXAS flashed across his mind again, and he frowned, unaccountably disturbed by the idea that New Orleans had been abandoned.

Stop, he told himself. *Focus on your own ghosts.*

And that was almost funny now. Almost.

When the white walls of the Ursuline Convent came into view, he quickened his step, flush with anticipation. At the end of this bizarre chase, like some kind of scavenger hunt for a city's memories, he'd find . . . what? Crazy Ray? Undoubtedly. Answers? He hoped so. He didn't know how many Moments the map was set to reveal, but he now wanted to locate them as quickly as he could.

The Old Ursuline Convent was the oldest building in the Mississippi River Valley. Most of what lay behind those high white walls consisted of a massive L-shaped building, as white as the walls, with a simple black roof. There were smaller buildings on the convent grounds, but as he crossed Ursulines Avenue, he focused on the face of the convent itself, with its five third-floor gables and the peak above the entrance. He'd always loved this building. He should have expected it to be on the map, because it was a renowned source of local ghost stories, and now he was more curious than afraid. The map had shown him moments of transcendent magic, and he wondered what the convent's tale would be.

The gate on Chartres Street was closed, so he started down the sidewalk to a second gate, which opened into a lot at the rear of the building. But even as he approached, he could see that there would be no entry there, either.

Max stood on the sidewalk, staring over the gate at the rear of the building. For the first time, he wondered if he'd always been mistaken, and whether this might actually be the front entrance. He'd never been inside the walls, but the two sides looked very similar, except that the northwest side, facing the corner, had a courtyard he'd once seen when the gates were open.

Not that it mattered. He couldn't get inside and everything around him felt ordinary. No visions, no voices from the past, no rain. He pulled the map out of his back pocket, wondering if he'd misinterpreted the location, but when he unfolded it he had no doubt.

He refolded the map and clutched it in his hand, looking around. There might not be many cops around, but if he tried to climb the gate, and somebody saw him, New Orleaneans weren't above taking the law into their own hands. Especially now. Someone would shoot him, or drag him down and beat him. It would be an idiotic risk.

No, he had to find out what the deal with the old convent was, when it would open, or if he could get someone to let him in. He had to find a bell or a buzzer, and a lie that would gain him entrance.

Max stepped up to the gate, searching for some means to communicate with those inside. He stood on his toes, and leaned one hand on the gate. At the moment of contact, his gut gave a lurch and his eyes fluttered. His fingertips felt cold and he fell heavily against the gate.

This is it. It's happening.

But as he blinked and his vision cleared, he realized there was no rain. He'd come to expect some kind of storm with every Moment on the map, but the pattern had been broken. The sunlight seemed to have dimmed, but it was still day, and the gate had not changed.

Then the cold sank its fingers deep into his bones, and he knew something *had* changed. Even in the dead of winter, it was rarely this cold in New Orleans.

A scream tore across the sky.

As Max searched for its source, from behind him he heard horses' hooves on stone, and the rattle of wheels. For a beat he thought of the carriages that took tourists around the Quarter. But even as he turned, he knew what he would see.

A pair of horses drew a closed carriage made of gleaming black wood. On the high seat, the mustachioed driver wore clothes from another era. Along the street there came a handful of men and women in rough garb that Max placed in the 19th century. As another scream punctured the calm of the winter's day, they all began to rush toward the gate, talking amongst themselves in French, faces etched with worry as they stared over Max's head at the roof of the convent.

A thin stork of a man in ill-fitting clothes walked through Max and grabbed hold of the gate. Max felt that familiar disorientation pass over him, as if the world was about to slip away beneath him and send him sliding back to his own time.

I'm the ghost, he thought. That couldn't be, *he* wasn't dead, but he had never felt so insubstantial.

A third scream rent the air and sent spiders of fear dancing up the back of his neck. Max turned toward the convent again, just one spectator amongst a dozen gathered there, and at last he saw.

Two nuns stood precariously on the slanted roof, affixing

ropes to two narrow chimneys. A third woman, older, leaned from a window below them, and it was she who had been screaming. There were red bloody gashes on her face.

Abruptly she was pulled inward and another face appeared at the window. She began to shout at the younger sisters up on the roof, commanding them in French to climb down.

Three more nuns climbed carelessly over the roof's ridge, all of them slight things, no more than girls, but instead of trying to rescue the others, they helped them secure the ropes to the chimneys.

And then all five of them began to sing.

A winter wind wrapped around Max and he hugged himself against the cold, but he did not take his eyes from those five young nuns. *Just girls,* he thought. And then he remembered the words that accompanied this moment on the map, and a terrible certainty gnawed at him.

Nuns who hadn't yet taken the vows to become full sisters were called "novices."

"No," he whispered.

The older nun screamed at them again from the window, and others filled the rest of the windows on the third floor, shouting and imploring them to climb down. The five novices ignored them, playing out the ropes that the first two had tied to the chimneys. Ropes that were now knotted around the first two girls' throats.

"Jesus," Max whispered. He lowered his gaze.

And then he shook his head. He couldn't just stand here. If this was magic, it was entirely different from the sort he'd seen thus far.

The novices chanted, crying out to God or whatever else might be listening. Max caught something about marking the city, or staining it, and the same refrain, over and over: *"Por Mireault, por Mireault, por Mireault."*

He blocked the sound out and hurled himself against the gate. Leaping, he grabbed the top, scrambling with his feet and getting purchase, dragging himself up and nearly falling back. Instead he hurled himself over the gate, fell onto his hands and knees, then rolled.

He sprang up, barely feeling the sting of scraped, bloody palms.

Looking up at the roof, he could see a couple of older nuns carefully edging their way toward the novices.

The five girls stopped chanting. They covered their faces with their hands, some sort of ritual gesture, and then, as one, threw their arms wide.

"Por Mireault, le Tordu!" they cried.

Tordu?

Max froze. And in that moment, the two girls who'd tied the ropes around their own necks jumped from the roof's edge. They plummeted with a terrible weight, and when the ropes had played out, the novices were jerked up short, limbs flailing like marionettes, and a double-crack of snapping bones echoed off the walls that surrounded the convent.

The Ursuline sisters in their windows cried out in horror. The people at the gate screamed.

And then the three girls who'd aided the sacrifice of the others came together, joined hands, and stepped off the roof. There was no rope to shorten their fall. They hit the ground with a sickening *crunch,* falling in a tangle of limbs. One of them twitched, and then all were still.

Max's stomach convulsed and he fell to all fours. Like a dog, he threw up into the dirt, retching again and again, trying to draw a clean breath, mind churning even worse than his gut. It wasn't supposed to be like this. The magic of the earlier moments had been pure—a Native American ritual to end a hurricane, the power of faith keeping an enemy at bay with song and rain—but this was something else. This magic, whatever its intent, was hideous.

And if he'd gathered static from those other moments, what had attached itself to him from this?

His stomach heaved again but he fought it, taking long, slow breaths. Vision clearing, he glanced up at the convent.

The dead girls were gone.

"Shit," Max hissed, forcing himself up. He staggered a bit, looked around, and he knew he was back. The vision had ended. The moment had passed. *Off the map,* he thought, and felt that edge of hysteria returning—

—because he was inside the walls of the convent. In his vision, or his haunting, or whatever kind of reality-shift it had been, he'd scaled the gate, and he must have done it for real.

Panicked, he ran back for the gate. He'd scraped his hands before, and they burned with pain as he grabbed the upper edge and dragged himself up.

When he landed on the other side he sprang to his feet immediately, looking around. From the other side of the gate he heard someone shouting after him, and he bolted, sprinting for Chartres Street. Around the corner he kept running, only stopping when his leg muscles began to burn and his chest tightened.

Even then, Max did not stop moving. Walking, he cut up St. Philip to Royal and took a left. The map crinkled in his back pocket. By now, the Third Moment would have faded and the fourth would have appeared, but his determination had faded along with it.

Right now he had no desire to know what the next Moment would bring.

Back at the hotel, Max paced his room. Every couple of minutes he sat on the edge of the bed and dialed Corinne's cell phone, and when she didn't answer, he dialed the home number she'd given him. Then he listened to that ring. The cell phone kicked over to voice mail, but the home number went unanswered, and in his mind he could see a phone on a kitchen counter just ringing and ringing into an empty house.

He didn't have the first clue where Corinne might be. She called the place in Lakeview her "aunt's house," but the old woman had died, leaving it to Corinne. It had been ruined by the flood. So where was "home" now? Where was that endlessly ringing phone? Because Corinne knew more about old Ray than she was letting on, and she damn well knew more about Coco. When he'd asked about Tordu, she had told him to go back to Boston, and he could still hear the fear in her voice. Maybe she didn't know *everything* he wanted to know . . . but she had the keys.

Slamming the phone down again, Max went to the window. The shadows were lengthening. He hadn't realized how late it was, and he wondered how long he'd been pacing the room and trying to call Corinne. He leaned his forehead against the window and stared down into the street.

Dusk had begun to slink in and coalesce, and for a moment he thought the world flickered and shifted. But nothing had really changed. He had simply grown accustomed to a fluid reality, and the whole aura of post-Katrina New Orleans felt like somewhere unknown.

Corinne could be anywhere. He didn't know where to *begin* looking for her, and even if he did, he had no easy way to get around. She'd offered to drive him, and not having a car at his disposal made him feel trapped.

But he couldn't just pace.

He tried her phone numbers again. Still no luck. He fought the temptation to hurl the phone across the room, dropping the receiver gently into the cradle instead.

Max picked up the remote control and turned on the television. He lay back and surfed through local and national news clips, hotel information, pay-per-view, old sitcoms, HBO, and then clicked it off again. Closing his eyes, he steadied his breathing, trying to calm down. His skin prickled with the horrifying memory of those young novices plunging to their deaths, but worse were the sounds of their dying. He would remember that every time he closed his eyes.

The idea of touching the magic of this city had begun to intrigue him, even excite him. Now he understood how foolish that had been. Tragedy came with triumph, horror with glee. He'd let himself be drawn in, and now he felt the taint of darkness in his heart.

"Where the fuck are you?" he said through gritted teeth.

He opened his eyes. Corinne had shut him out. She was not going to answer his calls, or return his messages. He had to try something else. She and Gabrielle had relatives in New Orleans, so if he had to track down every Doucette in the city, he'd do that.

And sitting in this hotel room wouldn't get him anywhere.

Max pushed up off the bed, checked his pockets to be sure he had his wallet and room key, and went out the door. Riding down in the elevator, he bounced on his heels, still overloaded with nervous energy. He'd seen death today, and had it whisper in his ear as it held a knife to his throat. In his room, he'd been tempted to call his sister, tell her what had been going on, but she would only have freaked out and told him to get the hell back to Boston.

And she'd have been right to do so.

But he wasn't going anywhere, not yet. People were haunted far more often, it seemed to him, by what they hadn't done instead of things they had. Regrets. Omissions. If onlys. He would not allow those ghosts to find him.

The elevator doors slid open at the lobby and he strode to the front desk.

"Can I help you, sir?" asked the black woman behind the counter. Her name tag identified her as Audrey.

"Does the hotel have a business office?"

Audrey frowned. "Sure. But it closes at four o'clock. I'm sorry."

Max ran a hand through his hair and took a deep breath. "Listen, I didn't bring a laptop because I didn't think I'd need it. But I need to get online desperately. Is there any way I could get in there? It's really important."

Audrey gave him a sympathetic look. "Fires to put out, huh?"

"Something like that."

"Hang on," she said, ducking through a doorway behind the counter.

She spoke quickly to someone there, and a moment later a man emerged, dark circles under his eyes suggesting that Katrina had left him with plenty of ghosts of his own.

"I've got it," the man said.

"Thanks, Jaime," Audrey said, and then she smiled at Max again. "Right this way, sir."

She led him out of the lobby into an alcove with several doors with glass inset windows. One bore a brass plate beside it with the words BUSINESS OFFICE, and Audrey fished a set of keys from her pocket and unlocked it for him. She turned on the light and gestured toward the computer. Silver fireworks exploded on the screen saver.

"Let me know if there's anything you need."

Max looked at her. "Is there, I don't know, a time limit or anything? How do I pay?"

"Don't worry about it," she said, her smile faltering a moment. "Just tell people, when you go home, that New Orleans is open for business."

Audrey left him there.

As Max sat down at the computer, he realized that some of his nervous energy had dissipated. The woman's kindness had done that, and he was grateful. He needed focus, and that feeling of spiders crawling under his skin, and the urge to take off at a run, wouldn't do him any good.

He opened up the web browser and went to a white-pages search, typing in "Doucette" and "New Orleans." Even as he did, he remembered Corinne saying something about the family evacuating, and wondered if any of them had come back. There were forty-two listings for "Doucette" in the city, including one for Corinne at the old Lakeview address. Many of the other addresses were probably ruined now as well. But he had to find the ones that still existed.

Max looked around and spotted a printer. He could just print up the list of Doucette phone numbers and start dialing, one by one.

As he glanced at the screen again, however, something else caught his eye. One of the menu options read *Reverse Directory Search*. He clicked on the link, opening a page that asked for a telephone number.

"Yes," he whispered, fishing into his pocket for the paper on which he'd written Corinne's two phone numbers.

Her cell wouldn't do him any good, but that home number was a landline. He typed the ten digits into the box and clicked search. The browser seemed to slow down, and for a second he worried it would crash.

Then the name and address came up, along with a small window containing a map. With a click of the mouse, he had a map showing directions to the home of Huey Kelton, who lived on Magazine Street in the Garden District. Max had no idea who this Kelton guy was, but that was the phone Corinne had called him from to tell him that Gabrielle was dead.

Max jumped up and went out into the lobby.

Audrey looked up from behind the desk. "Did you get what you needed?"

"I did, thank you. Any chance you could call me a cab?"

"Can't promise one will come, but I'll do my best."

Max had a feeling her best was pretty formidable. He thanked her and went back into the business office, printed up the page with the map and Huey Kelton's address, closed the browser, and shut off the lights, then left, pulling the door closed behind him.

The cab rolled slowly through the early-evening streets of the Garden District. No traffic appeared to clog the route, but the driver never accelerated above thirty miles an hour, content to go at his own pace. In the time he'd lived in New Orleans, Max had found that pretty much summed up the populace here. Frantic or laid back, everyone did their own thing.

It had taken nearly half an hour for the cab to arrive, during which time all of Max's nervous energy had returned. The waiting made him itchy and he'd stood on the street in front of the hotel, trying his best not to look like some kind of junkie, twitching and biting his nails. When the cab did arrive, the driver reeked of booze and kept an unlit cigar chomped between his teeth. He guided the car with one hand, the other one out the window, surfing his fingers through the wind like a kid.

When Max had told him the address, he'd only grunted his assent and started driving. They'd gone through the Warehouse District, but the clubs that had made the place trendy in the last decade were either still closed up after the storm or hadn't yet opened for the night.

As they passed through the Garden District, Max found himself distracted by a bizarre spectacle. Some of the side streets were dotted with refrigerators, left out at the end of driveways as if their owners expected the garbagemen to pick them up. They hit a section of Magazine where the same phenomenon was in evidence. Some of the fridges were still covered with magnets, and all of them were taped closed with duct or electrical tape.

"What's that all about?" he asked.

The driver grunted, this time a question.

"The refrigerators. I didn't think this neighborhood flooded."

"Didn't. But the power was out too long. Nothing but rot and E. coli and shit in those things. Who knows what's growing in there? I wouldn't open one. They got dump trucks and loaders goin' around, picking 'em up."

"Looks weird."

The cabbie grunted, as if the relative weirdness of the forest of fridges hadn't occurred to him. "Drove through Gentilly and the Seventh Ward a few days ago. There's places up there where the fridges are the only things still standing. Rather lose the fridge and keep the house."

Max shut up. What could he have said to that?

In the front seat of the cab, the driver took a swig from a flask. He didn't give a damn about being surreptitious.

Max had lost track of addresses a while ago, and he let the driver do his job. When the cab slowed, he looked around. There weren't a lot of gardens in this part of the Garden District. Trees and bushes, sure, though the hurricane had stripped most of them of any green. They were pitiful, skeletal things, and seemed lost in front of the rows of houses and apartments. The buildings were stacked up close together.

"Hard to make out numbers, but I think that's the one you want," the driver said, around his unlit cigar. He pointed to a small, gray, neatly kept house whose bay window had been boarded up. Smaller windows were still intact, though, and a light burned inside.

Max looked at the house. Now that he was here, uncertainty took hold.

"Any way I can get you to stick around for a few minutes, in case I've got the wrong house?"

"If that's not it, it's bound to be one of these. This here's the block, for sure."

"I just meant, if the person I came to see isn't home—"

"I'm going home now. Got dinner waiting. I'm not going back to the Quarter tonight."

Max looked into the rearview mirror. The driver wasn't even looking at him. The man's tone was flat and dull, and he knew the cabbie was lying. Nobody waited at home for this guy, especially not with dinner on the table. Maybe he'd go home to a bottle and his television, and something microwaved out of a can. He just didn't want to be bothered. But Max couldn't get angry. If their situations were reversed, he'd want to go home, too.

"Can I get a card with the number of the cab company?"

The guy nodded. "Sure, sure." He grabbed one and passed it back.

Max paid him, tipping him a few extra bucks for his trouble, and stepped out of the cab. The car rolled away, taking with it the stink of whiskey. Max stood in front of what he hoped was Huey Kelton's house and watched the windows for a minute, looking for any sign of life.

Screw it, you're here. Just go. He didn't have any options. His cell phone was wrecked, and if nobody was at home he'd have to walk back along Magazine until he came to a bar that'd let him make a call.

Tucking the cab company's card into his pocket, he walked up to the house. For just a second, he thought he saw something move in the darkness to the side of the house, but when he narrowed his eyes for a better look, there was nothing there. Just the night, growing darker.

He went to the door and knocked. It felt quiet and empty in there. Max didn't believe in any sort of preternatural awareness, but he thought sometimes people sensed things, foremost among them the absence of other people. The house felt as if nobody was home, so that even when he knocked again, harder this time, he wished the cabdriver had agreed to wait.

For the first time he noticed the doorbell. It was half a

foot from the door frame, round, with a metal button at its center, painted the same color as the house. The thing looked old and unused, and he felt sure it must be out of order.

But when he pressed the button, the bell rang, a traditional *ding-dong* that sounded muffled, as though it came up from the inside of a well. His feeling that no one was home intensified.

"Shit," Max said.

He counted to ten and knocked again, his last effort before setting off down Magazine Street in search of a bar with a phone. And maybe a drink or two as he waited for a cab to come and fetch him, however long that might take.

He reached out and pressed the doorbell again.

From inside there came the chime, accompanied by the sound of breaking glass. Max blinked, straightening up. What the hell was that? He'd been so sure the house was empty.

"Mr. Kelton?" he called, hammering on the door. "Corinne?"

Coming down off the stoop, he moved around some bushes to the nearest unboarded window and tried to see through the curtains. The front rooms were dark, but a light burned at the back of the house. Its illumination flickered as something passed in front of it.

"Corinne?" he called through the glass.

Inside, someone screamed.

"Fuck!" Max jumped back over the bushes and started pounding on the door. "Kelton? Open the door!"

A light flicked on in front of the neighbor's house and an old man poked his head out the door. "Get away from there, boy, or I'm'a call the cops."

Max paused, mind racing. He stared at the old man, remembering the shattering of glass and that scream. One scream only.

Then he threw himself at the door, slamming his shoulder against it once, twice, a third time. It gave a little, but not enough. He hauled back and aimed a kick at the wood right beside the knob. On the fourth kick, the lock tore through the frame, wood splintering, and the door banged open.

The neighbor was shouting. Other lights were coming on.

Max rushed into the house, calling for Corinne. He heard sounds deep in the house, the rustling of clothes, something wet, and then a dark laugh. He rushed along the narrow corridor toward the back, careening into the kitchen.

He saw the blood, a spray across the linoleum, but couldn't stop. His feet slipped out from under him, and he managed to twist as he fell so that he landed on his hands and knees. His fingers and palms smeared trails in the blood.

Corinne lay stretched out on the floor, her throat cut. The edges of the gash pouted as blood burbled from arteries and veins. Her shirt had been slashed and her gut sawed open from breastbone to below her navel, fistfuls of intestine yanked out and unfurled onto the floor. The stink was terrible.

Her eyes were still open, tears drying on her face.

She twitched.

Max scrabbled away from the corpse, glancing around to see if her killer was still here. The window at the back of the kitchen had been smashed, the curtain rod pulled down. Outside, it was dark. Whoever had done this had vanished into the night.

Pulling up his shirt to cover his nose and mouth against the stink of her exposed bowels, he managed to stand and spotted a telephone on the wall next to the cabinets. Shaking, he picked up the phone—the same phone Corinne had probably used to tell him Gabrielle was dead—only to have it slip from his bloody hands.

He retrieved it, and steadied himself long enough to dial 911.

"Murder," he said. "There's . . . there's been a murder here."

But death and murder, new as they were to Max, had been all too common in New Orleans of late, and like cabdrivers, the ranks of the police had thinned in the wake of the storm.

They told him to wait.

chapter

7

He tried waiting in a room at the front of the house, but the thought of Corinne's body lying alone in the kitchen preyed on his mind and drew him back. Her glassy stare welcomed him, and though he turned his face away, he sat and kept her company.

He could not stop shaking. Everything was falling apart. The last Moment had displayed the dark underside of the magic of New Orleans, and as if in response to that, he had walked in on this slaughter.

His teeth chattered. He'd always heard the expression, but he had never thought it possible or likely. His gums hurt, but however much he tried to clamp his jaws shut, the muscles spasmed and shook in concert with the rest of his body.

Where the hell were the cops?

Max glanced from the kitchen window, just catching sight of the red splash of Corinne's demise from the corner of his eye. The killer had gone through there. And the destruction wrought on her body had been performed between him hearing her scream and then bursting into the kitchen, a space of . . . how many seconds? He could guess, but there was no knowing for sure. His whole concept of time had been twisted. He had come from the eighteen hundreds to the terrible present, and seconds could be years.

He waited over an hour for the police to arrive. In that time, he never once looked back at Corinne's cooling body, but neither did he leave her. He was certain that she would not want to be alone right now.

And when they did arrive, their reaction was not what he had expected.

In retrospect, he should have anticipated what happened. If he'd been thinking straight he *would* have expected it, but he had an image of the way things should go from here, and that image was very, very wrong.

He heard a car screech to a halt outside, some muffled voices, and then the cautious footsteps of someone entering through the broken door and approaching along the hallway. A shadow projected into the kitchen, something long wrapped in its hand.

"Down!" a voice called.

Max gasped and glanced to his right. A shape stood at the open window, a short man silhouetted by the few lights still shining outside. Illuminated by the weak glow of the single kitchen light, Max saw the ugly end of a gun pointing directly at his chest.

The shadow emerged from the hallway, a big cop also carrying a gun. "You heard him. Down!"

"Holy shit," the cop at the window muttered.

Max held up his hands and shook his head, starting to protest. But he did not even have the chance to utter one word.

"I'll count to three," the short cop said. "One . . . two . . ."

Max dropped forward, easing himself to the floor, pushed the final few inches by the big cop's boot. He turned just in time to avoid crushing his nose, but his cheek cracked against the floor, and he tasted blood where he'd bitten his tongue.

"Please!" Max said. "I came here and found—"

"Shut it," the cop in the window said. "Paul, I'll come around."

"I got him," the big cop, Paul, said. "Move a muscle, fuckwit, and your brains will corrupt the crime scene."

Max closed his eyes and breathed deeply, the weight of the man's boot still pressing him down. He wouldn't have been able to move even if he wanted to, and he supposed that was the whole point.

The short cop entered along the hallway a few seconds later, gun still drawn and pointing now at Max's face. He glanced around the kitchen, his face twisting into a grimace of disgust. "Holy shit, you really did a piece on her."

"It wasn't me."

"Yeah, I heard that one before." A silent communication passed between the policemen, and Paul's foot pressed harder on Max's back as the other man bent his arms back and cuffed him.

"I don't believe this," Max whispered.

"From out of town?" the short cop asked.

Max nodded.

"Figures."

"Really, I came here to talk to her, heard a scream, found her like this. Ask the old guy outside, he saw me."

"Already talked to him," Paul said. "Let's get him up."

The two cops grabbed an arm each and lifted Max to his feet, dragging him from the kitchen and into the small, dark sitting room. They dropped him into a chair and hit the light. There were a couple of comfortable armchairs, a wall lined with books, and a selection of amateurish watercolors hanging from the other walls. Max saw an open book lying facedown on the arm of the other chair. *Was she reading that?* he thought. *When the murderer came, was she sitting there reading that, trying to distract herself from whatever it was she couldn't bear to tell me?* He turned his head sideways in an effort to see the cover, but he could not make out the title or author.

"Crime Scene on the way?" Paul asked.

"Should be." The short cop sat in the chair opposite Max, staring at him without blinking or averting his gaze. Max stared back for a moment, then glanced away and closed his eyes. He was still shaking, and his shoulders ached with his arms forced behind his back. He swallowed blood.

"Sick fuck," the short cop said. He took out a notebook and pen, scribbled a few lines, then looked at Max again. "I'm going to take a statement."

Max wasn't sure whether he was about to shout or cry. His breath came fast and shallow, and he ground his teeth together to stop them from chattering. *This is bad,* he thought, and the sound of those novice nuns striking the ground came to him again.

"Ask the old—"

"Told you, already talked to him," Paul said. "Said you were snooping around the house, started screaming the woman's name, then you shouldered the door, came in, and he heard her screams."

"She screamed *before* I forced the door."

"So why break in?"

Max frowned. "Because she was screaming."

"You in the habit of breakin' down a lady's door when she's screaming?" the short cop said. "How'd you know she wasn't just gettin' banged?"

"I heard glass breaking. The window you were at, I heard that break, and so—"

"So you stormed in to the rescue," Paul said. He was standing by the door, and even though Max was cuffed, the cop still cradled a gun in his hands.

"Aren't you going to arrest me?" Max said. He had no idea how this worked. Was this part of the statement? Were they recording this exchange, somehow? He'd seen the cop shows and movies, but he didn't have a clue whether they'd arrest him now or at the station, or if they should even be talking without them having read him his rights. *And what are my rights?* he wondered. *Are there even any lawyers still in New Orleans?* He'd heard reports of cops being the worst looters of them all, and suddenly he felt in danger as well as in deadly, unbelievable trouble.

"Old guy says you smelled like trouble and sounded worse, the way you were hollering for that gal."

"The broken window," Max said. He closed his eyes and tried to shed his memory of the blood, the smell, and the sound of people hitting the ground that for some reason he could not disassociate from Corinne's murder. "Shattered glass was on the floor inside. That's how the *murderer* got in. I came through the door, and he got in and out the window."

Paul shrugged, and the short cop threw him an uncomfortable glance. "Ain't for us to decide what glass went where," Paul said. "Fact is, we got you and a corpse, and your hands covered in blood."

"I stayed here. Waited for you." The situation was starting to feel unreal, and Max caught a fresh whiff of death from the kitchen.

"Ever heard of suicide by cop?" the short cop said. *Was that a threat in his voice?* Max glanced at him, but looked away again when he saw the look in the man's eye. He was almost smiling.

"That's ridiculous."

"New Orleans isn't a normal place nowadays. Right, Paul?"

"Right." Paul shifted the gun, as if to draw Max's attention to it. *He's going to tell me how many people he's shot since the storm,* Max thought. *Sweet Jesus, are these really even cops?*

"Can I see some ID?" Max asked.

The short cop's eyes widened, and he almost levitated from his chair, pen and notebook spilling to the floor. "ID? You want some ID? ID this, sick fuck!" And he pulled out his gun. "Down, on the floor."

"But . . ."

"Down. On. The. Floor."

Max complied, slipping from the chair to his knees and trying to lie down sideways, doing his best not to smash face-first onto the glass-strewn floor. They should be chasing the real murderer, he thought, but he said nothing. Silence was his best option right now.

The short cop knelt on Max's back, knocking the wind from him. Max felt fingers delving into his pockets, hands tapping his hips and thighs, and then the map was tugged from his back pocket, crinkling as if upset at being removed.

"What's this?" the short cop asked.

"A map."

"I can see that, sick fuck. I asked, what is it?"

Max frowned and shook his head, confused. *I can't really tell him, can I? What would he think?* "It's just a map of the city. I was looking around and . . ."

"Looking around for what?" Paul asked.

"Just . . . looking. I used to see Corinne's cousin, and——"

"Who's Corinne?" the short cop asked.

Max twisted his head so he could look up at the man kneeling on his back. "The dead girl."

"Right. And let me guess: her cousin's dead, too?"

"In the storm."

"Right." The cop nodded slowly, unfolding the map as he did so. "In the storm."

The opened map hid Max's view of Paul and the cop on his back, plunging him into shadow. The weak light shone through the paper, silhouetting the short guy and stretching the profile of his face so that he looked like something unnatural and deformed. As he turned, his elongated nose and chin pointed across the map, and for the first time Max saw the small box containing the Fourth Moment. He frowned, concentrating on the reversed words, but the sheet was moving too much for him to make them out.

The cop stood from his back quickly, paused, then knelt by Max's side and slammed the map down beside him. "What's this?" He was pointing directly at the handwritten Fourth Moment.

> *The Fourth Moment:*
> *Evil Defeats Badness for Its Own Ends*
> *Tordu Banishes the Yellow Fever*
> *September 18, 1853*

"The Fourth Moment," Max muttered.

"You wrote this?" Something about the short cop's voice had changed. There was a sense of unease there, and he tapped the map several times beside the boxed words, never actually touching them. "This? The yellow fever?" Another slight, loaded pause. "Tordu?"

"No, I didn't write it," Max said.

The cop stood and showed the map to his companion. They exchanged a few muttered words, but Max's blood was pulsing so hard in his ears that he could not make them out. He turned on his side and looked, and they were both staring down at him. The tall one, Paul, glanced at his watch.

The short cop darted across and kicked Max hard in the side.

Max gasped, from shock as well as pain. He tried to bring his knees up against his chest, roll into a defensive ball, but the cop kicked him again, this time in the back.

"Steady," Paul said, concern in his voice. But Max was not sure who the concern was aimed at.

"Where'd you get this?" the short cop asked. He kicked again, softer this time, more of a nudge. *"Where?"*

It's the Tordu *that's got him riled up,* Max thought. That name was appearing more and more. It reeked of trouble and dark deeds, and he still felt the dregs of its corrupted magic prickling his skin and haunting the byways of his memory.

"Where?" the cop asked again, and stepped over Max, turning and pulling his right leg back to kick him in the face.

"Coco gave it to me," Max said. It was a stab in the dark, but those five words changed everything.

The short cop froze, and Max heard Paul's sharp intake of breath. Max considered elaborating, taking advantage of the fear that man's name seemed to conjure, but then he would risk getting some small detail wrong.

The short cop folded the map and slipped it into his pocket.

"You need to leave," Paul said.

"What?" Max managed to sit up, and the short guy circled behind him. Max winced. What would it be, pistol-whipped? A kick in the throat? But then he heard the jangle of keys, and the cuffs fell away from his hands. He hugged his arms, cringing as the circulation returned.

"Get out of here," Paul said.

Max glanced past him into the hallway, and Corinne now seemed like an afterthought to these men. Her murderer was still out there. Maybe it was even Coco himself, whose mere name had shifted this situation from weird to surreal.

"The Tordu . . ." Max said, wanting to ask questions, plead for information, and maybe protect himself from who- or whatever they were.

The short cop raised his gun and pointed it at Max's face. He was sweating, his jaw clenched and unclenched, and Max realized that he was utterly terrified. "Out," he said, and it emerged as a croak.

Max stood and looked at the cop's pocket into which the map had disappeared.

"No," the cop said. "Consider this . . . bail payment." He lowered the gun, and the nervous glance he exchanged with his partner spoke volumes. "Don't leave the city."

"Would I be safer in custody?" Max asked. Neither man answered, but they both stared at him grimly, perhaps as they would at a dead man.

There were so many questions that Max wanted to ask, but any one of them could change things again. So he looked down at his feet as he exited the room, hurried along the hallway, and left the house, expecting at any moment to feel the impact of a bullet.

Corinne's old neighbor was looking from his front window as Max walked past. He dropped the curtain and retreated into the room, but Max could still see his shadow, alone and adrift with little to protect him against the dark.

Before long, Max started to run.

He paid little heed to direction.

They think I killed Corinne.

He ran along one street, turned a corner, and jogged along the next. The darkness swallowed his footfalls without echo.

They think I cut her open, pulled out her insides while she was still alive.

A dog barked, small shadows darted across the road before him, but the only signs of other people were the occasional dull glow of lights behind drawn curtains.

And they let me go.

He was convinced they were cops. He'd never been arrested, never even been involved with the police, but they had looked and spoken as he expected cops to look and speak. Their actions, however . . .

Max eventually stopped running because he could run no more, so he walked across a small square and into the shadows of another row of buildings. The night air was cool, and the sweat beaded across his back and sides made it feel cooler still. But when he sat down on a bench outside a boarded-up café, shivering, hugging himself, it was shock more than the cold that pulled him down. He bent over and stared at his feet, then looked at his hands. They were still speckled with dried flakes of Corinne's blood, dark in the weak street light. *I touched what was inside her,* he thought. *The last time we spoke, this blood was where it was meant to be. And now . . . now it's out, she's open, and everything she knew is gone.*

Something banged, wood against wood. Max drew in a sharp breath and sat up. The shakes receded as rapidly as they had arrived. The sound came again, and it seemed to originate inside one of the buildings opposite. There were several shops on the block, all but one of them boarded up, and that was a café closed for the night.

There must be ghosts, he thought, *because I've seen them.* The thought chilled him, but it did not feel quite right. What he had seen were not the spirits of people, but the ghosts of moments in time, echoing down through the decades and centuries and revealing themselves to those able or chosen to view them.

Whatever had been in crazy Ray's bottle had shown Max the correct way to see.

The banging came again, more frantic than before, and Max ran.

A few minutes later he stopped again, out of breath and realizing once more how unfit he had become. He looked around, trying to locate himself—but mapless, the street signs were all strange to him. He stood at a crossroads, and on the corner of the street opposite sat a burnt-out car.

There were a couple of weak lights behind the windows of houses, but not nearly enough to warm the scene. They looked like islands in the dark, and Max did not imagine that their owners would welcome a knock at the door at this early hour.

"Lost in New Orleans," he whispered to the dark, hoping for some response. But he was alone here, in this ruined city, and he reflected that perhaps he had been lost since the moment Gabrielle had left him.

Corinne was dead, and he could not go to the police.

He could sense the echoes of time gone by, the magic upon whose foundations the city was built, and the dark deeds buried in those foundations like bodies in a bridge's supports.

But he had no control over what he knew, nor the magical Moments he had witnessed.

And Coco might be looking for him even now.

Max was not streetwise. He was a history professor, a normal man who had found and lost love in a far from normal place. This was all too much for him, and his thoughts were a stew of ideas and fears, images and memories, and all those memories were bad.

He had to go to ground. Find somewhere safe and quiet, where he could think things through and decide what to do next.

And as the shadows around him suddenly grew thicker and deeper, as if becoming something solid rather than the absence of light, he knew that he had to get off the streets.

The place looked as if it'd had its last coat of paint sometime around the Civil War. Its façade was rotten and crumbled in places, several windows were cracked, the roof was missing tiles, and Max was sure that none of this was because of Katrina. This dilapidation was something only time could bestow, and the light emanating from inside barely found its way through the grubby glass.

He knew it was now well into the early hours, and he wondered how the owner would welcome a guest at this time of night.

The hand-painted wooden sign nailed up beside the door looked much newer than the rest of the building. BED AND BORED, it read, and somehow Max managed a smile. He tried the bell, but it depressed without him hearing a sound. It reminded him of the doorbell on the house where Corinne had been murdered, and a sudden, complete image leapt into his mind, shocking him with its intensity: Corinne, glancing up from her book as the bell rang, hearing glass break, placing her book facedown on the arm of the chair, and stalking into the kitchen, seeing the shadow sliding through the broken window . . . faceless, nameless . . . and then the knife, and the scream that had caused Max to force the door, rather than ring the bell again.

So quick! he thought. It was maybe fifteen seconds between when he'd heard the scream to when he skidded into the blood-spattered kitchen, and in that time the killer had . . .

Glancing around at the shadowy street behind him, Max rapped on the door; three quick, loud bangs. He waited a while then knocked again. After a third knock he heard someone approaching from the inside, grumbling and coughing, their feet dragging across a bare wooden floor.

"Got a gun!" they shouted through the door.

Max stood to one side, in case they decided to make a hole in their front door. "I only want a room," he said, his voice shockingly loud in the deserted street.

"It's late!"

"That's why I want a room."

"Thirty bucks through the flap."

"What?"

The metal cover over the letter slot in the door snapped shut three times, a rapid *crack crack crack* that echoed across the street like gunshots.

Max pulled three crumpled tens from his pocket, glad that the police hadn't searched him too thoroughly. He flattened them and pushed them through, and heard a grunt from the other side.

"You runnin'?" the voice asked.

"No," Max replied.

"Yeah, right." There was silence for a few beats, and Max wondered whether he had just given away thirty bucks for nothing. Then he heard locks being twisted, bolts withdrawn, and the door opened a crack, security chain in place. A sawed-off shotgun poked out at him, and above it he could make out a dark face haloed with a shock of white hair.

"Don't look like trouble," the old man said.

Max smiled and held out his hands. *See?*

"Sure smell of it, though." He closed the door, flipped

the chain, and opened it fully. "Thirty bucks's for the bed. I can do you breakfast, but that's another ten. An' you pay in advance, day by day."

Max nodded and smiled again, hoping it did not look too much like a grimace. "Fair enough."

The old man ushered him inside and resecured the door behind him. Then he led Max up a narrow staircase to the second floor, and along a series of damp-smelling corridors to a door adorned with a hand-painted 7. The key was already in the door, and the landlord pulled it out and handed it to Max.

"When's breakfast?" Max asked, shocked to discover how hungry he was even after everything he had been through, everything he had seen.

"'Bout four hours." The man nodded at him and squeezed by, retreating along the corridor with the same coughing and scraping Max had heard downstairs.

Max glanced at the three other doors on this corridor. All of them had keys hanging from their locks.

He opened the door, stepped into his room, and turned on the light. There was a single bed, a small chest of drawers with one whole drawer missing, and an open-fronted wardrobe that seemed to be filled with old coats. The curtain across the window had been pinned into place and would be impossible to take down without a knife. The ceiling and walls were yellow from years of cigarette smoke, and though there was a carpet, it was so worn that in places it was possible to see the joints between floorboards. He looked around for a bathroom door, but there was none.

Shared bathroom, then. The old guy hadn't told him where it was, but Max would find it when he had to. It was the least of his worries.

If Max had gone back to his hotel, he'd have been visible, easy to find if Coco or the police came looking. Here, he was invisible. It was just what he needed.

He flopped on the bed, exhausted, traumatized, but when he closed his eyes he could not sleep. Too much had happened in too short a time to allow escape that easily, and his mind was abuzz with events, and everything that might yet come.

The next day—or rather, later that same day—Max was booked on a flight back to Boston. It took him only a minute or two to decide not to go.

He could flee, he knew that. Run from Coco and whatever the Tordu were, or had been. Run from Corinne's murder, because he couldn't remember those two cops even taking down his name. And he could run from Gabrielle's memory, and the crazy notion that Ray had planted in his mind that he could actually save her from the past.

Yes, he could run. But he could not hide from his memories and guilt, or from the mysteries that were growing around him. He was not the Max he had been just a few days earlier, looking down on Louisiana from above and witnessing nothing he could understand. Now he knew something about this city, and though ingrained doubt still niggled at him about those visions, he could feel the effect they'd had upon him. The city had entered his blood and bones, and the bones and blood of the past had rooted in his memory. What would grow from them, he did not know.

But he could not leave.

He stared up at the ceiling, resigned to sleeplessness, and tried to decide what to do next. The cops' attitude had changed the moment they saw the word "Tordu" on the map, and they'd let him go as soon as he mentioned Coco. They were obviously afraid of the man and the organization, but Max thought there was something more than fear in what they had done. Respect? Complicity? Not that close, perhaps, but maybe they had simply known that, were Coco searching for him, it would be against their better interests to become involved.

Easier to find me if I'm in custody, Max thought. *But maybe not so easy to get to me.*

The more he dwelled on Coco, the more he felt hunted. He could not be certain that Corinne had been killed by Gabrielle's old lover, but if he *had* been the murderer, Max realized with a jolt why it had happened: he had called Corinne, and asked about the Tordu.

He groaned and rested one hand across his eyes, shaking his head slowly. *Me?* he thought. *Is it all because of me?* He'd found out about the Tordu accidentally after all. Coco himself had mentioned it first.

"Fuck," Max whispered. "Fuck fuck fuck." He wished there were an easy way he could discover more about Coco and his gang, but he didn't think the Tordu was the sort of thing he could just Google. Strange to think that in this modern world there could be anything still secret, still off the map. But if he'd learned anything these past few days, it was that there were whole worlds you couldn't find a whisper of on the Internet. Whether through magic or fear, some shadows remained shadows, no matter how much light the world might shine upon them.

Besides, he was out of circulation now. With the windows of his room covered, he might as well be underground. He could stay here for a day or two, lie low, and maybe when the time was right he'd find his way to a police station, speak to someone senior, tell them about Coco and Corinne, and what he'd seen and heard . . .

He wondered what the two cops had filed in their report. *Suspect sighted but lost after a chase?*

He needed help. He needed someone to talk to about Gabrielle, and perhaps through them he could find out more about the Tordu. If he was to remain in New Orleans and protect himself, that must be his main aim.

But who? Crazy Ray? Max laughed bitterly. Even if the old man allowed himself to be found, Max was sure he and the Tordu must be entangled somehow.

His friend Charlie, back at the university? Sitting there with his empty classrooms, emptied bottles, mourning whatever future he saw in the bottom of a glass? Charlie had been in New Orleans all his life, and he might well know about the Tordu, past or present. But the last thing Max wanted to do was to put his friend in danger.

Not after what had happened to Corinne.

Who, then? He stood and paced the room. His feet ground in grit on the carpet, and in one corner the floor gave a little where the floorboards were rotting. This was the second floor, and Max knew that this area hadn't been flooded that deeply, so it wasn't Katrina that had done this.

Not like in that attic where he and Gabrielle had loved, and she had died. Max had dreamed about that, he was sure, though only the vague shadows of images came back at him, not the scorched pain of memories. At least, not of the flood.

Months before, though . . .

The kid's name had been Joseph Noone, a student from Max's class, and Max had walked in on him and Gabrielle having sex.

"Joe Noone," Max muttered. Nothing changed around him, but inside he felt a flush of optimism. If anyone knew what Gabrielle had been embroiled in, it would be the kid she'd left him for.

He sat up on the bed and leaned back against the wall. On the opposite wall hung a picture, a cheap reproduction of an old New Orleans street scene, and he wondered where that place was. *Near the Fourth Moment?* he thought. *Tordu banishing the yellow fever in 1853?* He closed his eyes and tried to recall where exactly on the confiscated map that Moment had been located. If he thought about it some more, he'd be able to find that place, he was sure. And if he was a little way off . . . well, so long as he was in the locale, he'd find his own way there.

"'Cos I've got magic static," he whispered, and he remembered Corinne sitting across from him as they ate breakfast, and he started to cry.

Oh, Christ, she's dead.

The tears quickly stopped, but the grief did not. Guilt made certain of that.

And then the idea came that if Ray had been right, and

he *could* help Gabrielle . . . then maybe he could help Corinne, too.

For that, he would need to follow the Moments. And to do that, he needed a map.

He lay awake until dawn, staring at the ceiling and making a whole new world out of the cracks and spiderwebs across its surface.

chapter

8

Max ate breakfast alone. He'd come to believe that he was the only resident of this cheap hotel, although the noises issuing from the kitchen gave the impression that the old man was preparing breakfast for a dozen. The pancakes and bacon were excellent, though, and afterward Max found the offer of an omelet too tempting to turn down.

It was a brand-new day, and never had Max felt that so keenly. He had a plan for today, and that felt good; he was flushed with a sense of purpose. The old man served him quietly, inviting no conversation. Max was happy with that. He ate to the sound of '30s jazz crackling through a pair of speakers older than him, while the landlord clashed pans and dropped plates in the room next door.

"Stayin' tonight?" the man asked, clearing Max's plates.

"I'm not sure yet. Can you hold the room for me?"

"No one else comes, it's yours."

Max nodded, but the man did not catch his eye. "I owe you for the breakfast," he said.

"Leave it on the table, got wet hands." And the man retreated into the kitchen again, apparently dropping Max's dirtied crockery into the same pile as everything else.

Max dropped a twenty onto the table and left.

Daylight showed him just where he had ended up the previous night. The building he'd slept in was not the only run-down place here, but there were a couple of shops opposite that were already open, shelves of books standing on the pavement before one, clothes rails outside the other. A few cars drifted along the street, and lone pedestrians passed by, keeping to themselves. Max felt a quiet determination in the air, a sense of defiance at the waters now long gone, and his respect for this city grew another notch. He'd seen good things in its history as well as bad, and that was enough to maintain his hope.

He jogged across the street between traffic and approached the bookshop. A middle-aged woman was stacking a wooden bookshelf propped against the wall beside the entrance door, and she gave him an open, friendly smile.

"Day's going to be a nice one," she said. She glanced up at the sky, and Max took the opportunity to appraise her. She had a slender body, firm and athletic, and luxurious blond hair. It was her face that aged her; wrinkles, bags under her eyes, and the skin of a heavy smoker. Her habit had given her a yellow fringe. When she looked at him again, he saw the same guarded distance he'd found in many New Orleaneans, and not for the first time he wondered why it was so obvious that he was a stranger here.

"Sure hope so," he said. "How's business?"

The woman shrugged and looked away. "You searching for something in particular?"

"Well, yeah. Do you sell maps of the city?"

"As it is now?" she asked, and Max heard a cool challenge in her voice. *What does she think I am? A vulture?*

"No, just a city map. Street names, districts, that's all."

She smiled again and nodded inside the shop. "Rack on the left, by the counter. Find what you want, give me a call."

Max nodded his thanks and entered the shop. It was gloomy, and the shelves and walkway seemed to disappear deep into shadows at the rear of the large room. But he found the smell of old books as welcoming and comfortable as ever.

Corinne's hesitant smile played across his mind, and Max sighed, his shoulders sinking.

He found the rack and chose a folded tourist map of a similar size and scale to the one Ray had given him. The shopkeeper came in before he had a chance to call, and they concluded the deal silently. Perhaps she was waiting for him to ask something about the past or comment on the future, but his mind was elsewhere, his attention already drifting beyond the streets and buildings he could see and back toward Tulane University.

When he emerged from the shop, it felt like walking out

into danger. The watchers he had sensed in shadows were still there, but now the shadows had been replaced by the blank faces of strangers, and with every step he took, he was sure he was being followed. He walked quickly along the street, trying to look as though he had a purpose and an aim in mind, and he stopped frequently. Pausing in shop doorways, he would bend to tie his laces and look back the way he had come. Sometimes a person passed by, swapping an awkward stranger's glance with him, or more often not looking at him at all. A couple of times he changed direction completely, looking out for faces he had already seen.

When he reached a fenced parking lot, the Superdome hunkering on the horizon like a giant sleeping tortoise, Max slipped through the fence and sat on the ruin of a block wall. A couple of dogs were rooting through piles of refuse dumped on the opposite side of the lot, but apart from them he was alone.

He breathed deeply, trying to calm the cloying paranoia that threatened to darken the day.

Taking the map from his pocket, he cast his mind back to the terrible events of the previous night. He blinked away the memory of blood and the stink of Corinne's murder, trying to see past them to the moment when the short cop had opened the map, pointed at the Fourth Moment, and asked him what it meant.

Where had it been? Not too far from here, he was sure, but not the Quarter. Tremé, perhaps? He'd never visited that neighborhood, but knew that it was off the beaten track for most tourists—a private, proud place, laden with history much like the rest of New Orleans.

He opened the map, catching the whiff of new ink and printing chemicals. It felt and sounded different from the old map, its crinkles sharper, folds more defined. As he laid it out across his knees, pulling its edges to straighten it, angling it so that the sun did not reflect from its newness, the weight and feel of the paper changed.

It grew older.

Max gasped and his hands fisted, fingers breaking through more brittle paper. The colors before him faded, becoming more diffused. Shaded areas grew pale, and clear areas became built up. He blinked, certain that something was making his vision blur. But his eyes were clear.

He watched a small box appear on the map, and within its sketched edges manifested the words:

> *The Fourth Moment:*
> *Evil Defeats Badness for Its Own Ends*
> *Tordu Banishes the Yellow Fever*
> *September 18, 1853*

The box appeared to indicate an area north of the Superdome, on Perdido Street. Max wasn't sure what was there, but . . .

But this thing just changed in my hands!

He almost dropped the map. His grip loosened, but his fingers snagged on the paper, and the map rested on his legs in all innocence.

Ray had given him the Map of Moments, but the gift had been more than the physical map. The magic hadn't been imbued in the paper, but in Max himself. It traveled.

He folded the map quickly, suddenly needing to hide what had happened. Seconds later he had left the lot and was walking along the street once again, and minutes later he could even doubt what he had seen.

Or he could *try* to doubt, even though that did not really make him feel any better. With everything he had witnessed over the last couple of days, doubting his eyes was starting to feel like a fool's escape. His world had changed, and he had no choice but to go along for the ride.

Fishing into his pocket, Max found the card the taxi driver had given him the previous evening. He stood on a street corner and stared at it for a while, remembering the journey, wishing himself back there knowing what he knew now, so that Corinne could still be alive and he could pay the driver to go faster.

He found a working pay phone just inside the door of a pharmacy and dialed the number. The cab operator sounded tired and uninterested, but she told him the cab would be with him in ten minutes. It came in five. Max guessed taxi service was one of a thousand businesses hurting right now.

This driver was even quieter than the one who'd brought him to the Garden District last night. That did not bother Max. He rested his head back on the seat and used the fifteen-minute journey to try to clear his head.

"You walk from here," were the first and last words the driver spoke. Max paid, tipped, and started walking even before the taxi pulled away.

If there was any other way of getting Joe Noone's address, he'd take it. But this was all he could think of right now. His head was a mess, his heart thumped, and he felt the predatory touch of eyes on the back of his neck whichever way he turned.

They'd known he had called Corinne. How? Was her phone tapped, or was it his at the hotel? He didn't know.

He wanted to get in, find his old office, and hope his file of student information was in the place where he'd left it; look up Noone's address and contact details, turn around, and leave. He did not want to bump into Charlie, because he knew that if he did, he'd end up talking with him about the Tordu. And, impossible though it may be, he was sure they'd know about that conversation as well.

Max already had enough guilt to last a lifetime.

"In and out," he whispered to the warming morning air, and when he blinked he saw Gabrielle grinding herself onto Joe Noone's lap. They'd heard him leaving, and she had called him back, standing naked at the head of the narrow staircase. He'd always wondered whether she had known he was there all along.

The campus was still a mess, and he crossed it quickly, one of only a few people traveling these roads. The students were continuing with their lives somewhere else.

The history building's front door stood open, as it had the last time he'd visited. Things had been relatively normal then, with the memory of that first strange Moment sitting uncomfortably in his hungover head. Max entered quietly, wincing as his shoes ground on dried mud and grit still smeared across the floors. He walked along the corridor to the far end of the building.

It was silent, and felt deserted. A building with people inside didn't feel like this, whether they were out of sight or not. He was alone, and for the first time since leaving his dingy digs that morning, he no longer felt watched. Strange to feel so observed in a city so deserted. Maybe the relief was because he was somewhere familiar, somewhere that had once been safe, and a place of which most of his memories were good.

He went up the stairs and stood at the head of the second-floor corridor. It, too, was silent. At the far end was Charlie's office, and three doors from where he now stood had been his old room. The corridor looked very familiar, though much had changed in the months since he had left, both in New Orleans and within himself.

The sign on his former door named a stranger, but Max did not feel like an intruder as he went inside.

The office had been moved around. He'd had the desk against the wall just below the window, so that he could sit back sometimes and look out across the campus. Most of what he'd seen in those moments had been Gabrielle; her smile, her half-closed eyes, her breasts. Whoever had taken over when he'd left a month before the end of the semester had pushed the desk against the blank wall, and the only thing on that wall was a plaque printed with a quote from the Bible: *Consider that I labored not for myself only, but for all them that seek learning.*

Max shook his head and managed a smile.

The shelving and cabinets in the office looked the same as when he'd last been here. The files and books were different, but when he knelt beside a filing drawer and checked the labels, he was relieved to see one of them still marked in his own handwriting: *students.*

Of course, someone with a quote like that on the wall would lock their filing cabinets.

But luck breathed on Max, and the drawer slid open. He fingered through the files until he found Noone's details, grabbed a pen and pad from the desk, and jotted down his address. He replaced the file and closed the drawer, and as he backed out of the room he suddenly felt like an intruder. The office should be left as it was, he knew. This was not his place anymore, and he had no right being here.

Max stood there for a moment after he'd closed the door, looking at the stranger's name, crumpling in his right hand the piece of paper he'd ripped from the pad. What dangers would he be subjecting Noone to if he approached him now? He remembered the boy; a quiet, intelligent guy keen to learn about history, and determined to become a teacher himself, given time. He'd always worked studiously, been polite and courteous to Max and his fellow students, and his work had been of a consistently high standard. And as Max blinked, he saw Joe's soft hands grasping Gabrielle's buttocks as she raised and lowered herself onto him.

He liked to think there was no sense of petty revenge here, but he needed to know some truths. And if asking Joe certain questions put him in danger from the Tordu . . . so be it.

Max stared along the corridor, toward Charlie's office. Could the Tordu really stretch this far? They'd known about Corinne because she was Gabrielle's cousin, and Gabrielle had been in deep with whatever the Tordu were. Others knew their name—the two cops that had let him go from a murder scene, for instance—but perhaps just enough to know to stay away.

Maybe just knowing about them wasn't enough. Hell, half of New Orleans might know enough about them to be scared to even whisper their name, like some group of bogeymen. But Max was snooping. He was hearing their name breathed with fear in the present, and uttered during moments of the darkest magic from the past. Maybe the trouble came from asking questions, digging around, opening old wounds.

That made more sense to him than the idea that simply mentioning them could bring death down like lightning. And it meant that visiting Charlie wouldn't really do any harm. If he was right.

He started walking along the corridor. When Max reached it, Charlie's door was open several inches. There were three knives stuck in the wood of the door, forming a very precise equilateral triangle with its point facing downward, and each blade pierced a dried hunk of meat.

"Fuck," he whispered, all of the little, logical conversations he'd been having with himself crumbling. Logic had no place here.

The meat looked like organs. Dried parts of the body, belonging inside, not out.

Cattle organs, obviously. Yeah . . . *had* to be.

He nudged the door open with his foot.

The office had been cleared out. Papers and files lay scattered across the floor, and the shelves still held some books, but much of Charlie's presence had been removed. He had packed up and gone, warned away.

Charlie had been born and brought up in New Orleans. He must have known what this warning meant.

And Max could not plead ignorance, not really. This had to be a Tordu warning, which meant that they were already at least one step ahead of him. Whether he believed in magic or not didn't matter. They knew more about him than they should; about him and Gabrielle, Corinne, and his old job and friends at Tulane . . .

He ran from the building, Joseph Noone's address clasped tightly in his hand.

chapter
9

Max felt as though he'd been slogging through mud and now his limbs were free for the first time. Purpose gave him momentum. A call to the cab company had eventually brought a taxi—the same one that had run him out to Tulane to begin with—and promises to the mostly silent driver had persuaded the man to search with him for a working ATM machine. Though wary of being robbed, Max took a five-hundred-dollar advance on his Visa card just to have the cash in his pocket, and he'd paid the driver fifty dollars to take him out to Louis Armstrong International Airport.

The place felt deserted and hollow. Half of the car rental

desks were closed and of those that were open, it took him three tries before he found one with a vehicle to rent. The Toyota RAV4 smelled like mold inside, but Max didn't give a shit. He needed wheels. He cranked the windows down, turned the radio up, and looked at the map the lady at Dollar Rent A Car had given him, watching the mileage as he drove along I-10 back up toward Baton Rouge.

His destination sat about a third of the way to the state capital, off the highway and along the river. Given its size on the map, Peyroux Landing had probably only had a population of a couple of thousand, even before the storm.

The small town was mostly row houses and bars, and a big empty industrial structure loomed on the river, which must once have been a factory or a fishery keeping the town alive. Max felt confident that Peyroux Landing was the sort of place young people spent their lives trying to leave. It couldn't be anybody's idea of a haven.

Yet there were trucks in driveways, laundry hanging on lines behind the houses, and dogs in yards. To people who'd grown up here and stayed, it wasn't a matter of coming or going, it was just home.

Peyroux Landing didn't have a lot of streets, and Max found the address easily enough. He pulled to the curb in front of 124 Lizotte Road. As he killed the engine and popped the door, he gripped the keys in his hand. Having the car changed everything. He was still afraid, but he no longer felt trapped. When he needed to, he could get the hell out of town.

The Noone house was a two-story brick job with concrete steps that stood slightly off-kilter, or perhaps the steps were straight and the house was off-kilter. The brick had faded through decades of Louisiana weather, and the postage-stamp yard consisted mainly of weeds and hard-scrabble ground, but once upon a time someone had taken care of it. Rounded granite stones ran along both sides of the walkway up to the door, some of them jutting at odd angles like vandalized gravestones. Nobody cared about this place anymore, but that hadn't always been the case.

Max took a deep breath, thinking about the last time he'd walked up to the front door of a strange house. But he didn't slow down. Momentum could be disrupted too easily to allow hesitation. He went up the steps in two strides and rang the bell.

Rocking on his feet, feeling as if he'd had too much caffeine, Max rapped on the door for good measure.

"Coming!" a voice called from inside. Then, more quietly, "Jesus, give a guy a chance."

The door swung open. No chain lock, no dead bolt. The kid who answered couldn't have been more than eighteen, a good-looking boy with shoulder-length hair that framed his face without making him look feminine. His shoulders and biceps marked him as a weight lifter or football player, or both.

The kid gave Max a what-the-fuck look. "Yeah?"

Max peered past him into the house. Ratty carpeting covered the stairs going up to the second floor. The hall that led toward the rear had decent wooden molding, reinforcing his belief that someone had cared about this place once upon a time. Maybe it had been a previous owner.

"I'm looking for Joe Noone," he said.

The kid flinched, producing a snort of derision. "Yeah?"

Max fought the urge to ask if he knew any other words. In the car on the way over here he'd considered and discarded a dozen lies, and decided in the end to let the truth—or as much as he dared—pave the way.

"My name's Max Corbett. I used to teach at Tulane. Joe was a student of mine. I came back to New Orleans for the funeral of a mutual friend, and I was hoping to talk to him about her."

And it's possible someone might be trying to kill him, he thought. But that wasn't the sort of thing you blurted out on a stranger's doorstep.

A kind of understanding touched the kid's eyes, but it only made him look younger, and Max wondered if the kid might not be fifteen or sixteen and just big for his age. The football coach must love him.

"You been away a while?"

Max nodded. "Yeah." Give the kid a dose of his own monosyllabic medicine. "I missed the storm."

"That ain't all you missed," the kid sniffed, oddly superior. "Joe's dead."

He delivered the news like an insult.

Max deflated, searching the kid's face for some sign of deception. The Tordu had already gotten to Noone. How could that be?

"I'm sorry. That's terrible. Can I ask what happened?"

The kid's face softened, and for the first time, Max could see the grief behind his anger. "Were you really his teacher?"

"Yes. I really was."

The kid pushed his hands into his pockets and leaned against the door frame, seeming to shrink into himself. "I'm Drew. Joe's brother."

Max noticed the wording. Not "Joe was my brother" or something like that. All his life, Drew had been "Joe's brother," the younger Noone boy. And in the same instant, Max noticed something else as well. The way he'd talked about Joe dying, it hadn't just happened.

"Sorry to trouble you, Drew. How long ago did he die?"

The kid glanced back into the house, but nobody stood behind him. Max felt pretty sure nobody else was home, or they would have come to the door by now.

" 'Die' isn't the word. Not for what they did to him."

Dread trickled down the back of Max's neck. "Who?"

Drew shrugged in that way only teenagers can manage, hands still in his pockets. "Not a clue. The cops say they don't have a fucking clue, either. Joe didn't come back from classes one day, this was early May, and that was it. At first the cops didn't even want to look for him. Nineteen-year-old college guy? They figured he was shacked up with some girl or just off on a road trip or something. My mother pushed 'em pretty hard. Some fishermen found him in bushes on the shore of Lake Pontchartrain."

Max's skin prickled. The end of May. He wondered what day, exactly? Maybe the day he'd walked in on Gabrielle with Joe? Which would mean that other than Gabrielle, he was the last person to see Joe Noone alive.

Not something he planned to tell Joe's little brother.

"He drowned?" Max asked.

Drew sneered. "I know what you're thinking. Suicide? Not Joe. Anyway, he didn't drown, and the way they cut him open, it's not the kind of thing that's self-inflicted."

He sounded disgusted, but then he hitched slightly with emotion and his eyes grew moist.

"What do you mean?" Max asked.

Drew narrowed his eyes, pulling his hands out of his pockets. "Man, what's with you? Why does it matter? You came to tell him some kid he knew at school died in the storm, right? By the time Katrina rolled in, Joe had been dead for months. You want details, that makes you some kind of sick fuck. Why don't you get—"

"Did the police catch his killer?" Max pushed.

That stopped Drew. The kid looked at him a minute, then grabbed the door. "In New Orleans? Seriously? They'd have to care first. For four months, they could barely be bothered to take my mother's calls, and once the storm hit . . . well, they stopped taking everybody's calls, didn't they? They got more important shit to worry about in the Big Sleazy these days."

The two of them stared at each other for a moment, and then Max opened his hands, like he was talking to a church congregation. It was part of his almost unconscious professor's repertoire, and he regretted it immediately.

"I'm very sorry about Joe, and about bothering you."

"It's a sorry world, man." And Drew shut the door.

After a moment, Max retreated from the house, swept along on the current of this new information. Somewhere around the time he'd been involved with Gabrielle, Joe

Noone had been murdered. *Cut open,* his brother had said. And Max felt a terrible certainty that if Drew had been willing to talk about it, he would have learned that parts of Joe had been removed.

Gabrielle held the key to Noone's involvement. Her connection to Coco and the Tordu, whatever they were, had been a secret people were willing to kill for. But Gabrielle could tell Max nothing.

He climbed into the RAV4 and felt the map crinkle in his back pocket. He thought about Ray, and a conjure-man named Matrisse. Gabrielle couldn't tell Max anything, but if he could find Ray, or this Matrisse, both of them must know more about all of this than he did.

That meant going back to the place where he'd met Ray and asking around, and that would draw attention he couldn't afford.

Max started up the RAV4, and headed away from the river and back toward the highway. The nuns he had seen taking their own lives had chanted: *Por Mireault, le Tordu.* The same name Max had seen written on the map in the Third Moment. Ray hadn't given him any kind of warning, but there was no doubt it was all connected. Gabrielle, the Map of Moments, and the Tordu. So before he ran the risk of sticking his head back in the hornet's nest, he wanted to see the next Moment. Perhaps it held more clues.

Before *that,* though, he needed to take a breath and focus on the other Moments; what he'd seen and heard, and what they might have contained that he'd simply missed.

It was time for the history professor to learn.

Sitting in a research cubicle at the main branch of the New Orleans Public Library, Max should have felt at home. And simply being there amongst the books and the quiet did lend him a certain solace that the eerily vacant halls at Tulane had not. Yet he still felt out of place.

He knew he could have talked to librarians about the specific moments that interested him, perhaps even accessed special collections due to his prior connection to Tulane. But apart from the brief chat he'd had at the front desk—presenting his ID and congratulating the staff member behind the desk on their post-Katrina efforts, as though he had any idea what he was talking about—he shied away from contact. Those who weren't a threat to him might themselves be put under threat simply by talking to him.

Max wanted to be a ghost, moving unseen through the stacks.

A notice on one wall had laid out the current plight of the city library system. Eight of the city's thirteen libraries had been completely ruined by Katrina. Some of the others remained closed. But the city promised that the system would be rebuilt and upgraded to a 21st-century library system worthy of a world-class city.

After what Max had seen of New Orleans' current status, this seemed awfully optimistic. But all that really concerned him at the moment was that the main branch had power, and Internet access.

The stacks could wait. He still wasn't sure where he'd be sleeping tonight, and time felt valuable to him. For speed, Google came first.

He sat in a wooden chair, fingers on the keyboard. The back of his neck felt warm and he glanced around, always on edge now. He wanted to laugh it off as paranoia, but that would be foolish.

The First Moment he'd already figured out: an Indian ritual conducted to end a terrible storm, strange magic witnessed by the French scout who'd first identified the area as a good place to build a city. Exactly what the ritual had been, he had no idea. The attempt to drown the child had disturbed him at the time, but in retrospect seemed largely symbolic, a gesture to whatever primal deities the Biloxi Indians had prayed to.

The Second Moment, the spiritual power of the priest's voice, raised in song, seemed self-explanatory. These were both occasions of positive magic that had had dramatic effects on the fate of New Orleans.

But the Third Moment presented its own mysteries. The behavior of those novices had been ritualistic, and the map had referred to their deaths as a sacrifice. Yet their suicide had not had any magical effect that Max had seen. Whatever they had been attempting, it had been hideously dark magic, nothing like the first two Moments. And yet Max felt that the Third Moment must have been significant, and he needed to know why.

There were a hundred ways he could have started a web search. But even before he began typing, he knew what his first query would be. He tapped out the five letters, clicked on the search button, and Google went fishing in the pool of public knowledge for anything referring to the word "Tordu."

The search turned up more than 107,000 results. A lot of the pages were in French, and there were music pages, a porn site featuring girls with extreme piercings, and a European horror magazine. A town in Estonia had the name.

Por Mireault, le Tordu. He could still hear those young women at the Ursuline convent chanting.

He typed "Mireault," just the way it had been written on the map, adding it to the search. Fewer than a thousand results appeared. Still too many. Max added "New Orleans" to his search. There were three results, and none of them was what he sought.

"Right," he whispered to himself. "Did you think it would be that easy?"

The Tordu, whoever or whatever they were, kept people in fear by remaining little more than whispers and shadows . . . and yet sometimes, the opposite was true. They seemed able to *remain* shadows by sowing seeds of fear. At first he had believed that they were little more than a street gang, New Orleans style. But once he'd seen that Third Moment, Max had understood that they were far more than that. And far older.

That event had resonated through the magical history of the city enough to end up on the Map of Moments. There had to be some trace of it.

He stared at the search window, turning it over in his

mind. How to phrase the inquiry, that was the key. What words to include. Max added the word "Ursuline," and then hesitated a moment before deleting "Tordu" from the search. The Tordu were a secret. But the convent was real.

There were six results. Max stared at the fourth one. *Haunted History of the French Quarter.* It could have been like a hundred other sites operated by ghost story collectors, "haunted tour" operators, and true believers. Perhaps it was. But his focus was on the words in bold under the title of the page. His search words. "Ursuline. Mireault."

He clicked open the story and started to read, barely breathing as he scanned a written account of the suicide of five teenaged girls who had pledged themselves as novices at the Ursuline Convent. It had been discovered that Marie-Claire Bissonette, one of the girls, had been pregnant, though the Ursuline sisters tried their best to hush up this discovery.

> . . . the convent's Mother Superior made public accusations against a Creole aristocrat, Monsieur Henri Mireault, claiming that Mireault had corrupted not only Marie-Claire Bissonette, but the other two novices as well, and that he had fathered a child upon Bissonette and deflowered other Ursuline novices. The Ursuline sisters insisted that Mireault—of mixed French and Caribbean descent—had exerted the force of his will and sexual power over the young girls, in effect mesmerizing them, and that he had driven them to suicide. The Mother Superior went so far as to claim Mireault had commanded them to hang themselves.
>
> With no evidence save the sisters' claims, and scornful

of the suggestion that Mireault could have had such per-
suasive charms—particularly given his physical appear-
ance [Henri Alain Mireault suffered from a childhood
ailment that left his body bent and twisted, as pictured]—
the authorities recorded the deaths as suicides and per-
formed no further investigation.

All of this is a matter of public record. What is not a
part of that record are the stories that sprang up and per-
sisted from that horrible day in 1823 until at least 1951.
Many visitors to 1114 Chartres Street, the oldest extant
building in the entire Mississippi Valley, have seen appari-
tions in the corridors of the top floor. Passersby in the early
hours on winter mornings have sometimes seen similar ap-
paritions, dressed in nuns' habits, hanging from the roof.

A detailed listing of such sightings follows, but one
final observation seems appropriate. The Ursuline sisters re-
mained at the Chartres Street property barely a year after
the suicides took place. In 1824, the convent—and
school—was relocated across town and the original prop-
erty became storage and offices for Catholic archives dating
back to the early 18th century. Reportedly, at the time of
the move, the Mother Superior referred to the Old Convent
as "tainted ground."

No wonder the ghosts walk there still!

Specific accounts of alleged encounters with the novices'
ghosts followed, but Max ignored them. His throat felt dry.
He scanned what he'd read once more, first the words, and
then again and again he came back to the photographs of the

convent, the Mother Superior, and a flock of black-habited nuns on the grounds. Black-and-white, grainy images.

All of his scrutiny was merely to avoid focusing on the one photograph that troubled him most. It revealed a well-dressed man whose features and hue favored his Caribbean ancestors more than any French heritage. His dark hair implied a man of youth, but his face had a hardness and his eyes an awful gravity that spoke of age. He was stooped, his back crooked, and his arms and tiny, bent hands were held twisted against his body.

Monsieur Henri Mireault.

Mireault, le Tordu.

Nearly two hundred years had passed. It should have been easy for Max to brush away the connection. A 21st-century gangbanger named Coco couldn't have anything to do with a wealthy Creole aristocrat from the beginning of the 19th century. But the sick feeling in Max's stomach said otherwise. He was way too deep into this thing to allow himself to imagine, even for an instant, that the two could not be connected. Maybe the people Coco worked for, the ones he called "the Tordu," were the remnants of whatever organization Mireault had established in those dark days. Or perhaps they were just inspired by him, the way so many freaks in Europe seemed to worship the memory of Aleister Crowley.

Either way, he was looking at the man who had brought a terrible, dark magic to New Orleans and tainted the Old Ursuline Convent. Perhaps that was the significance of the Third Moment, a tilt in the balance between lightness and darkness in the city.

He needed to learn more about Mireault.

Max pushed back from the computer and glanced around for a librarian. He hadn't wanted to have contact or draw attention, but he needed to know where to begin searching for books covering the goings-on in the city during the 1820s.

As he stood, he felt heat flush the back of his neck. He turned around.

The man staring at him from across the room did not look away.

Max froze. The guy wore an elegant leather jacket. His hair hung in beaded cornrows to his shoulders and he had the biggest hands Max had ever seen. He stared with unblinking, stone-cold eyes, but did not make any move to approach.

Tordu, Max thought. *Has to be.*

He glanced at the computer screen, thought of pausing to wipe his search history, but fear seized him. He took a step away from the cubicle . . . and the cornrowed man took a step as well.

Max started walking, slowly, toward the front of the library. The man matched his progress with longer strides.

Max broke into a run.

The man came for him, the beads clinking in his hair.

An attractive fortyish black woman pushing a metal book cart emerged from behind a shelving stack. Max dodged around her and sprinted for the front desk, but his pursuer slammed into the woman and the cart, spilling books and knocking her down. She cried out, but Max didn't turn to see how badly she might be injured.

At the front desk, someone shouted at him as he ran between the security sensors and crashed through the doors. He leapt down the front steps, the sun glinting off of the railings. Cars passed by in both directions on Loyola Avenue. On this block, north- and south-bound sides of the street were separated by a thin grassy island.

The RAV4 sat at the curb just down the street. Max careened toward it. He heard the library door slam open behind him, glass shattering with the force of his pursuer's exit.

"Fuck," Max muttered. He repeated the word in his head as a mantra. Images of Corinne flashed in his mind and he could practically feel the cold, sharp metal of a Tordu knife splitting the skin of his belly. Desperation opened before him, an abyss into which he felt he might plummet forever.

He kept running, fishing the car keys from his pocket. He could not let terror seize him. If he surrendered to desperation, the knife would not be far behind.

He'd locked the car, of course. For a moment he panicked, but his thumb found the button on the key chain, and he heard the beep that signaled the locks disengaging.

An engine gunned to life nearby. From the corner of his eye he saw an old black Mercedes pull away from the curb maybe fifty yards farther up Loyola.

Max ran around to the driver's side and opened the door. He heard heavy footfalls and grunting breaths, and glanced up just as the guy hit the sidewalk and jumped. Those huge hands outthrust, he came flying over the RAV4's hood. Max dropped into the driver's seat and tried to slam the door behind him, but the man managed to get one hand on the door as he scrambled off the hood, half hanging from it.

"Nowhere to run, teacher."

Max used both hands and his left foot to ram the door open. The guy was still off balance and the door mashed his face, glass striking skull, blood blooming from one nostril. Then Max tried again to haul the door closed, but the bastard hung on with three fingers. Max dragged it closed anyway, even with the guy's weight on it, and slammed his fingers in the door.

With a shout of pain his attacker let go, falling backward into the road. Max hit the locks and started up the car, engine purring.

The impact from behind took him by surprise. With a crash of metal the RAV4 squealed forward, and Max whipped back in his seat. He swore and looked in the rearview, and there was the old black Mercedes.

He blinked, forcing himself to focus.

The cornrowed guy got to his feet, and Max saw him in the rearview mirror, signaling to the Mercedes with those huge hands.

"You not goin' anywhere, teacher!" the man called.

And he was right. If Max drove off, they would follow. And they knew the city better than he did. Heart pummeling so hard that it blurred his vision, Max slammed the RAV4 into reverse.

Just a nudge. Just to put him down, block the road in front of the Merc, give me time to——

His foot slipped from the clutch and the vehicle jarred

back. Still looking in the mirror, he saw the cornrowed man's eyes widen.

The RAV4 struck him with a *whump* and pushed him back against the Mercedes' bonnet. He screamed as his legs were crushed.

"Oh Jesus, oh shit . . ." Not wanting to see what he had done, Max shifted into drive and punched it, tearing away from the front of the library. *I hit that guy! Crushed him!* Shaking, he spared a single glance back, even now expecting to see the Mercedes giving chase. But the Tordu apparently took care of their own; the driver was out of the car, kneeling beside Max's broken and bleeding pursuer and lifting his face to cast a hate-filled gaze at the departing RAV4.

Coco, of course.

Max drove, blinking away tears or sweat. His heart refused to settle, and every squeal of brakes or creak of the car was an echo of the sound it had made hitting that man. *It was me or him,* Max thought, and he laughed out loud at that clichéd idea.

He took lefts and rights, getting himself lost in New Orleans, with no destination in mind. At last he pulled over and took the map from his back pocket, unfolding it and looking again at the marking on Perdido Street, and the words describing the Fourth Moment.

Leaving the map open on the seat, he started driving.

chapter

10

Max didn't need Google or the library to tell him about the yellow fever epidemic in New Orleans. Even before the possibility of teaching at Tulane had arisen, he'd covered it several times as both a student and an educator. He'd spent a semester at Boston University teaching a course entitled "Plague in History," and remembered the most prominent details, just as he did the bubonic plague, and epidemics in London, in Philadelphia, and in ancient societies. By its very nature, an epidemic could be a tilting point in the history of a city or region, changing its cultural fabric forever.

Yellow fever hit New Orleans nearly every summer from

the early 1800s until 1905, killing at least forty thousand people, though with the flow of immigrants arriving in that era, the death toll could have been much higher than official numbers reflected. Some years, only a handful of people were taken by the fever, and in others the angel of death might dim the lights in hundreds of homes, even thousands.

The darkest point came in 1853, when the yellow fever had raged out of control, striking down more than eight thousand New Orleaneans in a scant few months, the majority in the sweltering heat of a brutally tropical August. The streets had been deserted, the music halls silent, with most people dead, dying, or tending to the sick. Mass graves were dug and filled, and each morning in August an impromptu parade of hearses and dark carriages headed out to the cemeteries. That image, the burial parade, had remained fresh in Max's mind all the years since he had first read about it.

What he didn't understand was the phrasing of the Fourth Moment. Its meaning seemed clear—the Tordu had done something to rid the city of the yellow fever. But that seemed entirely opposite from what little he knew about them thus far. Had Mireault still been alive then? Why would he have cared how many people the fever took? Max had no idea what the population of New Orleans had been in 1853, or what percentage eight thousand dead would comprise, but it had to be enormous.

Max sighed. He clicked on the car radio and tuned through hip-hop and rap stations until he found a comforting bit of bluesy jazz. The only way for him to find answers was to follow the map, all the way to the end.

He'd managed to get himself tucked away on North Derbigny Street, just off Iberville. According to the map, he wasn't any farther from his destination than he'd been at the library. The only difference was that west of Canal, nearly every street was a one-way, and the map didn't account for that. More than once he had to turn around, but within minutes he found himself turning off Perdido Street onto a road that had no sign.

Both sides of Bertrand Street were vacant lots now. What they had been before Katrina, Max could not decipher. Whatever had been here before had been erased.

He parked the RAV4 on the hard earth of the shoulder and got out. The engine ticked, cooling, and he glanced around to make sure nobody would appear to question or challenge his presence. The neighborhood felt dangerous, even the slant of afternoon sunlight ominous.

Max slammed the car door and locked it. The RAV4 chirped and he surveyed the lot in front of him. When he encountered the Moments, they had a startling reality, and he knew enough about the yellow fever to make him hesitate. This was something he didn't really want to see.

But then he thought of the man he'd left broken and bleeding in front of the library, the hatred on Coco's face, and the dead, glassy eyes of Corinne's corpse. He'd made his choice and chosen his path back in the bar with Ray, when he'd taken the map and later drunk from that little stone bottle.

Max walked onto the vacant lot, stepping carefully over concrete fragments and hard, furrowed ground. He felt the frisson of shifting air around him and the small hairs on the back of his neck stood up.

The stench hit him first.

He staggered, queasy. His equilibrium shifted and he nearly fell, but the sense of dislocation seemed to decrease with every stop along the Map of Moments, and Max was prepared for a shift in the weather, the season, the angle of light.

Instead, he gasped in shock to find himself in a narrow corridor with rough wooden flooring and peeling fleur-de-lis wallpaper. Turning, he saw an entryway behind him and a heavy oak door hanging open. The air that swept past him in the hallway reeked of rot and filth and something much worse– -a sickness more revolting than anything he had ever smelled.

He walked back along the hall, reached out, and felt the turned-up edge of peeling wallpaper. His footfalls echoed on the wooden floor. *Christ, I can feel it. It isn't like a dream at all. It's like I'm here.*

The thought terrified him. Of all places, this was somewhere he did not want to be, with the yellow fever infecting the air of the city itself. *It's 1835. Jesus, this is 1835.* He looked out through the open door. The stone-and-dirt street was empty, save for an open carriage that rolled slowly down Perdido Street at the corner. The driver had a scarf across his face. The back of the carriage was laden with the dead, their clothes stained with blood and black bile, faces and other exposed flesh dominoed with purple lesions.

On the street corner, and just across from the building where Max stood, barrels belched flames and spewed black smoke. The wind carried the scent of burning tar, and he recalled the old belief that the scorched stench of the tar could cleanse infection from the air.

Panic touched his heart. Max remembered the map's description of the Fourth Moment, but he hadn't really been prepared for this.

He stepped back out into the street, away from the Moment, out of the past . . .

But nothing changed. Black smoke drifted across the sky. Grief-stricken wailing came from farther along the block. And an awful certainty formed within him: he'd entered the Moment, but he would not be able to leave until he had experienced what the map intended for him to see.

Max glanced around. What if he walked away? How far would he be able to wander through 1835 New Orleans, or the rest of the world in that year? Would he be little more than a ghost, as he'd been during past Moments? Where was he, physically, right now? In an empty New Orleans lot, or somehow slipped in between realities, as though time were sheaves of paper?

He could smell the stink of this world, hear its agonies, feel its texture.

Could he be infected by its ills?

Max hung his head, thinking, breathing evenly.

He had no choice. *Only forward.* But in this case, forward meant backward. He turned to face the building again and saw the sign above the door—GRANGE HALL. Taking a breath, Max crossed the threshold, leaving the door open.

The corridor rustled with shifting September breezes, carrying the acrid smell of burning tar in one direction, and the bilious stench of rot and death in the other.

Cries of despair and suffering came from deeper within the building, and the breeze grew stronger. Max pulled his shirt up over his mouth. Though he always thought such attempts to prevent disease illogical and feeble, instinct demanded it.

At the end of the hall, he entered a small kitchen. Two doors exited from the rear of the kitchen, one leading into some other living area, the other opening into a narrow corridor from which issued the moans and wails of anguish. He tried to make mental sense of the building. If this was a grange hall, it seemed an odd construction.

He turned a corner and went through another propped-open door, finding himself in the hall itself. The side he'd entered from must be the residence of the grange president or some other caretaker. On this side there were two large doors—one to the right, at the back of the hall, and a side entrance directly across from him—and the hall had the feeling of a vast church whose pews had been removed.

People lay on cots, blankets, and the rough beams of the wood floor. Every door was open, but somehow instead of taking away the smells, the moving air made them worse, disturbing the stink that rose from the bodies of both the living and the dead. The dead in the cart that had passed him on Perdido Street had not been as hideous as some of those who lay here.

There must have been more than two hundred people here, including several dozen who were tending to the sick or mourning the dead. The place seemed to have been broken up into three staging areas, with the ill at the back of the hall, the dying at the front, and the dead in the center, most of them wrapped in blankets that would have to be burned. Men with kerchiefs over their faces were carrying a corpse out through the side door as Max entered.

He'd studied plague, taught lessons about it, but seeing it brought home how little he'd really understood. Half of those infected would die. The fever started like a typical flu, but those patients wouldn't have been brought here yet. The grange hall was filled with end-stage victims, many of them close to death.

Max walked amongst the caregivers and the grief-stricken. Men huddled in tears over wives, mothers over children, people of all ages over parents. Doctors and nurses and patients alike spoke in a Babel of languages that made understanding impossible. Max heard Spanish, French, English, and German, as well as languages that must be Caribbean or African. All of those tongues, all of those words, flowed into a single prayer for the dying.

Some had boils on their skin; others were spotted with purplish blotches. A pale little girl of no more than twelve began to convulse just as Max passed her, and he flinched away. Then, ashamed, he forced himself to stay and watch as a nurse rushed to her side. The girl vomited black bile, which dribbled down her chin and stuck like tar in her long, lank blond hair.

Max fought back tears as he finally turned away.

When shouts rose from the back of the hall and he turned to see a group of healthy men storm in, he knew that the Fourth Moment had arrived. This was what he had come for, and he hated the relief that swept through him. He would willingly bear witness to whatever the map's magic demanded, as long as it meant he could be gone from this hall, from this Hell.

There were nine of them, all with their faces masked against the disease. It took a moment for Max to realize his mistake. Two of the nine were women, one white and one with the caramel hue shared by some Creoles. Three of the men appeared to be Creole as well; three were black and one white. Whatever the Tordu's origins, their work blurred the lines of race.

One of them carried a burlap sack, heavy with things that squirmed and chattered, struggling to be free.

Nurses shouted at them. They made their way into the building, passing the sick who lay near the rear door, intent upon those deeper in the hall: the dead or the dying.

"Le Tordu," a whisper went up from two nurses standing amidst the patients closest to death.

"*Non!*" a doctor said.

He started forward and confronted the leader of the group at the middle of the hall, amongst the blanket-shrouded dead.

"Monsieur, you have no business here!" the doctor said firmly, pressing one hand against the man's chest.

Dark eyes stared over the top of the cloth mask covering the Tordu man's face. "Ah, but we do," he said. "We are here to help."

The doctor gave him a hesitant shove.

The man took one step back, and his hand came round

in a silent arc. Max thought he would merely slap the doctor away. He didn't realize the Tordu held a knife until it slashed the doctor's throat; blood sprayed onto the white cloth the man wore as a mask.

Nurses screamed; men shouted.

But the Tordu marched forward, and no one else dared to stand in their way. Some of those who grieved for the dying lay themselves on top of their failing loved ones, as if to protect them. Coughs and moans and sobbing continued, but the doctors and nurses had moved to the sides of the hall now, and they did not interfere.

The nine Tordu weaved through the cots and blankets and bodies. One of the women muttered a name, and the leader, whose knife had already been bloodied, hurried to her. The others followed suit, until all nine of them surrounded the little girl whose black vomit stained her hair and chin.

"This one's perfect," the leader said.

"No," Max whispered.

They moved quickly. From their pockets the Tordu brought out half-melted black candles and placed them in a circle around her, lighting the wicks. They dragged and shoved other patients away from the girl without a care for their lives or comfort. Their only focus was the girl.

"You cannot—" one of the nurses began.

A doctor clapped his hand over her mouth and held her back.

The Creole woman took out bags of powder and began to sprinkle them first over the girl herself, and then in a careful circle around where she lay on the floor. Two men dropped and began to use half-burnt sticks of charcoal to etch symbols on the wooden floorboards around her.

"Wait," Max said. "What are you going to do?"

Stupid. They can't hear you.

The white woman produced a knife and stepped toward the girl. She began to chant in something that sounded vaguely like French, but was not. Max took a step closer, but the woman lifted her own hand and sliced her palm, wincing, then made a fist and let her blood spatter down onto the dying girl's face.

Where the blood dripped, it burned like acid. The girl opened her mouth in the beginning of a scream, and then convulsed again, more of that black vomit issuing from between her lips.

Two men tore away the blanket covering the girl and ripped open her clothing, showing her withered body and its pattern of awful lesions. Her lower back had turned entirely bruise-purple, like a corpse whose blood had settled into mortification.

The Tordu took up the chant. One by one, they cut their palms and bled onto her belly, legs, and face, and everywhere their blood showered her, the girl burned.

Max shook his head, hands clenched into fists at his side, damning the map and damning crazy Ray, and even damning Gabrielle. "Stop!" he screamed, stepping up to the one who was their leader.

The Tordu man raised a hand to hush the others and looked around in alarm, his eyes alert, but not as though he was searching for something. As though he was *listening*. He closed his eyes tightly, cocked his head.

"Did you hear me?" Max said aloud. Impossible. But . . . "Stop, you fucking bastards! Leave her alone!"

The man's eyes flashed open and shifted, and he stared right at Max, studying, trying to decipher whatever it was he saw, or thought he saw.

"Yes! I'm right here!" Max cried, frantic now. "Right in front of you! Get away from her!"

The man shook his head, as though working off a chill, and then turned away, signaling for the others to continue.

"No!" Max shouted.

The one with the squirming burlap sack stepped toward the girl. Max felt as though his mind would simply fall apart. To be unable to do anything but stand and bear witness was more than he could tolerate. He reminded himself what the map had said of the Fourth Moment: the Tordu were here to help. This day, evil banished the yellow fever. Thousands of lives might be saved, and without this Moment, the entire population of New Orleans might have died that year.

But this?

Was anything worth this?

The blood of the Tordu had burned holes in the girl's belly, chest, and cheek. The man upended the sack and dumped a squirming gray mass of rats onto her.

The doctors and nurses in the grange hall screamed.

Max screamed with them. He rushed at the nearest Tordu, the one he thought had been able to hear him, and tried to grab him. His hands passed through.

Two doctors, crying out in rage, ran to help the girl. One of the Tordu women threw a handful of powder into their eyes, and they fell, crying out in pain.

And all the while the rats tore at the little girl. She still twitched, still breathed, still lived. But she never opened her eyes. Consciousness never returned.

Max screamed epithets at God, full of venom and hysteria and helplessness. Then, quietly, turning his back, he prayed first for the girl, and then for himself. And as he prayed, the rats began to move away from the girl, who surely must be dead by now. Squeaking, sneaking, leaving tiny paw prints marked with the ink of her blood, they began to race through the hall toward the other patients.

"No!" Max pleaded, turning his gaze heavenward, wishing that God or even crazy Ray would hear him, that the magic of the Map of Moments would be taken from him. "I don't want to see any more. Please."

But the Moment had not ended yet.

The plague-stricken who were conscious screamed as the rats darted about. Some tried to stand and stagger from the place. The vermin seemed to target only the sickest amongst them, though, and those people were in no condition to move. They hardly seemed to notice as the rats began biting their fingers, toes, and faces. They had eaten of the girl and their snouts were daubed with her blood, but now they were not attempting to eat flesh, only to nip.

And then, as quickly as they had swarmed through the grange hall, they darted into corners, through doors, and beneath cots, vanishing in moments.

Instantly, the boils on the faces of the stricken began to shrink. Purple lesions faded, and if they did not vanish entirely, they might as well have. Those who'd seemed closest to death opened their eyes as fevers broke.

Whispered prayers came from the corners of the room where the remaining doctors and nurses had retreated. Now they rushed to their patients. Someone laughed, and then others took up the sound. The weeping that began was the sound of joy instead of anguish.

Max looked around, eyes wide. The Tordu had already left, but now those who had not yet been on their deathbeds were beginning to sit up, their symptoms departing, and the rats had not been anywhere near them. Those the rats had bitten were healed first, but their wellness was *contagious*.

The fever had been broken.

He heard, amongst the whispers and shouts, the word "miracle" in several languages. But how could anything that required the mutilation and death of a little girl be a miracle?

His mind could not contain any more. He ran for the door where he'd come in, through the kitchen, and down that corridor with the peeling wallpaper, to the front entrance. When he staggered into the street he fell to his knees and threw up, eyes watering.

A car horn blared.

He blinked and looked up at the oncoming car, forced himself to stand and move aside to let the rusted Chevy go by, then turned and stared at the vacant lot on the corner of Perdido and Bertrand.

The stink of disease and rot was still in his nose, and he didn't think he would ever be rid of it.

chapter

11

Back in the RAV4, driving through the streets of New Orleans, the stink of corruption from over a century before still on his clothes, Max felt in more danger than ever. He was the focus of this city's attention, as if every home he passed had someone standing behind its front window watching him. And yet he knew that whatever had set its awareness upon him was beneath and behind the city. Something deeper, and deadlier. The Tordu.

He had stood and watched them slaughtering that girl, that doctor, so that they could introduce a cure. He'd been able to touch and smell, hear and taste, but he had not been *there* enough to intervene. And that felt so unfair.

But if he *had* intervened? Stopped them, somehow? How many more would have died?

He cursed, stamping on the brakes and slewing around a corner, taking out his anger on the road.

Ray's words came back to him. *Follow it, magic yourself up, like runnin' your feet along a carpet to build up static, and at the end of the map you'll find Matrisse. Then maybe he'll help you through.*

Perhaps it was because it was fresher in his memory, but this Moment had felt much more real than the others. He had almost been taking up space in that replay of history rather than merely witnessing it. During the other Moments, all his senses had been delving into the past, but this time he had felt less like a bystander. It had affected him— involved him—in some way the others hadn't.

That man stared at me! Max thought. *He sensed me there, maybe even heard me.*

Maybe he *was* magicking himself up, as Ray had put it. Perhaps it was a cumulative thing, and every time he viewed a Moment, understanding came closer.

"But how will I know?" he muttered.

A gray sedan cut him off at the next intersection, horn blaring, and Max's heart jumped. He jerked the steering wheel to the right, bouncing over the curb at the corner and getting back on the street just in time to avoid hitting a parked car. The car that had cut him off slowed.

He caught his breath and slowed as well, staring at the sedan, almost expecting to see a man leaning out with a gun at the ready. What he actually saw were two small kids, turned in their seat and waving to the man their mother or father was likely cursing.

I *cut* them *off,* Max thought. He waved back and drifted to a stop at the curb, watching the other car drive away.

He glanced in the rearview mirror. Real though that Moment had been, it did not compare to the sound and feel of the RAV4 crushing that man against Coco's car. *Because* I *did that,* Max thought. And he wondered if the man was dead.

He breathed deeply and closed his eyes, letting the sounds of the street wash through his partially open window. *Had* he killed? He did not know, and there was no way he could find out. He was alone on the streets of this ruined city, and the sooner he left, the better. But not yet.

Each time he blinked, he witnessed that sick little girl dying beneath a shower of Tordu blood. He was still confused at what he'd seen—the brutal, heartless Tordu apparently curing the plague—but the more he dwelled on it, the less he understood. Why would those dark magicians use their magic to help the people of New Orleans?

"Hey!" Someone rapped on his window and Max jumped, heart fluttering in his chest. He reached for his keys, wincing against whatever violence was about to come.

"You're in my parking spot!"

Max looked at the old man standing beside the RAV4— tall, bald, face like a crumpled leather jacket, cigarette hanging from the corner of his mouth. He frowned at Max, pointing at the car, then down at the road.

Max smiled. Relief flooded him, relaxing his tensed muscles. Normality *did* still exist. He wound down his window.

"Sorry," he said. "Just taking a break."

"Yeah, well, break somewhere else. I gotta load up my car."

Max pulled away slowly, moving out into the road and waving at the tall guy.

He drove, edging south without realizing it and finding himself heading back toward the university. He tried to hunker down in his seat, but the vehicle was high, and he felt on display to anyone who might be looking for him.

And they *were* looking for him. After Max had crushed that guy who'd chased him from the library, Coco and his cronies would search until they found him. From the current of fear their name inspired and the way the police had responded to it, it seemed likely the Tordu had a web of contacts through the city. Some strands may have been snapped by Katrina, but it still felt as though a deeper, darker level of the city than most people saw was theirs.

I'm being hunted, he thought. The sights, sounds, and smells of the last Moment would remain with him forever, but this was reality. Corinne's death had implications in the here and now, rather than being a snapshot of old history. And in the reality of here and now, action remained his only recourse. Momentum.

He glanced in his mirror, then drifted to a stop before an empty, boarded-up house.

The map lay on the passenger seat, folded, enticing. The Fifth Moment would be on there now, the fourth already faded away to the memory it really was. He grabbed the map and opened it across the steering wheel, looking everywhere but at the map while he smoothed it out. A couple of cars passed by him, their drivers apparently uninterested.

Across the street, three men in overalls walked along the pavement, dragging their feet, heads bowed. One of them seemed to be talking, but Max could not see whether the other two were even paying attention. They carried long-handled tools over their shoulders. The buildings across the street from him were faceless, windows gleaming with reflected sun. If someone was watching him from there, he would not see them.

They can't be everywhere, he thought. *If they were, I'd be dead already.*

So, finally, he looked down at the map.

He scanned areas where no Moment had appeared before, but eventually his eyes were drawn back to the French Quarter, only a couple of blocks from Jackson Square, where the Second Moment had occurred. A small box had appeared there:

The Fifth Moment:
The Civil War Dead Unite to Avenge
a Heinous Tordu Crime
June 8, 1935

Later again. Each moment represented a shift forward in time, marching toward the present. He wondered how many more there could be after this one, and the strange sensation of something closing in on him made him shiver.

Maybe they don't always win, he thought, taking in those words again and trying to make sense of them. But he could make little sense, because he *knew* so little. He knew the Tordu existed, but not why. From his first meeting with

Coco, it had been apparent they were involved in drugs and prostitution, some kind of crime family, holding the city in a terrible grip. According to the Moments he had seen, they had been preying on New Orleans, living off the city, for centuries. But what did their rituals and conjurations have to do with any of that? Were they ruling this town with dark magic, the same way organized crime families controlled other cities with fear and money?

Their influence on New Orleans could not be denied. And Max felt certain that someone with an intimate understanding of the city would have to know at least something about the Tordu . . . even if they never spoke of it aloud. Even if fear made them erase such knowledge from their minds.

"Charlie," he said. His old friend from the university, chased away by the Tordu. There was only one reason for them to warn Charlie away: they'd been afraid he would speak of things meant to be secret.

Max sighed and folded the map. He had transportation now, and he could be at the site of the Fifth Moment in maybe fifteen minutes, but the streets were dangerous for him. The Tordu were looking for him and for this vehicle.

"Charlie, you can tell me," he whispered.

He couldn't break his momentum. He had to forge ahead to the next Moment, and witness its memory and truths. At first, he had not seen the pattern, not realized it at all, but the Map of Moments contained within it the story of the Tordu establishing a hold upon the heart of New Orleans. And if Max hoped to survive contact with them, he needed to reach the end of the map, the end of the story, and unravel the secrets of the Tordu. This wasn't just about making peace with losing Gabrielle anymore, or even some hope that he might reach back to save her, or forgive her, or forgive himself.

Now it was about getting out alive.

But the closer he got to the end of the map, and the more recent the Moments became, the more he felt a part of them. And last time . . .

Last time, amongst all the sickness and rot, the Tordu man had sensed him.

If the trend continued with the Fifth Moment, Max might find himself in mortal danger from the past.

True, forward was the only way to go. But he needed to discover as much as he could about the Tordu's past before he walked into it again.

The bar reminded him of the place where Ray had given him the map. Physically, it was much different, because it had not been touched by the floodwaters. But it *had* been irrevocably changed by Katrina. The owners played jazz through a stereo that sat behind the bar, but the drinkers' minds did not seem to be on music. They stared into a middle distance at something far away.

He approached the bar. The barman was short and fat, his bald head bubbled with perspiration, the pale skin of his jowls seeping sweat. His eyes bore an impression of lifelong fear, and Max wondered how someone like this could come to run such a place.

"Getcha?" the man asked. His voice was high, and any other time Max might have smiled.

"Coffee'd be fine," Max said. "Do you have a phone I could use?"

Something changed in the man's demeanor. He seemed to stand up taller, lifted his chin, and his eyes grew sharper. "Booth at the back, by the john."

Max nodded his thanks and weaved his way through the tables and chairs. Had he really upset that guy just by ordering coffee? He supposed it was possible. Everyone here nursed a beer or a whiskey. Maybe not drinking was enough to set Max apart from the rest. That, and the absence of a thousand-yard stare.

The phone was in an old booth at the end of a short hallway, restroom doors heading off left and right. Max tried to close the door, but it was rarely used in these times of cell phones, and it stuck halfway.

He sat there for a beat, eyes closed. The quiet jazz washed over him and took him back to the times he'd visited places like this with Gabrielle. A rush of memories came, their pureness pleasing him: Gabrielle grinning as they downed their fifth cocktail of the night; her delighted laughter as they were rained on rushing from one bar to the next; her softer, more sensual smile later, arms around his neck, lips brushing his as they waited for a cab. Good memories, untainted by what had happened recently, and as yet untouched by his discovering her with Joe Noone.

Noone's name shattered the memories into a thousand bloody fragments.

Max's eyes snapped open and focused on a piece of graf-
fitti on the wooden wall of the booth: *fuck suck pussy anal,* it
said, and then a number that had been scratched out. He
sighed. The grime was always so close to the surface, but in
that, at least, New Orleans was no different from any other
city.

The receiver was cold and greasy, and he wondered who
had used it before him. He rooted around in his wallet,
looking for a business card that had sat in one of the slots behind his medical insurance card for over a year. The card belonged to Cornelia Trask, who'd been head of the Tulane
English department when Max had taught at the university.
He'd never called the number on the front, but over the du-
ration of his employment at Tulane, on the back he'd scribbled eight or nine other numbers of colleagues and friends
he'd made. Since moving back to Boston, he'd never so
much as drawn the card out of his wallet, never mind called
any of them. It stuck to the leather as he tugged it out now.

There would be other ways to track down Charlie, if he
had long enough, but this was his first hope. Max had once
mentioned that he'd never visited Houston, and Charlie had
given him his parents' phone number, saying that if he ever
went, they'd happily put him up for a few days. They had a
big house, Charlie'd said, and rattled around it like two peas
in a pod. Max never would have taken him up on it, of
course. Southerners might really be comfortable offering
that kind of hospitality, but boys raised in the Northeast
would never be comfortable accepting it.

He'd dutifully written down the number, so as not to
appear rude. Now he stared at the digits and thought of the

organs he'd found pinned to Charlie's office door. Cattle organs, he'd tried to convince himself at the time. Not
human.

Max took a deep breath, then tapped in the number.

An old man answered—Charlie's father, Max figured.
When he put his son on the phone, Max wasn't really surprised.

"Hey, it's Max."

Charlie was silent for a long time. Max could hear his
friend breathing, fumbling at the other end of the phone,
and in the distance he heard the sound of a child's voice,
raised in delight or distress, he could not tell. Tempted
though he was to prod a response from Charlie, he knew he
should give him time.

"Max," Charlie said at last. "You home?"

"Not yet," Max said. "I'm still in New Orleans, and I
need—"

"What the hell are you still doing there?" Charlie tried
to sound angry, but his voice came across as scared.

Max looked along the small hallway. Although there was
no one there, he had the sense that someone was listening.

"I've got a feeling you know what I'm doing, Charlie.
You were pretty adamant about staying in New Orleans yesterday. Today you're in Texas."

"Yeah. Drove all afternoon and half the night. There was
no way I could stay. I'll never know why I ever thought of it
as somewhere to bring up a family. It's . . . not a place to call
home, Max."

Max frowned. "You were born and raised here."

"Yeah," Charlie replied. "Yeah, I was." His voice sounded

strange, forced. Charlie's breathing came faster, and Max was sure he heard the beginnings of a sob. Then it became muffled as Charlie covered the mouthpiece at his end.

"Charlie, I need your help," Max said. "The Tordu. I need to know what you know."

"There's nothing I can tell you." Charlie covered his mouthpiece again, as if afraid the truth would bleed through the lines.

"They're more than gangsters, Charlie. More than drugs and violence, aren't they?" Charlie said nothing. "You *have* to tell me!" Max continued. "Don't do this, man. They're after me."

For a while, Charlie's end of the line remained silent. No heavy breathing, no shuffling of his hand over the mouthpiece. Eventually he said, "I know."

"They warned you off."

Silence again. And then, "My family needs me here. There's nothing for me in New Orleans anymore, and there's nothing for you there, either. I told you, Max—"

"I *can't* leave."

"Then that's on you. If I were you, I'd get the fuck away from there, and never even think about going back."

"Charlie—"

"That's me talking as a friend."

"It's gone too far for me to leave."

"You're still alive, aren't you, for fuck's sake? It hasn't gone too far yet."

"Why would they cure the yellow fever?" Max asked.

"Because they think the city is theirs!" Charlie shouted.

"Its *people* are theirs! And you sticking your damn nose into places it shouldn't go . . . You've pissed off Mireault."

Mireault? The name those nuns were calling before they hanged themselves? Max frowned and shook his head.

"Mireault ran things two hundred years ago. Unless you're telling me he's risen from his grave."

Charlie said nothing. From shouting to silent, as though scared that someone would hear.

"Charlie?"

A man came around the corner from the bar, staggering slightly, pushing himself from the wall and through the door into the men's restroom. He didn't even seem to notice Max.

"Charlie?" More shuffling on the other end of the phone, more breathing, and in the background Max heard one of Charlie's kids screeching. "I'm only asking for your help. You're away from here now, and——"

"He doesn't have a grave, Max. He'll never need one."

Max frowned. "What are you——"

"I can't keep talking to you. It's not safe for me. No one's beyond their reach," Charlie whispered. "Just because they can't leave the city doesn't mean they won't send someone for me."

"Jesus, listen to you. I don't get it, Charlie. Why doesn't anyone do something? Talk to the cops, something? You need to help me!"

"You aren't listening. You need to comprehend what I'm saying. You can't fight them! Nobody can. The only thing they're scared of is Seddicus . . ."

He trailed off, and Max waited for Charlie to say more. The man stumbled from the bathroom and back out into the bar, and just before he disappeared around the corner he glanced back at Max.

"Everything I find out confuses me more," Max said.

Silence from Charlie; breathing; something scraping the mouthpiece.

"They kill people," Max rasped into the phone. "Rip them open and take their organs."

There was a click as Charlie hung up. Static for a while, then another click and the fast, annoying tone that came with disconnection.

Max hung up, then picked up the phone again. He dialed the number and let it ring and ring. No one answered. He imagined Charlie sitting there in his parents' home in Houston, his kids bustling around him, his wife pleased that they were together again and doing her best to make home of somewhere far away . . . and Charlie staring at the phone, perhaps regretting what he had said, and fearing everything else he *should* have said.

Max hung up and dialed again, just in case he'd gotten the wrong number. He got a busy signal, so rare in these days of call waiting. The phone had to be off the hook. Charlie had unplugged Max from his life.

He stared at the graffitied wall and thought through the little that Charlie had told him. The Tordu were old, he knew that, and it seemed that they were run by the Mireault family. So was it really just that? A crime family, twisted by their dabblings in dark magic, and using fear to control the people of New Orleans? *Because they think the city is theirs,*

Charlie had shouted. *Its* people *are theirs!* And what was that business about the Tordu not being able to the leave the city? And Mireault . . . *He doesn't have a grave.*

Max shivered. Did Charlie believe Mireault was still alive? He hadn't just said Mireault didn't have a grave, he'd said the man would never need one. So he was . . . immortal?

Only days ago, Max had not believed in magic at all. He'd been forced to change his view. But even magic seemed to have rules, patterns, and limits. Immortality . . . that was something else entirely. Could anyone or anything really live forever? He couldn't imagine it. The first rule of the universe was entropy. Things fell apart. Deterioration, death, and rot, these were constants. All anyone had to do was walk the streets of New Orleans in these days of disaster and learn a little about the sinking of the city, the ruin of the wetlands, the negligence of the government, and it seemed obvious that sooner rather than later *everything* ceased to be.

It was the way of things.

But rejecting the idea of immortality didn't necessarily mean Charlie had been wrong. Hell, maybe Mireault really was still alive. Or maybe it was just a myth the Tordu created about themselves, with the man's descendants posing as him down through the years.

Max realized it didn't matter. The answer to that riddle would not keep him alive.

He stood and walked back out into the bar. The fat barman nodded at Max's coffee, steaming on the bar. Max dropped a five-dollar bill and went to leave.

"Not staying?" the barman said.

"No, I've got to—"

"Best coffee in New Orleans." The man was smiling, but it was as if someone had painted the expression there; it touched only his mouth. He was sweating more than ever.

Max looked around at the other patrons. A couple were watching him, and they glanced away casually, lifting drinks to their lips. *Am I really so paranoid?*

He left the bar, jumped back into the RAV4, and pulled away. There were no more reasons to wait. Charlie had told him little, but the very fact of his fear communicated plenty. *Just because they can't leave . . .* he had said, and whatever that really meant, the same words now applied to Max.

For the first time in his life, he wished he owned a gun.

He drove back into the French Quarter. The sun was sinking behind him, but there was still an hour of daylight left, and he was determined to progress on to the Fifth Moment. He'd go back to the rooming house or find somewhere else to sleep. He'd worry about tomorrow when the Moment had passed.

Max reached over, grabbed the map, and sat up straight as a car slewed across the street in front of him. He stood on the brake, the RAV4's tires skidding, thinking, *I'm driving like an asshole.*

Then he recognized the vehicle. Last time he'd seen it, a guy with crushed legs had been collapsed in front of it, with Coco kneeling over him. And as if conjured by Max's memory, Coco stepped from the passenger door on the far side and stared across the car's roof at Max.

The bastard even smiled.

Max had an instant to make a decision, and in the blink of an eye, whether it was the right or wrong thing to do, he was committed. He stamped on the accelerator and gave thanks that he'd belted up.

Everything slowed down. He was aware of the startled looks of several pedestrians as they realized what was going to happen, the feel of warm air lifting his hair through the open window, the face of the car's driver—a man he'd never seen, black, with an ugly burn on one side of his face—as his eyes and mouth opened in surprise. And Coco, still smiling, and making no apparent attempt to escape the collision that would certainly hurt, if not kill, him.

Max braced himself back against the seat, clutching the steering wheel tightly and bending his elbows slightly. At the last instant he had a panicked thought: *air bag!* And then metal ground on metal, the world twisted and rolled, and something punched him hard in the face.

Someone groaned. There was blood. His mouth tasted of it, he felt it sticky on his face, and the groaning was coming from him. It sounded close and contained. And though he could see daylight, it seemed very far away.

The air bag started to wilt and deflate, and Max managed to move a hand to his face. He groaned again when he touched his nose. It did not feel broken, but it had taken a hard knock. His eyes watered, his face sang from the impact. Blood flowed freely. *I must look dead,* he thought, and then he remembered the Tordu.

Max tried to work his way out from behind the air bag. The RAV4 had spun across the street, and what little he could see consisted of the front of a two-story building, faces lined at the windows. They seemed ghostlike behind the glass, distorted and lit pink by the setting sun's light. At least the car hadn't rolled.

He reached for the keys, but they were swallowed behind the deflating bag.

Everything was silence. No shouting or screaming, no calls for help or voices raised in concern. No gunshots. He reached around painfully for his seat-belt catch and managed to click it open, releasing some of the tension across his chest and stomach. He pushed the bag away from him, hands slipping in his own blood, and looking to his left he saw what had become of the other car.

His RAV4 had knocked it aside, spinning it across the road and lifting its nose up onto the sidewalk. He could see the silhouette of the driver nursing his head in the front seat; in the back, someone else was kicking at the door, trying to get out. He hadn't noticed the person in the back before.

Of Coco, there was no sign.

People started running. Someone appeared at his open window and asked if he was all right, and when Max turned to her, the woman's eyes went wide and she staggered back a few steps. Max blinked slowly and lifted his hands to his face, wondering what he would find. Everything was in place. But blood dribbled and bubbled from his nose, and the flow did not seem to be lessening.

The faces at the windows of the building before him did

not move. They disturbed Max, and then he realized that they were cut-out images, placed there to lure tourists into some tacky souvenir shop selling "real" voodoo dolls, potions, and spells. Each face seemed to laugh at him.

Someone shouted, a deep, throaty roar.

Max looked across at the Tordu car again and saw a short, fat man climbing from the open back door. He waved one hand before him, and for a beat Max thought he was asking for help, looking for a hand to hold. But then he saw the flash of a blade in the man's hand, and the worried bystanders suddenly forgot their concern. The man locked eyes with Max. Even from that distance, maybe forty feet, Max heard the grunt.

Where the hell was Coco?

Max reached for the ignition key, praying that the RAV4 had only stalled, rather than having a chunk knocked out of the engine by the impact. When he turned the key the engine coughed, shuddered, then came to life.

"Hey, maybe you should . . ." the woman who had come to his window began. She was standing ten feet from the vehicle, hands clasped beneath her chin as if in prayer. Her eyes were wide, and her smooth coffee skin reminded him of Gabrielle.

"You don't want to get involved with me," Max said. He shifted the gear into reverse and backed quickly across the street.

The fat man was kneeling beside the Tordu's car. The driver was out now as well, and he, too, fell to his knees, looking under the car. Both men reached beneath the vehicle, and Max saw shadows moving there. They seemed to writhe and thrash, like the silhouettes of landed fish, and the two men quickly withdrew their arms.

Against every screaming instinct, Max paused with his car pointing directly across the street. *Drive!* he thought. *Get the fuck out of here, go, lose them, take the advantage and* get the fuck out of here!

But as Coco emerged from beneath the car, Max could only watch.

The two men stood back as Coco lifted himself to his knees, then up to his feet, like a marionette being drawn upright. He inspected himself for a few seconds, running his hands down the front of his legs, across his stomach and chest, then finally around his head and onto his face. There was no blood, no apparent injuries . . . only that smile.

He was still smiling at Max.

And then he started walking toward him.

Max threw the gear into first and slammed his foot on the gas, lifting the clutch too quickly, jerking the car across the road and stalling. He glanced to the left and saw Coco running at him now, the smile morphing slowly into a grimace as one hand emerged from his jacket pocket, a blade catching the setting sun as he drew it down by his side.

Max started the car again, slipped back into first, and pulled away.

An arm came in through his window and clamped around his neck. Coco squeezed. Max gagged. Then he pressed his foot on the gas, looking through squinted eyes at the lamppost at the edge of the sidewalk. He turned the steering wheel, front wheel mounting the sidewalk and heading for the lamppost.

Coco growled, then let go. A beat later the lamppost scraped along the side of the RAV4, snapping off the wing mirror and scoring paint from metal.

Max swung back onto the street and accelerated away, gasping in breath through his bruised throat but realizing, with a sickness that threatened to erupt at any moment, that it was fear that had stolen his breath.

He glanced in his rearview mirror and saw the three men climbing back into the car. It reversed from the sidewalk, and the tires smoked as its wheels spun, launching in pursuit.

"Oh fuck oh fuck oh fuck!" He was in a car chase. However ridiculous that was, he was in a car chase through the French Quarter of New Orleans, and trying to think of somewhere to hide, only one place leapt to mind.

The Fifth Moment. It was maybe three blocks away, he could be there in minutes, but *could they follow him in?* He had no idea, and it was not the sort of thing he could discover by experimentation. He had to believe that no, they could not. But Coco was Tordu, and the more Max saw of these moments, the more he knew that the Tordu were inextricably tied to the magical history of New Orleans.

He turned right, swerving across a road junction and hoping that nothing was coming the other way. The car behind him was out of sight for a beat, then it, too, drifted across the junction, and came after him.

Trying to shut down his panic, concentrating, Max attempted to think his situation through. A car full of men was chasing him, and if they caught him he'd be dead. Nothing like this had ever happened to him before. Since coming to New Orleans his life had been disintegrating like the city around him. It was as if Gabrielle's death had drowned the comfortable confines of his normal life, breaking the levees at the edges of his consciousness that held back the unknown and the dangerous.

These men knew the city well. They had likely lived here all their lives, and since Katrina they had seen what their home had become. They would know the streets that were closed, the buildings that were no longer there, and he could not delude himself that he had any advantage over them whatsoever.

The Fifth Moment was the only place he could think of that would take him away for a while.

He drove hard, dropping down a gear to take another junction, steering into the skid and amazing himself by keeping control of the vehicle. Jackson Square was to his right, and two blocks from here he would turn right again, heading for wherever the Moment might lie. He swiped blood from his mouth and chin with the back of his arm.

Don't let them come in, he thought. *Let it only be me . . . let it only be me . . .*

A sneeze was brewing. Max tried to hold it back, but it exploded, spattering the windscreen with blood and sending a lancing pain across his face and through his head. He groaned, but concentrated on keeping his eyes on the road. Blood dribbled down over his lips and into his lap.

He reached for the map from the seat beside him and spread it over the wheel, glancing down as he drove, looking in the rearview mirror at the car gaining on him, and he realized just how close he was to never getting away from New Orleans.

He skidded right, and when he saw the Beauregard-Keyes House, his memory reached forward to help him. *He had heard this story before.* Gabrielle had told it to him, one night when they sat in a smoky, bustling bar, and she talked him through the mixed history of her beloved New Orleans. He had listened, rapt, as she spoke of ghosts and battles, magic, and the wars that had swung through and around the city. The story of the Beauregard-Keyes House had made her smile. *This one's for the tourists,* she had said, relaying to him a tale of Civil War spirits reenacting a supernatural version of the Battle of Shiloh in the main hall, complete with mangled bodies and slaughtered mules.

Max screeched to a halt and leapt from the RAV4, knowing he would never drive it again. Hearing the screaming brakes of the Tordu's car behind him, he ran up the steps and plunged through the front door of the house, and into somewhere else entirely.

chapter

12

When Max saw the man without a face he could not contain his scream.

Perhaps it was fear that carried him through the familiar disorientation, or the adrenaline pumping through his system from the chase. One second he was in the reception hallway of the house, fading dusk bleeding through the windows, dust motes swimming through the air, Coco's car still squealing to a halt outside; a beat later, everything had changed. It was dark, silent, and cold, as if the house had never known the comforts of warmth. And a ghost walked before him.

The dead man wore the remains of a tattered uniform, and his left hand held the barrel of a rifle, its shattered stock trailing along the ground behind him as he walked. If he had been a living man, he would have been dead, because most of his face had been blown away. His teeth, streaked red with blood and gore, peered through the side of his face, and where his nose should be was a hole, home to blood and smoke.

Still, he turned to Max.

Max forgot everything—the Tordu pursuing him, Gabrielle, poor Corinne's corpse. This remnant from the past glared through him as it drifted into a wall. The ghost seemed to wash against the wall, like a wave striking a beach, and then it continued on and through. The last Max saw was the rifle's ruined stock, scraping along the floor without touching or marking the worn wood.

He let out his held breath. When he breathed in again he tasted candle smoke, and something less distinct that he could not quite place. *This is 1935,* he thought, and he turned to look back at the door he had entered through. It had drifted shut behind him—or maybe this door, in this here and now, was locked. Only starlight showed through the windows, and there was no sound of pursuit.

Am I there? he thought. *Standing inside the house's front doors, still and vacant, waiting for Coco to draw the knife across my throat?* But he could not believe that. He stamped on the floor and dust rose around him. He breathed in again, deeply, smelling the smoke and that other scent, vaguely familiar and yet not quite connecting with anything in his memory. He looked at the wall through which the ghost of the Civil War soldier had vanished, then walked the other way, aiming for a door set deep in a wall and surrounded by a carved hardwood frame. He touched the carving, felt the wood grain beneath his fingertips. He was *here*. He could taste the air and hear the creaks and groans of this house, settling in June of 1935.

And somewhere here, according to the Map of Moments, the Tordu were beats away from being confronted by the Civil War dead.

It won't happen until I see it, he thought. *I'm here to witness this.* He glanced back at the door again and wondered how far he could go if he stepped out into the street. If he had to witness the Moment before returning to his own time, could he spend more time here? Perhaps he could walk the nighttime streets of the New Orleans of 1935, visit the city as it had once been. And beyond . . . a United States recovering from the restrictions of Prohibition, and starting to deal with the organized crime that had arisen during those dry years.

How far could he walk? How long could he stay?

Max heard a voice, and for a few seconds he felt a terrifying sense of dislocation. He grabbed his own stomach and throat, feeling himself to make sure he was still there, and his current reality flooded back in.

The voice came again, muttering words so quickly that Max could not even tell what language was being spoken. It originated beyond the inset door, and as he listened it was joined by more voices, all of them chanting something low and unintelligible.

He pressed his hand flat against the door and pushed it open.

The room beyond was large, maybe thirty feet square. Its timber-paneled walls were dark, the ceiling an ornate spread of plasterwork, and the floor was of polished, aged oak. Its corners were illuminated by hundreds of candles, shadows flickering this way and that as air movement sent the myriad flames dancing.

There were a dozen people in the room. Most of them stood in a rough circle, and at its center were three people. Max recognized Coco instantly.

No! He backed away, ready to turn and run. But then he realized that this Coco was wearing different clothes from the Coco he had known up to now. His suit was dark, his shirt gleamed a creamy yellow, and the open collar displayed a necklace of what looked like teeth. His face was also different; not younger, but fresher, as though yet to gather decades of wear.

That can't be Coco. But he knew that he was wrong. This *was* Coco, and beside him stood a small, twisted man, with short hair and hands clawed inward, toward his chest. This could only be the Mireault that Max had read about . . . though he would have been over a hundred years old in 1935.

Before them, naked and shivering on the floor, lay a boy no older than fifteen. He moaned, and rolled his head, but his arms and legs were free, slumped on the floor in a vague crucifix shape. His voice slurred, and Max knew that he was drugged.

Coco held a long, thin, curved knife. He continued

muttering those words, and beside him Mireault joined in, his voice old and as gnarled as his body. The others echoed them, following a beat behind and lending the impression that Max was hearing this all in a large, echoing cave.

The smell of candles was strong in here, and beneath it he could still sense that other scent that so confused him. He looked around, trying to place its source, and then he saw the several metal tins arrayed around the prone boy. The light was poor, but he could see they were filled with liquid, and at last recognized the scent: vinegar.

He remembered the plague-ravaged girl and what they had done to her, and he stepped forward into the room. "Leave him alone," he said, and the sound of his own voice startled him. He drew back slightly, expecting all eyes to turn to him. But he could not be heard.

The boy rolled his eyes back in his head, staring directly at Max. His voice changed, from a low groan to a high-pitched plea.

The kid saw him.

Coco paused in his speech and looked across the room at Max. The man frowned, narrowing his eyes, and he looked to the left and right of Max, closing one eye and then the other. Beside him, the twisted shape of Mireault stepped around the boy.

Max tried to back away but could not. Mireault stood beside the boy's head, shoulders hunched, back bent, and yet in his eyes Max saw signs of a startling intelligence, and a cruelty he could barely comprehend.

Coco spoke, his words rising in a question.

Mireault shrugged, a grotesque movement. And then he

turned around, bent down with an audible creaking of joints, and drew a knife across the boy's throat.

Several people around the room gasped, and then their voices rose as one, launching into a loud and excited chant that seemed to drive back more shadows than the candle-light could touch.

Max watched the boy bleeding to death. He wanted to close his eyes and turn away, but an intense curiosity held him, because he knew that there was more to come. It was horrible to witness, but this boy's fate had been sealed many decades ago. What Max was about to see was essential to him steering his *own* fate.

Coco dropped to his knees and went to work. Even while the boy was still twitching, Coco slashed his stomach open, extended the cuts across his chest to his shoulders, and plunged his hands into the wound. He dug deep, sweating, muscles rippling on his arms, and with a dreadful crunching sound he ripped open the boy's chest.

Mireault laughed, a startlingly high sound from such a wizened man.

The other Tordu shifted and chanted, enrapt with what was happening.

Coco dug, cut, and dropped things into the tins of vinegar.

And then the ghosts in tattered uniforms arrived.

From the start, watching the slaughter, Max had the impression that there was more behind the ghosts than uneasy spirits. They emerged from the air itself, forming from shadows around the flickering candle flames, manifesting from the spaces between one circle of light and another, taking shape from the New Orleans air as if the city had sighed at the murder committed here, and in its sadness were these wraiths of murders past.

The dead were not silent. The sound of their arrival slid in along a tunnel of time; a single, indefinable roar to begin with, but soon opening into screams and shouts, shots and explosions, the whinnying of dying horses, and the cries of already-dead men. Chaos and confusion filled that room and made it seem much larger. And death soon followed.

Whatever the purpose of the Tordu's ritual here, it had offended the ghosts of the Civil War dead that had inhabited this home for decades.

The first Tordu to die was impaled on a flag staff. She screamed as two wraiths drove the metal pole through her chest, and the ghosts faded away to be replaced by others. The visions ebbed and flowed around the room, rarely existing for longer than a few seconds each. But each appearance was marked by murder.

Max backed into the doorway. There was something immediate about these ghosts, something out of time, and where and when he was became confused in his mind. Was this the Civil War or 1935, or was it still 2005, a place and time when many more spirits were lost to the wind and water? He shouted in confusion and fright, but everyone in the room ignored him.

The Tordu were panicking. All but Mireault and Coco, those two men who could not possibly be here, who were backing toward the rear of the room. They had both dipped their hands into the dead boy's open chest, and now they held them out, bloodied fingers flexing before their mouths as they uttered words lost to the chaos.

Gunfire sounded, different from the ghostly shots. Two of the Tordu—a man and a woman—had retreated to the far end of the room, and were hunkered down beneath paintings of proud-looking people Max did not know. They each held a heavy revolver. He could see panic in their wide eyes as they fired at the wraiths, and close to Max a Tordu man's head flipped back from a bullet's impact.

The woman with the revolver dropped her gun. Her head tipped to the side, bouncing from her shoulder and rolling forward. A ghost emerged from the wall behind her, passing straight through her slumping body even as it and its bloodied sword faded away once more. The Tordu man stared at the dead woman, then placed the barrel of the revolver beneath his chin and pulled the trigger.

Other Tordu tried to run. One man was trampled beneath a horse with terrible, gaping wounds across its stomach and flanks. Another was caught within a drifting cloud of smoke, and he screamed as a ghost manifested within him. Shots sounded, and Max saw two faces screaming as bullets ripped chests and throats apart, one of them melting back into the atmosphere of the room, the other crying lonely, desperate tears as he fell to the floor, dying.

Coco and Mireault had reached a door at the rear of the room and were backing through. Max knew that he was not meant to see them die here, and he wondered if he should follow. But then he looked at the chaos and death before him, unsure of whether he could.

The slaughter was almost over. There was no combating the ghosts, and the remaining two Tordu were quickly cut down by ethereal sword and bullet. The room stank of cordite and spilled blood, and the air still rang with the dying cries of those whom death had chosen. The ghosts wavered in and out of existence, and it was only when the last Tordu was dead that they began to fade away completely.

Max was left alone in a room of corpses. A mist seemed to hang over the scene, and he was not sure whether it was from the dead bodies opened up to the air, or a leftover from the ghostly apparitions.

He breathed deeply, trying to remember the texture and feel of everything he could sense, because he knew this was important.

A shape appeared in the corner of the room. It was the faceless man, still dragging his broken rifle behind him. He surveyed the scene with his blind eye, and only as he was fading again did he look up at Max. Then he was gone.

Max had to leave. He tried shifting his feet and they obeyed his command. But if he went back out the way he had entered, he had no idea what he would find, or who would be waiting for him there.

Maybe I can leave another way, he thought. He looked at the door through which Coco and Mireault had passed. It had drifted half-shut behind them, and beyond was only darkness. Before him lay a room of ruined bodies, which he would have to cross. Many of the candles had been tipped over or extinguished during the violence, but there was enough light left for him to see by.

The air shimmered. Max felt the world shift around

him, but the evidence of the ghostly slaughter was still there. He did not have long.

He started across the room, avoiding the bodies where he could. His feet splashed in a puddle of blood. *This is real!* he thought, and then a door slammed somewhere beyond.

When he reached the open door, he went through, plunging into a dark hallway that led toward the rear of the building. He passed several closed doors to his left, and on the right was a blank wall, broken up here and there with tall windows that looked out onto a shadowed garden. The plants and trees were silver and black, colored only by moonlight.

The end of the hallway was marked by another door standing ajar, and from beyond he heard someone kicking again and again at a locked door.

The world moved around him. The air seemed to take on the consistency of sand, grating against his skin, and when he tried to breathe he found the breath trapped in his lungs. *Breathing out of time,* he thought, and someone passed beyond the door in front of him.

Max knew him. He gasped and called out, "Ray?"

Dusk resolved itself around him again, and from the front of the building he heard the screech of brakes.

Car doors slammed. Men shouted.

I was only in there a heartbeat! No time had passed while he'd been in the Moment. Yet Max himself had moved from the front to the back of the house, traveling through it.

He hurried from the hallway and found himself in a small vestibule, an external door before him flanked by tall glazed screens. He looked around for Ray but there was no one else there. Still, it *had* been him. There was no mistaking his slight build and shock of white hair. Max stared at the door. *The door where Coco and Mireault smashed their way out,* he thought, *seventy years ago. And now* . . .

Now Coco was on his trail once again.

Max drew the bolts and tugged the door open. He closed it gently behind him, ran across the small garden, climbed a short fence, hurried along a narrow alleyway, and emerged onto a long street. Confused, shocked, and feeling as though time itself was laughing at him, he ran.

The map poked at him from his back pocket. He was relieved that he'd grabbed it before jumping from the car, but then he remembered that this was the second map, the first having been taken from him by the cops. If he'd left this one behind he could have bought another, and still he'd have been guided toward his destiny Moment by Moment. Maybe he could simply draw an outline of New Orleans in the mud left over by the floods, mark its main streets and parks and squares, and even then he would be shown where to go next.

Ray had gifted him with something. Or perhaps cursed him.

Max ran along the evening streets, changing direction as often as he could. He had no idea where he was going, and he hoped that if he got lost, then they would lose him, too.

Three big army trucks rolled along the street. Max stood in a doorway, leaning against the sunburned painted door and watching the vehicles trundle past. They carried nothing that he could make out, and he caught the eye of one driver. He was young, maybe twenty, and he tried to stare Max down, his eyes screaming, *You haven't seen the things I've seen!* But Max stared back and won, because the driver was wrong.

As the trucks rolled away, he looked around, startled. He'd been careless; the sound of the trucks' engines could have masked anyone approaching, and here in the doorway he was exposed. Max moved along the street and ducked through some wrought-iron gates, traversing a small court-yard and passing into a narrow walkway between two tall buildings. He emerged onto another street and turned left.

Back there in the Beauregard-Keyes House, would Coco be remembering the slaughter from so long ago? Ducking through that house, maybe for the first time in seventy years, would he be recalling the blood and pain and death brought down upon them by the ghosts that haunted that old, old place? How Coco could be so old was a mystery that Max was doing his best to ignore right now, because it made the shadows growing across the streets seem even darker, and gave the buildings he passed a sense of dread that he could not shake. He heard Charlie say, *You've pissed off Mireault,* and shook his head to lose the echo.

He doesn't have a grave. Charlie had said that, too. *He'll never need one.*

Mireault might not be immortal, but if he'd been alive still in 1935, how much harder was it to believe he could still be drawing breath now, seventy years later? And Coco, seventy years ago, looking just as he did now?

Max ran, and he thought about the other familiar face he'd seen in that house.

Ray. It *had* been him, passing beyond that door like a ghost himself. But had that still been part of the Moment? Max tried to pinpoint the exact time when the replayed past had turned once again into the rolling present, but he was confused now, and afraid.

At the end of a street, with two-story buildings crouching on either side and the smells of cooking and beer wafting from open doors, Max heard a shout. He ducked sideways and stood among some scattered tables below a balcony, looking back the way he had come. *They can't have found me!* he thought. He'd run fast, turning this way and that, and however well they knew the city—

Because they think the city is theirs! Charlie had shouted. *Its* people *are theirs!*

—they would have no idea which way he'd gone.

"Unless the ghosts told them," Max muttered.

"You don't wanna mess with old ghosts, honey," a woman's voice said. Max looked through the doorway behind him and saw an old black woman sitting at a café table, a bowl of fried shrimp before her. She smiled at him, and it lit up her whole face.

"Not much choice," Max said.

"Oh," the woman said; her smile vanished, face dropping, as if he'd told her he had two weeks left to live. She glanced down at his bloodied shirt, then back up at his face. "Then I'm sorry."

"Is there a back way?" Max said, nodding into the café.

"Depends who you're backin' away from."

If he said, *The Tordu,* he was certain that things would

change. So he merely smiled his thanks at the woman and ducked inside. It was a sparse, simple place, unadorned by the usual tourist trappings, and the smells of honest food set his stomach rumbling. After all he had seen, all that had happened, Max still felt hungry. He almost laughed, and it felt good. It felt normal.

Past the restrooms, past an open door looking into a shady kitchen, the back door stood propped open with a chair. He stepped out into a narrow alleyway, piled here and there with bags of refuse. A couple of rats darted away from him, fast shadows in the dusky light. A dog worried a bag farther along the alley. It cast him a baleful glance before returning to its foraging.

He listened for voices and footsteps, but the noises that came to him did not seem out of place here: the crashing of pans; a dog barking; someone raising their voice; someone else laughing.

Max decided to double back on himself, turning left along the alley and walking cautiously until it spilled out onto a street. And there in that alley mouth he waited, watching and listening, wondering just what the hell he would do next.

His life was full of questions and dangers. And with every question he answered, two more arose in its place.

His exclusive, one-way viewing of these significant Moments in New Orleans' history appeared to be compromised now. Back in the plague hospital, the Tordu man had seemed to sense something amiss. And in the Beauregard-Keyes House, both Mireault and the sacrificial victim had looked directly at him. What they had seen he could not guess. Not a whole, solid person, certainly, because Coco would have never let a witness live through that.

Next time, perhaps they would see more.

He backed away from the street and sat on a cold concrete step. He could see out into the street from here, but now that darkness had fallen, he hoped that no one could see this far in. Street lamps were lit, and a few bars and restaurants tried their best to stay in business. The French Quarter was still alive. He smelled food again and his stomach rumbled, but the next time he breathed in he smelled spilled blood and vinegar.

He'd seen Coco taking that boy's organs.

He sighed and leaned back against the steel door. When he closed his eyes, Gabrielle's image leapt out, surprising him with her easy smile and the way her hair always fell over one eye, however much she swept it back. He felt a sudden rush of love for her, and for a beat it was as if she were still there. His eyes snapped open and he felt the loss again, raw and harsh.

Two men walked past the mouth of the alley, talking in hushed tones, and Max sank lower so that he could not be seen. He peered from the shadows, and the men were unknown to him. When they passed the alley he missed their voices. He missed the ease with which they walked the streets, their casual acceptance of the night, and the friendship that seemed obvious between them. Once again, the city made him feel alone.

"Up," a voice whispered, so quietly that Max frowned and tilted his head to one side. "Up," it said again. And he felt the point of a blade touch his neck below the jaw.

Slowly, Max pushed himself up, pressed face-first against the metal door. He tried to turn, but the man behind him growled and nicked him with the knife.

Max felt the cool dribble of blood down his neck. He sniffed; this was not Coco. The car driver, then? Or the fat man from the back? If it was the driver, he'd seen the man nursing his head after the collision, so there could be a weakness there. If it was the fat man——

A fist crunched against his back, driving white-hot pain through his kidneys and around his torso. Max groaned and went to his knees, crying out when the knife touched his neck again.

"I said *up!*" the man said. He smelled of garlic and whiskey, cigarettes and sweat, and Max could tell that he'd been running.

How far behind are the others?

Max stood, hands raised in supplication, knowing that he had to get away.

Had they split up to look for him?

He leaned against the door, gasping as the pain settled into his side and back.

Were Coco and this goon in touch?

"Face the fucking door."

Max leaned against the door and heard a voice behind it, shouting very faintly.

"What's that in your pocket?"

Max glanced back at the man, taking the opportunity to press his ear to the door. Clanging, metal on metal, shouting, bustle . . . it sounded like a busy kitchen. "A map."

The fat man grunted and plucked the map from Max's

pocket. He wiped sweat from his big round head, flicking the droplets across Max's face and smiling. "What sort of map?"

"A magic one."

The fat guy's smile dropped from his face. Something flashed in Max's eye, and then the tip of the knife was pressed to his lower eyelid. Max rose onto his tiptoes but the knife followed him up, never more than half an inch away from his eye.

"Don't fuck with me, dead man," Fat Man said. "My brother's legs are shattered, they say he won't walk again, if he even lives. But Coco told me he don't want you dead. Least, not yet. But that doesn't mean I can't . . . cut you a bit. Soften you up for his questions. 'Cos he has plenty of questions for you, dead man."

Don't push don't push don't push, Max thought, feeling the knife's tip touch his inner eyelid.

Fat Man eased back on the knife, and when Max sighed with relief and lowered himself down, Fat Man flicked the blade.

Max gasped, from shock more than anything else. He felt a drizzle of blood on his face, and then the stinging came in, and the pain, like intense heat or extreme cold pressed in a line on his cheek.

His heart thumped quicker, and fear and anger sharpened his senses.

"What are you—?" he began.

Fat Man pointed the knife at his face. "You don't ask any fuckin' questions here. Got that?"

Max nodded, resting his head back against the door.

"Now be a good dead man while I give my friends a call." Fat Man took a cell phone from his pocket and flipped it open, knife still pointing at Max's face.

Max heard footsteps approaching beyond the door, echoing, setting the metal vibrating. A voice called inside, Max felt the door shake as bolts were drawn back, and a man laughed, deep and hearty.

Fat Man was dialing a number, frowning, large fingers clumsy on the small keypad.

The metal door shifted, and Max made sure he had his balance.

"Your brother screamed like a pussy when I ran him down."

Fat Man's eyes went wide.

The door swung inward, away from him, and Max let himself fall forward onto his hands and knees, twisting and kicking up at Fat Man's hand.

The guy who'd opened the door jumped backward, shouting in surprise.

Fat Man's knife hand was thrown back by the force of Max's kick, but he held on to the blade, fumbling and dropping the phone from his other hand instead.

Once again, Max was faced with a sudden choice: flight, through the kitchens and out into the streets once more; or fight. And he was sick of running.

He stood and swung, his fist glancing from Fat Man's cheek, thumbnail ripping his ear open. The man screeched and stumbled back, and Max heard the crunch of plastic as the man stepped on his own phone.

Behind Max, the man who had opened the door was

already retreating back inside the building, the door swinging shut. The man said nothing, but he moved quickly. Max didn't have long.

Fat Man started to swing the knife around again but Max shouldered him in the chest, reached up, and caught his forearm, gripping hard. He planted his feet and spun around, twisting the guy's arm as far and as hard as he could.

He heard a crack, and Fat Man screamed. Max had never done anything like this before. He'd had a fight in fifth grade when his combatant and he had both been sent to the head teacher with blood streaming from their noses. And once, out in Boston with a group of college friends, he'd helped break up a drunken scuffle between two of them, and a flailing fist had caught him in the mouth and made his lip bleed. But that was the sum of violence in his life. He didn't know how to hurt, and the thought of doing it had always been reprehensible to him.

But the Fat Man had grinned as he flicked the knife across Max's face. He had called him "dead man." And something deeper than memory, something more allied with instinct, kicked in.

Max let go of the man's arm and pushed. Fat Man shuffled backwards and hit the wall, grimacing as his useless right arm flapped at his side. Max stormed forward, aiming a kick at the man's balls and missing, but following up with punches to his face and neck. It was pathetic. Fat Man's knife gone, his arm out of action, he snotted and sniveled, and in what seemed like seconds he was begging for Max to stop. But to stop would be a mistake, Max knew, and he punched again and again. Fat Man slid to the ground, and Max kicked him in the face.

At last he stepped back. It could have been seconds or minutes, but the red mist of fight and fury lifted as quickly as it had arrived.

Fat Man started laughing. Each time his chest rose and fell Max heard something click, and blood bubbled at his cut and swollen mouth, his eyes seeing little. The beaten man lifted his good hand to his neck and laughed some more, shaking his head as if he'd heard the funniest joke ever told.

"What's so goddamn funny?" Max demanded, unnerved.

The man pointed at him first, and then with great effort his lips parted in a grin, splitting and spilling more blood down his slick jaw. "Dead . . . man."

Max glanced around. The metal door to the restaurant kitchens was still open, though there was no sign of any curious faces inside. *Someone else's problem,* he thought. In the borrowed streetlight he could see Fat Man's crushed phone, like a huge beetle someone had trodden on. He looked around, and moments later he saw the glint of the fallen knife.

He snatched up the weapon and knelt before the man, knowing even then that he could never kill. But he had to convey the possibility that he would.

Max pressed the knife beneath one of the Fat Man's eyes, reversing the situation from minutes before. "What did Gabrielle Doucette have to do with the Tordu?"

Fat Man smiled, and a croaky giggle escaped him.

"I'm going to kill you in five seconds if you don't start

talking," Max said. "Tell me about Coco, the Tordu, Gabrielle, and why you do what you do to people. What's the point of it all? Tell me, or in five seconds I'll cut your throat and watch you bleed to death. One."

Fat Man stared at him with one partly-open eye.

"Two."

A car passed by the end of the alley, and Max glanced up. Police car. It did not stop. He looked back down at Fat Man, whose smile had disappeared.

"Three."

The man stared at him blankly now, chest still clicking every time he took in a breath. His eye was watering. Blood bubbled at his mouth.

"Four."

Max moved the knife from the man's eye and pressed it to his throat. His own heart was racing, perhaps fooled into the possibility that he might actually go through with this. He tried reassuring himself that this was a bluff, but something inside didn't quite believe.

"Five." He stared at the man's eye, seeing nothing. "Last chance."

Fat Man closed his eyes, shutting out the world.

Max pressed the knife forward, his thoughts manic, searching for something that would rescue him from this failed situation, and all he could come up with was a name, dredged up from his memory of Charlie's ranting.

"Seddicus will laugh at you, Fat Man."

The man's eye opened again, with a soft *pop*. It went wider than it had before, and even swollen so badly, the other eye opened as well. The man pushed with his feet, struggling to back away from Max, and the fear on his face could not be feigned. He was moaning, and his good arm came up to wipe a sheen of blood from his face.

Max leaned forward, taking advantage of the man's state, and he felt a smile split his own face. "And after he laughs, Seddicus will want you."

The man's good arm lifted and slapped the wall behind him, fingers twitching.

"Tell me about Coco and the Tordu!"

"You know. You already *know*!"

Max heard voices behind him. He glanced back at the open doorway. Two people stood there now, the man who had first opened the door and another, bigger man.

"Cops on their way," the big man said.

"Fuck off and mind your own business," Max said.

The big man shrugged and the two faces disappeared again.

Max bent to the Fat Man and snatched the map from his jacket pocket. "Be seeing you," he said. When he stood up again, he saw a vague shape on the pale brick wall, drawn in blood. It was a circle with three lines through it, forming a triangle within the circle, each line trailing beyond its edge.

"Don't think that will help," he said.

Fat Man stopped breathing. His body froze in a moment, his hand raised, a blood bubble forming at the corner of his mouth and popping.

Max took one more look at the marking on the wall, then turned and sprinted away along the alley. For as long as the street light filtered in and lit his way, he felt Fat Man's eyes on his back, watching him go.

He reached the end of the alley and hit the street. He walked quickly, turning left and then right, working his way west, away from the Beauregard-Keyes House and what had happened there. Eventually he realized that being out on the street, bloodied as he was, would be more dangerous than holing up somewhere. Besides, he was thirsty, and he needed a place to look at the map.

Time was of the essence. However many Moments there were left for him to view, the faster he did so, the better.

He ducked into a café and went into the bathroom to wash the blood from his hands and arm and face—carefully, biting back groans of pain when his fingers touched his bruised nose and cut cheek. He looked in the mirror. In the dark café, and wearing dark clothes, the tacky drying blood would not be too noticeable. That was good. Using a wet paper towel he dabbed at the slash on his cheek. It was already clotting. He looked like a mugging victim, but little could change that.

When he came out, he took a table at the back and ordered a jug of coffee and a chicken po'boy. He was not really hungry anymore, but did not want to look too out of place.

The café was about a third full, most tables taken by couples or small groups. There were a few solo diners, some of them evidently self-conscious, the others quite comfortable in their own company. They read, or drank, or just looked into a distance that Max could never really know. He guessed that the ones not used to eating or drinking alone were from out of town, brought in to help with the cleanup.

He tucked a paper napkin into his collar, trying to hide the blood on his shirt.

No one looked too threatening. The waitress took no notice of Max's clothes. His nose hurt, so he breathed through his mouth.

A car swept by, a black-and-white with no blues flashing.

Coffee poured, waiting for his food to come, Max opened up the map and spread it across the table. He scanned it quickly, but the Sixth Moment did not leap out at him. Frowning, he fixed the location of the Moment he'd just visited, pleased that the boxed words had faded, but still confused. *Where is it?* he thought. *Just where the hell . . . ?*

"Didn't mark you for a tourist," the waitress said, standing beside him and pouring more coffee. She was a short white woman, very trim and athletic, her long hair tied back and hanging over one shoulder. She smiled at him and glanced down at the map.

"Visitor, not tourist," he said.

"There's a difference?"

"Tourists are happy to be here." He winced inwardly, hoping he hadn't caused offense. *Is she really flirting with me?*

But the waitress laughed. "Sure, *you* don't look like you're having too much fun. And I never met a tourist found what they expected here. 'Specially now."

"Yeah," Max said. "It's quite a place."

"Sure is that. Be quite a place again, too, just you see."

Max was moved by her confidence, and he felt a lump in

his throat. Senses heightened, his emotions had followed suit, and much as he knew he was in mortal danger, he still felt incredibly alive.

"Good to hear some optimism," he said.

The waitress leaned on his table across from him, looking him in the eye. "You tell everyone," she said. "When you go back to wherever you came from, you tell everyone that we're still here, and we'll survive."

Max smiled and nodded, and the waitress turned and went to wait on a neighboring table. He had the sense that he'd been honored somehow, and he watched her for a few minutes to see whether she repeated the performance. She did not. She had seen something in Max that drew that out of her.

Must have more of New Orleans in me than I realized, he thought. And terrible though the city was to him right now, he could not help liking that idea. The Tordu might have been tormenting the city for generations, tainting it with whatever dark magic they performed, but he recalled clearly the wondrous magic he had seen at the moment of the city's founding. The Tordu were a stain upon New Orleans, but they weren't the city. It had a powerful heart that had nothing to do with their darkness, and a sense of joy and hope that was unlike anywhere else in the world. New Orleans was hurting now, teetering, and maybe it would never fully recover. But the Tordu were like rats, infecting the city and feeding off its garbage.

He went back to the map, sipping his coffee, scanning the streets and districts, and then he saw the Sixth Moment. He'd not spotted it before because the blocked square fit so well into the streets of the Lower Ninth Ward.

The Sixth Moment:
Under Cover of Betsy
The End of a Ward
September 9, 1965

Lower Ninth Ward. He knew that had been hit hard during the storm, with the Industrial Canal flood walls being breached and sending billions of gallons of water raging through the streets. Then Hurricane Rita had flooded much of the neighborhood—and Gentilly as well—only a few weeks after Katrina. And he had read about Hurricane Betsy forty years ago, when the ward had suffered a similar fate. But what did "Under cover of Betsy" mean? What had the Tordu done during that hurricane?

Right now, the Lower Ninth would be a bad place to visit, and it was maybe two miles from where he sat. It was dark, he'd lost his rental car, and the city streets were not a safe place at night.

For him, they weren't a safe place by day, either.

But he *had* to get there. There was no mention of the Tordu for this Sixth Moment, but that did not mean they had not been involved. And then the sobering thought hit him that Coco might actually figure out the trail he was following, and why.

Max shook his head. He could not let suspicions like that derail him. He drank some more coffee, then the waitress returned with his food. She smiled a dazzling smile, and for a beat he even thought she was going to join him. She glanced at the map, then up at him again.

"You looking for someone?"

"Yes," Max said, without thinking. "Is it that obvious?"

"Yeah. Seen a lot like you, over the past few weeks."

"And you?" Max asked. The woman's smile faltered, and he silently berated himself for being too forward.

"We done okay," she said. "My family, at least. Lost an old friend from school, though. And my boyfriend . . . he's just gone."

"I'm sorry," Max said, thinking of stinking attics and houses lifted from their footings, and that warehouse by the Superdome where hundreds of unclaimed bodies still lay.

"Hope you find her," the waitress said. And with a smile, she turned to leave.

"Wait!" Max said. She glanced back, raising an eyebrow. "Can I ask you . . . a couple of questions?"

The waitress glanced around the café with a professional eye, then smiled. "Shoot."

"Who's Seddicus?" He did not know what to expect: fear? Disbelief? But the waitress frowned at first, then half smiled, as though trying to figure whether he was taking her for a ride.

"You yankin' my chain?"

Max shook his head. "It's a name I heard . . . "

The waitress laughed then, shaking her head and running her fingers down her neck. "Baby, someone's been fooling with you." She leaned on the table again. "Seddicus is a demon of the swamps."

What the fuck . . . ? Max thought. "A demon?"

"It's an old folk tale, the kind of stuff you hear on those Haunted New Orleans tours. Well, maybe you wouldn't hear that one, but you talk to Cajuns and the fishermen on Lake Pontchartrain, or any of them fake mojo women run the voodoo shops on Bourbon Street, and they'll tell you the story."

Max arched an eyebrow, showing her a smile he did not feel. "Which is?"

She glanced around again, making sure none of her customers needed tending to, then looked at him like she was sizing him up, seeing if he might be a little crazy, or just curious. The waitress shrugged.

"They say he arrived here long ago, in New Orleans' early days. No one knows where he came from. For a while he stalked the city, but he's banished from here now, livin' out in the bayou. My ol' gran used to say Seddicus was well fed when New Orleans was young, and here an' there you can read accounts of bodies that were found. Torn up, shredded, like they'd been eaten an' spat out again."

"A bogeyman story?" Max said.

"For the tourists, yeah. But it's said he only fed on bad folk. So maybe he ain't a bogeyman at all." Her eyes twinkled.

"A demon," he muttered, shaking his head as though they were on the same page about the foolishness of such superstition. And with that came total recall of what Charlie had said, and how he'd said it: *The only thing they're scared of is Seddicus.* The only *thing*. Not the only *man*.

"That help?" the waitress asked.

"Maybe," Max said. "So you don't believe the story?"

The waitress' smile hardened a little. Someone from another table signaled her. She nodded at them, then looked back at Max. "We're not all voodoo people down here, you know."

"No, I—" Max began, but the woman was already walking away.

He folded the map, ate a few mouthfuls of food, drained his coffee. He left thirty dollars on the table, then stood, and on his way out he looked for the waitress. She'd disappeared. *On the phone?* he wondered. *Calling Coco right now?* Paranoia grabbed him again, he looked around at the other diners, locking gazes with one of the other single customers and both of them looking away, embarrassed. Outside he sucked in a heavy breath, and jumped when a voice spoke next to him.

"Sorry," the waitress said. She was leaning against the café's front window, smoking.

Max shook his head. "I didn't mean—"

"No, I know you didn't. I know. And that's what frightened me, a little."

"I frightened you?"

"Your eyes, when you asked if I believed. Because *you* do."

Max didn't know what to say. She finished her cigarette, threw it into the gutter, and gave him a final smile.

"I hope you find who you're looking for," she said.

"I hope so, too," Max said. And turning around to head back into the café, she could have been Gabrielle, walking away from him all over again.

He knew that he should get a taxi, but the paranoia was still there, and he wanted to at least get out of the Quarter before stopping to call a cab. So he walked, and the streets were nowhere near as alive as they had once been. One night, amongst many he had spent on the streets with Gabrielle, they had come just to see the life and listen to the bustle. They had stopped in the occasional bar for a drink or some food, and it was not until early the next morning that they had hailed a cab and gone back to that house where she had died. They had snuggled in the back of the vehicle, and Gabrielle had smiled sweetly while unzipping him and slipping her hand into his trousers. She had stroked him, and agreed with the driver that there were so many things the tourists could never know.

Didn't mark you for a tourist, the waitress had said, and Max knew that he would never come to visit this place as a sightseer again. He knew too much to face these streets with such innocence. When he'd flown back to Boston after finding Gabrielle and Joe Noone fucking in the attic, he had left that place almost as he had arrived: a visitor who had gathered a mere haze of New Orleans about himself. It had not taken long for that haze to be washed away, eroded by his return to a safe life in the Northeast.

But now he had New Orleans inside him. He breathed its air, and it breathed him. He dreamed of the city when he slept, and though the city itself could never sleep, he knew that he was in its thoughts.

Max kept a watch out for faces he knew, or strangers who appeared to know him. He enjoyed the walk. Something about the warm evening air seemed to slough away the revulsion he felt at the beating he'd dealt Fat Man, and that was part of the city's gift. He thought of Coco and the

Tordu, the Moments he had witnessed and what Charlie had said about them only being afraid of Seddicus. And though little of what had happened could possibly make sense in Max's innocent Bostonian mind, this new Max of New Orleans had a mind that was opening more and more to such possibilities.

He smelled the air, smacked his lips, and once more tasted that bitter liquid that Ray had given him. *It's all coming closer,* he thought, and though that scared him immensely, he also found comfort in such an idea. He'd come here for a purpose, and every street, breeze, and breath of life left in this damaged city seemed to be driving him toward that end.

At the junction of two streets in Faubourg Marigny, the sound of jazz breathing through the open doors and windows of a bar along the street, Max found an idling taxi. He checked out the driver first and, satisfied that he'd not seen him before, jumped into the back.

"Off duty," the driver said.

"I'll pay double."

A sigh. "Where to?"

"Lower Ninth."

The driver looked in his mirror. "Nothin' there now for anyone with sense."

"Not now, no," Max said, staring back.

The man sighed again and started the car.

Max took the opportunity to rest, wondering just what atrocity, crime, or wonder he was about to witness.

chapter
13

The driver was not keen to drive into the Lower Ninth. Max had to promise him a forty-dollar tip, and even then he drove at a snail's pace. Max heard metal strike metal, saw that the man drove with one hand, and guessed that he was nursing a gun with the other. A week ago, he would have been shocked, but now he saw the sense in caution.

The moon was emerging in the dusky sky. Hesitant, as if uneager to view this devastation once again.

They passed two cars, one on top of the other, the one underneath flattened to half its normal height. A house lay across the road, its roof washed away and its insides laid bare. Max saw pictures hanging on inner walls, and he wondered how many people in those portraits were still alive, and where they were, and what they were thinking right now. He felt like an intruder, and he looked away from the ruined home.

But wherever he turned were more ruins. One house had slumped sideways, skewed almost forty-five degrees from the vertical, and its front yard was piled with appliances turning to rust. Another home had a name, KENNETH, spray-painted across its whitewashed front façade, and moonlight glinted from several framed photographs pinned there. Beneath the name, like a ghost, were the pale sprayed words indicating that the house had contained a body.

Cars had been washed along the street, houses carried from their foundations, roofs swept along in the flood and deposited almost whole in neighbors' front gardens. One vehicle was crushed front to back, maybe half its original length, and Max wondered at the forces that could do that.

It was an apocalyptic landscape, a scene of ruin and destruction that he would never get used to seeing. But something made him look.

"Where to?" the driver asked.

Max took out the map and examined it closer, leaning this way and that so that the moonlight would reveal relevant detail. "Where are we now?"

"This used to be North Claiborne."

"Left onto Lamanche," Max said.

"If I can find it, I'll take you there. This far south, water was up to the tops of the front doors. Farther north you go, deeper it was. Up to the eaves, higher. That's where a lot of people died. Then Rita came along, swamped it all again."

Max did not respond, because he could think of nothing meaningful to say.

After a few minutes, the car braked and came to a stop. "This is as far as we go," the driver said.

"Is that Lamanche?" Max asked. They were at a junction, of sorts, but the road had almost disappeared beneath a sea of broken wood, shingles, slates, smashed cars, and other detritus. Ahead of them, several cars were tangled with the ruin of a house, splayed across the street and preventing any further progress.

"Two, maybe three streets farther."

"Thanks." He handed the driver some money.

"This place isn't safe right now, you know that?" the man asked.

Max nodded. "I know."

"You got a gun?"

"No."

"Well . . . you should've brought one."

Max nodded his thanks and exited the car, standing there in the rubble and watching the driver perform a five-point turn before going back the way they'd come. As he stood alone, listening to the sound of the car engine diminishing in the distance, the weight of emerging moonlight was almost palpable.

A dog barked somewhere in the distance. The sound of something collapsing came from nearer; wood tumbling, metal clanking. And Max silently agreed with the driver.

He walked past the car wrecks and the ruined house, making his way along two more streets until he reached what he hoped was Lamanche Street. Here he turned left, counting the houses on his right. *What if it's been washed away?* he thought. *What if it's a ruin?* He would face that when he came to it.

The third house was collapsed, the roof sloping down to touch the front yard. The fifth house had a car buried in its front façade, just the rear trunk and wheels visible. The sixth house, which the Sixth Moment on the map pointed to, had vanished.

Max stood staring at the square concrete foundation, light gray in the dusk. There was still some grass on the front yard, though much of the lawn had been scored and scarred by objects being dragged across it. There was a set of three concrete steps leading up to a vanished front porch, and Max approached, each tentative footstep marking his route in dust.

More noises from far away . . . but this time, there was more than just distance between him and their source. He heard voices raised in argument, and then in triumph. A cheer. And behind the talking and the cheering, the unrelenting roar of a storm.

He walked up the concrete steps. Grit ground underfoot. At the top he faced where the house had once been, breathing in the scent of rain, feeling a cool breath on the back of his neck, and hearing raindrops hammering against glass, wood, and stone long gone.

Then he took a step forward, and the Moment erupted around him.

Noise, chaos, the crashing of wooden shutters, the smashing of glass, and the cheering of voices raised again from somewhere above him.

Max stumbled into the hallway of the large house, and something smacked him in the back. He fell, wincing at the pain. Rolling, he looked back, and the front door was in the grip of the storm, thrashing back and forth but never quite allowing the catch to click. He kicked out and sent the door swinging, then he crawled forward and pushed with both hands.

The noise of the storm lessened only slightly when the front door slammed shut.

He pulled a curtain aside and looked out into the face of Hurricane Betsy. Rain slashed down, driven almost horizontal by vicious gusts of wind, and a car was rolling slowly along the street, parking brake off. There was no one inside. He watched until it struck another car, its windows rattling with the potential to move on and do more damage.

This Moment is everywhere. He looked up and the sky was heavy with rain, violent with the forces slamming down upon the New Orleans of 1965.

More voices from behind and above, and it was as if they called him. *They* were what he was here to see. Not the storm, not this backward echo of the doom that would once again befall New Orleans . . . but the voices. The people. And whoever they were, they were about to destroy the ward.

He crept up the staircase, his caution natural. *Last time he almost saw me,* he thought. *And the time before that, I was just a glimpse. Maybe this time . . .*

He touched the walls and felt them shaking, breathed in and tasted rain and danger.

Maybe this time, I'm really here.

A woman appeared at the top of the stairs, looking directly down at him. Max froze. She was young, pretty, and she looked petrified.

"I . . ." Max began.

She started down, and her eyes looked past him. He flattened himself against the wall as she passed by, not wanting to sense her moving through him, or himself through her. She reached the bottom step and stared at the front door. After glancing around the hallway she ran back upstairs, turning left at the top. The sound of voices raised and lowered slightly as she opened and closed a door.

Max let out his held breath. The house creaked around him, timbers stretching and groaning in the wind.

He continued up the stairs, turning left to follow the young woman. He was faced with a closed door. Beyond, the sound of a single voice, low and sonorous, and Max closed his eyes because he had heard that voice before.

"Ray," he said. He reached for the handle, wondering what he would see when he opened the door. But the woman had looked through him. *I'm not really here,* he thought. *And maybe I'm not really back there, either.* He was at the balancing point between two moments in time, and to maintain the balance he had to bear witness.

He opened the door and walked through into a large bedroom. The bed had been pushed into the bay window, and Ray was sitting there, and he looked exactly as Max had seen him in 2005. Before him, a dozen people sat on the floor, some of them hugging, others apparently on their own.

In front of Ray stood a low, narrow wooden table. There was a large bowl there, in which some thick fluid seemed to be boiling. Beside the bowl was a mess of brown paper, open on the table like a large wilting bloom. At the bloom's heart, something wet and bloody.

"I trust you all to be here for good reasons, not bad," Ray said. "I trust you all to have made the right choice, the purest decision. I trust you all . . . and that's why Mireault and I have always been so different. I trust, he mistrusts." He nodded slowly, casting his gaze across all those present. Then he smiled, but there was little humor there. "Besides . . . I'd know if your being here was a lie."

A couple of people looked around, and there was an expectant air in the room. No one stood, no one spoke.

"You're good people," Ray said. "At their heart, everyone is. It's the bad that steals you away. Light is heavy, it has weight and mass, and if you bathe in light long enough, it will move you. Darkness . . . that's just an absence. It can be cured."

"For everyone?" a young man asked.

"Everyone."

"Mireault?" a woman's voice whispered, and outside the wind battered the house, rain smacking at the windows like shotgun pellets.

Ray looked at whoever had spoken, and that sad smile came again. "You've all suffered at his hand, and caused suffering in his name," he said. "You've all lived with the dark for a very long time. And I thank you from the bottom of my heart for shunning that darkness."

"Will you kill him?" someone said.

"I don't have the power for that. I never have." Ray looked down at the package before him, grimacing with distaste. "But because our friend Robert here brought that out with him . . ." He picked up the package and gasps came from around the room.

Max did not like the sound of those sighs. They were not shock, they were hunger. *What is that thing?* he thought.

"Did anyone know his or her name?"

"Marcus," a woman cooed. "Marcus, sweet boy."

"And you should fucking know!" another woman said. The tension in the room heightened.

"Enough!" Ray snapped. "There are no histories here. You all started your lives again the moment you walked through that door."

"No histories?" the loud woman said. "No justice?"

Ray shook his head. "Justice? If we punished everyone who'd ever helped or followed the Tordu, how many would be left?"

Max sidled across the back of the room, trying to edge closer to Ray. He did not want to see whatever he had in the paper before him—heart, kidney, brain—but there was something he wanted to try.

Mireault had sensed him. And now here was Ray, more involved than he had claimed, more a part of everything than Max had ever guessed. There was something incredibly ancient about this old man, as if he were carved from quartz, not built of flesh and blood. He and Mireault . . . *they* had histories.

"Ray?" Max called, startled by how loud his voice sounded. No one seemed to hear him.

"Now they've gone too far," Ray whispered. "And I'm getting too old to hold them off."

Something seemed to strike the house, rattling windows in frames and splitting wood. The people looked around in a panic, but Ray ignored the noise, picking up the raw, red organ and dipping it slowly into the bubbling bowl before him. He started a chant that troubled Max's hearing. It was made of words he did not know or understand, and sounds he could not make, and the others in the room quickly picked up on it, repeating the words slightly after Ray to form a group echo.

As Ray dipped the organ into the boiling bowl, Max felt something hot pressing against his right buttock. He snatched the folded map from his back pocket, certain that it was on fire, ready to open it up and stamp out flames. But when he did open it, there seemed to be nothing amiss. This Sixth Moment was still here, boxed and written against the Lower Ninth Ward.

Is Ray trying to flood the ward? he thought. He couldn't think what else the writing could mean.

Under Cover of Betsy
The End of a Ward

He knew that many people had died in this hurricane, drowned in their attics as they had been forty years later during and after Katrina. Was Ray really a killer? A mass murderer?

And if he was, what did that make Max?

Ray's chanting increased in tone and urgency, and the thing he held down in the bowl started to foam and froth. Pinkish bubbles overflowed, creeping up his arms and spilling across the wooden table. The other people in the room continued their chanted echo. *They were Tordu,* Max thought. *Ray brought them over.*

The Tordu, he knew, were bad. Maybe even evil. But that did not necessarily make Ray the good in all of this. Maybe—

He dropped the map. It had burned his fingers. Glancing around the room, aware that he was still unseen, Max opened the map on the floor. To the southeast of the city, where the swamps and lakes were marked with sparse symbols and vague shading, a faint glow had appeared.

"One ward in many," Ray said, "one of the farthest out. And Seddicus will welcome its fall."

Not the Lower NinthWard! Max thought. This was another ward entirely. He did not know what, or why, or what it was meant to do, but—

In superstition, a ward was a manner of protection. A method of warding something off, holding it back.

Keeping it out.

Max shivered. He knew only the name, Seddicus. And he knew that it was meant to be a demon. *It's said he only fed on bad folk,* the waitress had said. It was as if there was a lake of buried knowledge within him, an awareness of that unknown thing's true nature, and that lake was now being plumbed. He felt more terrified than he ever had of anything in his life before. A shadow closed over his mind, not quite touching him but smothering much of what he thought of as natural awareness. He tried to look beyond this moment, but he was locked here by fear. He could only watch Ray's hands covered with the bloodied foam of someone's dead organ, hear the chant, taste the wet, salty air as Hurricane Betsy prepared its assault on this great city, and as he looked back down at the map he saw a stain appear in the distant, primal swamps.

"It's working!" Ray said. And then he looked across his assembled audience's heads and directly at Max.

Max froze. *Ray,* he tried to say. But the man was not quite seeing him, not truly aware. There was a distance in his gaze as he said, "This is one of the city's most powerful Moments."

Then someone pulled a gun and shot Ray in the chest.

Others fell on the shooter, beating and kicking and slashing with knives, and outside, the storm's violence grew to match.

Ray gasped, blood staining the front of his clothing, as several people squatted around him. One of them held his hands and kept them pressed down in the boiling bowl, but Ray's jaw dropped, his eyes went wide, and he let out a piercing cry.

"All gone wrong," the old man gasped.

The shooter was dead, a bloodstained mess of meat and clothing in the corner of the room. Everyone stood now, all except for Ray and the man holding his hands. In their eyes, Max saw fear and hopelessness.

"Is the ward broken?" a woman asked.

"Wrong . . . wrong!" Ray whispered.

"Is it broken?"

"Mireault knew . . ." he gasped. "He knew about *all* of this, and now . . . he'll punish us . . . "

Max looked down at the map. The singed, darkened paper in the marshes grew light again, resolving the lines and shadings of that wild place. And another area, much closer to where he viewed this pivotal part of New Orleans' history, was starting to glow, and char.

From outside, through the violence of the storm, came the first of several massive booms. The house shook, the people gasped.

As one, they turned to look at Ray.

"I was so close," he said.

"What do we do?" someone asked. Another thudding explosion from the distance, and this one continued to shudder through the ground, as something monstrous approached.

"Run," Ray said. "The water's coming."

Max looked back down at the map. Spanning the Industrial Canal, the scorched spot writhed.

Was that Ray protecting the city, or destroying it?

As Max descended the stairs, the house was already fading away. In the last blink before this Moment disappeared, he thought he heard the roar of water in the distance, and the sound of buildings falling. Then he was standing on the concrete slab of the house, moonlight bathing him and silence surrounding him.

I don't know how many more of these I can take.

He looked at the map, watching the Sixth Moment fade away forever. He scanned for the Seventh Moment, but it did not appear. Even with the map flat on the concrete and held down by lumps of rubble, Max could not discern where the next Moment might be. He searched the city district by district, then out beyond the city, paying particular attention to the swamps and lakes to the southeast.

"Nothing," he whispered. "So is that it?" The night gave him no reply, and he sat down and wiped sweat from his face. Staring out at the road, he could see the place where he'd watched that abandoned car pushed along by the wind, nudging another car and waiting for the storm to carry it farther.

Ray was mixed up with the Tordu. No, not with them, *against* them.

As ever, the Moment had left him with a thousand more questions, so many that his mind felt full of them.

"So is it time to find Matrisse?" he muttered.

"Not yet," a voice said. Harsh, nasal, and filled with violence.

Fat Man.

Max went to turn, but something struck him in the face. He fell sideways onto the concrete slab, putting one hand out just fast enough to prevent his head striking too hard. He spit blood across the map.

How did you find me? he wanted to ask, but he would not give Fat Man the satisfaction.

More shadows closed in, four of them stepping up onto

the slab. One of them carried a machine pistol. Another flapped a bag in the air, which snapped in the wind like a gunshot.

"Coco requests an audience with you," Fat Man said, kneeling beside Max and clenching one meaty hand around his throat. He squeezed. "You, and your magic fucking map."

Fat Man pulled him upright again, and Max scanned the map. Brought out by a spray of his blood, a Seventh Moment began to manifest, nestled in the ruined streets of Gentilly.

Before Max could read what it said, the bag was pulled down over his head, a rope was tightened around his throat, and he was kicked in the head again and again.

chapter

14

The full moon silvered the buildings as Fat Man drove northeast, up through Gentilly and onto Chef Menteur Boulevard. Max sat in the backseat, disoriented from the beating and getting his revenge the only way he could—by bleeding all over the Cadillac's leather upholstery. That would teach them. Bloodstains would never come out. Fuckers.

He knew his thoughts were too sluggish, that he'd lost a lot of blood in the past few hours. But the basic situation was not lost on him. They had taken the hood off once the car picked up speed. Fat Man and his Tordu buddies didn't care if Max saw where he was going, which illustrated a fact that Max did not want to face: they did not expect him to be alive to tell anyone where they had taken him.

So he sat in the backseat, discouraged from trying to pop open the door and dive from the moving car by the presence of a gun pressed against his right side, aggravating his already bruised ribs. Hitting the pavement at fifty miles per hour did not appeal to him, either. On the other hand, since the alternative seemed to be dying, he tried to clear his mind enough to come up with a third option.

Chef Menteur Boulevard—also known as Chef Menteur Highway, aka Route 90—meandered northeast out along an isthmus that separated Lake Pontchartrain from the Gulf of Mexico. Technically, the whole area was part of the city of New Orleans, but civilization grew sparse out here and then disappeared entirely. There were a few suburban neighborhoods out this way, Max knew, dropped down in the middle of nowhere like they'd fallen from God's pockets by accident. But for the most part, off the highway there wasn't much more than forest and wetlands. Did this count as bayou country? He didn't know. But he knew there must be a million places out here to dump a body, or feed one piece by piece to 'gators.

There were three people in the car with him. Fat Man drove. The guy with the gun sat in the back with Max. In the passenger seat was a white woman with full lips and jet black hair pulled into a ponytail. She was anywhere between twenty-five and thirty-five, dressed in blue jeans and a green ribbed tank top. Tall and thin, she sat upright and remained grimly silent. Max thought it might be because she was uncomfortable with what they were doing, that she might turn out to be an ally in keeping him alive. But when she glanced back at him with the dull, lightless eyes of a predator, he gave up on that fantasy.

As in the past, the Tordu apparently did not discriminate based on hue or sex. They had only one requirement that Max had discerned—their members must be without mercy, as single-minded as the alligators that prowled the bayou.

"How you feelin' back there, dead man?" Fat Man asked, grinning into the rearview mirror.

Max sat right behind him, and when he hadn't been searching the sprawl of thick, green, mosquito heaven that unfurled on both sides of the road, he'd been staring at the sweaty rolls of fat at the back of the guy's neck. Now he stared there again, not wanting to meet the man's gaze in the mirror.

Over the past couple of days he had become more and more afraid that his search, and his life, might end this way, driving out into the middle of nowhere to eat a bullet. He'd always been a bit of a coward, avoiding pain whenever possible. If he'd ever imagined a scenario such as this, he would have pictured himself pleading, panicking, even praying. A lot of guys might try to think like tough action heroes and keep their jaws square and their repartee sharp, holding on to their dignity, but Max would have predicted only whimpering on his own part.

What he could never have prophesied was the particular stoicism with which he now confronted his fate. Certainly he felt fear; it shook him, within and without. And the thought of death, perhaps with torture beforehand, terrified him. Yet it all felt so inevitable that he could not muster a prayer or a plea.

"I'm talking to you," Fat Man said.

The barrel of the pistol jabbed his ribs and Max hissed air in through his teeth. He turned to glare at the Tordu son of a bitch beside him in the backseat. The guy had fine features, a long nose, and wavy, shoulder-length hair. His eyes were green and his skin a coffee hue that might have been Spanish Creole or ordinary Latino. He had expensive taste in clothes, and was now picking invisible lint off of his linen pants. The guy had an elegance about him and an arrogance, like he was some kind of foreign nobleman.

The thought made Max smile.

"What's funny to you?" the man asked, poking the barrel of the gun into Max's ribs again.

Max only shook his head and looked back at Fat Man's neck rolls. But the intensity of the glare in the rearview mirror was too powerful, and Max found himself staring back at last.

"Gerard," Fat Man said, "if he don't answer me, shoot him in the leg."

The guy beside Max nodded. "You have a preference of legs, Lamar?"

Max blinked, taking a moment to realize that Lamar was Fat Man's name. The silent woman continued to stare straight ahead during this exchange.

"Nah. Either one's fine." Lamar looked at Max in the rearview mirror again. "So, where were we, dead man? Yeah, how are you feelin'?"

"Like I just got my head kicked in," Max said.

But it was a lie. Fear filled him up to overflowing, but it wasn't alone. Something else was inside him as well, and he knew what he felt didn't only have to do with disorientation or loss of blood from the beating. Ironically, on a trip that would end with his death, he felt remarkably alive. His skin tingled, and the night air sparkled, suffused with a golden aura that should have gone with the setting sun. The Tordu in the car with him were voids in that aura, as if on a certain level of perception they did not even exist.

Just as Ray had predicted, he was suffused with magic. Max had taken Ecstasy once back in college, and it had felt something like this; it gave the world a sharpness, seeming to heighten his awareness and the clarity of his thoughts. That had been illusion, of course, an effect of the drug. But this . . . he felt the truth of it, saw clearly the connections that brought together so much of the information he'd already gathered. Mireault. Ray. The Tordu. Seddicus. The wards.

He knew what questions to ask, when the time came.

"Guess we have that in common," Lamar was saying. "You broke me up pretty good. Wasn't for a little mojo workin', I wouldn't be up and around. Too bad you don't have any of that going for you, huh, dead man?"

"Too bad," Max agreed numbly, barely paying attention.

"I think we rattled his brains," Gerard said.

"See, we're getting off topic," Lamar said, and his voice had a knife's edge. "I'm guessing the dead man thinks we're even. But Donte's dead. Fucker killed my brother." He kept his left arm straight out, pinning the steering wheel in place, and shifted his bulk to try to glance into the backseat. His fat neck wouldn't turn that far.

Still, nobody misunderstood that Lamar's next words were for Max only.

"Just want to be clear, fucker. Soon as Coco's done with you, I'm gonna kill you three, four times, keep you on the edge till I'm too tired to kill you anymore. And when I let you die for good, I'm gonna eat your heart and your liver. And whatever mojo you might've picked up down here's only gonna spice up the meal."

"Hope you choke on it," Max said.

Gerard poked him with the pistol barrel. Max winced.

"Careful," the Tordu gunman said.

"Why? Fat bastard just said he wasn't gonna start killing me until we got to Coco."

But Lamar had stopped paying attention. They were on a long, dark stretch of highway, but nothing moved in either direction. The night seemed to deepen as the car slowed.

Lamar took a right onto a narrow road, cypress trees forming an arched corridor overhead. The undergrowth infringed upon the road, and branches and leaves brushed the car as it swept past.

"Guess what?" Gerard said. "We're here."

Max blinked, eyes adjusting to the deeper darkness of the narrow road. The pavement went on for a hundred yards or so and then simply ran out, and they were on hard, rutted earth. Through gaps in the tangle of overgrowth on the right he caught glimpses of black water and swamp grass.

The back of his neck prickled with newborn fear.

The only thing he could think to do was strike back in kind.

"Good. I want to get this over with."

"You in a hurry to die?" Gerard asked.

"I'm not here to die. I'm here to give Coco a message from Seddicus."

Fat Boy Lamar flinched, jerked the wheel a little but then righted it, and kept his eyes front. The silent, nameless white woman turned toward Max at last, her hard features pale as alabaster in the dark.

"You lie," she said.

Max forced himself to smile. Unnerved, she faced front again. He liked that quite a bit.

But then Lamar turned carefully into an overgrown path cut into the brush on the side of the dirt road, and any thought of victory dissipated. It seemed petty to Max now. He'd soaked up magical static, just like Ray had instructed, but he had no idea how to use it. The map couldn't do anything for him, and he had no weapon.

To the right, they passed a large hump of earth that hadn't formed there naturally. He could see stone battlements on top, and then a whole wall of stone, and realized that the crumbling edifice had once been some kind of military fort. It reminded him of the one on Georges Island, out in Boston Harbor, and he guessed Civil War era.

Up ahead was the silhouette of a dark sedan, and beyond that nothing but water. Max did a quick calculation. They'd turned right, which meant south, so whatever inlet this was, it must weave out to the Gulf eventually. Or maybe not. What little he knew about New Orleans ended miles back. Out here he'd be lost, the highway his only touchstone.

Lamar rolled the Cadillac to a stop and killed the engine. The dashboard lights went dark, and Max could hear them all breathing. They didn't seem in any more of a rush than he was, now that he'd claimed affiliation with Seddicus. But this wasn't a swamp, and the flirty waitress had called Seddicus a swamp demon. The picture grew clearer for Max all the time. He began to understand the shape of things now, for all the good it would do him.

The woman opened her door first and Max followed suit. No reason to dawdle now. No delaying the inevitable.

He'd quite literally reached the end of the road.

The humid air caressed him as he walked toward Coco's dark sedan. That cocktail of fear and magic still roiled inside of him and Max felt jittery, as though he might jump out of his skin. More than once in his younger days he'd done what his friend John Cardiff had called "shrooms," and one of those times he'd sat for an hour just passing his hand back and forth in front of him, watching the movement blur and elongate like soap bubbles, vivid colors trailing from his fingers.

His whole body felt like that now. The effect upon him was so powerful that he found it astonishing none of the others seemed to notice. The stern woman walked ahead, but Lamar and gun-toting Gerard were behind him. Whatever magic or mojo he'd accumulated was invisible to them.

They marched him up to the sedan and he thought they would stop there, that Coco would be sitting in the car. But they kept going. There was no one behind the wheel. Exhausted but shuddery with manic energy, Max nearly stumbled walking down the grassy incline toward the water. Ahead of him the woman turned right, and he followed, Lamar shambling along behind him. They were single file and Gerard had the gun. With Lamar between them, Max could have made a break for it. But, really, where would he go?

The old Civil War fort rose up on the right, taller and more imposing now that they were right beside it, and to the left the moonlight painted dark water. The river had to be a hundred feet across, and in his imagination alligators cruised its banks.

Max wished he could call his sister one last time. She'd shown him nothing but love and tenderness, tried to look out for him, and he'd repay her now by washing up dead on some marshy shore. His heart ached for her. And for himself. He'd acquired an intimacy with magic and an unwelcome knowledge of some sort of vague afterlife. It might have comforted him once, to know that perhaps he could see Gabrielle again, but his memory of her was tainted by the things he had discovered. And this wasn't how it was meant to be. Ray had given him an impossible hope that he might speak into the past, deliver a message to her and interfere with her fate.

Instead, he'd come to his own end.

They arrived at an angle in the stone wall where the space between fort and water narrowed. Ahead of him, the woman went around the corner first. Max followed, but a moment later he heard a scuffle behind him and Lamar let out a little cry of fright. Turning, Max saw Gerard gripping Lamar by the arm, tugging him toward the wall of the fort, both of them staring at the edge of the footpath—at the water's edge—with eyes full of terror. Lamar had stumbled, but the two of them behaved as though he'd nearly fallen off a Himalayan precipice.

Gerard noticed Max looking at them and pointed the pistol at him. "Walk."

Max obeyed, tumblers clicking in his mind as a door opened there. Ahead of him, the silent woman walked carefully, back rigid. She didn't want to be here any more than her companions.

The path widened into a point of land protruding from the shadow of the fort. In the moonlight at the water's edge, a man stood waiting for them, a single silhouette. He cocked his head toward them and his profile confirmed what Max had already known. Coco smiled at him, handsome as ever. With his hair cut so close to his scalp and the carefully groomed goatee, he looked more like a lawyer than a killer, magician, serpent in the garden.

Coco wore expensive-looking trousers and a sheer white sleeveless undershirt. Max could picture the backseat of the man's car, where Coco's shirt would dangle neatly from a hanger. The image in his mind did not seem quite like something imagined; it was more as if he knew without seeing. Whatever work Coco was doing out here, he expected it to be messy or sweaty, or perhaps both.

And the man had been busy. Fat white candles burned

and flickered, set in a circle that would have been romantic in another setting. But Max doubted Coco had romance on his mind. Without a word, he crouched down, hands out, palms hovering over the soil, chanting whispered words that Max did not understand.

Coco picked up a small metal bucket, thrust his right hand into it, and drew out some kind of paste. Slight though the breeze was, it was sufficient to deliver to Max the awful stink from that bucket. Coco cupped a handful of stuff that reeked of piss and rot and burnt things, and, underneath those smells, of spices that ought to have made the odor less wretched but instead convulsed Max's stomach. He breathed through his nose and glanced at the bucket, wondering and yet not wishing to know.

As the silent woman led Max, Lamar, and Gerard to the edge of the circle of candles, Coco reached out with that filthy, disgusting hand and smeared it onto something that Max couldn't see.

Max realized that in the darkness, despite the moonlight, he'd somehow missed the other significant object there at the water's edge. The rock thrust up from the ground like a jagged, broken tooth. It tapered upward, and Max had the feeling it was like an iceberg, and that most of it extended far underground.

As he stared at it, the rock faded a little. Max narrowed his gaze and concentrated. His skin prickled with a frisson of magic, and the stone resolved itself in his vision once more.

Coco chanted his song, the tone rising and falling from whisper to guttural invocation. He reached into the bucket, cupped another handful of the filth, and smeared it across the face of the rock.

Smooth stone hissed and steamed, and shapes began to reveal themselves beneath the mucousy film. Coco traced the outlines, digging them more deeply, carving into the stone with his finger. Throughout this process, the rest of the Tordu observed in respectful silence, and Max watched in revulsion and fascination. Gerard kept the pistol more or less aimed in his direction, though his attention was on the man they'd all come to see.

Coco dipped his hand in the bucket again, but instead of coating the rock's face, he dropped the muck in a straight line from either side of the stone, marking off the tip of the shore that jutted into the river and creating a kind of boundary.

He crouched again, wiping his filthy hand off in the dirt. Then he paused, studying the work he'd done.

Max was tired of the silence. Tired of waiting.

"Ironic, isn't it?" he said.

Coco froze. The candles fluttered in the slight breeze, but none went out. He turned and looked at Max.

"You care to elaborate?"

Max glanced at the strange, almost hieroglyphic symbols etched in the stone, and then he met Coco's gaze. The man's eyes were wide and inquisitive, dancing with a kind of wild light that might have been a reflection of the candles, or something that came from within.

"The last time you almost lost a ward was also in a hurricane. And here you are, repairing one of them again . . . "

He trailed off because he saw Coco flinch, eyes narrowing. The light in them went out, and his gaze turned flat and reptilian.

"Well, that's what you're doing, isn't it?"

Gerard cocked the pistol. The silent woman took a step away from Max. Lamar said nothing, but Max could feel the tension in all of them. Coco only stared at him expectantly.

Max shrugged. "I'm betting this isn't the only one that got damaged by Katrina. Just seems ironic to me that you've spent all these years making them, hiding them, and protecting them from your enemies. And pretty successfully at that. But every time, it's Mother Nature who fucks with you."

Now Coco smiled, but those alligator eyes remained. "Yeah. What do you make of that?"

"I don't know. But maybe there's a message there. Natural versus unnatural, that sort of thing."

Coco shook his head, laughing softly. "You think you've got it all worked out."

"More than you know." Max delivered the line with such calmness and precision that it brought Coco up short. The Tordu man—a leader amongst them—paused and regarded him more closely. Then he shook his head again, but with less confidence this time.

"You don't know shit. Gabrielle told you nothing; that was part of the deal, part of the price. And whatever you think you learned since coming back to this city, you only see what New Orleans wants you to see. That's the way it's always been."

Coco looked at Lamar. "Give me the map."

The Fat Man had taken it from Max back in the ruin of the Ninth Ward, and now he tugged it out of his back pocket and handed it over.

Coco opened it in the moonlight, scanning it carefully. "This just some tourist map," he said, frowning, speaking in a patois that had been absent before, losing his cultured edge. "No juju here. Just shit."

He shot an accusatory glance at Lamar, who opened his hands in supplication.

"You said get the map, Coco. I got the map. He didn't have anythin' else on him."

Coco stared at it a moment longer and then began tearing the map into long strips, tossing them into the air. Some fluttered to the ground, others danced on the breeze and landed in the river, eddying away.

Max still felt that new sensitivity coursing through him, the strange clarity of thought, and with each new piece of information he felt doors opening in his head. *Gabrielle told you nothing,* Coco had said. *That was part of the deal, part of the price.* But the price for what? Ugly thoughts entered his mind, but he sealed them away for the moment, needing to focus.

"You're right, Mr. Corbett," Coco said, his tone polished again. "Ever since the bitch blew into town, I've been checking on the wards, each and every one. This is the sixth one I've found damaged or weakened, and I've repaired them all. But none of them broke. They're strong. Very strong."

Max silently agreed. The wards would have to be strong.

But the Tordu had not just forged them in the physical world. The rock had been invisible to him when he had arrived, and even now he doubted he would see it at all were it not for the static he'd picked up following the Map of Moments. Anyone else coming this way wouldn't even know the rock was there. Max figured some of the spells that had been cast would keep people away, make them avoid the place without even knowing why. The ward was both physical and mystical, and it would probably require a combination of both forces to destroy it.

"I've been out here three hours," Coco went on, "but you're wrong about one thing. I haven't finished repairing this one yet. There's one last element missing."

Max didn't want to ask, but heard his own voice say, "And what's that?"

Coco smiled. "You, Mr. Corbett. Whatever errand you're after, whatever map you're following, however you know what you know, all that matters is that you're asking the wrong questions. People see you're not afraid, and we can't have that. But just killing you would be wasteful. The wards get their strength from death, and from blood. So you and I are going to finish repairing this one together."

Max shivered. His skin felt terribly cold all of a sudden. A leaden sadness pressed down upon him, not despair so much as sorrow and exhaustion, and some of the static he'd felt crackling in him diminished.

He'd known they would kill him out here. They had made no secret of it. But the conversation was winding down. He didn't interest Coco anymore. The time had come.

Coco reached into a shoulder bag at his feet and withdrew a filleting knife. He let its sheath fall back into the bag and looked at Max. The moonlight glinted on the blade, a steel smile.

He stepped out of the circle of candles.

"Coco, wait," Lamar started. "I claim him."

"Lamar," the silent woman warned.

But Coco looked at Lamar, narrowed eyes. "For Donte?" Lamar nodded.

Coco considered a moment and then nodded in return. "All right. You can carve him. But we share the rest—"

"He fucking killed my brother!" Lamar snapped.

Coco shot the Fat Man a glance that cowed him. "We share the rest, as we always do."

Max blinked, glancing back and forth between them, but then he caught the way the silent woman stared at him, the eagerness in her eyes, and he remembered what Lamar had said in the car about eating his heart and liver. He thought about the way Joe Noone had died, and a vision of Corinne's bloody corpse flashed across his mind, body torn open, organs ripped out. More tumblers clicked over in his mind, more doors opened that he wished had remained closed.

"Oh, Jesus," Max whispered. And for a moment, the frisson he felt was entirely the prickle of fear, with no mystical static to interfere.

Coco grinned, eyes widening. "Oh, so there are some things you don't know."

Max had only one card to play. "Don't you want to hear the message I have for you?"

Coco sighed. "Lamar, Gerard, bring him into the circle."

"Wait," the woman said.

Coco looked at her. "Felicia?"

"In the car . . ." She faltered, glancing away from him, looking frightened. "He said he had a message from Seddicus."

Coco lowered his head, brows knitted, and then slowly lifted his gaze again. "Did he?"

He walked toward Max, filleting knife rising. That mad light danced in his eyes again, and this time it was clear that it was not a reflection. The candles were behind him. "What's your message, then?"

Max swallowed. He'd barely thought through what he might say, but there were some secrets of the Tordu he knew for certain.

"Seddicus says that if you repair the wards, you can also break them. He offers you a bargain. If you destroy one ward—if you let him in—he'll spare you when he comes for the others."

For a long moment, Coco stared at him, blank-faced, and Max had hope. The others seemed to hold their breath.

Then Coco laughed, and Max felt the others relax. And he knew that he was dead.

"You keep revealing what you don't know, Corbett," Coco said, his own grin matching the curving glint of the knife. "That isn't how it works. My fate has been sealed for more than a century. And Seddicus doesn't bargain. He only eats."

Coco stepped up to Max and pressed the filleting knife against the side of his throat. When he spoke again, it was in a whisper.

"You're a long way from home now. You come to a city you don't know, you really ought to take what it's offering, what it wants to show you, not try to look under the mask. Especially this city. 'Cos under *this* mask, it's *ours*."

He nodded at the candles. "Step into the circle."

Max held his breath. Gerard still held the gun, but in a second he was going to have to choose between that or helping Lamar restrain a screaming, panicked college professor. *And I will be screaming,* Max thought. He didn't want to die. Anyone who wouldn't scream for their life probably didn't value it very much.

He blinked, trembling. His skin prickled with that mystical energy, but fear raced through his veins, and his stomach churned. His perception had been altered, but he wondered if all along it had been adrenaline, and this was just what terror felt like. Perhaps he'd been a fool to ever perceive anything magical in it.

Open your mouth, he told himself. *Breathe.*

But he couldn't. The fear had closed his throat. No breathing, so perhaps he wouldn't scream after all. He'd just run, and if they caught up with him, he'd fight. Escape was too much to hope for, but he would rather force Gerard to shoot him than be pinned to the ground while Coco cut him open, carved him alive.

"I said, Step. Into. The circle." Coco pricked him with the point of the filleting knife, and Max felt a bead of blood run down the small of his back.

He stared at the ward, and then the circle in front of it.

Enough space separated each candle that he could have walked between them, but Max stepped over them as though they created a barrier to be hurdled, setting his left foot inside the circle. Coco and his knife were right behind him. Felicia watched, but the other two Tordu were moving to follow. Max might be cooperating now, but every one of them knew that wouldn't last. Lamar, at least, clearly relished the idea of having to hold Max down while Coco cut him open.

"Gerard, put away the gun," Coco said. "He's not going anywh—"

Max brought his right foot down inside the circle, and Coco's voice ceased, cut off in the middle of a word without even leaving an echo behind.

The air shifted. Max's skin prickled again, but differently. It felt as though a thousand butterflies had been at rest upon him, and now the brush of their wings was the last thing he felt before their absence exposed his skin to the elements.

The sensation overwhelmed him and he bent slightly, shaking. The stink of the paste from Coco's metal pail remained, and he pressed his hand over his nose and mouth to block it out. He stared at the candles at the edge of the circle.

Motion in his peripheral vision drew his gaze up to the bent, twisted figure now standing in front of the ward. Without turning toward Max, he dipped a clawed hand into a black metal pot and smeared it across the rock.

Mireault.

Max froze, taking a tiny breath, barely a sip of air.

Mireault stiffened. Slowly, eyes narrowed, the twisted little man turned. For a second, he peered at Max as though uncertain of what he might be looking at. Then he muttered something in French and returned to his work.

Beyond Mireault, the river looked different. Its banks were more ragged, more overgrown, cypress trees hanging out over the water. Taking long, slow, silent breaths, Max turned around, half expecting a poke from Coco's filleting knife. But deep down he knew that no such assault would be forthcoming.

When Max turned, Coco and the other Tordu were gone.

He trembled, glancing back at the busy Mireault, then looked again at the place where the Tordu had been an instant ago.

No, not had *been. They're still there.* You're *still there.*

Max stood now in the space between Moments. He felt flushed, his skin warm as though radiating heat from within. The hair on the back of his neck stood up, filled with static.

The stone and gray brick of the old military fort shone in the moonlight, clean and new. Its upper portions were ragged, but not because the fort lay in ruins. Though all work had ceased for the night, the place was still being built. Max turned once more toward Mireault, mind racing, wondering how this was possible.

This can't be one of the places Ray had in mind. It's beyond the edge. We're off the map. This wasn't the Seventh Moment, yet here he was. Whatever power Coco had put into this spot, whatever magic Mireault had invested the ward with over the previous two centuries, it resonated. Max was tuned in, humming along on the frequency of New Orleans' magical history.

What it meant—what might happen at other wards, or other places of magical power in New Orleans, now that his whole body was suffused with that static—he wasn't sure. He'd been following the map according to Ray's plan, but now it really struck him just how little he knew about the magic, and what other side effects it might have.

Stop, he told himself. *Worry about this shit later.*

Frantic, he glanced around again, thoughts falling into place, a surreal calm descending upon him. Tumblers clicked. Doors opened. Would the Moment pass? How long until it did, and he slipped back into the flow of 2005 to let Coco carve out his organs? No telling. But he looked at Mireault again, carving symbols into solid stone with his crooked finger, and thought that when Mireault finished, this Moment would be over.

He stared at the ward. At the river. And he smiled. At the Beauregard-Keyes House, he'd gone in the front door with the Tordu right behind him, but in the midst of the Moment he'd moved from the front of the house to the back. From the Tordu's perspective, he had stepped through the front door and out the back in the blink of an eye. Several times now, as he'd borne witness to the past, he had wondered how far he could wander inside a Moment.

It was time to find out.

"Catch me if you can, fuckers," Max whispered.

Mireault whipped around, faster than it seemed he ought to be able to move that contorted body. He scanned the night and his eyes narrowed, staring right at Max.

"Quelle êtes-vous?"

Max ran at him. Mireault's lips peeled back in a savage sneer and he raised his gnarled hands with their hooked fingers, muttering some kind of incantation under his breath. Max didn't slow. He raced past Mireault, past the ward, and dived into the river, swimming as hard as he could.

After four strokes, he kicked off his shoes. He heard a shout behind him but did not slow until he'd gotten three quarters of the way across. When he risked a glance back, Mireault had returned to the task of preparing the ward. It wouldn't be finished until he had sacrificed a life within that circle, but the gnarled man worked feverishly now, as though whatever he'd seen had spooked even him.

The river's current was lazy, and Max reached the other side in no time. Breathing hard, he stood and slogged to the bank, moving into the trees. He turned to peer across the water at Mireault working in the moonlight. The current had brought him a little off course, and the angle gave him a clear view of Mireault. Catching his breath, he watched for a minute or two.

When Mireault stepped back from the ward and began to dab the ground beside the stone with the revolting concoction, Max knew that Mireault had concluded his preparations. All that remained was the sacrifice, the blood, the fucking cannibalism.

Max shuddered, feeling the wind shift and the humidity pounce as though it had been stalking him all along. He knew before he saw it start to happen. For a beat he saw the past and present together, as if perceiving 19th-century Mireault with one eye, and 2005 Coco and his Tordu posse with the other. And then there was only the present, and the four people standing in the candlelit circle at the river's edge.

"What the fuck?" Lamar shouted, looking around.

Gerard swung the gun in quick arcs, searching. Coco stormed into the circle, crouched, and ran his hands through the grass, reached out and touched the ward, then stood and looked around, eyes wide with astonishment. It was almost comical.

Felicia had a hand over her mouth, staring at the place where Max had been only a moment before.

"Where did he go?" Gerard snapped. "Where the hell did he go, Coco?"

"How did he do that?" Lamar demanded. "What kind of mojo is *that* shit?"

"Coco!" Gerard shouted. "Where the hell——"

Enraged, Coco spun on him. "I don't know!"

Max should have fled, but their confusion amused him. He wanted to savor it as a small shred of vengeance. The three Tordu men flapped and squawked like fools. But their antics drew his focus, and he didn't pay enough attention to Felicia. So when she pointed across the river and shouted, it caught him by surprise.

"There!" she said. "He's right there."

He'd thought the tangle of overgrowth dark enough to hide him. But she had seen, and he wished she had remained the silent woman forever.

Gerard swung the pistol up and squeezed off a shot. It snapped through the trees seven or eight feet from where Max crouched, echo rolling along the river. But Lamar had no patience. He knew that Gerard had little hope of hitting his target.

Max had crushed his brother's legs, killing the man.

Lamar threw back his head and let loose a howl of primal rage, and then ran for the river. Felicia called for him to stop. Coco even reached for him, grabbing Lamar's sweaty arm, but could not hold on. Lamar tore free and thundered past, knocking over a couple of candles as he hurled himself down the bank and into the water.

Right past the ward.

"You got nowhere to run, dead man!" Lamar screamed as he first waded, then started to swim. "Where you gonna go?"

He continued with a stream of profanity and promises of pain, and all the while, Coco and Gerard and Felicia were shouting, trying to make him hear them. Lamar could not see the way the woman gestured for him to return to the riverbank, nor the way Coco shook his head as though the sad matter had already concluded.

"You dumb asshole!" Gerard screamed, his voice rising an octave.

Nothing seemed to get through to Lamar. In fact, when the moment came that he faltered, standing man-tits deep in the river, and looked around in utter bafflement at the result of his blind rage, it was clear the revelation had come from somewhere deep inside his primitive brain. Their words hadn't reached him, but somehow, he had come to his senses.

Max watched from in amongst the trees as Lamar glanced around at the dark water, head moving in quick jerks as though every ripple on the surface threatened him.

"Oh, Mama," he said. And though it must have been only a whisper, Max could hear it fine.

The giant black Buddha-man began to retreat, shambling back toward the riverbank, and the ward that marked the outer edge of the city Mireault had claimed so long ago. Gerard and Felicia exhorted him to hurry, but both kept well back from the ward that separated Tordu territory from the rest of the world.

Coco said nothing. When Max looked over, he found the Tordu leader staring at him. Though the trees partially hid him, he knew that Coco saw him very well. That handsome face was no longer alarmed, but resigned.

No splash of water revealed the demon's presence. The river did not even part to flow around it.

But Lamar started to scream. Unseen hands plucked him out of the river, held him dripping in the moonlight, and turned him upside down. He hung there for a second, and then a wet tearing noise filled the air as Lamar was ripped apart.

Gerard shrieked.

Pieces of Lamar began to vanish as though swallowed by the air.

Coco screamed at Gerard, slapped his face. "Hurry! The ward's weak. If it senses the weakness, it could try to get through!"

Max stared in confusion, unsure what Coco had in mind. What could he do? The ritual had not been completed.

Gerard and Coco fell on Felicia. They dragged her sobbing into the circle and the filleting knife rose and fell, reflecting moon- and candlelight. They would be cutting pieces of her free now—her heart, her liver, her kidneys. They would have to complete the ritual. In Max's place, it was Felicia who would be eaten alive.

Felicia had become the silent woman forever.

As the last shreds of Lamar vanished above the river, Max turned at last and began to flee through the trees, working his way back toward the road.

chapter

15

The battered Ford pickup rattled along Chef Menteur Highway, slowly disintegrating. Max sat in the rear of the truck staring at the rust-eaten floor of the flatbed, where metal flakes sifted down through holes and shook and jittered like sand. He thought of trips home from the beach with his dad at the wheel of Mom's station wagon, Max and his sister in the backseat, and the way the drying sand flaked from their feet and legs and accumulated on the floormats, a thousand little grains, jumping and sifting with every bump in the road.

That had been long ago and far away. God, how he wished he could go back.

Humid or not, it was November, and with the wind whipping around his wet clothes, Max shivered and huddled down behind the pickup's cab. He didn't say a word, nor had he complained when the driver had balked about letting him sit up front. It wasn't like his wet jeans were going to do much damage to the upholstery of the ancient pickup, but how could he argue? The guy had stopped for a stranger hitchhiking on a lonely stretch of highway, sopping wet and with no shoes on . . .

And where were his shoes now—or more accurately, when were they? How could his clothes be saturated by water from the 19th century?

It seemed that with each Moment he experienced, he was there more and more.

A few cars had passed him by before the graying, bearded pickup driver stopped, and Max felt nothing but gratitude.

They drove past warehouses and shipping docks on the canal that ran along the north side of Chef Menteur Highway. Eighteen-wheelers sat in parking lots, silent monoliths, and small cargo ships were moored at the docks. Not a lot of fishing boats up this way. The occasional gas station or liquor store broke up the landscape, and once or twice a mile, a lonely house. They'd rolled right on past a wealthy suburban development that seemed remarkably out of place, and then across the bridge that spanned Chef Menteur Pass, and now Max's jeans and shirt were stiffening as they began to dry.

With every mile he moved away from the city, the pull of New Orleans grew stronger. He fought the urge to tell the driver to pull over so he could turn back. It was barely past midnight, but he felt the seconds hurrying past. Max needed a place to stop for a few moments, to think and take a breath, but he knew he would have to return to New Orleans, and quickly.

Outside of the wards that marked their territory, the Tordu could not follow him, but they would never let him go. No one he loved would be safe if he left New Orleans behind.

If there was a way to survive, he wouldn't find it anywhere else but here.

The pickup began to slow, and the driver turned into the half-full parking lot of a squat little place with neon beer emblems in the windows. A sign at the edge of the lot announced it as Mattie's All-Night Crab Shack. The post leaned to one side, maybe nudged by an errant car bumper.

A pair of thirtyish women laughed about something as they walked toward the door. One of them, an attractive brunette with librarian glasses, gave Max a curious look as the pickup slid into a parking spot, but then lost interest.

The driver popped his door and stepped out, slamming the door behind him. The impact made the rust flecks in the truck bed sift with a sandpaper rasp.

"This'll do ya," the driver said.

Clothes plastered to him, Max climbed stiffly from the back of the pickup and dropped to the pavement. He'd shed his wet socks back in the woods, and the tar still held some of the warmth of the day. It felt good.

"You think it's okay for me to go in there like this?"

The driver smiled, blue eyes bright in the light from the

restaurant. "Mattie's has seen worse. 'Sides, you had a rough night already. Nobody gonna give you a hard time now. Least, not if you come in with me. Might be Mattie can fix you up with something for your feet."

Max cocked his head. "Thanks. But why are you bothering?"

The man laughed, stroking his graying beard. "I didn't say it wouldn't cost you nothin'. For my part, you can buy me a beer if you still got a wallet in them pants."

Max patted his back pocket, though he'd already checked and knew his wallet was there. The cash would be soaked, but the credit cards ought to still work. He'd given the driver one fat lie on the side of the road—said he'd been out fishing in a rented boat and hit a rock, holed the hull, nearly drowned, and had had to kick his shoes off in the water. It sounded like bullshit even to him, and he had no idea what the driver thought had really happened. But all that mattered was the guy had picked him up.

"Still got it," Max assured him. "And I'll go you one better. If you're hungry, I'll pick up the tab."

"That's a deal," the man said, pointing at him. He thrust out his hand. "Archie Baldwin."

They shook.

"Max Corbett."

"All right, Mr. Corbett. You follow me."

Archie led him inside. If he was troubled by the sign on the door that said NO SHIRT NO SHOES NO SERVICE, he didn't show it. The place came alive the moment the door swung open, laughter and clinking glasses and the low susurrus of human voices. Max's stomach purred at the smells of frying seafood and cooking spices. Music played low from hidden speakers, and colored lights and mirrors behind the bar gave the place a surprising glitter. Mattie's All-Night Crab Shack wasn't the shithole dive he'd been expecting, and it made him feel even more out of place.

A waitress with red hair and a spray of freckles across her cheeks and nose whooped when they came in and made a beeline for Archie.

"Hey, honey, what you doin' out here tonight?" she asked, giving him a hug.

"Oh, you know, Beth. Just wanted to see your pretty face. Plus, my friend here ain't never had Mattie's crab cakes, and I told him he can't go home until he's had a taste."

Beth cocked a hip, studying Max up and down. "What happen to you, baby?"

Max shrugged. "Fell in the river."

"Now, come on, darlin'. Max's had a hard day. Don't be making him feel even stupider than he already does."

"All right, all right," Beth said, smiling up at Artie, eyes sparking. He might be twenty years her senior, but Max could see she wasn't just flirting. He charmed her. "But you know he can't come in here in his bare feet like that. After the way Mattie's done the place over, it's a class joint."

Artie smiled. "Come on, now. Nobody's gonna notice if you hustle us into one of them booths by the bar." He gestured. "Anyway, I was hopin' Mattie could open the bait shop. You know she sells them Timberlands or whatever they are in there, the waterproof boots. Max could buy a pair, maybe a sweatshirt or something."

Max was impressed. Artie might drive a rattletrap, but

there was nothing rusty about his brain. The guy had it all worked out. Max had noticed the extension on the side of the building but hadn't paid any attention to the sign there, because the windows were dark and the place looked locked up tight. If they sold boots and sweatshirts, it sounded more like a full-service fishing supply store than a bait shop.

Beth dashed his hopes with a shake of her head. "I'm sorry, honey, but Mattie don't work this late at night. And you know she don't let Jasper have a key to the place."

She looked at Max, and brightened a little. "We can fix you up with a dry shirt, though. Got Mattie's Crab Shack T-shirts behind the bar, only twelve dollars. Sweatshirts are twenty-five. Got caps, too, but that won't help much."

Max smiled. Dry clothes of any sort sounded good. "No pants or shoes with the Mattie's Crab Shack logo on 'em, huh?"

Beth laughed. "Not much call, sorry to say. Used to carry aprons, but they didn't sell."

She hooked her arm through Artie's and guided them both to a booth across from the bar. They passed a few tables where people were eating and drinking, and though several people tossed Max curious looks, nobody mentioned his bare feet.

"You don't happen to sell maps, do you?" Max asked as he slid into the booth.

Both Beth and Artie looked at him, obviously wondering what he was really up to.

"Sorry," Beth said. "In the bait shop, yeah, but not here in the shack."

Disappointed, trying to figure out how he could work out the location of the next Moment, Max forced a smile.

"No worries. Thanks."

Beth slipped them menus. "You boys figure out what you want, and I'll see what I can dig up." She looked at Max. "You a large?"

"I'll take extra large if you've got them. The T-shirt and the sweatshirt both. And two of whatever beer Artie wants—"

"Corona," the man chimed in.

Max nodded. "Corona's fine."

Beth strutted away, promising two guys at the next booth that she'd check on their food. Artie and Max sat together and silently perused the menu for a couple of minutes, but Max spotted what he wanted pretty much immediately. Mattie's menu called them Creole Crab Cakes, and that sounded fantastic to him.

"You're not going to ask, huh?" Max said at last.

Artie shrugged. "You already told me a story. Figured the details were none of my business."

Max noticed the wording—*you already told me a story.* Not the truth, in other words.

"I appreciate that."

Artie's expression grew serious. "We learned a lot of lessons down here not long ago. People reach out for a hand, you got to help them up. Do what you can. We're all in this together, and we can't expect the authorities to do a damn thing for us. We got to do for ourselves, and for each other."

"It's a hard lesson to learn," Max said. "But it means a lot. I won't forget."

"See you don't," Artie said.

As Beth reappeared, so did Artie's smile. She delivered their Coronas, then went behind the bar and returned with a blue T-shirt and a pale red sweatshirt, both neatly folded, and promised to be right back. Hurrying away, she vanished into the kitchen.

Good as her word, she came back less than a minute later with two dishes for the guys at the next booth, then whipped out her order pad and stood with her pencil poised.

"Okay, shoot."

"Crab cakes and dirty rice," Artie said.

Max pointed at him. "Times two."

"You boys make it easy," Beth said, gliding away again.

Max sat back, sinking into the cushioned seat of the booth, and tipped back the bottle of Corona. No one had asked if he wanted a glass, but he didn't mind at all. The bottle was cold and the beer quenched his thirst.

Artie took a couple of pulls from his own beer. Max leaned forward and clinked the bottles together.

"Thank you, Artie. Samaritan in a pickup truck."

Behind his beard, Artie's grin made him look like Santa. "I am my brother's keeper."

Max took another sip, then slid out of the booth. "And now it's my turn to disappear."

He took the T-shirt and sweatshirt off the table and headed for the bathroom. The fluorescent lights within were grimly unforgiving, giving the tiled room the feel of a morgue. Max tried to avoid looking too closely at the floor, which felt sticky underfoot. Walking through the woods he'd gotten his feet muddy and scratched, and the instep of his left foot had a little slice in it. But he was more worried about it getting infected standing on the bathroom floor than from anything he'd stepped in outside in the woods. Dirty was one thing, but filthy was another entirely.

Balancing first on one foot and then the other, Max washed his feet in the sink, grateful that no one came in during the operation. He stripped off his shirt and threw it in the trash, washed his face delicately around the cut, and then put on the soft, dry T-shirt and sweatshirt, admiring their identical Mattie's Crab Shack logos.

Hating the way his underpants chafed and clung, he was tempted to go into a stall and strip them off, leaving just his stiff but drying jeans. But that would have meant walking barefoot into the stall. Treading on twelve brands of piss did not appeal to him, and he decided to live with the discomfort.

His stomach rumbled again and he realized how ravenous he was. The rest of his beer was calling to him, too, so he ran fingers through his hair and went out the door, returning to his booth.

By the time he got there, Artie had started on his second beer. On the floor just beside Max's seat were a pair of grimy, grease-and-paint-spotted men's work boots with frayed laces and deeper creases than his grandfather's forehead.

Max stared stupidly down at the boots. "I don't get it. The shoe fairy came by?"

"Drink your beer," Artie said.

Max slid into the booth. "So?"

"Beth told the guys in the kitchen about the poor S.O.B. who lost his shoes. I guess the fry cook's some kinda snappy dresser, keeps these in back for when he works and changes into street shoes when he goes home."

"So he was just wearing them?"

Artie tipped back his beer. Max noticed a lime floating in the bottle and envied him.

"You gonna get picky now, man with no shoes? Only, the cook ain't as sweet as Beth. He's takin' advantage of the situation."

"How's that?" Max asked.

Artie smiled. "He wants fifty bucks for the boots."

Max laughed. "You've gotta be shitting me."

But Artie wasn't. Max sighed, ran a hand over his face, and then looked down at the boots. He swung sideways in the booth and lined one up next to his right foot. They were going to be a couple of sizes too large, but at least he couldn't smell them from three feet up.

He pushed his bare feet in, upper lip curling at the touch of damp leather and rubber. The cook had sweaty feet.

"Too bad the sock fairy couldn't have dropped by, too."

"I recommend you keep drinking. Good advice on the best and worst of days."

Max took that advice and tipped back his beer, trying not to think about his feet, the sweaty cook, or the tight hunger in his stomach.

When he put the bottle down, he noticed the condensation ring that had appeared on the paper place mat. The mat had that familiar happy crab logo and a picture of what the place must look like in the daytime, plus the history of

Mattie's All-Night Crab Shack. But his focus was on that damp circle. Up in Maine, he'd been to plenty of dives where the place mats had maps of the local area on them, maybe with little box advertisements around the perimeter.

Too bad they don't use those sort here, he thought.

Then he frowned, staring at the circle. He pressed the bottle partway down, making a semi-circle that looked roughly similar to the arc the Mississippi made as it snaked past the French Quarter. He could picture it in his mind. In fact, staring at that paper, he came to realize that he'd looked at the city map so often in the past few days that he could picture the basic outline of New Orleans in his head; the main thoroughfares, the river, the parks, the neighborhoods. Not many individual streets, but a general sketch.

"What's the matter with you, Max?"

As he glanced up at Artie, Beth arrived with their crab cakes. The smell practically had him salivating, but he needed to keep his mind clear another minute.

"Thanks for all your help," he told the waitress. "Can I put an extra fifty on my credit card for the cook? Call it a tip, for the boots."

"That'd be fine, darlin'."

Artie dug in the second his plate hit the table.

"Do you have a pen I could borrow?" Max asked.

Beth pulled one from her apron and laid it on the table. "Anything else I can get you boys?"

Max didn't even reply. He slid his plate aside, turned over the place mat, and stared at the drying marks from his beer bottle, trying to keep the map image in his mind. He started to sketch with the pen, marring the plain white paper, drawing in the turn of the Mississippi, the spokes of Esplanade and Canal and other streets that jutted off from it, the rough shapes of Treme and the Quarter, Gentilly and the Garden District, and half a dozen others.

Artie and Beth only watched, and in their silence Max became aware that he wasn't really the one creating the map on the back of that place mat. It had started out that way, with an image in his mind, but the details were too fine, the distances too exact, to ever have been drawn by him. He could barely draw stick figures in correct proportion, and would have made a shitty cartographer.

Max wasn't drawing. The map was in him, whenever he wanted it. Whenever he *needed* it. Like now.

"I guess we've got everything we need," Artie said, more than a little mystified.

Max looked up in time to see Beth giving Artie a peculiar look, a stay-away-from-this-flake sort of look, then she headed back toward the kitchen.

But he only let his gaze wander from the map for a few seconds, and then his right hand moved again, adding detail, and moving out toward the limits of what he now understood was Tordu territory.

At last he took a breath.

"Max," Artie said. And then again, "Max."

"Huh? Yeah, sorry. Just a little carried away. It's . . . kind of a hobby of mine."

Artie's smile had the same quality as that look Beth had given him. "Okay. But aren't you hungry, man? You don't want those crab cakes, they're callin' to me."

"No, no, I'm starved. But get more if you like."

Artie shrugged. "I'm good. Maybe another beer, though."

Max's attention returned to the map. He couldn't have looked away now if he tried, not while the small box gradually appeared with an arrow pointing to an intersection in Gentilly.

The Seventh Moment:
The Hollow Man Tempts
The Oracle's Faithless Heir
She Succumbs

"The Hollow Man?" Max whispered to himself, trying to interpret the riddle.

"What's that?" Artie asked.

Idly, Max cut into a crab cake with his fork and started to eat. Chewing, he pointed with his fork at the map.

"Do you know this part of New Orleans?" Max asked. "Could you figure out where this was, even without the street names?"

Artie reached out and turned the small map toward him. He shook his head in amazement. "Pretty damn good work for a hobby, son. Might not be able to find the right corner, but in the ballpark for sure, if the map's accurate."

"It is," Max said. He knew it was. The details hadn't come from him; they'd been given *to* him by old Ray and that stone bottle drink. He looked over at Artie. "Any way I can persuade you to run me back into the city? Dinner and drinks are already on me, but I'll get cash from a money machine if you can find one."

Artie frowned. "It ain't like that, son. I told you. We're all in it together. Course, gas isn't cheap, and I've always wanted one of them Maggie's Crab Shack T-shirts."

"Take your pick," Max said. "On me. Only one condition, though."

Artie didn't seem to like the idea of conditions. "What's that?"

"This time, I get to ride up front."

The wards would have been placed where they could be hidden, and where they would have the most power. The one on the river beside that old fort seemed to have been chosen because it put up a barrier on the narrow strip of land that ran between Lake Pontchartrain and the Gulf. Maybe the water made a natural boundary, but after what had happened to Lamar, Max doubted that.

And so, as Artie's rusty Ford pickup rolled along Chef Menteur Highway back toward New Orleans, Max could not pinpoint the exact moment when he passed back into the realm of Mireault's dark influence. Several times he shivered a little. And once he slid lower in the seat, wondering if the Tordu would be watching for him.

That seemed unlikely. Anyone with half a brain would have been heading back to Boston by now, and since the last glimpse the Tordu had of Max had been of him rabbiting into the woods, Coco probably thought they'd seen the last of him. So no, they probably weren't expecting him to return.

But maybe they'll feel *me,* he thought, studying the shadows beneath the trees along the side of the road. That seemed plausible enough to give him the shivers. They had managed to find him several times in the city. Some of those occasions could be explained away as whispers, nervous phone calls from frightened people who'd heard him asking around about Coco. But a couple of times it had certainly felt as though they were tracking him, could sense him. Once, that would have seemed far-fetched, but not now.

From the moment he had jumped into the truck with Artie and started back, the clock had been ticking.

"You're awful quiet," Artie said.

Max glanced at him, teeth rattling as the Ford juddered along the road on long-dead shock absorbers. "Contemplating the glories of Mattie's crab cakes."

Artie didn't smile. "You don't want to talk about it, okay. But I been real good about not askin' questions, and now I'm gonna dump you off in the middle of a neighborhood that's still halfway abandoned since Katrina came knockin'. So you can't blame me for wonderin'."

"I don't blame you."

"That's good. But you're still too quiet. Maybe you need some help, Max. I'm not necessarily offerin'. I'd have to hear what kind of trouble you're in before I decided it's worth putting my own ass on the line. But . . ."

Max looked out through the windshield and saw the edges of the city ahead, dark silhouettes of buildings, some of them illuminated but others just silent shadows.

For the first time, it occurred to him that he'd put Artie

in danger, that he could get his Good Samaritan killed, and he didn't like that idea one bit.

"I used to live here," Max said, surprising himself by speaking. "I came back to New Orleans for the funeral of an old girlfriend."

Artie's eyes narrowed and he gave a slow nod. It wasn't sympathy so much as empathy. This made sense to him.

"I ran into some trouble with another guy she used to see."

"There you go." Artie smiled. "And where I'm dumpin' you? You gonna need any help?"

Max didn't hesitate. "I'll be all right. I appreciate it. I mean, you don't know me from Adam and here you're coming to my rescue—"

"Hey, I got beers and some damn fine crab cakes out of it."

The smile this brought to Max's face was entirely genuine. "And a T-shirt, don't forget that." The Mattie's Crab Shack shirt he'd bought for Artie lay folded up in the tight space behind the driver's seat. "Seriously, I'm good. I just need to take care of some unfinished business and then I'm putting the Big Easy behind me."

Artie sniffed. "The Big Easy. I got a feelin' nobody's gonna be callin' it that anymore."

They fell quiet again. Max watched as the outskirts of New Orleans evolved into neighborhoods of houses and bars, restaurants and stores. A fish market on one corner remained open, despite the lateness of the hour. A man in baggy shorts and a pink, hooded jacket more suited to a teenaged girl leaned against the metal grated windows at the front of a liquor store.

Down a side street, a dozen or more ghosts danced half-naked around a dull orange fire.

Max blinked, twisted around to get a better look, staring down the street. The men and women were both topless, their skin an array of brown hues but also transparent. The fire seemed pale and cold and very far away.

"What?" Artie asked.

The street was behind them, and though Max still looked back, all he could see now were the buildings at the corner.

"What's wrong?"

Max shook his head, righting himself in his seat. "Nothing. Sorry. Just thought that might be the corner we wanted."

"Nah. We got a way to go yet. Judgin' by the map you drew, you want to be up past Elysian Fields, a little south of Mirabeau Avenue. You sure about that map?"

"Very."

"All right, then."

Artie took a right, threading through a neighborhood where the tide mark from Katrina lingered like a scar on most of the buildings, then turned left. Max peered at every house, down every street and alley. He ought to have been prepared; when Coco had forced him into the ritual circle in front of the ward, he had slipped into a Moment that wasn't on the map. He felt certain he'd just glimpsed another. The static he'd accumulated spilled off of him now, filled him so much that his altered perceptions were seeing more than just what Ray had intended.

He took a breath, tried to focus. The neighborhood

improved dramatically as they drove, but Katrina hadn't chosen her victims by their social status. Roofs had caved in. Chimneys had collapsed. One house was missing half its second floor. Blue tarps were everywhere, though in the moonlight they seemed closer to black. Gentilly had been hit hard, but already the repairs had begun, and that was the difference between this place and some of the others Max had been through. Here, there were homes left to repair.

Movement in his peripheral vision caught his eye, and he glanced up just in time to see a young boy throw himself from a third-story window. Max's breath hitched and he reached for the dash to brace himself, nearly screaming at Artie to stop.

The phantasm vanished halfway to the ground.

"I'm startin' to think maybe it ain't healthy for you to be hanging out down here. You're spooking me a little, son. Maybe there're some meds you supposed to be takin' and forgot?"

Max's face felt cold and he could only imagine how pale he must have been. He smiled and shook his head. "I'm good."

"So you keep sayin', but that don't make it true."

Unable to stop himself, Max shot Artie a dark look. For a guy who had made noise about not prying into other people's business, about just helping, no questions asked, he certainly seemed to have gotten more comfortable with both questions and opinions.

Artie got the message. He raised his eyebrows with a sniff, as if to say *Ain't that a fine thing, try to help a guy out and that's the thanks you get.* But he didn't say anything else.

A few more blocks and Artie pulled over to consult the map Max had drawn. He scratched his beard again, peered out through the windshield, then put the map aside. Another couple of turns and he pulled over again, but this time he threw the truck into park and looked over at Max.

"Here you go, partner. Far as I can tell, this is where you want to be. Look familiar?"

Max looked around at the houses. Only a few had lights burning inside. The rest of the buildings on the block were dark, and two had sustained massive wind damage.

"Nope. But it will."

He popped the door, which opened with a shriek of rusty metal, stepped out with his hand-drawn map in his hand, then peered back in at Artie.

"Look, you really saved my ass tonight. I'm grateful for that. I'm sorry if I—"

"Don't mention it. None of my business, anyway. Good luck to you, Max. I hope you find what you're lookin' for."

Max nodded. That might be a blessing or a curse, but he knew Artie meant well. "You have a good night."

Artie hesitated one last second; it was clear he didn't like the idea of dropping Max off out here. But then he gave a small wave before driving away, leaving Max alone on a Gentilly street without a clue where he was supposed to go next.

If he'd thought about it, he could have asked Artie to stop so he could buy a tourist map, but it was too late now. He could feel time constricting, funneling down into this instant. For once, the Moment he was in seemed just as vital as the ones New Orleans had left behind.

Studying each house on the block, he started walking along the street. He looked at the map in the moonlight, turning around and around, but kept going in the same direction because that felt right. Just as, after a few minutes, he knew he had gone too far, and turned around.

Far off, he could hear cars going by. In one house a TV had been turned up loud enough to deafen. But no headlights turned down the narrow, residential street, and for that he was glad. Paranoia held him in its grip. At the approach of any car, he was liable to run for cover, fearing that Coco and his cronies had found him again.

Frustrated, Max stepped up onto the scruffy, postage stamp–sized yard of a little house. A fallen tree had been cleared off the road, waiting to be cut up and taken away. There were branches and scraps of debris scattered everywhere. Max picked up a twig and tried digging into the soil at the edge of the yard, sketching lines to represent the street he was on and the few blocks around it. But whatever had inspired him in Mattie's Crab Shack had abandoned him for the moment.

He started back the way he'd come, thinking he'd have to try each house individually. He could start with the ruined ones and hope that he would not have to disturb those with their lights on. A strange man showing up after dark in a crab-logo sweatshirt and filthy boots two sizes too big for him? He could get shot. At the very least they'd call the police, and that he could not afford.

One side of a duplex ahead had its lights on, and Max started to cross the street, trying not to draw attention. Something on the front walk caught his eye and he paused, then cut back toward the two-family. He glanced at the house to confirm he was unobserved, and crouched down, reaching out to pick up a piece of pale chalk. Half a dozen pieces in various pastels had been left scattered about. On the walk were crude renderings he recognized as Sponge-Bob SquarePants and some of the other characters from that show.

With the piece of chalk in hand, he moved on down the street to a spot as distant from any of the lighted windows as he could get without actually moving to another block. Dropping to his knees, feet sliding inside the big work boots, he began to draw, outlining the street he was on and several blocks in each direction.

When the box appeared, and the words describing the Seventh Moment, they were in pale yellow chalk, and there could be no mistaking which house the arrow pointed at.

The little one, with the downed tree lying half across its yard.

Max steeled himself but did not hesitate. The time for hesitation had passed. Retracing his steps, he returned to the little house with its bay window and the single gable above the front door. Some of the roof had been stripped away and the bay window shattered. Unlike some of the other darkened houses, no one had bothered to board this one up.

An icy prickle went down the back of his spine. The

magic crackling that had suffused him all afternoon and night had receded but not departed. He looked around once more, waiting for menacing figures to emerge from the shadows or for headlights to snap on, engines to rev, enemies to appear. And when none of these things happened, he walked quickly and quietly to the front door.

Sometimes when he slept wrong, maybe with his arm trapped underneath him, he'd wake up with a sensation like a million tiny needles gently tapping his skin. As a boy, his father had referred to this as his arm having fallen asleep. But Max remembered his mother's phrase best. She'd always called that feeling "pins and needles."

He had it now, over every inch of his body.

As he reached for the door, the temperature changed. The night turned sweltering, the heat beating down on him, the air so thick with dampness that he could barely breathe. He remembered many nights such as this, though he'd trained himself to forget.

Summer in New Orleans.

The bay window was no longer shattered. He didn't need to glance over his shoulder to see that the tree was still standing. But other than that, the place looked much the same. Whatever year this was, it had to be recently.

Max paused with his hand on the door, troubled. What year *was* it? Every Moment had been clearly dated, except for this one. The place mat upon which he'd drawn a map sat folded in his back pocket and now, knowing he had to enter the house but also curious and unsettled, he took it out and unfolded it.

There were the words again, just as they'd been before.

The Seventh Moment:
The Hollow Man Tempts
The Oracle's Faithless Heir
She Succumbs

Only something had changed. There had been no date when he looked before, but it was there now, at the bottom of the message. And as he looked at the date, and it took root in his mind, he understood that the magic he had been accumulating was not his own, and never had been. The Map of Moments had led him where he needed to be, but it did not serve Max Corbett. The map served the man who had given it to him, along with that little stone bottle to drink from. The date in which he now stood, when the Seventh Moment took place, had been withheld from him until now.

This was the worst night of his life.

The night he'd walked in on Gabrielle and Joe Noone, in the attic of the house over in Lakeview.

Jaw clenched, Max let the place mat flutter from his hand, gripped the doorknob, and turned it. To others it might have been locked, but not to him. The door swung open. Even as he stepped inside he heard the chanting, its cadence now familiar to him, its intent making him recoil.

He forced himself on, down a short corridor, through the kitchen, and into a kind of den at the rear of the house, where the lights were off and the shades were drawn, and where a circle of candles provided all the light he would ever need.

Max had seen Gabrielle in candlelight before, and when he glimpsed her now, in silhouette, he could not breathe for the tears that began to choke him. For Gabrielle was crying as well, shaking her head as Coco pressed the knife into her hand and the others continued to chant.

"You have to, girl," Coco said. "You know you do." The sincerity in his eyes was hideous and painful to watch. He cared for her. He meant her well. "You don't have his strength, and Mireault won't hesitate to kill you. You're with us, or you're alone."

"I can't!" Gabrielle wailed, her anguish stabbing at Max.

Coco's eyes flashed with anger and his lips tightened in a grim line. "You swore to me, girl! You made a promise. I let the teacher go and you don't fight anymore. I even let you pick the one to substitute for him. You go back on your word now, and when Mireault comes for you, I'll be the one to hold you down."

Gabrielle stared at the gagged figure on the floor, in the midst of that circle. He squirmed, but the other Tordu gathered for the ritual held him tightly. She turned to Coco, eyes imploring, but his gaze had gone flat and merciless. Gabrielle squeezed her eyes tightly shut, tears streaming down her cheeks, and then she whipped her head around to look again at the man on the floor.

He shook his head wildly from side to side, eyes huge, staring up at her, pleas muffled by the gag in his mouth.

And Max knew.

"Gaby, no!" he screamed.

Coco spun as though he'd heard, stared at Max, eyes narrowed as though he couldn't focus.

But Gabrielle *had not* heard. With a cry of sorrow, utterly devoid of hope, she knelt, raised the knife in both hands and brought it down, driving it into the struggling man's heart. Blood sprayed into her face, but she brought the blade down again, and then a third time, and she might have done it again if Coco had not stilled her hands.

"Good girl," he said, kissing the blood on her cheek.

She had stopped crying, arms and expression slackening at the same time.

"I'll take it from here," Coco said.

And he started to carve into the corpse of Joe Noone.

chapter

16

Max staggered down a nameless street—no sign, no identity, just one more empty place left hollow by Katrina's passing. The sidewalks were strewn with debris, but unlike some of the other areas he'd passed through in New Orleans, the flotsam and jetsam left behind by the storm and the lives that had been lost or abandoned here had been gathered into heaps. Every twenty or thirty feet there were piles of refuse—children's toys, broken furniture, roofing and siding, ruined appliances—but no one had come by to pick it up. Some order had been brought to the chaos in this one neighborhood. Compared to other places, it was moving on.

For a while, Max had stopped noticing the debris. He'd become numb to it.

Now it drove him on, and he forced himself to keep putting one foot in front of the other. His thoughts were a swirl of bitterness and regret. He seesawed between despair and the laughter that came with disbelief. Had he really thought he could save Gabrielle, reach back in time and pluck her from the path of the storm? *For a smart man, you're one stupid motherfucker.* In his mind he'd pictured himself the knight in shining armor, selfless in his return to New Orleans for the funeral of a girl who'd betrayed him, then risking his life and perhaps more for the chance to save a woman who didn't love him.

But it wouldn't be enough to save her life. He had to save her from herself, or none of it would matter. *No, you have to save her from* you, *because she* did *love you, and she gave up her soul to protect you.*

He tripped on something, staggered again, and turned to stare uncomprehending at a metal prosthetic leg. It still had a sneaker on the foot. What had happened in the storm to the man who owned that leg—a soldier, maybe, home from Iraq? Had he drowned?

Max sat down hard on the sidewalk and buried his face in his hands. There were no tears. He was too empty for tears. Coco's words, back in the woods by the river, echoed in his head. *Gabrielle told you nothing, that was part of the deal, part of the price.* And now he'd seen, firsthand, the rest of it.

In that Moment he wished he had never seen, Coco had made it plain. The Tordu had forced her to become one of them, and to do so, she had to give up her past and some part of herself. She had to commit murder. Coco had wanted Max, "the teacher," to be her victim. But Gabrielle had bartered for his life, and she had chosen Joe Noone to die in his place.

Max cried out, there on the sidewalk amidst the wreckage the storm had left behind, grabbing his hair in tight fists and letting loose a tortured howl.

His walking in on her and Joe that night had been no accident. It was so obvious now. Gabrielle had set it up so that Max would catch them, so that his heart would be broken, so that he would go away and *stay* away. Stay safe.

But there was more to the equation. She had been involved with Coco before she ever met Max. The Tordu had been trying to seduce her for a long time, and what he'd seen was the culmination of that. But the murder of Joe Noone had not only been to save Max. Coco's words had made it clear that if she didn't go through with it, Mireault would kill her.

She'd saved and damned herself at the same time.

Had she partaken in the hideous sacrament afterward? Once Coco had cut out Joe Noone's organs, had Gabrielle eaten? Max shook his head, sagging further into himself.

"Gaby, no," he whispered, an unconscious echo of the words he'd shouted minutes and months ago.

Lost and broken amongst a city of the lost and broken, he felt something sifting itself up out of the wreckage inside him. A question. Of all the things Coco had said, there had been one Max did not understand. *You don't have his strength.* Whose strength? What he had seen in that little house had been the Seventh Moment, and there could be no denying the words that had appeared on the street in chalk had been about Coco and Gabrielle. *The Hollow Man Tempts the Oracle's Faithless Heir. She Succumbs.*

But if Coco was the Hollow Man, and Gabrielle the Faithless Heir, then who was the Oracle?

Tumblers, clicking into place once more . . .

Max had learned a great many things tonight, and intuited others. Really, there were only two men the Oracle could be, and he knew one of them. Had seen him shot in a little house in 1965, with Hurricane Betsy howling outside. And he'd drunk with him after Gabrielle's funeral.

Ray had the answers, and always had. Either Ray was the Oracle, or it was the conjure-man, Matrisse, who was supposed to help Max go back and stop Gabrielle from dying. But he had no way of finding Ray. And the crazy old man had said that in the end, when Max had followed the map to his final destination, Matrisse would find him.

"Bastard," he whispered. "Fucking son of a bitch." What had Ray said, exactly, that day he'd given Max the map? Something about Gabrielle having the potential to be someone special. Or some*thing* special. How much of this journey had Ray manipulated from the beginning? Enough so that the map had not shown him the date of the Seventh Moment at first, withholding a vital piece of information. And why? Because Max might not have continued if he'd known what he was in for? Might not have been able to force himself to witness that scene?

He stood, still trembling. But now his shaking had less to do with shock and grief than it did with the magic that hummed through his body. He'd dragged his feet across the carpet of the Seventh Moment, picking up even more static, and as he walked it crackled on his skin, sparks cascading invisibly to the ground.

"Hey!" someone called.

Max spun, a scowl on his face, and saw the two young black guys watching him from the stoop of a house on the opposite side of the street. They had bottles of beer, and one—larger and more formidable than the other—had a lit cigarette dangling from his hand.

Fucking Tordu.

Max tensed, ready to run, ready to fight.

"You all right, man?" the big guy asked, pointing at him with the burning tip of his cigarette. Concerned.

The thinner, younger guy tapped the other's shoulder and murmured something in a low voice. He looked anxious, almost afraid, and Max realized that they weren't Tordu after all, just a couple of guys having a beer, wondering if the crazy-looking white man stalking down their street needed help.

Max remembered the night he'd taken the bike out to Lakeview, and the threat of violence he'd witnessed on the street. Every shadow had seemed filled with the promise of pain, of attack, of sudden death. Desperate, dangerous people prowled the city without anyone to rein them in. And now he'd come full circle. To the guys on the stoop, he was one of those people.

What could he have said to them?

Max hurried to the corner, glancing in both directions. To the right there seemed to be only dark buildings and a few distant streetlights. Several blocks to the left he saw the lights of a convenience store and a street where a few cars were passing, busy traffic by post-Katrina standards.

He also saw ghosts. People walking, laughing, dying. Carriages and cars. A phantasmagorical circus displaying the history of New Orleans in spectral figures. Max turned left and walked through them as though they were nothing more than mist. With every one he touched, he felt their Moments—the shifts in reality, air, weather, and time—but the dirty, too-big boots trod only on the pavement of 2005. He kept his eyes focused on the lights of the convenience store.

Lost and broken, no doubt.

And when you were lost, what you needed more than anything was a map.

He bought a map in the store. The skinny white clerk had black-rimmed glasses, a stubbly shaved head, and a one-inch strip of beard on his chin that hadn't earned the right to be considered a goatee. His arms were covered with demon tattoos that snaked around his biceps and striped his fore-arms. He didn't look like he had much of a sense of humor, but he took one look at Max in his Mattie's All-Night Crab Shack sweatshirt and then down at the map and he grinned.

"Yeah, you *look* like you took a wrong turn somewhere."

Max nudged a ten-spot toward him. "More than one."

The guy gave a small shrug, rang up the purchase, and handed him his change. Max took the map, but only as far as a metal rack loaded with chips and pretzels, where he un-folded it and stared as three words took form—"The Last

Moment." The arrow came next, but it took him a moment to realize that it pointed to a place he had been before.

Folding the map, Max turned to the clerk.

"Hey. Any chance you could call me a cab?"

In the couple of days since Max had first pulled up to the curb near Cooper's, with Ray behind the wheel of that little sports car, the place showed some signs of improvement. Two sections of cracked and taped window had been revealed, plywood taken down and added to the heaps of debris in the alley beside the building. Some enterprising soul had hand-painted a new sign, and the Coopers had hung it from the bent metal hanger out front.

The convenience-store clerk hadn't been able to get him anything resembling a real cab, but he knew a guy who'd started running a taxi service in the aftermath of the storm. The silver Cadillac gleamed in dawn's early light, a glimpse of sheer perfection right off the assembly line, except for the painted TAXI sign strapped to the roof. Max figured it for stolen, but didn't much care at this point. A ride was a ride. He and the driver, an amiable white guy with a bit of a Cajun accent, had agreed on twenty bucks. Max had been able to get money out of an ATM machine in the store, and when the Cadillac pulled up in front of Cooper's, Max gave the driver thirty instead.

Now he stood in front of the bar, staring at the duct tape that had been used to seal cracks in the windows. Dawn was breaking over the city, and the lights were on in Cooper's. Edgy funk music spilled out through the open door, along with the strong smell of coffee, and something frying in a breakfast pan. Max stepped inside . . .

. . . and into the Final Moment.

He'd been here before. Not just this place, but this *Moment*. The brothers who owned the place now that their parents were dead were off toward the back by the bar they'd thrown together. Tires and plywood had been rigged for some of the tables. Fans whirred. Outside the window, the sun blazed again.

And at one table, he saw himself sitting across from crazy old Ray.

This was an earlier version of Max. Calmer, more innocent, less afraid. And though the dislocation of seeing himself struck Max hard initially, he realized that in reality, he was looking at a very different person.

He noticed something he had not seen before; Ray claimed to have been drinking in Cooper's for thirty years, but nobody even really looked at that table. The attention of the people around it wandered away. Gazes slid past as though they knew to look anywhere but at Ray and his guest. It might have been magic, but another possible explanation occurred to Max: fear.

"End of the journey," he said.

The Cadillac cab ride to Cooper's had not taken long, but he had seen dozens of magical Moments on the way, bits of history unfolding, and hundreds of the ghosts of New Orleans. Max had watched them go by with no more interest than if he'd been gazing out at the passing landscape from the window of a train.

This Moment had much more substance. The stale stink

of mold remained in the air. He heard the clink of glasses. Max thought that if he went up to the bar he would be able to pick up a bottle of beer, that he'd be able to drink it and have it quench his thirst. He was in this Moment more than he'd been in any other before.

He weaved a path amongst the tables until he stood only a few feet away from Ray. From *himself*. He watched as Ray produced the small clay bottle as if from nowhere, and saw his own surprised reaction, the disbelief in those past-Max features and the spark of hope in the younger Max's eyes.

I so wanted to believe, he thought. He wished he could interfere, slap himself and tell himself not to drink it, not to take the map, that it would show him things he would soon wish never to have seen. Yet no matter how much pain it had brought him, he knew he would be lying to himself. For Gabrielle's sake, this more innocent Max needed to have his eyes opened.

"Just humor an old man," Ray said. "Ain't nothin' in this bottle gonna hurt you. And you know I ain't lyin', just like you know the rest of it's true."

Ah, Max thought, watching his own reaction, *there it is. The promise.* Nothing in the bottle would hurt him. But there's hurt, and then there's hurt. Ray's promise had been the sort the devil made, one with too many meanings. No, there was no poison in the bottle, but poison would only have killed him. Magic had damaged him far more.

"You're crazy," the past-Max said.

Ray chuckled and thanked him, and the past-Max stood, snatched up the Map of Moments and the little clay bottle and started for the door.

Max watched himself, not at all surprised to see a sway in his steps. He'd had too much whiskey and not enough to eat. He could barely believe that this had been only days before. It felt like a lifetime.

He turned to look at Ray, but flinched in surprise when he found Ray staring at him. Looking *right at* him, but not the way Coco and Mireault had been able to see him in previous Moments.

"Welcome back," the old man said, no smile at all. "Have a seat. You'll have questions, but we gotta be quick about it before the magic you picked up starts to bleed off."

Max glared at him with a hardened heart. "You're him."

Ray cocked his head. "Sit down, Max."

Reluctantly, Max slipped into the chair that past-Max had just vacated. He stared over the top of a fresh bottle of whiskey that Ray had just opened. The old man's glass was full.

"You're him," he said again. "You're Matrisse. The fucking conjure-man. And apparently you're also called the Oracle, whatever the hell that means. But you're him. It's the only thing that makes any sense. I saw you in that house in the Ninth Ward in 1965, working some mojo, trying to blow one of the Tordu's wards and let Seddicus in, and you didn't look any different then than you do now. You were shot, but you pulled through just fine, didn't you? And I saw you earlier than that, decades earlier, and maybe your hair wasn't as white. But other than that, you looked the same. Just like Mireault."

Ray's eyes blazed. "I'm nothing like Mireault."

"Could've fooled me. Oh, wait, you did."

"What can I say?" Ray gestured with his hands, nodded, and gave an annoying, dismissive shrug that Max remembered from their first meeting. "I dress mighty fine, but I'm ordinary enough to look at. I'm the man behind the curtain, Max, and for you to believe in magic, you had to think the conjure-man had the big juju. You had to think Matrisse was the Great and Powerful Oz."

Ray reached inside his jacket pocket and pulled out a small glass vial with a glass stopper.

"Now, wait a second," Max said, shaking his head. "I'm not drinking a goddamn thing until I get some answers."

Carefully, Ray poured a few drops into the glass that past-Max had just left behind, and followed it with a dash of whiskey. He slid the glass across the table and smiled.

"Seems to me you've already got the answers. You followed the map. You just about brimmin' with magic, Max; I can see it all around you. You're lit up like a Christmas tree to these old eyes."

Max frowned at the glass, spiked with whatever new liquid mojo Ray wanted him to inflict upon himself, and he remembered this moment. He turned and saw himself, drunk as a skunk, standing by the door; past-Max watched Ray curiously for a moment, then turned and stumbled out of Cooper's, into the street, where soon he would steal a bicycle, and tonight he would find his way into City Park and the First Moment.

"I know a lot. But I don't know it all." Max didn't touch the glass.

Ray nodded, took a long sip of whiskey, and smacked his lips. Then he sat back in his chair, cradling his own glass.

"All right, boy. Shoot."

Max stared at him, aware of the whiskey glass before him. Whatever Ray had spiked it with had to be the last ingredient, the final bit of magic to let him reach the destination he'd been seeking when he'd set out from this very chair. But he wondered now if he even needed it. The way he saw the Moments all around him now, the ghosts and the magic—and the way Coco and even one of the Tordu's victims back in 1935 had been able to see him—he thought maybe he had enough mojo on his own.

"I know what you're thinkin'," Ray said.

"You're psychic now, too?"

"Not the least bit. But you watch people's eyes for as many years as I have and you get to knowin' what's in their heads and hearts. I warned you already; you take too long, the magic starts slippin' away. A conjure-man, he knows how to hang on to it, keep it close. But you're just a teacher, Max. You went to all that trouble gatherin' up the sparkle you got around you now, but you need a little help if you want to hold on to it long enough to do what needs doin'." Ray nodded toward Max's glass. "That right there'll do the job."

"Fine. But not yet."

With another shrug, Ray rocked a little in his chair and sipped his whiskey.

"How old are you?" Max asked.

Ray arched an eyebrow. "All the things you've seen and that's the question—"

"How old?"

"Two hundred and thirty-three, this past July. I was born

on the island of Martinique. My father was a French aristocrat, and my mother an African slave."

Max closed his eyes. He'd worked out so much of the
truth already, and logic had dictated the answer would be
something like this. But to hear it out of the man's mouth so
casually, as if everyone lived to be that age, made it all real.
Wonder and horror shook him in equal measures.

"Who's Seddicus?"

Ray gave him a stern look. "Now, Max, don't waste time
with things you already know. I can smell him on you. You
been close enough to not have to ask that question. He's a
devil, come from the old world to the new the same time as
I did."

"Following you?"

"Mireault."

Max sighed. "Now who's wasting time? Why does the
demon want Mireault? He and the Tordu put up all these
wards to keep the demon out of New Orleans—"

"They don't care anythin' about New Orleans, except to
keep it for themselves. Their little hunting ground,
Mireault's kingdom of fear. Most people live here never
even know. They might hear about the Tordu, but they think
it's gang business that don't concern them, an' part of that's
true. The Tordu, they got long lives, and they like to live
well. So there's drugs, and women, an' guns, an' that part of
it's all about money. But the people of New Orleans are his
subjects just the same. His cattle. Anytime he wants, he'll
kill 'em, twist 'em, throw shadows into their lives, unless
somebody's there to stand against him."

"And that'd be you?"

Ray nodded. "For now."

"What about Seddicus?"

"The wards keep the demon away, but Seddicus wouldn't touch most people. If he was in this bar with us right now, he wouldn't even know we were here. That old boy's blind, Max. As for the rest of his senses . . . well, the only thing he's hungry for is the hollow ones, the ones without souls. The ones who owe him."

Max stared at the whiskey glass in front of him. It might have been his imagination, but the prickling pins and needles feeling of magic crackling on his skin seemed to have diminished.

He picked up the glass, stared at Ray over the rim.

"The Tordu sold their souls to Seddicus?"

Ray raised his own glass in a silent toast. " 'Sold' is the wrong word. They surrender their souls to make room for darkness, and the long lives they lead. Murder's a part of it. And eatin' the organs, but you know that much. That's what twists 'em. Mireault le Tordu, that's what they called him even in Martinique, twisted up by the dark magic he practiced, even as a boy. He wanted more. More life, more power, more magic.

"Seddicus is an ancient power, bound by ancient covenants," Ray continued, eyes bright with terrible knowledge. "Mireault surrendered his soul, and as long as he continues performin' the ritual every few years—killin' some innocent, offerin' up their life to Seddicus, consuming the vitals—he won't ever die. Not until Seddicus finds a way in to claim him. That's the pact all Mireault's followers enter into, and old, old laws means the demon honors it."

Max saw it clearly now. They made their offerings, and Seddicus was bound by some kind of infernal law to fulfill his end. But as long as the Tordu kept the wards in place around New Orleans, Seddicus couldn't get in to claim them.

"They're immortal," he said.

"No such thing as immortal for someone flesh and blood," Ray replied. "One day a mistake will be made and the wards will fail and Seddicus will take them. Mireault knows this. But he lives as he lives until then, and he'll put off the day as long as possible."

Max studied him. "So in 1965 when you tried—"

"Enough!" Ray said, banging his now-empty glass on the table hard enough to make Max jump, to make a little drop of whiskey slosh out of his own glass.

No one so much as glanced at them. The talking continued, and Max wondered if Ray himself had somehow stepped out of time.

"You don't drink that now, and you're gonna miss your chance to do anything for Gabrielle," Ray said. "I know you loved her."

Max narrowed his eyes. The whiskey glass felt warm in his hand. Something glittered like diamonds inside the brown liquid.

"So did you," he said.

Ray nodded. "All right. So did I. But not the way you mean."

"And Corinne?"

"Corinne's dead an' gone. Gaby's the one you might still save."

"That's not—"

"Fair?" Ray sighed, and suddenly he looked so tired. He nodded at the drink.

Max tilted the glass to his lips. He drained the whiskey in one go, no sipping for him, and it burned all the way down.

"You tried taking out a ward in '65 and you fucked it up," Max rasped. "Why didn't you try again?"

Ray poured them both another whiskey. "I'm not strong enough. I'm just a conjure-man, not some kinda sorcerer."

"Then why doesn't Mireault just kill you?"

At that, Ray smiled. He picked up his whiskey glass, knocked it against the one he'd poured for Max, and raised it in a toast.

"That's one I thought you'd figured out. He don't want to kill his own brother. Our daddy's the one taught us our first conjurin', but he showed Mireault magic he never shared with me. Maybe because I was younger, and by the time I got a little older he'd already disappeared."

Tumblers clicked. Doors opened. Of course they were brothers.

"Seddicus took your father?"

"Oh, yes. And we ran. Well, Mireault ran, and I followed him. And so did the demon. And here we've been, ever since."

"And now you're some kind of oracle?"

Ray smiled. "Didn't start out that way. Oracle's the heart of a city, or at least someone who's got the city's best interests at heart. Every big old city's got one. But, understand, bein' the Oracle ain't where my magic comes from.

I'm a conjure-man through and through, and the conjurin's what has kept me alive this long. It's what I use to keep Mireault from takin' over entirely.

"Bein' the Oracle . . . that's like havin' a second job. But it makes it easier for me to fight Mireault 'cos I got the heart of New Orleans in me now. Used to be I had to try to protect the Oracle from Mireault—he was always tryin' to kill them. Guess New Orleans finally decided it made more sense to just give me the job. The city's had three Oracles just in the time since I've lived here . . . three before me, I mean. But I've been playin' the part for goin' on seventy years now, since the Tordu killed the last one, a young man—"

"In the Beauregard-Keyes House," Max said, thinking of the screaming, struggling victim who'd seen him there. "And you were there."

"I tried to stop it. Got there too late. The city chose me next."

"And you chose Gabrielle to take your place."

Ray sipped whiskey, savored it. "I'm dying. The city conspired to bring me and the girl together. I taught her everything I know about conjurin', but she didn't have it in her as strong as my family does. She needed every bit of magic I could give her to stand against Mireault. She wouldn't have the power to destroy the wards or to kill him, but she could be the light in the darkness, keep the Tordu from truly controlling the city. Stop Mireault from ever getting the shadow kingdom he's always wanted." Ray leaned forward, and his next words were a whisper. "If no one stood against him, my brother would turn everyone. Then even Seddicus would bother him no more."

Max felt a fresh wave of grief, images of Gabrielle flooding his mind. She'd been just a girl, nineteen years old. It must have been terrifying for her to think that Ray would die and she would have to face Mireault on her own.

"She didn't have faith in herself," Max said. "She was afraid she wouldn't be strong enough."

"Maybe she wouldn't have been. But I trained her. And I had enough faith for both of us. And then the city chose her to be the next Oracle, too, so I knew my choice had been the right one. She'll be like me, mojo in one hand, heart of the city in the other. Burnin' the candle at both ends. My clock is winding down, Max. Won't be long now. If I could do this for Gabrielle myself, I would've done it already. But if I step out of time, then there's no one here and now to fight the Tordu. We got one chance to fix it, Max, to make sure Gaby doesn't die in that attic, so she can do the job I trained her for."

The last of the tumblers clicked into place.

Max stared at him. "Jesus. You set this up right from the beginning, didn't you? You and Corinne."

Ray breathed an old man's sigh. "Poor Corinne was just an innocent. The girl loved her cousin, an' she stood by her when no one else did. Messin' with me is what made Gabrielle's family shut Gaby out in the first place. They heard of me, you understand? My name's spoken in the same breath as the Tordu, by people too ignorant to under-stand the difference.

"So when Gaby died and Corinne tol' me about you, I asked her to get you down here. Corinne called you 'cos of me. I set you on this path 'cos I can't do it, but *you can save Gaby*. If you stop—"

"You used Corinne, like you used everyone?"

Ray shrugged. "Stop asking so many goddamn questions. You can still save Gabrielle's life and put things right."

"But—"

"Out of time, Max," Ray said. He threw back the last of his whiskey and slid the glass across the table. "It's now or never."

"That's really all I have to do?" Max asked.

Ray pointed at the door. "You go out there, an' you'll step right into the Moment you need. You'll still have to get to her house, but you'll be *when* you need to be. Getting *where* you need to get will be your problem."

Even with all that he'd seen and done, Max might have argued, but he still felt the frisson of magic in him, the high voltage passing through his veins and bones. He'd spent all this time gathering the mojo into him so he could have this moment, this opportunity.

Now his thoughts raced ahead. With all he'd been through, he'd thought very little about what he would actually say if and when he saw Gabrielle again. If he didn't speak the right words, if he couldn't persuade her to have faith in herself, then she would give in to her fear and to Coco, and it would all have been for nothing.

I've never been eloquent, Max thought.

But he would have to be. It had occurred to him that he

could go back to the beginning of their relationship and simply make it so that they had never met, or never fallen in love. Max would be protected that way. The selfish part of him felt tempted, but that would also mean never having experienced the love he'd felt for Gabrielle, the good times they'd shared, and though he'd have saved himself some pain, Mireault and the Tordu would still end up controlling New Orleans. They'd win. And though the implications of that were still vague in his mind—

If no one stood against him, my brother would turn everyone. Then even Seddicus would bother him no more.

—he could not allow it. Not after the way they'd twisted Gabrielle. Seeing the anguish in her, seeing her ruin herself . . . Max didn't have the power to make Mireault pay for what they'd done to Gaby, but he could take away the Tordu's victory.

And if he could get to her before she slept with Joe Noone—or even after, as long as it was before she gave Noone up to the Tordu—then maybe the thing he'd wished for all along could come true.

Maybe Max could have her back.

Deep, booming laughter came from the back of the bar. Max glanced over and saw one of the Cooper brothers with one hand clapped to the side of his head, rocking from side to side with mirth. The other brother rolled his eyes and shot him the middle finger. A man and woman who were huddled back there with them also seemed amused.

A waitress teased a flirty customer. Fresh beers were opened. Morose faces slumped on tables, but others were alight with humor and warmth—with survival. In the wake of the storm, people were recovering as best they could, and each in their own way.

So would Max and Gabrielle, when this was all over. Each in their own way.

It was his greatest wish.

"Max . . ." Ray began.

"I'm going."

The two of them stood by the door. Outside, the street sounded quiet.

"I'm trying to think of a reason to thank you," Max said.

"Don't trouble yourself. I didn't do it for you."

"I know." Taking a deep breath, Max looked at the door. Then he pushed it open and stepped outside, hearing it creak shut behind him.

"What the fuck?" he whispered.

Because it was all wrong.

The wind hit him, making him stagger, and the rain pelted his face. He raised his hands to protect his eyes as he took two steps out into the street. The moonlight had gone away. The storm howled along the street, tugging at shutters. Trash skittered in the wind, flapping down the sidewalk.

A gust pushed at him again.

"This isn't it," he said quietly, and then his voice rose to match the roar of the storm. "This isn't the right time. This isn't it!"

The night he'd walked in on Gabrielle and Joe Noone had been months before Hurricane Katrina. But here was the storm. Dark as it was, it might only be hours before landfall. Right now, at this moment, she would be up in her attic, waiting and hoping for the storm to kill her so she would not have to face the evil she'd done, the person she'd become.

"You fucker!" he screamed into the storm, turning back toward Cooper's.

The old sign still hung there. But the door was boarded over now, the façade covered with wood and nailed down tight. The words WE SHOOT LOOTERS had already been spray-painted across the boarding. The Cooper boys weren't taking any chances. The only thing missing was the brown tidal line, but that would be here soon enough.

The worst had already happened. Gabrielle had given up her soul to Seddicus. She'd murdered Joe Noone. After all Max had been through, Ray's conjuring had fucked him again. He had arrived too late to save Gabrielle from herself.

But if he hurried, there was still time to save her from Katrina.

chapter
17

This time it was real.

The Katrina-battered street knew that Max was here. Wind howled around him, rain sliced through the air to sting his exposed skin, and he could feel a rumble through the ground, like the approach of something terrible. But it was when two men struggled past him along the street that he knew this was not just another Moment. Because they both looked at him, and one of them grinned. The man shouted something that sounded like, "Here we go again!" and then they were gone, arms around each other's shoulders to help move along the road.

Max started after them. There was an urgency in him,

inspired by both the incoming storm and the sense that his time here was not without limit. Perhaps it would be dictated by the strength of the drink Ray had given him, or maybe his accumulated magical aura would determine exactly how long he could live this moment again. *Am I reliving it, or is it reliving me?* he thought, confused and terrified at what this meant for time, and existence, and everything he had ever known.

Viewing the Moments had been like witnessing the past, and he had been unable to influence what he saw. Here, when he placed one foot in front of another, he was changing events with every motion, every heartbeat. The man who had just grinned at him had been at this point before, and that time Max had not been here for him to smile at. How could that affect the future? How much could it change the past? He knew the saying about a butterfly flapping its wings and causing a hurricane. Well, here he was in the path of one of the greatest storms known, and he had no wish to be a butterfly at its mercy.

Time.

Ticking away, for him, and for Gabrielle.

Max started running.

This was a very different New Orleans from the one he had been immersed in for the past few days, yet there were striking portents of the tragedy to come. Many businesses and homes had been boarded up, and some of this temporary protection would remain for months to come. Several homes had small boats already moored in their dry yards, tied to the buildings or stakes in the ground with long ropes, ready for the water. And more than once Max saw the glare of lights behind drawn shutters, evidence of those who had been unwilling or unable to leave. He wondered how many of them would die tomorrow.

And then he wondered if *he* could die here, and the answer came back fast, obvious, and terrifying.

As he jogged, he tried to figure out in his mind the quickest route to the house in Lakeview. Frustratingly, after days of staring at maps of the city, he could not conjure an image of the New Orleans streets, so he simply headed west, knowing he would have to traverse City Park to reach Gabrielle's neighborhood.

A lot of people were just leaving, finally realizing that the Big Easy wasn't going to skate by this time. On the main roads there were cars jammed with evacuees, and trucks piled high with what some seemed to value: suitcases; furniture; bedding; boxes of food. In a couple of trucks, Max saw someone quite literally riding shotgun in the passenger seat, the barrel of their weapon on display. *Go into a disaster with that mind-set, come out the other side the same,* he thought. But he berated himself for being so judgmental; this was not his city, and this had never been his disaster.

It is now. Maybe it already was. I wasn't even here and it ruined me.

Somehow, though, the terrible wind and rain seemed to partition him from the New Orleans he had known. Filled with panic and held breath, raging with storm, this was a strange place to him, almost as strange as the ruined city to which he had returned just days ago.

Max ran, slipped, fell, and rose without slowing, propelling himself forward. His heart beat in time with some internal clock. He tried peering through the rain, hoping to see some clock tower or a bank building with a digital sign. How much time did he have? How long before Gabrielle's lungs filled with water?

Goddamn you, Ray. You old bastard. Goddamn you.

Think, Max.

In the midst of the maelstrom, it would be so dark that it would be difficult to tell what time of day or night it might be. But shutters weren't tearing off, signs weren't pinwheeling across the street. Katrina hadn't yet made landfall. What he raced through now was just the first flirtation of storm and city.

He tried to remember. Landfall would be right around dawn. And then the flooding would start, first breaching the levees off the Intracoastal Waterway into New Orleans east, then battering down parts of the levees to flood the Ninth Ward, Bywater, Chalmette . . . so many neighborhoods.

Focus. Why didn't this matter before? They aren't just details, they're people's lives.

Maybe two hours after landfall, Lake Pontchartrain would be so pregnant with the storm surge that it would overtop the floodwalls. And that would be it for City Park, Gentilly, and other northside neighborhoods.

So how long until the 17th Street Canal floodwall failed, and a tidal wave swept through Lakeview? How long until the water filled Gabrielle's house and rose up into the attic? Three, maybe four hours after dawn?

But when was dawn?

Max let out a scream of frustration, lost in the howl of wind and rain, and ran on. His chest burned, his muscles ached. His clothes were soaked through and his hair was plastered to his scalp. He reached City Park and started through, shocked at how different it looked from the last time he had seen it. Old oaks bent and creaked, but at least they were still standing. Grasses danced as the wind made exotic patterns across the ground, and soon they would be smothered with water and muck. Trees that had stood for hundreds of years vainly swayed and bent to the whim of the wind . . . but soon, they would fall.

Nothing, he realized, lasts forever.

Immortality was a lie.

Ray was dying. Old and powerful though he might be, and ruthless in his manipulations of lesser mortals, he was fading. And this storm had snatched his last hope for leaving an enduring legacy behind: Gabrielle. Like one of those old oaks, Ray could rage against the storm, but there were never any guarantees.

Max felt a weight of responsibility crushing him down, and he did not want to become a part of the mud. *I could die here,* he thought, still coming to grips with the reality of it. This place where he had never been, this tragedy he had never seen, could become his grave. Yet there was something incredibly potent about such a possibility, and for a moment he realized just what Ray must feel.

"I don't *want* the power!" he shouted, but his voice was lost to the wind, and the only thing that heard was Katrina.

Landry Street, Lakeview. He wanted to smash down each door, shout at anyone left behind that they had to leave, flee, abandon the city to its terrible fate. And he tried, knocking at one door several houses away from Gabrielle's aunt's house. A frightened old man opened his front door on a chain and Max started screaming at him.

The man slammed the door in his face, and Max tried to remember what he had seen of this house after the storm. But his memories were no longer clear. His mind, buoyed though it was with magic, was not well suited to what it had been through, and what it was still going through now. Perhaps this juggling with time would affect his memories and perceptions . . . but perhaps, also, he would never know. What would he remember? What, God help him, would he forget?

At last, he stood before Gabrielle's aunt's house. The last time he had been here, it was a ruin, with *1 IN ATTIC* spray-painted across the dormer. He was here now to ensure that message was never left.

There were no lights, and he could see no sign of anyone being inside.

As he mounted the steps the storm seemed to shift up a notch. A sheet of corrugated iron flipped along the street, scoring the road and smashing a car windshield as it sailed by. Water gushed along gutters, carrying litter down into the sewers. Rain dashed horizontally, and in the distance Max heard a sound like a siren, rising and falling and casting its doom-laden notes across this condemned city.

Nature angry at his interference, perhaps.

He tried the door, found it open, and entered without knocking.

Max climbed the staircase, then and now and on a day yet to come, simultaneously, as though he existed in this place in all of those moments at once. The first time, Gabrielle had been leading him by the hand, smiling back down at him, her smile so gorgeous that he had been looking at that instead of her naked behind. The second time he had gone alone, because Gabrielle had promised that she would be waiting for him up there. True to her promise, she had, with a bottle of wine, and a hundred candles turning the attic into a golden dream. Several times after that blurred into one, all ending in the same passionate, sweaty embrace on the wooden floor. And the last time . . . when he had walked in on Gabrielle astride . . .

Joe Noone.

The name conjured images Max wished he could forget.

He walked slowly up the staircase, his progress masked by the sounds of Katrina's fury. As he reached the narrow door at the top and gripped the knob, he wondered if this would be the final time he ascended these stairs. He looked around at the shadows, searching for observers from past, present, or future, but he saw or sensed no one.

Alone, he opened the door.

Gabrielle sat on a mess of blankets piled on the floor. An empty wine bottle stood beside her, and another, half-full, was cupped in her hands. The attic was lit unevenly by a dozen fat, squat candles, and shadows danced around her. She was fully dressed in shapeless clothes that seemed to match what she had become—a shape where a woman had been. Though the hands around the bottle's neck seemed clean, Max saw them stained with Joe Noone's blood. He'd never be able to look at her again and not see those stains.

"Hello, Gabrielle," Max said.

Her eyes opened wide, then wider still when she saw him, and she let out a small, strangled cry.

He'd thought he might cry, that his heart would swell with hope. He'd sacrificed everything he had believed about the world to reach this moment, given up his own past and perhaps his future just to stand here, to be able to reach out and try to reclaim the happiness she'd stolen from him. Perhaps even the love she'd thrown away. At the very least, her life.

But the woman before him was broken and empty. He had seen what she had done, and felt a dreadful certainty that no matter what havoc magic wreaked on his memory after this, the sight of her plunging a blade into Joe Noone was something he would never be able to forget.

He silently cursed Ray yet again. *Why couldn't you even give us a chance?*

"You went back to Boston!" Gabrielle gasped. Candle flames flickered and swayed, and the shadows seemed alive. "I made sure."

"I did," Max said. "But I had to come back."

"Why?"

"For your funeral."

"Max . . ." Her eyes sparkled with panic, and she looked past his shoulder at the dark staircase behind him.

"Don't worry, I'm alone. The Tordu don't even know I'm here."

She gasped. "You know about . . . ?"

"Coco? Mireault? The Tordu? Seddicus?" He saw her shiver as he uttered the demonic name, and for a beat he almost went to hold her. But this was an empty woman before him, someone who had already given her soul to the demon in return for . . . what? Power? If what Ray said was true, yes. But here she sat, more powerful than any normal person in New Orleans, yet still readying herself to die.

"You left," she said. "I sent you away so you didn't have to know any of that."

Frozen, he couldn't approach her. His hands ached to touch her but he stopped himself. Anguish stabbed him, twisted.

"What do you think is going to happen, Gabrielle?" he said, shouting to be heard over the howl of the wind and the trembling of the house. "You're going to die in the morning. And then Corinne will call me, and I won't be able to stay away—"

"You were supposed to—"

"I can't. You know I can't! So when Corinne calls, I'll come, and I'll find out everything. What you did, and what you gave up."

"Why?" she screamed, voice matching the cry of the storm.

"Because . . ." *Because I love you?* If he said that, would it mean anything to her now? To this soulless girl with blood on her hands? "Because Ray tells me," he said instead.

Gabrielle glanced away at the mention of the Oracle's name, but he could also see understanding in her eyes.

"What'll happen if you're both gone? You're betraying him if you let yourself die."

"He betrayed me!" she spat. "He *destroyed* me! Said because I didn't have the same magic in my blood that he did, the only way to be strong enough was to be empty, *soulless,* like them. Ray said I had to be able to use all kinds of magic if I was gonna fight them. He *allowed* Coco to take me from him, turn me into what it is those sick bastards are, and I had to . . ." A single tear dribbled down her cheek, and she touched it as though surprised.

"He betrayed me, too," Max whispered, realizing at last that this was always the moment Ray had intended returning him to. The bastard had wanted her to be tainted by the Tordu's dark magic, and he couldn't afford to let Max rescue her before she had given up her soul.

"I had to . . ." Gabrielle looked at her hand, fisted around the shaft of an invisible knife.

And then Max couldn't help it. To hell with the stakes, with what it meant for Ray or Gabrielle or the city of New Orleans. For just a moment all of his illusions about his motivations slipped and the only thing that mattered was what she'd done to him.

"Joe Noone," he said. "I saw what you did." He closed his eyes, and what Gabrielle said next could have come from the mouth of the woman he had loved.

"Better him than you."

"Why would Ray let you do that?" Max asked, shaking

his head. "If you've given up your soul, how could he think you wouldn't really be tainted, that you wouldn't just hand the city over to Mireault?"

Gaby wiped away her tears, staring at the dampness on her fingers. "When Ray dies, I'll be the Oracle. I'll have the soul of the city in me. I guess he figured that would be enough. But in between, after what I did, what I gave up . . . I'm in Hell, Max. Maybe I'd feel different if I were the Oracle, but why would the city want me now? Like this?"

Her despair tore at him. This was what Ray had done, manipulated her into murder and ruin and black magic, and if he had some greater plan for her, full of hope, in her current state she could not believe in it.

Max opened his eyes and leaned against a support beam. "You die in here. Katrina's worse than anyone predicted. The lake surges, the levees break, thousands die. You're just one of them. They leave you up here for weeks, even though someone sprays a message." He stepped forward and tapped the dormer cheek. "Outside. It says *1 in attic*. That's you, Gabrielle. One in attic. You die alone."

"It's what I deserve," she whispered, surrendering, drinking more wine. Abruptly she turned to focus on Max, as if seeing him for the first time. "What time of year is it where you are?"

He shook his head, threw his hands open. "I'm here. Right here!"

She smiled through her tears. "For a moment."

So she understood. Of course she did. Ray had taught her well. The conjure-man Matrisse. How strange to think that when Max had first met her, all he'd seen had been a nineteen-year-old girl, and already she had been one of the most powerful people in New Orleans.

"It's November," he said, barely able to hear himself over the storm. "Your body's in the ground. The city's a disaster. The government isn't doing shit. The people are on their own."

"They always are," Gabrielle said.

Max stared at her, thinking back, now, to their first meeting. She'd walked in this shadow world that ordinary people could never see, knew ancient secrets that would shake the world. And finally, he thought he understood.

"Is it because I was normal?" he asked. "Is that why you fell in love with me?"

"Love?" she asked, and for a beat he was terrified that she was about to laugh. How that would change things. How that would knock out of shape everything he thought he understood. But instead she looked at him, her eyes now dry, and a great sadness exuded from her. "Max, I can't remember what that means anymore."

"But you did," he says. "And I still do."

"Even after everything?"

"What Ray did to me . . . I *saw* you kill Joe Noone!"

Gabrielle turned her eyes away.

"It repulsed me," Max said. His voice was low. Over the storm, neither of them should have been able to hear the words, but they were strangely loud. "But I know why you did it, and I can only begin to imagine what it cost you, what you gave up for me . . ." He shook his head, and the house creaked and groaned as the gale strove to tear it away. "I've tried telling myself I can't love you, but it isn't that simple.

Whatever you did to yourself that day, you did it to me as well. We've both got blood on our hands."

Gabrielle looked so lost. "So you're here to rescue me?" she asked.

"To save your life, yes," he said. *I wanted so much from this Moment! Once, I even hoped . . .* "But we both know it's too late to rescue you. I couldn't go back that far." As he said this last, his voice broke. "That Moment can't be changed." God, how he wanted to go to her, to hold her and try to lend her solace. But he had none to give. "You've got to get out of here, Gaby. Get to high ground. I don't know how long you have, but we're talking hours. You need to go right now."

"And do what?" she cried, and in those three words he heard the despair of falling angels.

Max steeled himself to take her out of there by force if it came to that. "You've got to go back to Ray. You've got to be what you promised, otherwise Coco and Mireault win, and what they made you do—"

"I can *never* change that!"

"No, you can't. But you can stop it being their victory, and make it yours."

"I'm so tired . . ."

"You're nineteen!"

She laughed, but it was bitter and sharp. "What, I have my whole life ahead of me? All two centuries of it, fighting the Tordu? The conjure-woman, Gabrielle? What kind of life is that, Max?"

"What kind of death is this?"

She snorted, but did not answer. She drank more wine,

her eyes distant, and the storm made itself known once more. Something smashed against the side of the house and was lifted, scraping, across the roof.

"Some of the wards are damaged in the storm," Max said.

"Seddicus . . . ?" Her eyes were wide and filled with terror.

Max shook his head. "Not this time. But if you die here, and Ray dies, then they won't worry about Seddicus anymore. They'll have the city for themselves, and they'll grow strong and fat on its people. Then they'll be able to keep their demon at bay forever."

"You sound like you care."

"I do," Max said. And he surprised himself by meaning it. He hated Ray for what he had done to Gabrielle, and what he had steered Max into. But he also understood why the old conjure-man had done it. He remembered a scene from a film his mother had loved, *The Cruel Sea,* where the captain of a destroyer steered his boat through a group of shipwrecked, drowning men so that he could depth-charge a U-boat. He'd known the U-boat would sink many more ships, and kill many more men if he did not destroy it there and then. But the expression on that captain's face had stuck with Max for a long time. The pain, the hopelessness, the shame. His mother had cried every time she watched the movie, and as a kid Max had needed to ask her why.

But he lived, and he learned.

He wondered whether he should go to sit beside Gabrielle, but decided against it. So he watched her finish the bottle of wine, and then stand, and when she came to him he remained leaning against the wall, hoping against everything he had seen and heard that she would reach out and stroke his face, just once.

But this Gabrielle was a stranger.

She walked to the stairs and started to descend.

Max went after her. "Ray's waiting for you at——"

"Cooper's," she said. "Yeah. Ray's always waiting for you at Cooper's." She smiled back up at him, and when she next spoke, he tried hard to hear something more than her words suggested, more than sorrow, and regret, and something approaching love. But there was nothing.

"I'm sorry for what I did to you," Gabrielle said. She disappeared from view, and moments later Max heard the front door open and the storm blow in.

Then silence descended, and Max swayed, disoriented, and slumped to the floor of a very different place.

He didn't sleep, exactly. But he did rest. It felt as if he'd run a marathon. The attic room was bare now; no blankets, no empty wine bottles. The house smelled stale, but there was no odor of rot.

When he stirred at last, and found the strength to go outside, the street was a ruin, and there was an old truck parked in a driveway a few houses away. A man jumped from the truck, and for a beat Max hoped it would be the old man he had shouted at to get away. But fate, he knew, could never be so kind, nor so neat. This man was younger, and whatever grief he carried he kept to himself.

Max looked up at the house. The dormer was bare of those spray-painted words. No one had died in this attic.

He had changed the world forever.

For a while, he thought of simply going to the airport and flying out of New Orleans, never to return. But after everything that had happened to him, this journey felt incomplete. There was something tugging at him, a part of him that had become forever New Orleans.

He had to know what had happened to Gabrielle.

He had to know if it had worked.

Standing outside Cooper's once again, Max sniffed the air, wondering whether he would smell Gabrielle's perfume. He closed his eyes and tried to feel the crackle of magic within him, tried to get some sense of what waited for him inside the building, but whatever static he'd accumulated, he had spent it. He felt empty of potential, shorn of power. But at least he still possessed a soul.

What Ray had led her to . . . what that old bastard had allowed to happen to Gabrielle . . .

Max was not the man he used to be. The violence he had committed weighed upon him. He'd struck a man with a car, killed him. He'd watched people die. He'd fought a man, beaten him, and he had witnessed the woman he loved commit murder, surrendering her soul to eternal damnation.

I could kill him, Max thought. He imagined his hands

closing around Ray's throat, squeezing, and Corinne's smile floated before him, and Gabrielle's laughter seemed to fill the air. But even in his imagination his hands soon loosened, and the old man fell away. Max might have killed, but he was no murderer.

He pushed the door open and went inside. Ray and Gabrielle were sitting at the usual spot, the two of them engrossed in conversation. A half-empty whiskey bottle stood before them, and two glasses, and Max wondered how long they had been here. How long had he been out, lying on the floor of that attic? A day, a week, a year? He had no way of telling. *Messes with your body clock,* his sister had once said after flying from Boston to the UK, and Max smiled as he remembered that. *Try this,* he thought.

When they looked up at last, there was no surprise in Ray's eyes. Of course not.

But Gabrielle looked amazed.

"I thought you'd gone back to Boston!"

His breath caught in his throat, brows knitting. Could it be that she didn't remember? Of course. Her eyes held no guile.

"I came back," Max said.

Ray, the old bastard, actually laughed. He remembered well enough.

"Why?" she asked.

"Unfinished business."

Ray's smile faded and his old, hooded eyes drooped. "Nothin' left unfinished," he said. "That's it now. That's all."

"You can't just leave it like this," Max said.

"Why not?"

"Because . . ." He sat at the table with them. She was staring at him, and her eyes were so very different. "Because . . ." But he could think of no reasons that involved the old man. Max and his interests no longer mattered to Ray.

Not at all.

"It's done," Ray whispered firmly. His voice sounded as old as the years he claimed, and when Max caught his eye, he was shocked at Ray's expression. He was almost crying.

"So you've got the mojo now?" Max asked, looking at Gabrielle.

"All kinds," she said darkly.

"And you're the Oracle," he said.

"She will be," Ray answered for her. "There's just one more Moment to pass, and then the balance will be reestablished. For a time, at least."

Max did not understand. But then the door of Cooper's burst open, Coco entered, and the time for questions was over.

Rising from his chair, Max moved to Gabrielle's side, putting himself between her and Coco. Ray leaned back, seemingly resigned to what was to come, and with a whisper Coco cleared the room. Chairs scraped, and the half a dozen other patrons left, along with the Cooper brothers.

Coco took another step forward, and then he saw past Max, to Gabrielle sitting there. His eyes went wide and his mouth hung agape.

Mireault entered the bar. Old, withered, pathetic, his power surged before him in a wave that took Max's breath away. A chill like winter's first frost settled on the room. Mireault moved with painful determination, wheezing, and then he looked at the three of them and stopped, staring, a statue of an impossibly old man.

Then he started laughing. It was a cheerful chuckle, the sort of laughter a place like this heard many times each and every day.

"So," said Mireault le Tordu, "everything *has* changed."

"But . . ." Coco began, shaking his head, baffled.

Tumblers clicked, and more doors opened in Max's mind.

Several other Tordu entered, some carrying guns, and they all paused as they saw Gabrielle.

Mireault waved his hand back over his shoulder, as if dismissing everyone behind him. Then he came forward and gently, carefully, lowered himself into the chair Max had just vacated. The old man's eyes had not left Gabrielle for a second. He stared at her for a while, nodding, grunting now and then, as if the truth of what had happened was presenting itself fully to his mind.

"Very good, Matrisse," he said at last. "Father would have been delighted at your deceptions."

"You expected me to do nothing?" Ray asked.

"You were bound to try," Mireault said. A smell came off of him, something older than age, and Max thought of the stinking mess he'd seen this man smearing across a ward centuries before. "But I knew you were all but powerless. Dying. My dear brother, dying." And then the withered old man did something that amazed Max—he reached across the table and took Ray's hand.

"Death comes for us all," Ray said.

"So they say." Mireault nodded slowly. "Clever of you.

Very clever. You'd have never survived the Moments your-self." He kept his gaze on Ray, and Ray stared back. *How long since they've spoken like this?* Max thought. *How long since they've even seen each other?*

"Never was about my survival."

"The lengths you go to," Mireault said. "You can never win."

"But I must never lose."

Mireault chuckled. "That boy's heart tasted good, and strong. The boy Gabrielle delivered to me. I thank you, brother."

Ray's smile slipped. "A necessary evil."

"Are you really going to let him leave," Mireault whis-pered, "with all he knows?"

Max realized with a sickening jolt that the old man was talking about him.

"Gabrielle will take him to the airport and—"

"No, brother," Mireault said, smiling. "She's still vulner-able. Still . . . not all here. We'll have her yet, and you'll die, and I'll let Coco have the young professor. More blood on my brother's hands."

Ray frowned. "He's served his purpose, Mireault. Why not jus'—"

"He knows too much! About us, and about you." He glanced at Gabrielle. "About *her!*"

"Gabrielle—" Coco began, but he said no more. Mireault raised one hand and the Tordu man's eyes bulged, his mouth gaping open.

"You speak when I tell you to speak," Mireault whis-pered. "Fucking idiot!" In those two hissed words, Max heard the pent-up fury and blame that simmered in this old man, emotions that spoke of some form of defeat. And it was terrifying.

Ray glanced at Max. His expression was unreadable. Then he looked at Gabrielle, and Max saw something there that he had seen in his own mirrored reflection many times since leaving New Orleans: love, and loss.

"You know," Ray said.

Gabrielle nodded.

Mireault, twisted and withered as he was, suddenly sat up straighter. "What does she——?"

Ray stood and leaned across the table. As he did so he pulled Mireault closer to him, reached for his head, for all the world looking as if he wanted to give his brother a kiss.

Gabrielle grabbed Max's hand—her skin cool, dry, distant—and shoved him to one side.

"Now's the time, brother," Ray said. Mireault squealed something that Max could not hear . . .

But then Coco moved, and Max understood.

As Mireault lifted his clawed hand to frantically wave his men back, Coco pulled a gun, stepped forward, and shot Ray through the head.

"No!" Mireault wailed, his voice that of a child.

Ray slumped to the table, whining as he turned his head and reached for Mireault once more.

Coco shot him two more times.

Beside Max, Gabrielle gasped and went rigid, her eyes wide, mouth slack. She squeezed his hand so tight that he felt the bones crunched together, knuckles popping, and he tugged hard to remove his hand from her grip. Some dreg of the magic he'd gathered and used remained, because he sensed what was happening to her—smelled the history of New Orleans, saw its present sad state, and tasted the hope that existed once again in its future.

Mireault was laughing and crying. Coco looked aghast at what he had done, and he had already dropped the gun, both hands reaching hesitantly for his master as confusion and fear took hold.

Oh, you'll get yours, Max thought, and he found it in himself to smile at Coco's stunned expression.

Mireault's tears and laughter filled the bar, and the sound of Ray's blood dripping from the table seemed just as loud.

Gabrielle went slack, sitting back down next to the dead man. As her hand loosened around Max's and she let him go at last, he felt a dreadful loss. *Hold me,* he thought. *Hold on to me forever; maybe you can no longer love but I can, and can't that be enough?*

But she was already different, already changed. "Mireault," she said, breathing heavily.

"Oracle," he said, tears still streaming from his eyes. "We'll be seeing . . ." He waved a hand, shook his head.

"I'm sure," Gabrielle said.

The old man stood and his Tordu helpers, Coco among them, held his arms and guided him backward out of the bar. His gaze never left the face of his dead brother.

Max left her in the bar, and as the door closed gently behind him, he was no longer certain that Gabrielle was even in there at all. From outside, the building looked and felt deserted and abandoned, and the street echoed with noises that all originated elsewhere.

He walked, and after a while he managed to hail a cab. He told the driver to take him to the airport. The young guy raised an eyebrow and shrugged, as if barely understanding why anyone would ever wish to leave the city.

Max leaned against the window and watched the streets, the squares, the ruined places passing by. Gabrielle's parting words echoed to him, and they were already taking on the tone of a haunting. *Max, it was always you in that attic with me.*

They passed a large market that the driver said had been gutted by fire soon after the flood. There was a small crowd of people on the sidewalk in front of the building, a few of them standing behind trestle tables piled high with bottled water, gas canisters, food containers, clothes in boxes, a hundred more things. The others browsed in front of the tables, and here and there money was changing hands.

"They're managing," the young driver said. "Can't never beat the storm, but can't let it win, either."

"It's all about balance," Max muttered.

"Yeah," the driver said. *"Yeah!"* And he drove the rest of the way in contemplative silence.

A while before they reached the airport Max drifted off to sleep. In his dream, Gabrielle still loved him.

And when he awoke, she was still alive.

About the Authors

CHRISTOPHER GOLDEN'S novels include *The Lost Ones*, *The Myth Hunters*, *Wildwood Road*, *The Boys Are Back in Town*, *The Ferryman*, *Strangewood*, *Of Saints and Shadows*, and *The Borderkind*. Golden co-wrote the lavishly illustrated novel *Baltimore, or, The Steadfast Tin Soldier and the Vampire* with Mike Mignola, and they are currently scripting it as a feature film for New Regency. He has also written books for teens and young adults, including the thriller series *Body of Evidence*, honored by the New York Public Library and chosen as one of YALSA's Best Books for Young Readers. Upcoming teen novels include *Poison Ink* for Delacorte, *Soulless* for MTV Books, and *The Secret Journeys of Jack London*, a collaboration with Tim Lebbon. With Thomas E. Sniegoski, he is the co-author of the dark fantasy series *The Menagerie* as well as the young readers fantasy series *OutCast* and the comic book miniseries *Talent*, both of which were recently acquired by Universal Pictures. Golden and Sniegoski also wrote the upcoming comic book miniseries *The Sisterhood*, currently in development as a feature film. Golden was born and raised in Massachusetts, where he still lives with his family. Please visit him at www.christophergolden.com.

TIM LEBBON lives in South Wales with his wife and two children. His books include the British Fantasy Award—winning *Dusk* and its sequel *Dawn, Fallen, Berserk, The Everlasting, Hellboy: Unnatural Selection,* and the *New York Times* bestseller *30 Days of Night.* Forthcoming books include the new fantasy novel *The Island,* two YA novels making up *The Secret Journeys of Jack London* (in collaboration with Christopher Golden), the collection *Last Exit for the Lost* from Cemetery Dance Publications, and further books with Night Shade Books, Necessary Evil Press, and Humdrumming, among others. He has won three British Fantasy Awards, a Bram Stoker Award, a Shocker, and a Tombstone Award, and has been a finalist for International Horror Guild and World Fantasy awards. His novella *White* is soon to be a major Hollywood movie, and several other novels and novellas are currently in development in the US and the UK. Find out more about Tim at his websites: www.timlebbon.net and www.noreela.com.